FROM RAGE TO RAPTURE

With a violent heave, Hunter flung Caroline on her back and rolled on top of her. "I could kill you," he snarled. "Scratching and clawing, you wildcat. I've had enough of this and plenty."

His body stretched atop hers and bore down upon her. He was much too heavy, yet she struggled against him. Angrily, she bucked up, thrusting her heels into the floor. The violent movement brought her body in the most intimate contact with his.

Their faces only inches apart, their breaths commingling, they stared.

"Damn you, Angel," he whispered as his mouth came down hard on her own.

Suddenly, her own passion answered his. Shameful excitement shot through her as inexorably he pulled her wrists over her head. "Monster," she hissed. "What do you think you're doing?"

His only answer was to kiss her again as he coupled her wrists in his left hand and freed his right to roam over her luscious body. . . .

Captive Angel

DEANA JAMES

ZEBRA BOOKS
KENSINGTON PUBLISHING CORP.

ZEBRA BOOKS

are published by

Kensington Publishing Corp.
475 Park Avenue South
New York, NY 10016

First printing: December, 1988

Printed in the United States of America

Dreams indeed are ambition,
for the very substance of the ambition is merely
the shadow of a dream.

—A dream itself is but a shadow.

To Pesha—

Who gave my shadow substance.

ACKNOWLEDGMENTS

Thanks to Paul Merritt for his expertise on the raising and curing of tobacco. Not only did he play the gracious host but also the reference source with equal aplomb.

Thanks to my good friend Constance O'Banyon for the loan of her book *Boston, a Topographical History.* Who says friendship is spoiled when one person raids another's library?

Thanks to Professor Raymond K. Kent for his scholarly work *Early Kingdoms in Madagascar 1500–1700,* without which the last part of the book would have been without substance.

Deana James
Dallas, Texas

Part I

England's Fancy, 1815

Chapter One

With the warm darkness all around them, he thrust into her.

Bathed in the scents and sounds of the Carolina night, she parted for him, welcomed him, gasped aloud as the slick, hot length of him slid into her. Her breath hissed out between teeth clenched tightly in their effort to maintain the ecstasy as long as possible. Her fingernails dug into the bunched muscles of his upper arms.

His breath dampened the long strands of dark auburn hair spread like a silken sheet across her pillow. Delicately, he nibbled upward along the smooth skin of her throat until he came to the lobe of her ear. She shuddered as he took the sensitive flesh between his teeth.

The vibration caressed his staff buried deep within her. Deliberately, he closed his teeth. All her muscles convulsed at the tiny pain. Her hands slid round his back to clasp him tighter; her thighs hugged him to her, striving to pull him deeper into her. The hard bones at the bottom of his belly pressed down against her mount. "Hunter," she moaned. "You're . . . hurting . . ."

Instantly, he pulled back, then pushed forward again, establishing a rhythm at the same time he asserted complete domination of her body. Like an angry stallion, he tossed back his tangled black mane as he locked his elbows to support himself on his hands. His arms extended at full stretch while he bore down on her in the fierce work of love. "Angel," he prompted. His jaw set in his efforts to check himself.

She rolled her head from side to side on the pillow. Perspiration gleamed on her forehead. Her eyebrows drew together in a tight frown. The external world was nothing. Only the internal throbbing mattered. Only the blood racing through her veins and the heat centered in her loins. Where his maleness filled her again and again, she was a supple sheath, clasping the sword he slid back and forth into her.

"Angel . . ." His tone peremptory; he drove forward harder.

She arched her back to accommodate him. The movement spread her nether lips and brought the throbbing nub of pleasure into contact with the thick base of his staff. She cried out sharply. Hot liquid jetted inside her as the painful tension of her loins suddenly dissolved in a river of pleasure.

"Angel, oh, Angel," he whispered, sinking down, his face buried in the pillow beside her head.

She could hear the mockingbird singing at midnight. Perhaps because of the rising gusts of wind, its sleepy tones sounded faintly irritated. They called her back to consciousness. The lace curtains billowed out from the jalousied windows. *Good. A little rain will cool things off.*

Hunter stirred beside her, flopping over onto his back to relieve her of his weight. Her skin felt chilled where his arm and thigh had covered it. Outside, the first drops of water spattered against the broad magnolia leaves. With a little shiver, she sat up and reached for the covers pushed carelessly to the front of the bed.

"Cold?" His voice was deep and warm.

She turned back into his arms, dragging the edge of the sheet with her. "The rain . . ."

"I'll warm you." He pushed the sheet away.

"Hunter," she protested.

"Come here, Angel." With a low growl, he rolled over on her again, guiding himself in between her legs, pulling her rounded knee up over his hip.

"For heaven's sake," she chuckled softly.

"So long as I have you down," he murmured silkily as he nudged the moist opening between her thighs. Almost at leisure, he filled her, while his hands played with her breasts, weighing their double handfuls of firm soft flesh, squeezing them, flicking his thumbs over the hardened nipples.

On her back beneath him, she stirred restlessly, torn between irritation at his demands and the animal heat she could not control. The moisture of her response sheathed him, so that he sighed with the ecstasy of it.

Rearing up over her, he cupped the back of her head. "Kiss me, Angel."

Obediently, she opened her lips to the hardened nubs on his chest, licked aside the curls of black hair, and laved them with her tongue.

"Ah, so good," he crooned. "So good."

Delicately, she suckled him, then gradually her attentions grew rougher. Her teeth nipped his hardened flesh.

"Damn," he moaned. "Oh, damn."

His free hand squeezed her breast, pinching the nipple in swift retribution. Involuntarily, her muscles tensed.

"Sweet angel," he encouraged her. "Sweet. That's

right. That's right. Soft. Warm." The words matched the rhythm of his strokes. She fell back against the pillow then, her climax coming with devastating force and swiftness. She cried out sharply as her ecstasy peaked.

But he was not finished. Implacably, he continued, driving again and again into her, while she groaned, then moaned, then pleaded, not knowing what she did or said, a prisoner of his merciless desire. The time he took to achieve his own release might have been minutes or hours. She writhed and twisted on a peak where time had no meaning.

Then he grunted harshly. An animal growl ripped from him as he stiffened over her. At last, sighing gustily, he slipped to one side and drew her into the circle of his arm. He did not even feel her hand smooth his disordered hair and kiss his throat before she drew the sheet over them both.

Faint blue smudges beneath her eyes made them look bigger and deeper than ever as she stared at him. The sheet tucked decently across her breasts, she watched him button his pants and draw on his boots.

His body still excited her, even with the night's loving behind them. He was only a little bit thicker through the middle than when she had married him ten years ago. She stirred uncomfortably in her bed at the thought of her own extra flesh.

As she watched, he donned a white shirt, then tied a neat, simple cravat about his neck. A tiny frown marred her forehead as she watched him pull a leather grip from the back of the wardrobe. "A trip to Charleston?" she hazarded.

He paused in collecting his shaving razors and strop from the washstand. "Yes." He did not turn toward

14

her. Instead, he glanced at her reflection in the mirror, then hastily looked away as their eyes met.

"I wish you'd told me earlier. I'd have liked to go with you."

He tossed the things into the bag and closed it with a snap. "You can't come."

She caught the edge of the sheet and sat up. "Whyever not?"

"Because I'm not stopping in Charleston." Taking a deep, steadying breath, he turned purposefully and took his coat from the wardrobe. It was not his best coat, she noted, but a rather old one of thick heavy wool, a French *frac* that came down around his knees rather than cutting away from the waist as the new popular style did.

"Where are you going?"

"To sea."

The simple words stopped her cold. She could not comprehend their meaning. "To . . . sea?"

"That's right."

She waved one hand helplessly. "But . . ."

Still avoiding her eyes, he plucked her green silk robe off the chair and tossed it to her. "Put this on and come downstairs, Caroline Fancy. We have to talk."

He had called her by her given name. He never called her Caroline Fancy unless she had done something terribly wrong. Chills, unrelated to her nudity, played along her spine as she heard the thud of his boots in the hall, heard him open the door to their son's room, heard her son's voice. The sheet fell to her waist where she clutched at it with both hands, pressing her fists into her midriff.

The clouds still lowered, although the rain had ceased for the moment. The breeze slipping in between the jalousies felt unseasonably cool even though common sense told her the day would be steamy.

15

Catching her bottom lip between her teeth, she climbed down from the high bed.

What could he be thinking of, planning a voyage at this time of year? He knew the importance of the end of summer on the plantation. At the end of July, tobacco was within days of being ripe for harvest. Every ablebodied man on England's Fancy stood poised for the herculean effort required to get the crop in at its peak. No one could waste an hour. The tobacco had to be gathered and suspended from long sticks in the flue-curing barns to dry. Behind the tobacco came the rice to be harvested, the fertilizer to be spread, and the second crop to be planted. Ever present, in the back of every planter's mind, was the threat of a hurricane whirling up out of the Caribbees and leveling everything in its path.

No. No master of a plantation of any size could afford to leave it for even one day at this time of year.

With her robe in her hands, she moved to look at her nude body in the cheval glass. Hastily, she slid her arms into the green silk and tied it firmly at the waist. Her lip curled in distaste as she tried to smooth the material over the bulges of hip and thigh and belly. When she had married Hunter and even after Alexander's birth, she had been almost too slim. Now she stared discouragingly at the results of months of neglect after the tragic loss of her baby daughter.

With a sigh, she turned her attention to something that she could do something about. Her long red hair hung down her back in tangles. Catching up her brush from the dressing table, she swung the heavy hank around to her left shoulder and began to brush it smooth. The loose sleeves of her robe fell back from her plump white arms.

A low knock came before she was half finished. "Yes?"

"Maitresse Gillard." The soft liquid voice of the mulatto housekeeper, Holy Dulcibella, summoned her. "Maitre Gillard is waiting."

Caroline shot a look of pure dislike at the reflection in the mirror before dropping the brush noisily. "I'll be right there. Tell him to hold his horses."

A ribbon was the only solution. She rummaged through the mess in the middle drawer of the dresser. Finally, a length of pink moire taffeta was in place. As she tied the bow on the top of her head, she grimaced at her reflection. Morning was not her best time. With no sleep the night before, she would not have looked beautiful ten years ago.

Hunter was not in the breakfast room, although he had eaten as had Alex, the son who trod in his father's footsteps like a small dark-haired shadow. She poured herself a cup of strong black coffee, carrying it and the saucer into the back parlor.

"So you finally came down."

"You're slow, Mama." Alex accused rudely.

"Mind your manners," she snapped.

The boy said nothing, but his lip thrust out stubbornly.

"Sit down, Caroline," Hunter advised. He rested his hand on the back of the brocade-covered sofa.

Her robe fell open, exposing one plump knee as she struggled with the opening and the cup and saucer. "Really, Hunter, why all the urgency?" she demanded querulously. "I'm not even dressed."

"We will leave you time for your dressing, madam," he replied stiffly. He watched her grimly as she arranged the robe over her limbs and balanced the teacup in her lap. Then he cleared his throat. "I have been very unhappy of late."

She looked at him uncertainly, then shot a wary glance at their son, whose dark brown eyes fastened alertly on his father's face. "Perhaps you should go and have another muffin, Alex," she interrupted.

"No."

Hunter sighed. "Go on, Alex." When the boy had stomped out, he cleared his throat again.

Fancy looked at him uncertainly. "Are we going to have a bad argument, Hunter?"

He continued as if he had not heard her attempt at levity. "I have been very unhappy of late." Shoulders squared, chest out, he rocked forward on his toes. "Although I have the greatest respect for you as a lady and as mistress of this plantation, I have come to the conclusion that we are not suited."

She took a deep hot breath. The cup rattled in the saucer as her hand shook. She set it hastily aside. "Why would you say we were not suited? We have scraped along rather well together for the last ten years. I have been a good wife and mother. We have everything that any two people could possibly want."

He shook his head. "You have everything that you want, Caroline Fancy. I have nothing that I want."

"I would not have thought so last night," she reminded him dryly.

The color rose in his dark cheeks. He took a deep breath. Hands at his side, his head thrown back in a look of stubborn defiance, he announced the words as if for a judge. "I mean for us to separate for a time. Alex is growing up here in this uncultured backwater. The boy's horizons need to be expanded. He needs to know the world beyond England's Fancy."

"Alex!" she exclaimed. "He's only ten years old."

"Exactly. The perfect age to be a cabin boy on a ship. To see—"

"On a ship?" she shook her head in bewilderment.

"I intend to take him with me on a voyage."

For several slow seconds she stared up into her

husband's face, sure that at any minute now he would break into a grin and declare that he had fooled her. But he did nothing of the sort. The blood began to pound in her temples. Desperately, she reached for the handle of the coffee cup in an attempt to raise it to her lips. It shook so badly that the dark liquid slopped over the rim into the saucer. She set it back down again.

Hunter cleared his throat. "I'm glad you're taking this so well. I was afraid you'd have a fit of some kind." He swung his arms wide in a gesture surprisingly awkward for a man who was usually so graceful. "The last two years have been a nightmare since—since the baby died."

Her hands were shaking so badly that she pressed them down between her thighs. "Yes."

Turning away, he stalked over to the window to stare outward at the dark wet expanse of green lawn. "I'm as sorry as you are that it . . . she died, but those things happen."

Her voice was low. "I can't ever have any more children."

"That's another thing." He turned around. "You don't know that for certain."

"I know," she insisted.

"Instead of getting out and exercising—riding again, for instance—you've sat inside and moped." He gave another impatient sweep of his arm. "You've done nothing but eat and drink and feel sorry for yourself."

"I almost died," she reminded him.

"Many women have almost died in childbirth. But they don't take the rest of their lives to get over it," he told her hardily.

"It's just that I—I can't have any more children," she repeated dumbly.

"For God's sake! Do I care?"

The tears began to trickle down her cheeks. "I care."

19

"You have a son."

"I'm an only child and I hate it."

He threw up his hands. "That's about all I can stand!" He pointed an accusing finger at her. "You sit around and cry about the things you can't change. Just let the least little thing go the wrong way and the fountain starts to flow."

"I can't help it." Still sobbing, she fumbled in her pocket for a handkerchief. The robe fell open across her knees, exposing her thighs.

"Look at you!" His tirade continued. "You're not the woman I married. She was spirited and gay and slim."

The handkerchief fell to the floor as she clutched at the robe. Her face, wet from crying, now reddened even brighter with embarrassment.

In a couple of quick strides, he crossed the room and caught her by the chin. "Up," he commanded.

"No." She twisted her face away and flung up a hand to cover it. "Oh, no."

"Yes." Once unleashed, his resentment turned cruel. Catching her under the arm, he pulled her to her feet and led her over to the mirror. "Look at yourself. Are you spirited? Are you gay?" He did not ask the next question. But it was there by implication.

Sobbing bitterly, she wrenched herself out of his hands and stumbled back across the room to the sofa. "For pity's sake," she moaned.

He followed her, merciless as the very devil. The disgust and resentment he had built up over the past months poured out, sluicing over her trembling body. "Almost from the time I married you, all you ever wanted was someone to work this patch of dirt and give you a brood of children. I felt like a mule half the time and a stud horse the rest."

"Hunter . . ." she pleaded.

But he swept on, as unstoppable as the tide once his

20

feelings were unleashed. "Then when that baby died, you didn't even want me for a stud horse anymore."

"Hunter!" She glanced hastily around her in painful discomfiture.

He raised his voice even louder. "And I will not be a damn mule anymore. I hate grabbling in the dirt. The sea's for me, and by God, I'm going to smell it and taste it and feel it again before I die."

As he swung away from her, she managed to catch the skirt of his coat. "What about me?" she whispered hoarsely.

He looked down at her with a mixture of pity and contempt. "You don't need me," he insisted. "Anyone will do. You don't love me."

She gaped at him. "I do. I do." She shook her head wildly. Her fingernails sank like talons into the heavy dark wool.

He bent to pry one of her hands loose. "You never did. You just wanted a man to do your work."

"How can you say I don't love you? I've made a beautiful home for you," she cried desperately as he managed to disengage her hands and drag her to her feet by her wrists. "I've done everything a wife should do."

He laughed harshly. "Oh, I grant if a house mattered, then you've kept a nice enough one. But these last two years you haven't even been a wife to me. So many nights when I've wanted a woman's tenderness, where were you?"

She cried out then and tugged herself away from him. In breaking his grip, she stumbled back and sat down hard on the sofa. "I was hurt. I couldn't bear to . . . I didn't think I would ever . . . You don't understand how I feel."

"And you don't care how I feel."

"I do care," she insisted. "If I didn't, would I have

given you everything?"

He stepped back and drew a steadying breath. "You've kept me from the one thing I want most in the world."

She huddled on the sofa, her shoulders shaking. The robe had become more disarranged in her struggles, until the whole expanse of her leg was bare to his gaze. Her skin was too pale and tiny dimples showed in the flesh of her thigh.

He waited for a minute, staring at her. His lip curled in distaste. The mantel clock struck the half hour. They both flinched.

She flung up her head to glance at it fearfully, then back at him. He tugged at his lapels, straightening his coat minutely. "I must be going." He took a quick step toward the door.

She put out her hand. "Wait. Just one more minute. Listen to me." Her sobs had become gasps as her heart raced in her chest and blood pounded in her ears. Her hands were numb with cold, yet her cheeks were hot.

He looked at her unemotionally.

She dropped her hands into her lap and took a deep breath. "Very well. I won't keep you anymore," she breathed. "Only, please say you'll come back to me when you—when you get through."

He crossed his arms over his chest. "We should both be free to pursue our own desires," he suggested.

"No," she gasped. "That is . . . No. I don't desire anything but to be your wife and Alex's . . . Oh, God . . . Alex's mother. Please don't take my baby to sea, Hunter."

"I'll not leave him here to let you turn him into a farmer."

She struggled to her feet. "He can go to school in Charleston. He can study to become a lawyer. He's quick and bright. I'm sure—"

22

"I don't want him to bury himself under a mound of books any more than I want him to root in the mud for the rest of his life."

"But he's just a boy, a little boy. He might get hurt. . . . He might be swept overboard and drown. . . . Your ship might be wrecked. . . ."

"There are just as many ways to die here on this farm. He might step on a nail and die of lockjaw."

With an effort, she steadied her voice. "Hunter, you're not being reasonable. I repeat. He's just a little boy. . . ."

"No, I'm not, Mama. I'm big. I'm as big as Daddy was when he went to sea." Alex burst into the room and planted himself, arms akimbo, feet apart, by his father's side.

"Alex." Hunter put a hand on his son's shoulder. "You shouldn't interrupt a grown-up conversation."

The little boy looked up proudly. "I ate a big breakfast and now I'm through. Are we ready to go?"

Fancy held out trembling arms to her son. "C—come here," she begged.

He stared at her. For an instant, his face crumpled, then he shook his head vigorously. "Daddy and I are leaving. I'm going to sea. With him."

She blinked back new tears. "I know, sweetheart. I know. Your father told me."

"And you're not mad?"

She shot Hunter a glance, but his forbidding expression made her drop her eyes again. She shook her head. "N—no. I'm not really mad. I'm just . . . I'll miss you terribly. I won't see you grow up. You'll be gone for so very long."

"But I'll be having lots of fun and learning to be a man." Realizing that his mother was not going to beg him to stay, he relaxed slightly. He pulled his lower lip back in and smiled.

23

The smile cut through Fancy like a knife. The only child she would ever have was smiling his beautiful smile at her. In another minute he would be gone, perhaps forever. When he returned, he would be older, taller, his voice might have changed, his body would have probably lost its little-boy look. And she would not have been with him to see it. She clamped a trembling hand to her mouth.

"Go hug your mother and give her a kiss," Hunter bade him, giving him a slight push at the shoulder.

"I'm too old to kiss," came the stubborn reply.

"Go on," Hunter said sternly.

With a show of great reluctance, Alex went into his mother's outstretched arms. Fancy's chest heaved with the effort to draw a breath as she caught him to her. He smelled of soap and bacon. A faint roughness scraped her cheek at the corner of his mouth—crumbs from his breakfast.

They gave her a reason to act normally. Her eyes smarting, she hugged him tightly, then pulled back to fumble for her handkerchief. With one arm around him, she picked it up from the floor and dabbed at his face.

"Mama," he protested, pulling back.

Instantly, she stopped, her eyes bright as she stared into his dear face, with Hunter's coloring and strong cleft chin. Yet she could see so much of her father in him. Around the mouth and across his nose and cheeks, he was clearly Richard England's grandson. As she again realized the family resemblance, her heart pounded so hard she had to clasp her hand beneath her breast.

"Ready, son?" This from Hunter, who shifted restively from one foot to the other. His face might have been carved out of stone.

"Ready, Daddy. Good-bye, Mama." Alex planted a

24

quick kiss on her cheek and turned away.

"Oh, God . . ." she whispered.

The little boy turned back. "You mustn't cry, Mama. We'll be back. When did you say, Daddy? In a year?"

"If all goes well." Hunter nodded, not looking at his wife.

Alex turned back to flash his mother a charming smile. With a smothered cry, she caught him by the shoulders and kissed him hard on the mouth, then on both cheeks.

"Mama!" He drew back, pushing his small hands against her shoulders. As Hunter opened the door, he dashed through it and out into the hall.

As she pressed her shaking hands to her mouth, she heard his shoes thudding across the porch and down the steps.

"Good-bye, Caroline Fancy."

She did not answer. The pain in her chest was so great that she could scarcely breathe. She sank back on the sofa, turning her shoulder to him.

He shrugged, then went out, closing the door silently behind him.

Chapter Two

She willed herself to die.

Long after the rattle of the carriage wheels had faded away on the Charleston road, she sat, feeling her heart pound against the side of her chest, wondering when it would stop. Would the next beat be the last? *Please. Please. Please, God.* She could not bear to think about what he had said to her. If she were dead, she would no longer have to think of what lay ahead of her.

The door opened cautiously. Amos, the butler, paused in the doorway, waiting for the mistress of England's Fancy to turn her head and acknowledge him. When she made no move to do so, he cleared his throat. Still, she stared at the polished hardwood floor with half-closed eyes. Finally, he bowed stiffly and went away.

The mantel clock continued to tick, its pendulum swinging back and forth, the only movement in the still room. Several times it chimed, but Fancy did not mark the numbers.

Again Amos entered. Disturbed to find her sitting in exactly the same position as he had left her at midmorning, he called her name gently. "Dinner is served, maitresse," he announced in a deep gentle voice.

"I'm not hungry." Coming after several seconds, her answer was spoken in a strained dry whisper.

"But, maitresse . . ."

"Go away."

Narrow rectangles of sunlight appeared on the floor in front of the windows. Gradually, they lengthened as they moved across the polished hardwood. In the midst of the humid Carolina summer, no one used the west parlor in the afternoon. Yet Fancy sat, oblivious to the temperature rising in the suffocating room. Sweat bedewed her temples where the blue veins pulsed with painful regularity. At her hairline a tiny droplet formed and trickled down the side of her jaw, but she made no move to wipe it away. Her stiffened fingers remained tightly intertwined.

At long last the door swung open before an authoritative hand.

"All glory to God. Have you finished your grieving, Fancy, maitresse?" A tall straight-backed woman stood in the doorway. Her midnight black skin stretched like crêpe over her cheekbones and sagged slightly into the hollows beneath them. Her age could not be guessed at because her body was so straight and spare. Furthermore, her hair, which might have gone gray, was completely concealed beneath a swathing of bright yellow silk.

No ordinary kerchief was this, such as the lesser servant women wore. It was not tied in the traditional bandanna fashion, with ends sticking up from the forehead like an uneven pair of ears. Instead, it was wrapped round and round the crown of her head in intricate folds and pinned with an ornate gold pin set with a piece of yellow glass the size of a pigeon's egg.

When she received no answer to her question, the woman strode forward. Her rusty black dress billowed around her like a ship under full sail. "I say, have you finished your grieving, Fancy, maitresse?"

Her accent combined a clipped manner of speech peculiar to British English with occasional French words. She crossed the room and flung open one of the western windows. "A cross breeze make you not so hot, yes. Soon you will feel more the thing." She pulled the bell cord. "I caused to be brought cold tea, made strong then doctored with lemon and whiskey."

A young girl in a full white pinafore apron brought a single small tray with a tall glass on it. She curtsied as she looked curiously at her mistress.

The black woman motioned to her imperiously. "Take up the morning things and be gone, foolish one. Do not stare at pain."

Ashamed, the girl dropped her eyes, collected the cups and saucers, and hurried out. The tall woman put her hand on Fancy's shoulder. "Drink," she commanded.

Fancy shook her head slowly.

Long fingers, made to appear longer by the sharply pointed almond-shaped nails, tightened, tugging at the younger woman. "Drink."

A deep frown creased Fancy's forehead. She shrugged irritably.

"Drink." The black woman lifted the glass.

"No."

"Ah, so you can talk. Praise God. I feared you had lost the power of speech. I feared it had gone when your ability to move went. You have sat here in this chair so long, I feared we would have to bury you in it."

"Go away."

"Drink, Fancy, maitresse."

Fancy set her lips stubbornly and shook her head.

"I say, drink. If I have to tell you one more time, you will be sorry."

"I'm not a child."

"How can I tell? You sit sulking and pouting. Drink." The black woman held the glass only a couple of inches from Fancy's mouth.

Defiantly, Fancy raised tired golden eyes drowned in sudden bright tears. "Oh, Dulci, he's gone. And he took my son with him." Her voice cracked and quavered before it could get to the last words.

"Don't weep. Drink, feel better, grow strong."

"I can't help it." The effort to suppress her sobs was a dismal failure. Her body was wracked by harsh snubbing sounds that tore out of her throat. The tears spilled from her eyes and streamed down her cheeks.

The black woman waited, immovable as a stone, holding before Fancy's eyes the glass of tea that she was expected to drink. The sobs ceased at last.

Fancy suddenly realized dully that she wanted the refreshing liquid. With hands that trembled, she managed to take the beaded glass to her lips. Half-heartedly, she took a sip so small it had no effect on her raw, swollen throat. But when she would have set it aside, the woman stopped her.

"No. You must drink it all."

"No."

"Yes."

"For mercy's sake, Holy Dulcibella, I feel as if I'm bleeding to death. Cold tea won't help."

"It will close the wound around the knife," the black woman insisted implacably.

"Damn you."

"Good." Her lips pulled back in a grin from her uneven teeth. "Good. You show anger. Feel the pain, but do not weep. Anger will sustain you."

"How can I be angry with my son and my husband?" But she took another swallow. This time she could taste the whiskey. With a grimace of distaste, she tried again to put it aside, but Holy Dulcibella closed her long,

30

withered fingers over Fancy's and held the glass firmly.

The women's eyes met, clashing stubbornly. Fancy's lips tightened.

Holy Dulcibella laid a gentle hand on the girl's cheek. "Drink, sweet baby. It can only help the sore soul."

With poor grace, Fancy lifted the glass to her mouth again. This time she drained it before setting it aside. Within a minute, the heat from the alcohol suffused her body.

"Good. Now we go get you dressed and you eat supper."

Too benumbed with grief to resist, her thoughts in a muddle, Fancy allowed herself to be guided up the stairs to where a warm bath had been drawn. Holy Dulcibella herself pulled the sweat-soaked robe and gown from Fancy's body and helped her into the tub.

As the water rose around her hips and the scent of rose-scented soap filled her nostrils, Fancy began to weep again. Silent, ceaseless tears trickled down her face and dripped onto the white slopes of her breasts.

Using a silk sponge, the black woman quietly washed them away while she kept up a gentle monotone of homely chatter. At length, Fancy braced her elbow on the edge of the bath and covered her eyes with her hand. "Why did he do it, Dulci? I can't understand how I could have done anything so bad that he would have left me and taken Alex, too. I can't understand. I just can't."

The black woman pursed her lips, then made a clicking sound with her tongue. "You will never understand if you don't stop crying and begin to think."

Fancy turned her head dully. "That's what he said. He said I cried all the time. Pouted and sulked."

Dulcibella's eyebrows shot up. Then she shrugged.

31

"Men are not allowed to cry themselves. They say they feel contempt for whoever does. But they do not always tell the truth. Sometimes they envy them."

"He said my grief for my baby wasn't normal."

The older woman's long fingers sank into the soft flesh of Fancy's shoulders. "What means normal? I think he had something else to say but could not find the words."

Fancy shuddered convulsively. "No, he said all he intended to say."

Holy Dulcibella's lips compressed tightly. Her brow wrinkled. Then she shrugged. "Get out now. Any longer in the water and you be weak as a little animal. You need to dress now and come downstairs. You have not eaten since yesterday."

Wearily, Fancy pushed herself to her feet. "I don't want anything to eat. He thinks I'm grotesque." The word came out on a quavering sob.

The housekeeper wrapped the big cotton towel around her. "You don't believe that yourself," she observed dryly.

"I do." Fancy hugged the towel tightly over her curves. "I do." Hastily, she glanced at the mirror, then shivered. "I believe it with all my heart. Otherwise, why would he have left me?"

Holy Dulcibella shook her head from side to side. "I say he might have many reasons, but your size not one of them."

"Even Alex wanted to go with his father. He didn't want to stay with me, his mother." Head down, bare wet feet leaving footprints across the hardwood floor, Fancy stumbled toward the bed. "I just want to die."

The black woman intercepted her, holding out a soft velvet robe with lace collar and cuffs. "No. I say you will not die. Nor will you talk about dying anymore. You listen to me. Praise God you live for thirty years.

32

You have health, you have home, you have son." She thrust the heavy material in Fancy's direction.

Obedient as a child to the signal, Fancy turned around, dropped the towel, and slipped her arms into the garment. *"Had* a son, Dulci. *Had."*

"I say you *have* a son. Turn around so I may button you into this. Amos be here soon with some food."

"Alex went with his father."

"Of course he would go with his father. What would you expect? His father promises him a trip on a ship. The child will go where he thinks he can see something new and exciting. He will soon be bored and wish he had stayed at home. He will miss his mother. He will behave like a child. He will cause trouble. His father will grow disgusted with him and will not tolerate him as you would. Then he will long for his mother and his home."

Fancy dropped her head back on her shoulders. Her damp hair fell down her back in a long dark red tangle. "Oh, God! My son will return to me because I tolerate him. Please, just let me die. I can't stand any more of this."

Holy Dulcibella finished the last button and stepped back. She dropped her hands from Fancy's shoulders and crossed her arms in front of her starched black front. "You have too much too easy for too long. Too much of soft life has left you weak."

Fancy's voice rose to a shriek. "God, yes, what a soft life I've led! My father dies more than fifteen years ago. My mother waited less than a year to marry that damned Puritan, then couldn't wait until my wedding bouquet had withered to leave England's Fancy for Boston. My baby daughter died before she even breathed. I almost died myself. Now my husband . . ." The stream of words exhausted themselves before the sentence was finished.

The black woman nodded. "Always you have a strong shoulder to lean on. You were allowed to collapse in your grief. Who hold you now?"

"Dulci . . ."

"Who hold you now?" she repeated implacably. Hands raised aloft, she stepped back. "Go on. Fall down and die."

"Dulcibella."

"Praise God, you still standing, maitresse. If you keep standing, you never need a single thing to hold onto again."

Fancy drew a shuddering breath. "But what's the use?" She shook her head. Her hair fell forward to veil her face, swollen and unlovely with crying.

Holy Dulcibella's face softened for only an instant. Then she turned away and glided toward the door. "You need food," she threw over her shoulder. "I say, come along. After you eat, you begin to count your blessings."

When she descended to the formal dining room, Amos pulled out the chair at the head of the table. Holy Dulcibella's hands hovered above her charge's shoulders, but Fancy slipped into the master's chair without comment.

The black woman shook out the napkin and spread it across her lap, while Amos brought a plate of food. A few bites of chicken, a bit of rice, a spear of asparagus were all that Fancy could manage. But she held the wineglass for the butler to refill it with the pale golden liquid.

Until then, Holy Dulcibella had encouraged every bite, but now she sought to intervene. "No. No more wine. You only feel worse tomorrow if you drink wine tonight."

"I don't want to think. I can't sleep. I'll only think about Hunter and Alex all night long."

34

"Praise God. I hope so. Thinking would be a change from grieving."

Fancy leaned her aching head on the heel of her hand. "I can't bear your cruelty," she whispered. "Get out. Both of you get out."

The two exchanged glances. Fancy looked up to catch their expressions. "Get out!" she commanded sternly. "Leave me. Don't forget, I'm mistress here."

A tiny smirk might have curled the black woman's mouth, but it was erased the next moment by a stern compression of the lips. Curtly, as if she were angry and frustrated, Dulcibella nodded. "Take the tray, Amos."

"But leave me the wine . . ." Fancy made a grab for the neck of the bottle, succeeding in dragging it off the tray.

"Maitresse . . ." the man objected softly.

Defiantly, Fancy filled her glass to within a quarter inch of the rim.

Dulcibella shrugged. "We leave her then." Her eyebrows rose almost to the edge of her turban. "You sure one bottle be enough, Fancy, maitresse. Your grandfather Great Edward in his youth was a four bottle man. Since you drink like a man, perhaps you would like some of his port."

Fancy stared at the woman suspiciously, then a tiny humorless smile—the first one that day—quirked one corner of her mouth. "The very thing. Bring a bottle from the cabinet, Amos."

"Maitresse." The butler bowed obsequiously.

The huge yellow glass pin in Holy Dulcibella's turban winked in the lamplight as she sailed by Fancy. Her wrinkled hands were folded neatly away beneath her apron; her lips were fixed in a straight thin line.

Amos returned as Fancy was lifting her glass to her mouth for the second time. "Shall I uncork it, maitresse?"

"Of course. Let it breathe. That's what Hunter always said about the strong wines."

Her moment of victory over, she watched disconsolately while he did as she bid, then bowed and left. As the door closed behind him, the last of her spirit went out in a shuddering sigh. She did not really want to drink herself into oblivion until every other avenue was exhausted.

Closing her eyes, she leaned her head back against the chair. Images marched across her eyelids in agonizing progression. Hunter as he had been when he had courted her. His pride in her. His laughing face. His mouth bending to kiss her at the birth of their son.

Their son. Her son. Alex. Harsh sobs tore from her throat.

She opened her eyes, fumbling for the stem of the wineglass even as the stinging salt tears blurred her vision. A swallow of wine and then another. The pale golden stuff tasted like salty water.

Making a face, Fancy pushed herself back from the small table and slowly stood. Her back and shoulders ached dully from the unaccustomed slump she had assumed all day. One hand at the back of her waist, she made a slow circuit of the formal dining room, seeing and not seeing the familiar things.

As she moved, she realized she could not live here among all these pieces of furniture and fabrics, each one touched by Hunter. Arriving back at the table, she drained the offensive pale wine from the glass. Shuddering as the unaccustomed amount of alcohol went down her throat, she reached with grim determination for the bottle of ruby port.

It splashed into her glass like blood.

Like blood. Does a broken heart bleed?

Wrapping her third, fourth, and little fingers around the neck of the bottle and carrying the glass between

36

her index finger and thumb, she made her way out of the dining room and up the stairs, lifting the skirt of her robe to keep from tripping over it.

Once in her room, she carried the glass and bottle to the chaise lounge stretched before the curtained window. The skirt of her robe fell open above her knees as she stretched out on it, set the bottle handily on the floor, and rested the foot of the glass on her stomach. To look out at the gathering darkness through the windows was oppressive, so she turned her head to the steady flames from the candles.

Wine certainly did have a way of making things seem a little better. But only a little. What could she do to get him back? Her mind twisted and turned like a mouse in a maze.

She had not even had a chance to talk to him. He had done all the talking, all the accusing, all the fault-finding.

Suddenly, she sat up, taking another drink of port. She had not had a chance to have her say. He would listen to her and she would make perfect sense of this situation after she had reflected upon it for a day.

Excitedly, she swung her legs over the side of the chaise lounge. She would follow him to Charleston in the morning. He would not have set sail immediately. A ship took days, sometimes weeks, to outfit. The chances were remote that he would be able to sail before perhaps a month had passed.

She would ride on horseback herself. He would see how earnest she was to have him back. He was probably having second thoughts about his leaving. She took another drink of port. He might have been testing her, testing her love. She had neglected him, but she would make it up to him. She would be so good, so very good.

Setting down the empty glass, she rose and posed in

front of the tall standing mirror. Turned sideways, her stomach pulled in as tight as she could hold it, she did not look so bad.

Bedeviled by a sense of urgency, she was determined to ride to Charleston on horseback. She would travel ahead of her luggage, which could come after her as soon as Holy Dulcibella could pack a trunk and send it along in a wagon. When Fancy got to Charleston, she would find Hunter immediately. A hot blush suffused her face as she took another drink of port.

Hunter would be amazed. He would never expect her to ride so far nor so fast. He would pull her into his room, kiss her again and again. His strong arms would lift her. He would carry her to the bed. As she lifted the port to her lips, she remembered his lovemaking. Had it really happened only last night? Her mouth curved in an anguished smile. She took another drink of port.

She must hurry! Swaying away from the mirror, she pulled open the double doors to the wardrobe and stared at the contents. A pang knifed through her. Her clothes were disgraceful. For almost three years counting her pregnancy, she had had nothing new.

She pulled out skirt after skirt, muttering to herself in disgust before letting them fall back. Depressed almost to the point of tears, she took another drink. At last she selected a loose-fitting round gown of sprigged muslin with eyelet panniers on the sides. It was out of style, but the dusty rose color had not faded appreciably. The white eyelet still presented a fresh appearance, though she realized it would not compare favorably with the new materials arriving from France and England since the end of the war.

Belligerently, she pulled it from the wardrobe and slammed the heavy oak doors. She would have Dulci pack only this, with suitable petticoats, hose, and slippers, for her to carry in a satchel on horseback.

38

She discarded the idea of taking any other garments. She would purchase new ones when she got there. Her new clothes would be part of her promise of a new life to Hunter. He would be glad to see her in new bright colors and styles.

Throwing the dress across the end of the chaise, she turned back to the wardrobe. Sliding aside hanger after hanger, she finally located what she sought, hanging in the far end against the panel—her riding habit. Foreboding prickled the skin on her forearms as she drew forth the rusty black velvet. It was seven years old. Its long sweeping skirt was wrinkled where it had been folded over a hanger. The jacket and silver-gray waistcoat to be worn underneath had been fitted to a seventeen-inch waistline. Hesitantly, fearing the worst, she crossed to her bed, examining it as she went. Her eyes filled with tears that she resolutely dashed away. With an impatient gesture, she flung the garments on the bed. She dared not look down at herself but kept her eyes firmly fixed on the habit.

With a tiny prayer, she dropped the robe and reached for the jacket. It still fitted well enough across the shoulders, but as she tried to fasten the buttons from the neck down, she began to cry. It gapped a full six inches at the waist.

Yet she must wear it. She must.

The corsets. Naked as the day she was born except for the riding jacket buttoned at the neck, she flew across the room to fall on her knees in front of the highboy. Her maternity corsets. She had kept them, unable to throw them away, as if their loss would ensure that she would never conceive again.

She started to ring for Holy Dulcibella, then glanced at the clock. Five minutes to eleven. Where had the day gone? She would have to wait until morning to summon her maid to lace her into the heavy casing of

39

silk, canvas, whalebone, and steel.

Feeling guilty at her procrastination, she swept the garments off the bed and spread them carefully over the chaise. Standing beside it, she removed the jacket and put on her bedgown.

The lamp flame died beneath her hand as she turned it down to its lowest point. It would go out on its own accord in another minute. Hope made her stomach quiver. She had eaten almost nothing today. Perhaps by tomorrow her stomach would have shrunk. She reached for the port again. Without bothering to pour it into a glass, she turned up the bottle.

This time she neither coughed nor shuddered at the taste. With the bottle in her hand, she crossed to the bed and slipped between the sheets. The bottle she cradled between her breasts. Before she even took another sip, her thoughts were becoming comfortably muzzy. She was going to be able to sleep for at least a few hours.

Thankfully, she plopped over in bed to set the half-empty bottle on the floor. With one hand still dangling over the edge of the mattress, she remained on her stomach. The last glow of the lamp faded as she closed her eyes.

She regretted her choice of mounts. She should have taken her mare, even though the animal was upwards of fifteen years old and had not been ridden in two. Despite the groom's pleas, she had insisted upon the huge black foxhunter with a shockingly hard mouth and a heavy head. Furthermore, for the first ten or fifteen miles, he kept tossing about and straining at the bit as he sensed an unfamiliar, weaker hand on the rein.

However, his long powerful stride had swiftly covered the miles on the Charleston road. She would be in the city by early evening, since the strong light lasted late in July.

The strong light was fortuitous, but not the heat. Hot damp air rose from the roadbed into her nostrils. She tried to take a deep breath but was forestalled by the cage in which she traveled. Moaning slightly, she tugged at the edge of her waistcoat.

When Holy Dulcibella had been called upon to lace up the corset, she had flatly refused. "You cannot ride to Charleston in the first place," she pronounced. "You surely cannot ride if you are laced into that casing. You will faint and lie by the roadside."

"But I can't button the damn clothes," Fancy had wailed.

Taking a pair of scissors, the black woman slit the vest up the back seam. "Slip this on and button it," she commanded.

"But Dulci . . ."

"Do it. What difference if you ride with your back bare beneath your jacket? People think you crazy anyway."

When the vest was in place and the jacket slipped on over it to remain unbuttoned, Fancy saw the effect was not too bad. Then Dulcibella had drawn up the skirt over her corset cover and pantalettes and fastened its buttons as high as they would go.

With a hat and a veil to protect herself from the sun, as well as heavy black boots and long gray hose made of cotton stockinet, she was completely covered by her clothing. Only her hands remained free, for she had forgotten her gloves in her haste to depart. Now she regretted their omission, for her hands were sore from sawing at the reins.

A milepost pointed the way to Charleston—ten miles. Fancy shifted gingerly in the saddle, biting her lip. Her legs ached, particularly the one slung between

41

the saddle horns. Her entire posterior was completely raw. Her throat was dry as a bone and she was extremely hungry, having resolutely refused breakfast despite Dulcibella's protests. Until she was as thin as she had been on her wedding day, she would not eat unless absolutely necessary to keep from fainting. Her stomach growled as she straightened her weary back.

In fact, the only thing that did not ache was her head. When she had awakened this morning, she had given herself fifteen minutes to rid herself of the hangover, consuming a number of cups of strong coffee. Now both alcohol and coffee were long gone from her system, and she felt more clearheaded than she had in months.

This was surely a good sign. She would get him back. He would see her seriousness. The sight of her sitting tall on the heavy hunter would rekindle his old love. He would come and take her down. She would slide down his body as she had done when they had finished their rides together in the old days. He would kiss her, hold her against him. Their son would frolic around them, ecstatic at seeing them reunited.

Despite the road becoming more crowded as they approached the outskirts of Charleston, she increased the hunter's pace. The great horse was tired now. He had alternately walked and trotted over fifty miles that day. His black hide was lathered with dried sweat and reddened with the dust from the roadbed. He had long since stopped pulling the bit and now moved gingerly as if his feet hurt. He stumbled as she heeled him in the side to move around a slow-moving wagon, but picked up his pace gamely.

Her eagerness to see her husband again led her past the Stuart Hotel, where she usually stayed, and on to the waterfront, near her stepfather's shipping office. A fine inn, the Drake stood across the street and down the lane from Shepperton's Offices. Further reflection had led her to suppose Hunter would have taken quarters there for the night.

Smiling wearily, she guided the horse down the street. Her right hand fumbled in the pocket of her jacket and drew out a handkerchief. Clumsily, she pushed it beneath the heavy veil and mopped at her face. She could not doubt that despite the fine material, her skin had acquired a layer of road grime to match the horse's hide. She should make no effort to see Hunter until she could wash and change into the gown she had packed in her satchel.

But her eagerness would not let her wait. The clerk at the desk confirmed that Mr. Hunter Gillard and his son were having late refreshment in the private dining room.

"Are you expected, ma'am?" he asked reluctantly.

"No, but I'm his wife."

Startled, the man cleared his throat as he looked over his spectacles at her. "Perhaps I'd better show you first to his rooms so you can freshen up," he suggested.

"Nonsense. He'll be glad to see me," she insisted eagerly. "If you'll just point the way . . ."

"Perhaps I'd better announce you. . . ." The man all but skipped from behind the desk. "If you'll just wait here, Mrs. Gillard . . ."

But she did not wait. Hard on his heels, she followed, her heart pounding, her lips stretched in a weary but eager smile. With hands that trembled slightly, she pushed back her hair. Dusty tendrils, escaping from the long French braid, lay plastered to her forehead and cheeks, but she could not take the time to wash her face. She could not wait to see him. She longed so for his touch. He would not refuse her. He would not.

The clerk knocked discreetly on the door with the name of The Colonial Rose on its brass plate. There was a pause in which the clerk half turned around, smiling uneasily. Then came an impatient rumble.

Shouldering the man aside, Fancy pushed the door open.

"Mama!" Alex spotted her instantly. His face spread in a smile. He sprang up from the carpeted floor and trotted toward her.

"Fancy. My God!"

Over Alex's head, Fancy saw him. He rose, his eyes colliding with hers, then shifting away guiltily. She followed his look.

Suddenly, as if her whole world had crashed around her, she took a step back, bumping against the chest of the clerk who shrugged eloquently and apologetically over her head.

Jessica Rutledge met her eyes. Her teacup rattled in the saucer as she set it down carefully on the carved table beside the loveseat.

Chapter Three

"Caroline! What are you doing here?" Hunter's voice was hoarse. Stumbling in his haste, he sprang to his feet between the two women. The color began to drain from his face.

"Mama," Alex repeated happily. "Did you come to see us off?" He flung himself against her, wrapping his arms around her waist and pressing his face against her midriff.

Automatically, Fancy's arms went round her son, but her eyes remained focused on her husband while her stunned brain refused to make sense of the scene.

Hunter halted a yard from her, glancing nervously over his shoulder, then back at her. His arms, too, were spread, but she had the distinct impression that he was barring her way, her vision if he could.

They stared at each other as the painful silence grew between them.

The clerk from the desk cleared his throat. "Shall I fetch more coffee?"

"Yes!"

"No!"

Man and wife spoke simultaneously, their voices explosive. As if a bolt of lightning had struck and left its energy to linger, the atmosphere in the room fairly crackled.

The clerk took a step backward. With an unintelligible murmur, he ducked out and pulled the door closed behind him.

The tableau might have remained frozen indefinitely had not Alex dropped his head back. Wrinkling his small nose, he smiled ingenuously up at his mother. "Mama, you smell dusty."

Automatically, she answered him, her voice distracted, her eyes riveted on Hunter's face. "I've ridden all day to get here." Lifting shaking fingers, she unwrapped the veiling from about her head and tugged off the hat. The heavy braid of auburn hair fell down her back. Stepping back from Alex, she laid the hat and veil together on the table.

Alex made a disapproving face. "You need a bath."

She nodded absently as her gaze flicked past Hunter to Jessica Rutledge. The woman's face was presented in profile, her chin up. With all the appearance of intense concentration, she studied a clumsily executed cross-stitch sampler hanging on the wall. Her glance flickered sideways to collide with Fancy's, then return instantly to her study. Snapping open a painted fan, she began fanning herself nervously with a lace-gloved hand. Apart from that single frantic motion, she sat very still, a charming diminutive figure like a porcelain doll from Dresden. Fancy's heart sank. Not only was she graceful and young, but her waist could have measured no more than sixteen inches.

Hunter cleared his throat again. "What a surprise!"

Her eyes darted back to his face. "I—I had hoped we might talk," she began lamely. Her lips were so dry that she felt them crack as she said the words.

"Yes, certainly." He nodded with false heartiness. "Alex, let your mother go. Step back there. Caroline,

46

let me escort you to your room. I know you must be fatigued. . . ."

"I don't have a room."

"But, surely . . . Well, that's quite all right. I'm sure the hotel has plenty."

"I had thought we might stay together."

His face reddened as he raised his voice in an effort to drown out anything else she might have said. "Oh, not here. That is, this hotel isn't exactly suitable for you. You must stay at the Stuart. That's where you usually stay. I'm sure you'll be more comfortable there." Still keeping himself between her and the silent woman on the loveseat, he came forward to put a hand under her elbow.

She pulled away as if he had burned her. Putting her son away from her, she stepped past him. "Good day, Mistress Rutledge."

The woman compressed her lips. Her fan rustled, then closed with a snap. Unmindful of its fragile sticks, she thrust the unfortunate object into her reticule and pulled its drawstrings closed. "Good day, Mistress Gillard. I really must be going, Mr. Gillard." Her voice held a nervous quaver.

Both father and son turned around. "Oh, no, please don't go." This from Alex, who dashed across the carpet and threw himself down on his knees. "Mama, look. She brought me this toy ship. Isn't it wonderful? It's just like the one we're sailing on." He held up a very fine model of a merchantman.

Fancy shuddered. "It's very nice, Alex. And so generous of Mistress Rutledge. And how is Mr. Rutledge?" she inquired icily, advancing another step while Hunter hovered helplessly at her shoulder.

Two spots of color flamed on Jessica's cheeks. "I have not entertained correspondence from my husband since he sold out and returned to England before

47

the war."

"Oh, how unfortunate that politics should come between a man and his wife," Fancy offered sweetly. "Still, I'm sure it's a nobler reason than something . . . personal." Her golden eyes flashed as she raked Jessica from top to toe. The younger woman's chin quivered.

"Caroline," Hunter interposed. "You're tired. Have you really ridden all the way from England's Fancy today? Why that's—"

"—over fifty miles. On horseback." She looked up into his face. "I can imagine how surprised you must be to know that I'm riding again." Despite her veil, her complexion had reddened beneath the sun's bright rays. Perspiration and dust had mixed on her skin, accentuating the fine lines at the corners of her eyes. Dust had likewise settled into the wrinkles in her clothing and heavily coated the hem of her skirt.

Hunter managed to look shamefaced and arrogant at the same time. "I did not doubt that you could, madam. In fact, I was sure that you could."

"Were you, Hunter? Somehow, I think not."

A muscle twitched in his jaw.

Hoping to leave while the two were concentrating on each other, the blond-haired woman took a hesitant step forward. "Perhaps I should go to my room now that your wife has arrived."

Flashing her a look of relief, Hunter turned, extending his hand. "I think . . ."

"Oh, are you staying at this hotel, Mistress Rutledge?" Fancy interrupted, shrilly flashing an angry look at her husband. "Why, I'm surprised! I thought this place would not be suitable."

"Yes," came the soft whisper. Jessica Rutledge ducked her head and pulled aside her skirts as she tried to slip past Hunter to get to the door.

"Staying at the same hotel, taking tea with my

husband and my son in a private parlor." Fancy stepped back to intercept her. When the woman reached for the doorknob, Fancy caught her wrist. "Are you by chance accompanying my husband on this voyage?"

Hampered by Fancy's hand, Jessica Rutledge struggled with the doorknob, which unfortunately had stuck. She gave a little smothered whimper at Fancy's question.

His face stern, Hunter caught Fancy by the shoulder. "It's not what you think, Angel. . . ."

"Don't call me that." She shrugged his hand away. High color had rushed into her cheeks; her whole body was stiff with righteous indignation. Her breath came short. "Are you sailing with my husband?"

While the younger woman hesitated, sucking in her breath through clenched teeth, Alex climbed to his feet. Carrying his boat in both hands, he ducked in between his mother and father. "Oh, yes, Mama. Aunt Jessica is going with us. Daddy said she would take care of me if I got seasick. So you won't need to worry about me at all."

"Aunt Jessica!" A thousand images flashed through Fancy's brain. Her hand tightened around Jessica Rutledge's wrist. The golden eyes spat molten fire. Then Hunter interposed himself between the two. His hard fingers reached for Fancy's hand and tugged it free.

The instant Jessica was free, she threw both hands about the knob and jerked open the door.

"Slut!" Fancy hissed.

The other woman shot her a look of extreme dislike and darted out.

"Harlot!" Fancy yelled after her, twisting her hand free from Hunter's grip and launching herself into the hall.

Hunter caught her around the waist and dragged her back into the room before she could pursue the other woman. "Fancy, get back in here."

"Let me go, you damned swine!" She swung on him, beating his shoulders and chest with her fists, kicking at his shins.

"Caroline Fancy! For God's sake!" Hunter grunted as the toe of her riding boot connected with his ankle. "You wildcat. Settle down. Remember where you are."

"Billy-be-damned. I remember where I am." She swung at his jaw, but he turned his head so the blow flashed harmlessly past his ear.

"Mama!"

Cursing deeply, Hunter caught her striking arm and twisted it behind her. "Caroline Fancy! Behave yourself. Do you want your child to see?" Wrestling her around in his arms, he lifted her off her feet and carried her into the center of the room.

"What do I have to show him?" she screamed. Clawing and kicking, she managed to hurt Hunter enough to make him drop her. Then she fled behind the loveseat. As she whirled, the wide skirt of the riding habit swept the floor around her. "You!" She pointed her finger at him. "You've brought him into this hotel and shown him your whore."

Hunter clenched his fists at his sides. "She is not a whore."

"Oh, no! What do you call her then? Mistress. Harlot."

His face dark red, he cleared his throat and extended his hands in front of him. "Caroline Fancy, calm yourself."

She drew herself up with tremulous dignity. Her son was staring at her with wide dark eyes. His small mouth hung open in amazement. She smiled shakily. "I think perhaps you'd better go up to your room, Alex."

50

Swiftly, he looked from one parent to the other, then hugged the toy boat to his chest. "You won't change your mind about taking me on the big boat, will you, Daddy?"

"I won't change my mind."

While they waited in silence, Alex cast a mutinous look at his mother before he trudged out and closed the door behind him.

No sooner had it shut than Hunter put forth a restraining hand. "Don't say anything you'll be sorry for, Caroline."

"I don't intend to," she hissed. "I shall be pleased with everything that I say now. I shall relish every word I utter. I rode fifty miles today through the dust and heat to reach you."

"You should not have come."

Her voice was lightly mocking, her hand waving an imaginary perfumed handkerchief through the air. "Oh-la, sir, of course not. How inconvenient for you that I should have found out about your real reason for this sea voyage!"

Dark brows drew together in a threatening frown. "Careful, Caroline," he warned.

She dropped into a belligerent crouch. "'I have been very unhappy of late,'" she quoted. "'I think we should separate for a time. I am going on a voyage, but you cannot go, Caroline.'" Roughened with anger and pain, her voice sounded like a travesty of its former self. "Of course, you could not have taken me. Not with 'Aunt Jessica' along."

He shook his head. "This is not what you think. Mistress Rutledge had merely proposed that since I was sailing to France, she might accompany me that far and then take ship to England to join her husband. Being a gentleman . . ."

"Oh, and does she intend to surprise him? Since she

51

has not 'entertained correspondence' since the war with him, she may have trouble locating him immediately."

Impossibly, Hunter's flush deepened. He bit his lip. "Damn it all, Caroline, this is your own fault." He spun away and began to stride up and down the room.

"I fail to see how your adultery can be my fault."

"If you had been a wife to me . . ."

She came out from behind the loveseat to intercept him. Toe to toe they stood, she looking up into his face. "I *am* a wife to you. And the mother of your son who, as you are trying to forget, is my son, too."

"I have no intention of forgetting that." His dark eyes shifted from her face to a spot somewhere on the wall beyond her left shoulder.

She stared up at the implacable set of his jaw. "Hunter." She put one hand on his lapel, the other over her heart. "Hunter. Please allow me to correct what I've done wrong. I swear I can change it. I came here today to do whatever you wanted me to in order to—" she swallowed hard against the lump in her throat, her voice wavering, "to be what you want."

"Fancy . . ."

Tears were very near the surface now as anger began to give way to exhaustion. "I love you, Hunter. I do above all things. Please let's begin again here. Now. I'll forgive you if you'll forgive me. And I'll change. I swear I will. Do you want me to starve myself? I'll do it. Do you want me to ride for miles every day? I'll ride them and more. I can do anything. Anything. So long as I have your love to strengthen me." Her face was only inches below his, her golden eyes soft with pleading.

He drew his head back. "Fancy, don't. For God's sake. That's enough."

"No, it's not nearly enough." Stepping back, she held out her arms. "As I rode today, I rehearsed all the things I was going to say to you. The promises I was going to make." As she spoke she turned away, the black skirt sweeping the floor behind her.

She paced the length of the room, then halted, her head tilted back, her chin jutting forward. In that moment, she had gained strength and a bit of self-control. "As I rode, I acknowledged your right to condemn me. I had disappointed you in so many ways. I had allowed myself to grow weak. Fear of death and dying—my baby daughter's and my own—had made me a coward. I had almost drowned myself in self-pity."

Decidedly uncomfortable in the presence of her candor, at a loss about what to say, he pressed his lips together sternly.

"I could hardly see the road sometimes through my tears, thinking how you must have suffered. I was dying of love for you and praying so hard that you would forgive me. I painted foolish little fantasies of your taking me in your arms and kissing me. Of the three of us sailing off together." She gritted her teeth until the muscles beneath her jaw strutted. "You would have laughed to see me."

"I would not have laughed," he denied angrily.

"I think you would have. The sight of your old fat wife riding down the dusty road in the steamy noonday sun, weeping and praying." She smiled mirthlessly. "Come now. Admit it. Doesn't the picture tickle you?"

"I would *not* have laughed."

"Of course, I was crying as much in pain as in grief," she admitted, her eyes suddenly bleak as stones. "I must be one solid bruise from the back of my knees up to the middle of my back. And my shoulders don't bear thinking about. That big black hunter of yours has a heavy head and a hard mouth." She searched his face hopefully for some sign of softening, of acceptance.

Hunter stirred restively. "Caroline Fancy, this isn't

getting us anywhere."

A great void opened up beneath her heart. She had delivered all her speeches, yet he remained coldly immovable. Pain cut through her with a jagged edge. Humiliation made a bitter taste in her mouth. She sucked in a deep quick breath.

Narrowly, he watched her as she struggled heroically for enough control to keep from crumpling to the floor before his eyes. "Now, Fancy . . ."

Her pride surfaced and she made a slashing motion with her hand. "Yes, Hunter. You're surely right. This isn't getting us anywhere. You will not give me the chance to change."

"I didn't say this separation was to be permanent," he inserted, his voice gruff.

She shook her head. "Spare me the sop. I'll come directly to the point and get out of your way. I'm going to take a room at this"—she looked contemptuously toward the loveseat where Jessica had sat—"bordello. In the morning I'll take the carriage, since you won't be needing it any longer, and Alex and I will be returning to England's Fancy."

Her husband's eyes narrowed dangerously. "You'll do no such thing," he contradicted.

"Oh, I think I will," she sneered. "But don't worry. I'll leave you the horse, so you may *vary the riding* before you sail. After that, you may *ride* the waves—or whatever you will."

"That's enough." He came toward her, his movements menacing.

She did not retreat. "Surely you can't imagine that I would allow you to take my son on this voyage now. He shan't be exposed to your vice and corruption."

"I warn you, Caroline Fancy."

Refusing to look at him any longer, she turned on her heel. With the long braid of dusty auburn hair twitching from side to side down her back, she swaggered to the door.

His voice caught her. "I'll not let you take Alex back to England's Fancy to turn him into a farmer."

She drew herself up haughtily, one hand on the doorknob. "Try and stop me. The Englands were a power in South Carolina while your relatives were still working off their indentures."

With those words, she left him. The door slammed behind her.

She had intended to make an early start, but the next morning her body betrayed her. When she tried to get out of bed, she found she could not move. Muscles from neck to heels were frozen. Likewise injured were the palms of her hands, blistered from the reins, and her shoulders, stiff from fighting the head of a horse too big for her to handle. Only by the most agonizing efforts could she crawl from her bed and stagger the few feet across the floor to the bellpull.

When at last the maidservant appeared, surly of face and frowzy of hair, Fancy had regained the bed and begged only for a pot of tea and a chance to die in peace. By midafternoon, she could move with difficulty about her room, but in no way could she attempt the steep stairs. The steamy heat of the Charleston dockside floated in through the single window of her room, bathing her in misery. Her cheekbones and the bridge of her nose were covered with tiny water blisters where the sun had burned her. Where the corset had been so tightly laced around her waist her skin was covered with a twelve-inch band of fiery prickly heat.

Her message sent to her husband demanding that he bring Alex to her bedside went unanswered. A different servant who brought her a tray of food at suppertime could give Fancy no information at all.

As night fell and no one came near her, the full extent of her predicament added to her misery and her self-condemnation. She was virtually crippled, her few garments a wreck; there was no maidservant to help her, no funds to pay her bill. When Fancy had set out on this ill-starred expedition, she had naively and foolishly trusted to her husband to take care of all the details.

Memories of Holy Dulcibella's skeptical words ran through her mind. Her trusted servant had suspected, perhaps known of Hunter's woman. Yet she had not warned her, not given her even a hint.

"Damn you, Dulci," she whispered. "Damn you. Damn you. I can't bear your cruelty. Step back and stand alone. Damn you."

As the sounds and smells of the dockside drifted in through the open window, she acknowledged herself a fool and worthy of nothing but contempt. Her anger at her betrayal by everyone she felt she could trust kept her from crying. Instead, she lay on her bed and recounted the injustices Hunter had done to her. Granted they were few and far between, but her pain and discomfort magnified them.

Far into the night she lay, her mind twisting and turning futilely as she could find no excuse for her multitude of sins. Finally, toward dawn, she fell into a shallow sleep from which she awoke periodically as her limbs twitched and jerked.

For forty-eight hours she remained alone, attended only by surly servants.

Shortly after noon of the third day, she pulled herself out of bed determined to ring for a bath. While she soaked in the tub of tepid water, she sent the maid away to press the only dress she had brought with her. The impudent woman unsuccessfully stifled a giggle when she picked up the waistcoat of the riding habit and guessed the reason for the slit back seam.

Fancy flushed with anger and embarrassment as she sank lower into the tub. If she never ate again, she vowed to regain the shape she had lost. The woman's sneering was the last straw. Hastily, she clapped the washcloth to her flaming cheeks, stemming the tears of anger and unhappiness before they could fall.

At last dried and dressed in clean, pressed clothing, she seated herself at the small dressing table.

With arms so sore she could barely raise them above her head, she unbraided her hair and began to brush it. The task was exhausting and tears stood in her eyes when the brush encountered the tangles and snarls. It had not been taken down since Holy Dulcibella had braided it four days ago.

From the crown to the softly curling tips at the back was a good yard. In happier days, Hunter had loved to spread it about her like a veil, hiding everything but the tips of her breasts and her long white limbs.

At least it was unchanged. It was still thick and wavy. The color was still the same rich auburn. No white strands appeared in it, though she searched as she brushed, fully expecting to see them.

If Hunter could see her now, what would he say? Jessica Rutledge's hair had been a pale buttercup-yellow and short. Any length she might have had was undoubtedly bound up in a tiny knot under that exquisitely modish bonnet, Fancy thought waspishly. For a deserted wife, Mistress Rutledge had certainly been able to afford elegant clothes.

Horrified, Fancy sat bolt upright, staring unseeing at the mirror as the picture of that dress materialized in her mind. The very latest style, beautiful sheer pink gauze over a taffeta slip of rose. A rose taffeta ribbon below her tiny breasts. The low neck trimmed with the same rose taffeta. Her little fan, her tiny lace gloves, her . . .

Suddenly, Fancy began to choke. Hunter had bought that dress for Jessica Rutledge. If he had had his monogram embroidered on the skirt, Fancy could not have been more sure.

Flinging down the hairbrush, she covered her eyes with her hand. Her own dress that she had chosen to wear was close to ten years old. Despite the good quality of the material, it was sadly out of style. She had no matching bonnet, no stylish gloves; even her shoes were old.

Pain like a lance through her breastbone made her catch her breath. Had she really been such a terrible failure to him?

Stifling a sob, she wiped the tears from her cheeks with the heel of her hand. Torturing herself would do no good. Her main concern now was Alex. Under no circumstances would she allow Hunter to sail away with her son in the care of "Aunt Jessica."

Gritting her teeth, she rose and straightened her stiff, bruised body. Her long auburn hair she swung around to the back, smoothing it away from her temples and tucking it behind her ears. Turning sideways, she threw a glance at herself in the mirror. Perhaps her stomach was smaller, but not much.

In order to descend the stairs, she had to hold on to the bannister with both hands. However, the muscles seemed to be loosening. At last she drew a deep breath, removed her hand from the newel post, and managed to walk almost normally across the lobby to the desk.

"What room is assigned to Master Alex Gillard?"

The clerk was the same one who had ushered her to the door of The Colonial Rose. He glanced up as she approached, then let his eyes fall again to the register in front of him. "I . . . that is, we have no one registered by that name."

She tapped one finger imperiously on the scarred cypress desk. "Of course he's not registered. He's staying with his father, Hunter Gillard. However, you cannot have so many small boys staying in this inn that you would have trouble remembering the room."

"We have no one registered by that name, either."

A dark premonition rose in her brain. "What?" Her clear voice sank to a hoarse whisper.

"They are no longer staying here. They paid their bill and left."

"Where have they gone?"

The man met her eyes then, his face expressionless. If he knew the right of her story, he gave no sign. "I believe they have moved their things to a ship. . . ."

"A ship! . . . What ship?"

He hesitated, then shrugged. "The porter carried their luggage to the *Carolina*."

Fancy swayed where she stood. "The *Carolina*! The new merchantman of the Shepperton Lines."

"That's the one. A real beauty."

"When does she sail?"

The man refused to meet her eyes. "I'm not sure."

Fancy struck the desk with her fist. "Damn it. When?"

"At the end of the week."

She turned away from the desk, her mind in turmoil. She had just over two days to get Alex away from Hunter. And she was without funds, without proper clothing. Straightening her back and assuming her haughtiest expression, she turned back to the clerk. "I presume the Gillard carriage and horses were stabled at this inn."

"Yes, ma'am."

"Please send them round immediately."

The clerk frowned. "I'd have to go for them myself.

There's nobody but me on duty right now in the middle of the day."

She gave him a look of icy dignity. "I assume you are on duty alone because no one is likely to come in at this time. In the unlikely event that anyone should come in, I'm sure he can wait a few moments until you return."

The clerk shook his head. "I don't think I can, ma'am. I'm the only one on duty. . . ."

Her control snapped. She slammed her fist down on the desk so hard that the inkwell jumped and the quill pen fell out onto the register. "Damn you! Go for those horses and that carriage this very instant."

The clerk fell back against the wall, then ducked from behind the desk. "Yes, ma'am. Right away, ma'am."

She strove for calm. "I'll stay right here by the desk," she informed him. "If anyone comes, I'll tell him you are on an errand for me. I'm sure that will be satisfactory." The dark auburn brows rose and fell above her golden eyes.

The clerk stumbled over his own feet as he spun away and raced for the door.

Chapter Four

"Excuse me, madam. You can't go in there. Mr. Wentworth is a very busy man." The secretary all but fell over his desk, but Fancy ignored him and thrust open the door. "Madam!"

As she swept into the interior office, Reginald Wentworth rose from behind the desk. The secretary hovered behind her, his hands outstretched, fingers twitching futilely. He shrugged hopelessly as Wentworth's bushy gray eyebrows rose almost to his hairline, then snapped together in a frown.

"He'll see me," Fancy advised the man briskly. "Mr. Wentworth, I am Caroline England Gillard." She paused for effect, but the man made no response other than a slight tightening of his mouth.

"I tried to stop her, Mr. Wentworth," the secretary bleated. "But she barged . . . that is, hurried right past me."

Wentworth's frown deepened. Doubling his hands into fists, he pressed them into the desk and leaned forward. "Young woman," he began sternly, "I'm a busy man. Perhaps you'd better make an appointment with my secretary. . . ."

Fancy halted directly in front of Wentworth's desk.

The thick pall of smoke from his cigar made her eyes water, but she did not retreat. "I am Josiah Shepperton's stepdaughter."

Wentworth's frown deepened. He stared her up and down. Under his intense scrutiny, Fancy stiffened, clenching her bare hands around the small cloth reticule. The appraising stare of the man's slightly bloodshot eyes made her supremely aware of her disreputable state. She should have gone to a dressmaker and had a proper outfit sewn for herself. She would have done so had she not been so desperate for time.

Left at the hotel without funds, she had enlisted the services of one of the chambermaids, a blowzy woman whose duties were mainly limited to cleaning and bedmaking. The woman had been competent enough with an iron. The old-fashioned dress had been pressed properly. Unfortunately, with no gloves or bonnet and with riding boots showing beneath the hem of the skirt, the garment looked worse than it really was. Furthermore, the maid's best efforts at coiffure had resulted in Fancy's bright red hair being scraped back and braided into a crooked coronet. Fancy had known after her first glance in the dim mirror on the washstand that the effect was unsatisfactory.

Now the expression on Wentworth's face confirmed Fancy's fears. The manager of the shipping line thought her peculiar, perhaps even deranged. She pressed her lips together and clutched her empty reticule so tightly that her knuckles whitened. The unfortunate impression created by her dress only added to her nervousness. She had never dealt with a man of business before. "I am Caroline England Gillard," she repeated through dry lips.

His expression did not change. If anything, he looked more repressive than before.

"Of England's Fancy," she continued, her voice drawing strength. "The largest tobacco plantation in Colleton County."

The secretary hovered behind her. "Perhaps you'd like to wait in the outer office until Mr. Wentworth is able to see you. He's a very busy man and—"

Fancy raised her shoulder irritably. "I haven't got time to wait. I came about the *Carolina*. She sails with the tide Friday."

Wentworth stirred restively, straightening his body and picking up a pencil.

The secretary pounced upon her statement. "Ah, madam, you've come to the wrong place. You don't book passage here. You must purchase your ticket at the shipping office. I'll be happy to escort you there," he informed her helpfully.

Fancy's full attention remained fixed on Wentworth. She directed her answer to him. "I'm not here to purchase a ticket, Mr. Wentworth. Indeed, I may want the refund of a ticket. A child is in danger. I assure you, this won't take up any more of Mr. Wentworth's time than is absolutely necessary."

The men exchanged looks. Wentworth nodded curtly. "I'll see Mrs. Gillard now, Biggers. But be sure to inform me in plenty of time for my next appointment."

"Yes, sir." The secretary bowed his way out and closed the door.

Wentworth reseated himself and pushed aside several papers on his desk. "Now, Mrs. Gillard, what was this about a child in danger?" His voice revealed his skepticism.

Fancy nodded hastily. "The fact is that I need your help, Mr. Wentworth. As my stepfather's representative, I was sure you would be happy to assist me." She made an effort to smile winningly at him, but his frown

63

remained firmly in place.

Suddenly, she was conscious that he had not asked her to sit down. With marked rudeness, he had reseated himself without offering her a chair. The heat rising in her cheeks, she clutched the small cloth reticule as she sought to control her temper. The man was not to be condemned. From his point of view, she had all but broken into his office and refused to leave when his secretary had asked her to. Still . . .

He cleared his throat noisily. "Well, what can I do, Mrs. Gillard? Please state your problem. I'm a busy man. . . ."

"I can't believe you don't know who I am," she countered.

He sighed. "I know who you are, Mrs. Gillard."

"Then you know that my mother is Mrs. Blanche Stoddart Shepperton of Boston, your employer's wife."

His face stony, he raised his eyes and regarded her sternly. "I am a very busy man, Mrs. Gillard. This is a place of business."

She flushed uncomfortably. "My son—my mother's grandson—is being taken away. Kidnapped," she blurted.

He leaned back in his chair. "Kidnapped?"

He was not reacting as she had foreseen. "Yes, kidnapped. Taken away from me. On board the *Carolina*."

He folded his arms across his chest, a most unusual position for a man sitting down. With his belly bulging out over his huge thighs, he looked like an implacable Buddha.

She cleared her throat. "You must help me. The *Carolina* must not sail with my son aboard."

"Have you been to the proper authorities? The magistrates?"

"Well, no, but—"

"Why do you think he is being kidnapped?"

The question was delivered in a tone that snapped her control. "Damn you. What kind of a man are you? I tell you my son's been kidnapped and you sit there, with arms folded, questioning me."

"A cautious man, Mrs. Gillard." His eyes narrowed. His jaw tightened. He heaved his bulk onto his feet. "I think perhaps you'd better leave."

"No!" She met him at the corner of the desk. Toe to toe, she challenged him. "You're the manager of this branch of Shepperton Lines. You can hold a ship until the proper authorities can act."

"The *Carolina* does not sail until Friday as you know, Mrs. Gillard. Any *authorities*"—his voice was heavy with sarcasm—"you would wish to summon would be able to board the *Carolina* before she sails."

"Then I must speak to the captain."

"He is a very busy man. As I am." He strode to the door and held it open.

She stubbornly held her ground. "My son is being taken away from me."

"By his father."

She reeled. "How did you know that?"

"Mr. Gillard has already made all the arrangements. He warned me that you were not amicable about the separation."

"Mr. Gillard has already warned you!"

"He told me that you were in ill health, not quite right in your mind," he added with breathtaking insensitivity. He stared at her. "I can see that he told the truth. Perhaps you would be better served to—"

The condescending tone infuriated her. "Damn it! My son is being taken away from his home and mother. He is only ten years old. His father is the one who has lost his mind. If you do not act, your

65

employer's grandson will be—"

"Mr. Gillard has my confidence," he interrupted, coming back to take her arm above the elbow.

"How much has he paid you to betray your employer?" she snarled, jerking her arm out of his grasp.

He puffed his chest out angrily. "I assure you, my loyalty to Shepperton's best interest is above reproach."

"Then I cannot believe you would not be willing to act to prevent a grave injustice. The man can go as a passenger on your ship. But you must hold the ship until I can take my son back." As she spoke, she backed away from the door until the backs of her thighs came in contact with the edge of his desk. "You must."

He gestured peremptorily, his patience clearly strained. "Mrs. Gillard, I am a very busy man. I have given you a fair hearing."

"Your mind was already made up."

He sighed. "My mind was not made up. I told Mr. Gillard that I had grave reservations about the entire proceeding. And so I did—until I met you."

She made a sharp exclamation of protest.

"Mrs. Gillard, be reasonable." His tone implied that he clearly believed her incapable of being so. "You thrust your way into my presence in a manner most indecorous. Likewise, your dress and demeanor suggest that you have not been well. You have used a tone of voice and language unbefitting a lady. As you spoke, I watched and listened closely. I am forced to agree with your husband that the boy would in every respect benefit from this voyage while you have a chance to recover your health and mind."

Fancy shook her head; her face contorted. Her voice sank to a desperate growl. "I am not crazy."

His manner switched to unctuous sympathy. "Mrs.

Gillard, calm yourself. You've allowed yourself to become overwrought."

"Damn you. I'll report you to my stepfather. He'll see that you receive a reprimand for this business."

An angry flush mottled Wentworth's already-florid face. Advancing steadily, he herded her across the office with his bulky body. "Please leave."

She caught hold of the connecting door. "At least give me the name of the captain of the ship so I may speak with him."

All but prying her fingers from their grip, Wentworth hustled her across his secretary's office and opened the door to the street. "The name will do you no good."

On the sidewalk, she caught at the arm that thrust her there. "Billy-be-damned!" she shouted. "Give me that name!"

Her furious violence drove him back a step. He gritted his teeth and lowered his head. His shoulders hunched; his big frame totally blocked the door. The secretary's white face hovered openmouthed above his shoulder. "Very well then, Mistress Gillard. You shall have it. James Hunter Gillard is to captain the *Carolina*, by order of Josiah Shepperton himself. Good day, madam." He slammed the door in her face.

Hunter must have planned this move for months. Correspondence of which she had no knowledge must have passed back and forth between England's Fancy and Boston.

Stunned, she turned away. Like a wraith, her face white as paper, she drifted down the street toward the hotel, her mind turning round and round on one inescapable fact. They had all plotted against her. Hunter, Josiah, perhaps even her own mother. Blanche had had no patience with grief even when Fancy's father had died. Within months, she had left the plantation to visit friends in Boston. Within a year, she had married.

No. No one cared about Fancy's feelings, Fancy's grief.

Somehow she made her way back to the hotel. As if she had walked in her sleep, she awakened in her room to stare around her in some surprise. Without bothering to slip out of her clothes, she climbed up on the bed and stretched out with closed eyes, hoping to force her mind to remain witless.

How much could she face? How much without dying? The contempt of other people—the people who should have loved her—was overpowering. Her husband's desertion had been a crushing blow. She had accepted it and tried to rise above it. Now on the crest of that loss, she had been delivered another blow of even greater magnitude than the first. Her mother and stepfather had sided with her husband. They had actually participated in his desertion.

Alex's grandmother thought he should leave his mother and go to sea.

She had no tears. Instead, she kept her eyes closed lest they be so dry that the very air would wither them. Not only her body, but her mind and her soul must be useless. Everyone who she had believed loved her believed she was unfit to raise her own son.

At last she fell asleep, awakening in darkness. Gripped by profound depression, she could not bring herself to move. From far away, she could hear someone calling her name. Hunter's voice was calling her name. She heard a knocking at the door, then Hunter's voice calling her name.

Was she mad? Had her mind, faced with such a tragic present, slipped into a safe past? She listened again, fearful to hear and fearful not to hear.

"Caroline . . ." And again the light knocking.

She tried to call out, but her throat was too dry. Swinging her legs over the edge of the bed, she stood and trudged to the door. "Yes."

"Caroline. Are you all right?"

She chuckled faintly. "No."

There was silence. "No?"

"I'm dying. . . ."

A long pause, then his voice came again through the thick oak. "Open this door."

Her fingers took instructions from him rather than from her. She pushed the bolt back and swung the door open. He stood there, looking tall and handsome, his face carefully closed to all emotion. If the dead whiteness and the deep lines of her face shocked him, he gave no sign. Still, after a minute, his voice registered some concern. "Are you all right?"

This time she did not bother to answer him. Instead, she concentrated on clinging to the door facing to keep from crumpling to the floor. An instant after her haunted eyes found him, they fell to staring at a spot on the floor between the toes of his boots.

"You've been feeling sorry for yourself," he accused.

"Holy Dulcibella has already told me that," she muttered dully.

His eyebrows rose, black wings in his tanned face. "She's right."

The silence grew between them. He shifted from one foot to the other. At length, he shrugged. "I've paid your bill at the hotel. You can go home tomorrow in the carriage."

Her stiff lips moved in an absolutely still face. "Why?"

"Why what?"

"Why do me a favor?"

"You're still my wife."

"I'd rather you killed me than treat me as you are."

"Angel." His voice was only a whisper.

Her eyes flew to his face.

Instantly, he stepped back, the expression gone. "Go home, Caroline Fancy. Grow up. I'll see you in a year."

Before he could turn away, she shut the door quietly in his face and leaned against it. In the silence, she could imagine him, frowning at the dark wood, perhaps rubbing a hand across the lower half of his face. Perhaps doubling up his fist to knock again. A tiny hope grew inside her, then died as she heard the scuffle of his boots, then the thud of his heels as he strode away.

For a minute, she thought his visit had been a dream. Then a fierce spirit of rebellion, born of fiery hot temper, rose in her again. He would not take her son. She still had one more day. She would go to court tomorrow. No judge in his right mind would separate a mother from her child. She would prevent this sailing, come hell or high water.

At dawn the next morning, Fancy rousted the dressmaker out of bed.

The woman was recalcitrant. She recognized Fancy, of course, but had had no trade from her in over two years. She made no effort to conceal her contempt at the sight of her former customer dressed in a frumpish old gown, years out of style.

Furthermore, a consultation of the latest measurements of Fancy's last garments proved embarrassing in the extreme. Fancy blushed red as fire as the tape went round her hips, waist, and bosom. Obviously amused, the woman announced the new measurements in a loud, clear voice as she jotted them down on a pad at her elbow.

For three hours Fancy suffered measureless humiliation. By mid-morning, she emerged in a dress of serviceable blue wool, with high waist—"so flattering to the fuller figure," the woman had cattily informed her—and long sleeves. Since Fancy could not allow the time to have the costume decorated, the dress would have been distressingly plain had not the dressmaker taken pity on her. Inside the high plain neck she had pinned a Betsie of fine batiste. The effect was more of a young girl than a mature woman embarked on a serious mission, but at least the style was right.

The dressmaker had sent to other shops after they opened, and she had purchased bonnet, gloves, parasol, and shoes. She had added the prices to her bill with a ten percent fee for her trouble, but Fancy had the security of knowing that they were correct.

As she had stood for the gown to be hemmed on her, she had thought through the argument she would present to the lawyer who would take her case immediately to the judge. No barging in unprepared this time. No cursing. She would be polite and well-bred. No angry denunciations. She would be a mother deprived of her son. She would have the voice of sweet reason on her side.

Taking a last critical glance at herself in the dressmaker's cheval glass, she smiled a tremulous smile. The color went well with her hair and her pale face. She was as ready as she would ever be.

Leaving the old dusty rose dress with instructions to burn it, she stepped out onto Church Street. Shame kept her from going directly to any of the homes of her friends. How could she go to them with her story and beg for help? They would gossip about this for weeks.

Her name would be on every tongue. She would be the subject of pity and scorn. She could imagine some of the women who had envied her marriage to Hunter. What delight they would take in her humiliation. How she prayed that Jessica Rutledge had at least had the decency to be discreet!

Vaguely, she remembered her father had spoken highly of a lawyer named Thomas Aiken. When she had inquired after him, the desk clerk had nodded sagely as if he recognized the name. The man's address was on Queen Street off the more fashionable Battery and Church Streets, but still a respectable neighborhood. Gathering her courage about her, she gave the direction to the driver of her carriage.

At Aiken's door, she paused to gather her courage. Then she thought of Alex taken across the sea, gone from her for a year. An accident, a storm, pirates, anything might occur. And "Aunt Jessica."

Furling her parasol, she lifted the knocker and let it fall with a determined thud. Once inside, she asked the butler to announce her as Miss England.

Trembling inwardly, she was ushered into Aiken's study in less than a minute. The lawyer rose from behind his desk. "Miss England," he began, coming toward her. "My dear Miss England. Caroline, is it not?"

"Yes," she whispered. "Yes, it is I, Caroline. I am Miss England." Her voice was so low he could not be sure he heard the words. "I am Richard England's daughter and the granddaughter of Edward England, who came here in the eighteenth century and founded England's Fancy." She was pleased to hear her voice gaining strength.

"I knew them both. And I remember you as a little girl, with long red curls." He glanced at her face framed by the blue bonnet, then took her hand and drew her to

72

an Adam chair in front of his desk. "They were both fine men. I was sorry to hear of your father's death. In the midst of life." He took a deep breath.

"It was a great loss," she agreed. "I miss him still. Sometimes so much I can hardly keep from crying." She stilled the impulse to touch her gloved finger to her eye. Tilting back her head, she kept the tears from falling.

Aiken patted her shoulder sympathetically. "And how may I serve the daughter of my old friend?"

"I am married now," she told him. "Or at least I believed myself to be."

He regarded her narrowly. "My dear Mrs.—"

"—Gillard. Oh, I am still married legally, but my husband has decided that we should separate for a time." The lawyer seated himself behind his desk and laced his fingers together over its polished top. His expression was carefully neutral. Quickly, she looked at him, then turned away, concentrating on the play of sunlight through the tree that shaded the window behind him. Even as she spoke, she cringed from having to tell the entire sordid tale again. The repetition clawed at her belly like a knife's blade.

Briefly, she outlined the death of their daughter and her subsequent illness. She spared herself the story of Jessica.

"I can understand his desire to return to the sea, which was his first love," she stated in a flat, dry voice. "But I cannot allow him to take Alexander on an extended voyage. It is too dangerous. Storms, accidents, diseases, even pirates. I cannot lose my son." Her voice faltered to a whisper. He had to lean forward to hear it. "I cannot have any more children."

Aiken shook his head faintly at the end of the short recital. The situation was without hope. The least he could do was to try to ease her grief. "I'm sure your love

73

and fear have made you oversensitive to the danger, Caroline. May I call you Caroline? Why, with your husband to look after him, this trip should turn into every boy's dream. I can't say I don't envy him."

During the recital she had bowed her head, only allowing herself to look out from under her eyelashes in what she hoped was a helpless, pretty way. Now her head snapped up. "Envy him?"

"Surely. He's a lucky boy, getting to go to sea with his father. He'll come back broadened by the travel and matured amazingly by association with men. A good experience for a boy. It's bound to develop his character."

"His education will be neglected," she began desperately.

Aiken nodded reassuringly. "And, of course, you would consider that first, good mother that you are, but don't you see? He has the opportunity to sail to foreign ports, to speak the languages and hear them spoken by the people who are native. He'll see their customs firsthand. Surely you must see that this experience is far more valuable than a history lesson taught by some dull tutor who learned his information from some out-of-date book."

"But his mathematics, his science, his—"

"I'm sure those can wait for just a year."

She took a tighter grip on her parasol. When she finally allowed herself to speak, she spaced the words evenly. "I don't want him to go. The danger is far too great."

"With your husband—the boy's father—watching his every step?"

Fancy took a deep breath. Pride be damned. She would tell the truth. "I fear my husband will have other things to watch."

The lawyer looked at her shrewdly. "Such as?"

If she lived to be a hundred, she would never know greater shame than that moment. The words rasped from her throat. "His mistress is accompanying them on this trip. I do not want my son exposed to such depravity. Alexander is not stupid. He will soon figure out what his father and this . . . woman are doing."

Aiken exhaled a long, slow breath. "So that is the way of it."

"Exactly."

The silence grew in the room. Through the open window at his back, a bird hopped from branch to branch. It twittered faintly, then flew away. Aiken stared at the woman before him. Two spots of color rode her cheeks in an otherwise white face. Her faintly slanted eyes, startlingly gold beneath dark lashes and brows, reminded him markedly of her father. He would have recognized her anywhere. He drew a deep breath. "I cannot help you."

She clutched the handle of the parasol with one hand. The other was clenched in a tight fist at her waist. "You must. Surely you can meet with a judge right now. Explain the situation. Get him to issue an order to prevent the sailing of the *Carolina*. If necessary, place James Hunter Gillard under arrest for kidnapping."

"A father cannot kidnap his own child."

She stood abruptly. The tip of her parasol struck the floor sharply as she came to the far side of his desk. "Then you won't help me?"

He looked up into the white face, up into the exotic golden eyes. "Believe me, Mrs. Gillard, I would if I could. But at this late hour, I cannot get an order that would delay the sailing."

"Then secure an order for his arrest. I will swear he kidnapped my child. I will swear to anything." Her voice sank till it was heavy with threat.

Aiken shook his head. "You would waste your time,

dear lady, and be exposed to shame and embarrassment. And when all was said and done, I can almost swear that the court would find against you."

"But she was having tea with him in a private parlor. Neither of them even bothered to deny anything."

"But you have no witnesses. There is no law that a man and woman may not have tea together. You have no proof."

"Dear God!" She spun away, pressing a hand to her throat. "I saw them with my own eyes and heard them with my own ears."

He came round the desk to her side, putting one arm around her shoulders.

"My dear Caroline, your son will be quite all right. His father cherishes him as much as you do. He will allow no harm to come to him. Surely you can wait a little while. A voyage is not such a long time."

Her voice was muffled. "It could very well be forever."

He patted her shoulder helplessly. "Dear lady, dear child, I wish I could help you. I can only offer you words of advice from one who has lived longer than you and seen much. These things have a way of running their course. Your husband may have strayed, but he will soon see the error he has fallen into and come home."

"I don't want him to come home!"

"Caroline! Don't say something you don't mean. You are a lovely young woman and perhaps have a right to be a little jealous, but I'm sure you have exaggerated the situation in your own mind. A man must be allowed a little license." His voice had taken on the unctuous tone he used to sway magistrates and juries.

Stepping out from under his arm, she turned to face him. His hair was gray and thinning; his face deeply lined. This man was older than her father would be had he lived. He was a man of the law. He should be aligning with her on the side of right, instead of paying her fatuous compliments and babbling about license.

Thinking he had reached her with his arguments, he smiled winningly. His expression faded, however, when she spoke again.

"Will you take my case to a judge?" she asked flatly. The golden eyes took his measure.

He turned away. Hands clasped behind him, he began an aimless prowl of the carpet. "It would be useless."

"Then I'll bid you good day." She turned and started for the door, but he overtook her and planted himself straight in her path.

"I'm sure you are overwrought. Your husband could not be so foolish nor so heartless as to abandon a pretty, sweet, good girl like yourself. He is a responsible man, is he not?"

"I had always believed him to be so."

"Then there you have it."

"Until now," she insisted with savage persistence.

"A leopard does not change his spots. He will return to you at the end of the year with your son. You will be able to overlook this little peccadillo. As you grow old together, you will forget it entirely."

"I don't want to forget it."

"What?"

"I shall never, never forget it."

"My dear Caroline . . ."

"Please spare me further humiliation, Mr. Aiken."

He drew himself up irritably. "I am trying to, Mrs. Gillard."

She looked him squarely in the eye. "You have been a great disappointment to me, Mr. Aiken. My father thought highly of you, therefore I came to you with

77

my problem."

"My dear, I am trying to think of your best interests. Your husband may be angered if you do not have more faith in him."

She made an inelegant sound. "I think he can survive the blow. He has called me everything but faithless. Perhaps he should add that to the sins already in his catalog." She stepped around him deliberately and strode to the door.

He pivoted to watch her, his hands folded behind his back. "I would advise you to do nothing foolish. Keep yourself above reproach, so he will have nothing to overlook when he does return."

"You don't understand," she told him, one hand on the knob, the other holding her parasol, tip down, as if it were a walking stick. "You don't understand at all. I don't want him back. I hate him. I don't care if I never see him again. But he shan't have my son."

"No judge can help you," he warned.

"Do you think I give a damn?" she shot back.

Chapter Five

The desk clerk had a younger brother whose clothes Fancy commandeered.

Dressed in long shabby trousers and a belted three-quarter jacket, her hair stuffed up under a loose peaked cap, she stared critically at herself in the small mirror. No one would notice her in the dusk of the street.

Under cover of darkness, she would walk to the berth of the *Carolina* and sneak aboard. Somehow she would locate Alex's cabin and . . .

She dared not think beyond that point. She could not lift him into her arms as she had when he was a baby. Would he obey her? Not without a protest. Her only hope lay in the fact that he would be more than half asleep. If she came to his bedside and woke him gently and led him, she just might be able to get him off the ship. The horses would be hitched to the carriage, her small carpetbag was packed. Hunter had paid her bill. She would leave in the dead of night.

Alex would fall asleep again as the carriage swayed out of town. He always did. Take him for a ride and he was asleep before the carriage cleared the lane of magnolias leading to the great house.

Hunter would sail with the morning tide. He might

not even bother to look in on his son before the ship cleared the harbor. Still, to be on the safe side, she would not return to England's Fancy for a week. She and Alex would take a little vacation south to Port Royal. In that way, she would assuage his disappointment for not getting to go on a ship with his father.

She turned sideways and stared over her shoulder at her back. Disgustedly, she pulled the three-quarter-length jacket down over her ample hips. Thank goodness the darkness would hide her.

Swinging back, she took a last critical look. Her face was too white, her skin too fine to be a lad's. Spitting on her hands, she rubbed them over the floor in the corner, then smeared her cheeks and forehead with grime. Her lip curled in self-disgust.

Hunter had brought her to this pass.

A quick last look, then she nodded tremulously at her reflection. Cupping her hand above the lamp chimney, she blew out the flame and opened the door.

The street along the dockside was busy. Men passed back and forth. Local merchants and tradespeople bustled about their business. Seamen were distinguished by their rolling walks as well as their seamen's bags slung over their shoulders. Aping their walk as best she could, Fancy struck out down toward the *Carolina*'s berth. Her disguise, coupled with the gathering dusk, kept her unnoticed.

As she neared the ship, she slowed in the shelter of a stack of heavy crates. Leaning against them as if she were loitering unconcernedly, she watched the final preparations being made for the *Carolina*'s departure with the early morning tide.

Scanning the deck, she caught no sight of Alex. Instead, men worked steadily under the direction of a man in a billed cap. Fresh provisions were being brought aboard: chickens and pigs in coops, a goat, as well as crates of vegetables. Local longshoremen rolled heavy-looking barrels of water and kegs of ale up a ramp.

If she were to work her way forward and just put her hands to one, the man assigned to the task would probably not protest. In such a manner, she might be able to get on board.

She started forward, then drew back. Once on board, then what? She did not know a ship well enough to be able to hide herself without being discovered. If she were discovered, Hunter would be alerted to her plan. Better to wait where she was until late at night. By that time, Alex would have fallen asleep. Wherever he was, he was sure to be bubbling with excitement, probably chattering a mile a minute in his boyish treble.

A lump grew in her throat at the thought of her little boy, so happy, so pleased. She was going to hurt him prodigiously. Still, he was so young. This would not be the only time he would have an opportunity to go on a voyage. She could not let him go with Hunter and "Aunt Jessica."

The lantern lights streamed out of the windows of a public house not far down the street. She longed to go inside and have a bite to eat and drink, but her disguise was too shallow.

Patiently, she slid down the side of the crate, drew up her knees, and rested her chin on her folded arms. From here she could watch until the activity all but ceased and Alexander was sure to be soundly tucked away.

One hour passed, then two. No one paid her the slightest attention. The moon swung high overhead. The activity on the dock continued unabated, but the

Carolina's deck was clear. The man in the peaked cap posted a watch and went below for a well-earned rest.

She dozed, only to awake with a start. Running a hand over her face, she wiped the sleep from her eyes. No one stood on the deck of the *Carolina*. The loading planks had been taken away, but the gangplank still stretched from the dock to the ship's deck.

As Fancy climbed to her feet, the stiffness in her limbs made her draw in her breath with a sharp hiss. Nevertheless, she pushed herself away from the crates and moved at a crouch toward the dark hulk of the ship. Her heart accelerated its rhythm in her chest; her nerves jumped and twitched in her belly; her scalp prickled.

A long look to right and left. At that moment, the street seemed to be practically deserted except for a carriage and a pair of horses near the hotel. Again she scanned the deck of the ship. Empty. The sails were furled, so the masts and spars stood clearly empty in silhouette against the bright moonlit sky. She wiped her sweating palms against the sides of the desk clerk's brother's pants.

One step, two, the gangplank was in front of her. Her foot was on it. Suddenly, a powerful hand seized her arm and spun her away. She gave a muffled cry and swung wildly at her captor.

The man ducked and chuckled softly as he dragged her back against him. "Enjoyed your rest, Caroline?"

"Hunter!" She relaxed against his hard chest, no longer afraid. His body was familiar to her, its height, its shape, its warmth. A tiny thrill went through her at his nearness.

His breath came warm only inches from her ear. "I had about decided that you were going to sleep all night long and wake up in the morning to find we had sailed."

Aghast and resentful, she tried to jerk away from

him. "You've known I was here all along."

He tightened his grip on her arm as he hustled her along the street past the windows of the public house. In the light spill, he stopped to turn her so he could see her face. "You've been a very busy girl, Caroline."

Her overwrought emotions dreaded what he was going to say to her. He would laugh at her, belittle her efforts, gloat over her failure. She bared her teeth in a snarl. "Let go of me!"

He shook his head. His face was in darkness, but she could hear the smile in his voice. "I watched you fall asleep. I signaled Bart to move in closer so nobody would bother you."

"You let me sit there all afternoon?" she asked bitterly.

She felt him shrug. "You were doing no one any harm."

"You must have known I came to try to get Alexander."

"I know everything."

"How nice for you."

"You never used to be sarcastic," he observed.

"I never had my son taken away from me. I never had my husband desert me for a whore."

"Jessica Rutledge is not a whore."

"Pardon me if I don't agree with you. I'll bet you've paid all her bills and bought her the elegant clothes she's wearing."

His silence was confirmation.

"What is she if she isn't a whore?" Fancy hissed. "Two a penny or two hundred. It's all the same."

"Shut your mouth."

"Her husband left her, so she takes up with mine to pay her bills and buy her clothes. I hope she's good in bed. I hope you feel you're getting your money's worth."

83

"Shut up."

She drove her elbow into the pit of his stomach at the same time she swung the toe of her boot with all her might against his shin.

He grunted and doubled over, one hand clutching his belly, the other groping for his injured leg. Her own leg was numb to the knee with the force of her kick. Nevertheless, she lunged away, limp-hopping into the pub. "Help! Help! Robbery! Murder!" Not pausing to judge the effect of her screams, she dashed headlong through the room.

By the time her husband had recovered sufficiently to pursue her, Fancy had already located the back door and flung it open. Hunter's dash into the pub was apprehended by the owner, flanked by two stalwarts whom he engaged to handle recalcitrant drunks.

Before Hunter could offer an explanation, the three manhandled him around and shoved him out onto the street. "Don't bring your troubles in here" was the succinct command as the publican dusted his hands.

Hunter would have forced his way back in had he not caught a glimpse of a fleeing figure. His mouth curved in a mirthless smile.

Fancy's only plan was to waste no time. While her husband was delayed with explanations, she would board the *Carolina* and take Alex. Panting as much from nervousness as from anything else, she dashed up the gangplank. On the deck she paused, glancing around her anxiously at the doors to the right and left below the quarterdeck. Breathing a quick prayer, she chose the one on the right.

It opened into a tiny closet of an entry, dark as pitch. Her heart pounding like a trip-hammer, she stretched out one hand before her and kept the other on the wall. A couple of steps and her questing fingers encountered a heavy curtain. Brushing it aside, she found herself in

84

a small cabin. A mooring lantern hanging from the outside of the ship revealed a small swinging cot.

It was too small for Hunter or even Jessica. Clasping her hands in thankfulness, she crept forward to look down into it. She could see nothing. It was like looking into a black box.

"Alex," she whispered. "Alex, sweetheart . . ."

Cautiously, she touched the side of the bed. It swung back and forth on its ropes. Too light. Disappointment surged inside her. This was not Alex's room. Or at any rate, he was not there.

Turning, she stumbled out, barking her shin over a chest and bruising her shoulder against the facing of the door as the ship lifted on her moorings. The wind had begun to freshen.

As she reached the other door beneath the quarter deck, Hunter stepped off the gangplank.

"Leave it, Caroline Fancy," he commanded.

She froze, then turned. "Give me my son, Hunter."

"No. He goes with me and you're going home."

She knotted her hands into fists and ground them into her hips. "You'll not be allowed to sail in the morning. I've—"

"You've made a fool of yourself," he interrupted curtly. "And embarrassed me."

"Give me Alex tonight and I'll call off the attorney. . . ." It was a bluff, but it was her last card.

"Caroline . . . Caroline . . ." He shook his head. "You never were a good liar. I've followed your trail ever since you managed to pull yourself out of bed twenty-four hours ago."

She straightened with outrage. How could he do her the injustice of thinking that she was lazy, when in fact she had been in too much pain to move? But he had not cared. Somehow, that thought hurt her. He was watching her closely, but the darkness effectively veiled her change of expression. "I don't intend to give Alex up" was all she said.

"Come." He held out his hand.

Instantly, she pulled back, but he just as quickly raised his hands shoulder height. "Just into my quarters. I've a bottle of sherry."

"I don't want to drink with you."

"Then we won't drink, but come."

She hesitated, staring around her in the darkness. Was she imagining things or was there the faintest hint of gray at the edge of the horizon? She shivered suddenly in dread. "L—lead the way."

Turning, he swung down the hatchway of the forward compartment. The merchantman was deep. Beneath the captain's cabins below the quarterdeck was another set of compartments. He led her into one of these. It was fitted with a sea chest, a table, and three chairs.

The significance of the arrangements struck her forcibly. She caught her lower lip between her teeth.

Hunter opened the door to a paneled cabinet and folded down a small tray. From a decanter, he poured two heavy glasses with dark brown liquid. Turning around with one in each hand, he caught her staring with fixed attention at the furniture. He pushed one glass into her line of vision.

She looked at him as she took it from his hand. As she watched, he drank, then motioned for her to do the same.

"Now," he said. "Drink up." He pulled out a chair and motioned her into it. Then he seated himself across from her.

She set the drink down untouched on the polished table.

"Wentworth was upset at your behavior," he began reproachfully. "Understandably so. The man was just doing his job."

"His job's in hell," she replied evenly. "I intend to take this directly to Josiah."

"He already knows."

"He can't know the whole of it. He's a proper Bostonian. He would never allow you the means to go on a cruise with your mistress. You've commandeered this ship under false colors. Unless you give up this wild scheme now, you could be faced with charges of piracy." She was talking wildly now, hardly making sense, the desperation like a shrill cutting edge in her voice.

Hunter leaned back in his chair, shaking his head. "Shepperton and I agreed that your illness was not getting better. For the sake of Alex, I convinced both him and your mother that—"

"My mother! . . ."

"Alex is her grandchild, after all."

"You told my mother lies about me!"

"They weren't lies."

"Of course you told her about Jessica Rutledge."

"Jessica Rutledge's name is on the passenger list."

She shook her head, her gold eyes accusing. "Hunter, I always thought you were a decent man."

His eyes narrowed. "If you've finished your drink, I'll take you to your carriage."

"I'll go straight to the police."

"Leave it, Caroline. Your lawyer told you the truth."

"You know about that?"

"I told you. I know about everything."

"Damn you!" She caught the glass of sherry from the table and flung it at his head. He ducked, but the glass shattered against the wall, the alcohol spraying in a wide arc across the room.

In the next movement, she launched herself at him, her fingernails arched in claws. His patronizing attitude infuriated her. He had had men follow her and report back to him as she struggled from one embarrassing, futile confrontation to another. Primal rage roared out of her throat as she crashed into him.

The heavy chair went over backward, propelled as much as anything by his effort to escape her clawing. They crashed together to the floor, Hunter underneath, their legs in the air, their bodies entangled in the arms and legs of the chair.

"Caroline, damn you!"

"No!" she screamed. "Damn you! *Damn you!* How much do you think I can stand?"

He caught at her wrists, wresting her hands away from his face where four white parallel scratches instantly beaded red. With a violent heave, he flung her over onto her back and rolled out of the chair on top of her. "I could kill you," he snarled. "Scratching and clawing, you wildcat. I've had enough of this and plenty."

His body stretched atop hers and bore down upon her. He was much too heavy, yet she struggled against him. Angrily, she bucked up, thrusting her heels into the floor. The violent movement brought her loins in contact with his. Shocked, she realized he was aroused.

Their faces only inches apart, their breaths commingling, they stared.

"Damn you, Angel," he whispered as his mouth came down hard on her own.

The kiss was without the slightest tenderness. Indeed, it was meant as a punishment. She squirmed, but he was relentless.

Suddenly, her own passion answered his. Kissing the ruthless tongue, laving it with her own, she welcomed the painful grinding of his loins against her mound. Shameful excitement shot through her as inexorably he stretched her wrists over her head. "Monster," she hissed. "What do you think you're doing?"

His only answer was to kiss her again as he coupled her wrists in his left hand and freed his right hand to roam over her body.

Through the covering layers of cloth, he found her breast with practiced ease. The kiss ceased to punish. Instead, his mouth moved over hers, nibbling at her upper lip. He ran his tongue along the edge of her teeth and felt her shudder beneath him. As her flesh betrayed her, he drew back, staring down into her face.

The light glinted in her eyes, turning them to gold-rimmed pools of darkest night. His own mouth lifted in a self-deprecatory sneer. "You still have the power, Caroline." Holding her with his eyes, he stripped away the boy's clothing from her breast. When it was bare, he stared down at it. The nipple was erect, the whole mound stiff with desire.

Her breath hissed from between her clenched teeth as he lowered his mouth then to her. At first he took the nipple delicately between his teeth as his knee wedged itself between her thighs.

"Stop, Hunter," she moaned. "Don't do this to me."

He did not stop. Instead, he suckled harder, nibbling at the stiffened nub of flesh. "Why not, Angel? You're here. I'm here. We both want it."

Adamantly, she shook her head back and forth. "I don't want it. I don't want anything at all from you. At least, nothing that you're willing to give," she amended. Her voice was cold, but its very breathlessness betrayed her.

"You're lying," he teased, his voice muffled as his lips trailed kisses up the mound of her breast and into the hollow at the base of her throat.

"I'm not lying." She pushed hard against his shoulders. "I don't want—"

"Pride is a cold companion, Caroline." He kissed her

again, long and lovingly.

Suddenly, tears trickled from the corners of her eyes. She loved him so. Despite everything. Unable and unwilling to deny herself, she arched her body up to his.

"Angel," he whispered. "That's right." He released her wrists to cup his hands under her buttocks and fit her tighter against him.

"Oh, Hunter . . ." Her body twisted and arched, rubbing against his.

He reared back on his heels to unbutton his trousers. She fumbled for the unfamiliar buttons of her own until he pushed her hands aside and finished the job. With her cooperation, he peeled the male garments down over her buttocks. Then she bent her knees, and he stripped her naked and flung the clothes aside.

"The cap," he whispered.

Obediently, she tugged it off and flung it after the other garments.

He threaded ungentle fingers through the red masses at her temples, spreading the wavy locks in a fan around her face. "Now," he muttered thickly. "Now."

With practiced grace, he eased himself between her thighs as she opened to accept him. Instead of thrusting into her, however, he brushed his fingers over the mound, feeling the throbbing nub of pleasure with his thumb.

"Hunter," she moaned. "Oh, Hunter."

She was moist and ready when he pushed two fingers into her, still pressing with his thumb.

"Hunter." Her voice was a wail this time as she arched wildly, following his fingers when he pulled them half out of her.

"So you don't want anything I'm willing to give," he teased. Circling the moist flesh with his thumb, he slipped a third finger inside her. "My sweet, lying wife."

Not knowing what she did, she clutched at him. As

90

her fingers slid into his thick hair, her palms pressed against his cheeks. Beneath one hand were the sticky smears of blood where she had scratched him.

Instantly repentant, she lifted her mouth to the wounds, her kisses a plea for forgiveness. One hand slipped between their bodies and closed around him.

"Angel," he moaned. "Oh, God . . ."

"Oh, yes, Hunter. Oh, yes, dearest . . ."

"That's right. That's right. Angel . . . My God . . . Angel . . . Don't . . ."

"But I want to."

"It's too much. Too much . . . Angel . . ."

Cradling him between her thighs, she traced the strong line of his jaw with her lips and the tip of her tongue.

He swallowed convulsively, biting back a moan of pleasure. The skin of his chin was prickly beneath her lips, but his throat was smooth and warm, the pulse a frenzied throb. Her hands slid down over his chest slick with perspiration, the hair curled in black fishhooks, then over his belly. Finally, her hands encompassed his hard male organ.

"Oh, Angel." His forehead braced against the smooth floorboard beside her head, tugging at her red hair where it spread in tangled waves around them. Ignoring the slight pain, she guided him into her body. As she closed around him, she arched ecstatically, taking the whole length of him in one swift thrust that wrung a groan from her.

"Angel?"

"Hunter . . ."

He never allowed her to finish the sentence. His back arched and his hips drove forward. "Angel!"

Even as his muscles weakened and his body began to settle, she attained her own climax. Her breath hissed between her clenched teeth; her fingernails clawed at

91

his back. Then breathless, temporarily sated, they sank together.

When her senses returned, she did not allow her arms to fall away. Instead, she held him tightly against her. Emotion welled in her until her throat hurt from the effort to choke back the sobs. Tears dampened her hair at the temples as his breathing evened and his heartbeat slowed to its normal rhythm. The hard floor bruised her shoulder blades, but his weight was welcome. He was her husband and she loved him beyond life.

Lazily, she opened her eyes, staring into the lamplight, allowing the flame to hypnotize her. Everything had worked out for the best. Now he knew she was determined in her quest. He would return with her and give up this insane expedition. Alex would be safe. They would be a family again. Jessica Rutledge . . . Jessica Rutledge could go to England or to hell for all she cared.

At last he stirred. "Did you enjoy that?"

"More than ever," she whispered. "Did you?" She kissed his wounded cheek again.

"You know the answer to that." He sighed and pushed up on his hands, his arms at full stretch. "It was very good."

"I love you."

Grimacing, he reared back on his heels. "I care for you too," he said carefully.

Alarm streaked through her. "What does that mean?"

Reaching for his breeches, he rose and stepped into them. Staring down at her, he buckled his belt with supreme casualness. "I must get you to your carriage."

A hot flush rose in her cheeks and instantly died away as her skin drained of all color. "You bastard," she whispered. "Look at me."

He shrugged his shoulders. "I see you." His face was

like a stone. "Get your clothes on."

Embarrassed, she scrambled to her feet. When he would have helped her, she angrily shrugged off his hand and pulled on the unfamiliar trousers by herself.

"I just gave you what you wanted." He defended himself resentfully.

She fastened the last button and straightened. "You didn't give me what I wanted. You took what you wanted."

"Tuck that hair up under your cap, unless you want everyone in Charleston to know what you've been doing."

She obeyed him after a fashion, but her hands shook so that she lost strands. They straggled untidily down the back of her neck and around her ears. No one with eyes to see would have taken her for a boy.

He waited impatiently, then pulled a gold watch from his pocket and flipped open the case. "Let's go."

She shuddered with fury. Had mere minutes passed since she had trembled and gasped with love? The change had been like a flash of heat lightning illuminating a summer night.

"I'll hate you till I die," she breathed.

His mouth tightened as he took her arm. "Let's go."

The first streaks of dawn pinkened the horizon. Sailors were already about their morning tasks. The activity on the dock had increased. She dug in her heels. "At least let me see Alex."

He shook his head. "No. You've said your good-byes twice. Again would serve no purpose except to upset you both."

"I never really knew you," she accused, all color drained from her angry face. "You're a monster."

The men on the deck of the *Carolina* looked at her curiously.

"Come on." With his hand under arm, he hurried her

down the gangplank.

At the foot, she stumbled and went down to her knees. He stared down at her, his mouth set tight, then bent and scooped her up in his arms.

Her head fell back and the billed cap fell to the dock. The long red hair spilled out over his arm.

"Let me down," she whispered. "I can walk."

"You're out on your feet," he informed her curtly. His long stride ate up the distance between the ship and the carriage. At their approach, the driver roused himself on the box and climbed down to open the door.

Hunter set her down in front of it and stepped back. Immediately, she sidled away from the carriage. "Do I have to tie and gag you?" he growled.

"You wouldn't dare."

"Try me."

She stared into the midnight eyes. "No," she murmured. She staggered back a single step and leaned against the leather that padded the inside of the door.

"Get in."

"No."

He pushed her then. One rude hand on her chest shoved her into the interior of the carriage. The other caught her legs at the ankles and swept them up, stuffing her in helter-skelter as if she were a rag doll. "Take her back to England's Fancy," he instructed the driver.

The man tipped his hat and mounted to the box.

Hunter swung around and began to lope back toward the *Carolina*. His face was grim, his scowl black.

"I'll never forgive you," she screamed after him. "So help me God, Hunter Gillard, I'll never ever forgive you. I'll hate you forever. Do you hear me, Hunter? I'll never ever forgive you."

The carriage started with a jolt. The driver could not

94

turn it in the busy street. His way led past the pub, past the gangplank of the *Carolina*. As Hunter topped the gangplank, it rattled past the foot.

Hunter turned in time to catch sight of her contorted white face. "I hate you!" she screamed again. "I'll never forgive you."

The driver had to pull up the team to follow a slow-moving dray. As Fancy looked back, she saw a slight figure move across the deck to join him. Jessica Rutledge placed a proprietary hand on his arm.

He seemed to start, to look down at her, and then he placed his hand over hers.

The driver managed to swing the carriage out and around the dray, then he whipped up the horses. They turned a corner and left the dock behind.

Chapter Six

Out of sight of the docks, Fancy rapped on the roof of the carriage. When the driver did not stop, she put her head out the window. "Take me to the Drake."

Once she would have sat fuming helplessly, allowing him to drive her where he willed. No more! Angered when he ignored her, she pulled herself through the window on the door. Perched on the sill, her long red hair blowing in the wind, she held on with one hand while she pounded on the roof with her fist. "Either take me to the Drake as I bid or, so help me, I'll climb out on top and knock you off the box."

Shocked at the disturbance, the driver twisted around. The sight of the blazing eyes, yellow as the hottest flames of hell, and the long red hair swirling around her head almost accomplished what she threatened. He hauled back on the reins as he braked the coach to a halt. "Y—yes, ma'am, of course. Where to, ma'am?"

"The Drake." He had already slapped the reins against the haunches of the horses and tugged their heads around before she slid back into the interior of the coach.

The throbbing heat of fury cooled to an icy composure that judged the whole world to be against her. Her husband and her son, her mother and her stepfather who had aided and abetted their own daughter's abandonment. These people were far away. They had done their worst and left her wounded; but, she resolved, people who worked for her would obey her commands. Or she would know the reason why! Her mouth a thin white line, her hands clenched at her sides, she alighted at the Drake.

Across the lobby she stalked, conscious of the anxious stares of the desk clerk and his younger brother whose clothes she wore. At the foot of the stairs, she halted. Her chin lifted fractionally. "Send someone up with a bath and breakfast."

Later, dressed in her new blue wool dress, her hair severely done up under her bonnet, her parasol erect in her gloved hand, she walked down those stairs with great dignity. At her cold command, the desk clerk placed her single satchel in the carriage, after which the driver took her first to Thomas Aiken's house on Queen Street.

"You will immediately take steps to secure a divorce for me."

"My dear Mrs. Gillard . . ." The lawyer was clearly flabbergasted. "Such a step. My dear . . . Please sit down. Have you thought carefully about this? I'm sure that you have misunderstood. . . ."

She remained standing, the tip of her parasol boring a hole in his fine Turkey carpet. "I have misunderstood nothing."

"But you have no grounds."

"Adultery, Mr. Aiken. Adultery."

He shook his head. "You must have proof."

"He sailed away with that . . . woman."

"The fact that they are both on the same ship—"

She stamped her foot. "Then desertion."

"He is merely pursuing a new career . . . I'm sure if you will return home and give this matter long and deep thought . . . You might pray about this. A wife should cleave to her husband. . . ."

She stalked to the door and jerked it open. "Will you help me get a divorce, Mr. Aiken?"

He clamped his jaw fiercely as he clasped his hands behind his back.

"Then, damn you, sir!" She slammed the door behind her.

"Mr. Wentworth, I wish to know the exact details of the correspondence between my stepfather and my husband."

The man regarded her with ill-concealed malice. "I couldn't give that to you, Mrs. Gillard. The records of Shepperton Lines are all very private and confidential."

"Since they concerned me directly, I can hardly see how they could be considered private to me."

Wentworth crossed his arms before his barrel chest. "They are private," he insisted. "Furthermore, I am a very busy man. The *Carolina* has sailed and that is the end of it."

She raised her chin. "No, sir. That is not the end of it. I am here to serve notice on you that your behavior toward me throughout this unfortunate affair has been rude and uncooperative. I intend to write so to my stepfather." She raised her hand when he started to protest. "When this is sorted out—and it will be—you will receive a stiff reprimand."

His chest swelled in anger. "As an employee of Mr. Shepperton, I have followed my instructions to the letter."

"You are employed as a manager, but you have used no judgment at all," she accused bitterly. "Hunter Gillard has deceived both my stepfather and mother as to the true state of affairs and as to his intention toward me. When Josiah Shepperton sees his error, he will hold you responsible."

Wentworth stood up. "For the second time in as many days, Mrs. Gillard, I must ask you to leave. I am a very busy man."

She too stood. "With pleasure, Mr. Wentworth. I merely came to warn you."

As the carriage rumbled out of Charleston, Fancy leaned back on the seats. Her words of warning were just so much false bravado. They only served to make her feel more despairing than ever. Both Wentworth and Aiken had defeated her. Her pride was torn to shreds by their obdurate support of her husband.

Taking off her bonnet, she set it on the seat across from her. With a faint sigh, she pulled the pins from her hair and massaged her aching temples. As comfortable as possible in the sweltering heat of the Carolina afternoon, she leaned back wearily against the squabs. At least tonight she would sleep in her own bed.

England's Fancy. The one sure and steadfast thing in a fast dissolving world.

Her eyelids drooped. Lifting the satchel onto the seat beside her, she pillowed her head against it and drew her feet up beside her. In a minute she was asleep, rocked gently by the swaying motion of the carriage.

She wakened to the scents of jasmine and tobacco. In the darkness of the carriage interior, she pushed herself erect. The horses' hooves clopped rhythmically with no sign of slowing, but still she knew that she was home.

The moon lighted the broad acres of tobacco plants growing right up to the road and beyond them to the river flowing silver.

She scooted across the seat to the other side of the carriage. There before her tired eyes the land rolled gently up to the big white house. England's Fancy. She blinked. The entire scene swam in the moonlight as the tears started.

Blindly, she snatched up her parasol to rap with its handle against the roof. The driver stopped instantly. But quick as he was, she was quicker. Flinging open the door, she swung herself to the ground before the wheels had stopped turning. The sandy loam on the shoulder of the road immediately filled the soft slippers that she had bought to match the new blue wool dress. Hanging onto the door of the carriage, she pulled loose their ties and stripped her shoes off.

"Ma'am? . . ." The driver started down from the box.

"Stay where you are."

He pulled himself back with alacrity.

She tossed the shoes onto the floor of the carriage. Her new silk stockings followed. Shutting the door with a swing of her hand, she caught up her skirts. "Drive on by the road," she commanded.

"Ma'am . . ."

She had already turned her back. Unhesitating, she stepped into the sea of tobacco. The broad leaves embraced her, brushing against her knees, her thighs, her waist. Her feet sank into the hot, damp earth as soft as any carpet ever made.

"Ma'am? . . ."

She put out her arms in swimming motions as she walked through the mass of silvery bright leaves. They washed her mind as they comforted her body. These were hers. These were the legacy from her father and before him from her grandfather, that shadowy old man Edward England. Had he really been a privateer as her father claimed? Or a pirate as her mother had insisted disdainfully?

Her imagination stirred with the certain sense of fitness of things. The cold, hard pieces of Spanish silver torn from the earth by unwilling hands had returned to the earth in the dark, warm roots beneath her feet.

Halfway up the slope, she paused to look back at the river. Flowing slowly in a wide long loop, it circled around the hill on which the great house stood and drifted lazily on toward the ocean.

The thought of the ocean sent a sharp pang through her. How was Alex tonight? Had he enjoyed his first day at sea? Had he been seasick? Had he missed her?

Loneliness swept over her and Fancy's eyes flooded with tears. Again, she turned toward the house whose white columns swam in the bright moonlight. The leaves rustled around her as a sudden breeze swirled up the slope. The carriage had almost reached the drive.

Only by thinking of practical things, she decided, could she survive. If she worried about Alex, if she thought about Hunter and her own loneliness, she would go mad. Just those few involuntary thoughts had destroyed the peace that the tobacco and the warm soil had imparted.

A light suddenly appeared in the black cave beneath the columns. Then another and another. The windows in the drawing room suddenly became bright rectangles of shining yellow. Another minute and the two windows at the top of the house on the east corner also began to glow.

With a tired sigh, Fancy visualized the activity even now occurring in her rooms. For the first time that entire horrible day, she began to hurry. At last, a little breathless from her exertions in the damp heat, she stepped out of the field at the curve of the drive and let her skirts fall sedately around her ankles. Lifting her hands, she smoothed her hair back from her face. With as much dignity as she could muster barefooted, she walked calmly up the drive toward the house.

Holy Dulcibella stood like a tall straight-backed statue on the porch. The lights from the carriage lamps on each pillar glinted off the yellow glass pin that held her turban. "We are waiting for you, maitresse," she announced loudly.

As he had done every morning for two weeks, the iron-mouthed black stallion that had carried her on her futile journey to Charleston plunged out of his box stall, snorting and stamping. Two grooms trotted along in front him, stepping lively to avoid his snapping jaws and potentially lethal front hooves. Fancy watched impassively as they bridled him and snubbed his head around the hitching post.

The stableman came up behind her. "You're not going to ride this black devil again, maitresse."

She did not turn. "He suits me perfectly. I need his strength."

"But his temper, maitresse. He's the very devil."

As if to punctuate his statement, the horse neighed shrilly and kicked out with his back heels. The groom trying to tighten the girth around the heavy barrel cursed angrily.

"Watch your language there," the one at the horse's head warned.

The horse quieted suddenly. His eye rolled in Fancy's direction. As if he sent her a cue, she stepped onto the mounting block. The groom dropped the irons and held one. She put her toe into it and swung her other leg over the saddle in a smooth motion.

The second groom released the horse's head. He rose on his hind legs, not high, but testing. Her thighs clamped firmly, she touched his withers with her crop. He dropped to all fours. A tug at the rein and he cantered out of the yard. No, she would not ride a tamer animal. The horse's bad behavior suited her mood perfectly.

Fancy squinted at the shimmering heat rising in waves out of the rows of bright green tobacco. Sweat trickled past her eyebrows and down the sides of her face. Salt stung the corners of her eyes, making her squint even tighter.

The armpits of her father's white shirt, the back between her shoulder blades, the front between her breasts, were all soaked. The tops of her thighs burned beneath buff wool breeches, unearthed from the clothespress in the attic. Pulled up around her waist and belted there, they reached the tops of her boots. Beneath the black leather, her toes felt as if they were on fire.

Never had she considered donning any of Hunter's clothes. The door to his wardrobe stayed firmly closed. Eventually perhaps, she would have to touch them, but for now she did not so much as enter his room.

Other than the tightening of her facial muscles, she might have been a statue sitting on the horse's back surveying the field before her. Beneath sun so hot that steam rose from the ground, workers moved methodically. Men, women, and children crept between the rows of broad tobacco leaves, pulling the sphinx moth larvae off with their bare hands.

As the workers' shadows fell across the bright curving leaves, each ugly green caterpillar with a tiny hook at the end of its body would rear up. In this

104

posture it would freeze, its head curled down over the front half of its belly. Its bluff exhausted, the tiny monster could easily be plucked off and flicked into a bucket or pail.

A buzzard swung lazily in the sky over the southeast. His movement roused Fancy from her trance. She clicked her tongue. The big black horse tested his strength against the bit, found her hand authoritative, and moved forward amenably enough. Along the end of the rows, she rode, her back straight, her face shaded from the sun only by the brim of her father's hat.

Ferris MacCullough stepped out from a row of waist-high "Sweet-Scented." His scowl black as thunder, he crossed his arms firmly over his chest. His hat remained on his head as he waited until she came abreast. The fair skin of his face had long ago been covered with freckles everywhere that it was not covered with bristling honey-blond hair. He was dressed much the same as she, except instead of boots reaching the bottom of his breeches, he wore thick cotton stockings and stout brogans.

He shook his head as she halted the stallion in front of him. "Ye shouldn't be ridin' in this heat."

She shrugged. "The heat doesn't bother me." She spoke the truth. Sweating might be unladylike, but the layer of water on her skin insulated her against the hot air. She shifted in the saddle to look out over the fields. "I like what I see."

"'Tisn't fittin' for a lady like yerself—"

She interrupted him. "When will we begin the actual cutting?"

He tilted his head to one side to squint up at her from beneath the brim of his hat. "When that field is cleared of the worms we can move in behind and cut."

She smiled faintly, looking back over her shoulder at the broad expanse of green and the bent figures moving through it. "The crop looks good."

He followed her glance. His chest swelled with pride, then he remembered with whom he spoke. "And how would ye know?" he challenged gruffly.

She flashed him a hard glance, then shrugged. His censure was her due. She had failed as a woman. Perhaps she would as a planter. She could only ride beside the field hands and watch ignorantly. "They're bright green and at least a dozen inches across," she ventured.

He did not reply. When he pressed his lips together stubbornly, they disappeared in the bristly yellow beard.

She shifted in the saddle again. "Do you think the clouds are building up to the south?"

At that he twisted around. "Mayhap," he muttered. "In which case, I ha' no time to be gawkin' here." Without a tip of his hat, he strode away. The broad leaves enveloped his hips. He shouted in Gullah to the nearest black man.

Fancy dropped her eyes to her hands clasped tightly over the saddlebow. She should be used to such treatment from males now, but still their curt dismissals hurt.

The black horse stirred impatiently under her, slinging his head up and down and tugging at the bit. Lifting the reins, she allowed him to pick his way forward. As she rode, she concentrated on the crop and the people harvesting it. Her people. She owned them, but in a very real way they owned her, too. They were her responsibility, for food, clothing, and shelter.

Tonight they would empty the worms from their buckets onto a great pile of wood soaked in coal-oil. It would be lighted and the whole odorous mess would be gone in a burst of bright orange flame and thick black smoke. Immediately thereafter, the workers would line up for tinplates heaping with slices of the hog that had been roasting for hours in the firepit and great spoonfuls of rice and okra from iron cauldrons.

For England's Fancy fed her people well. The mass meals at cutting time had been initiated by her grandfather. The thought of her grandfather strengthened her. She would continue everything as it had been. He had made this plantation from nothing. She would maintain it.

Smiling now, Fancy glanced down at her right hand resting on her thigh. The skin was a deep golden tan, as was her face. Furthermore, the thin white cotton shirt had not been able to turn away all the rays of the sun. Her back, shoulders, and arms had first turned faintly pink, then taken on a pale golden hue. If her mother could see her now, she would no doubt berate her soundly. All the years Fancy had spent under veils, masks, and parasols had been destroyed in less than a month.

Blanche Stoddart England, now Shepperton, would castigate her too for riding astride, saying that no man would want her if the softness of her body became calloused and manlike. Fancy took a deep breath of the hot, sultry air. No man wanted her anyway.

Another of her mother's favorite themes was the ruination of the body for childbearing. Fancy bit her lower lip; her heart beat a little faster. Her monthly courses were more than ten days late. She pressed her right hand against the lower part of her belly. She dared not hope she carried a child, yet with each day, the dream grew a little closer to reality.

A faint sound disturbed her reverie. Had she heard the rumble of distant thunder? She swung the horse around to the southeast to stare at the horizon intently. Was the blue of the sky darkening significantly?

A shower at this time of year could do little harm,

although the leaves needed to be as dry as possible when they were hung in the barns. The more dampness in them, the more heat required to dry them to a bright lemon-yellow.

More serious was a heavy rain that would delay the cuttings. A storm with pelting downpour, perhaps with some hail, would drive the plants to earth, lowering their value as the leaves were damaged. Even after that the crop could be salvaged.

But every day in the field increased the likelihood of the thing feared by every farmer along the southeastern coast of the newly formed United States of America.

Hurricane!

She shivered in the heat. Twice in her lifetime one had blown in. Once three of the workers had been swept away and drowned in the rush of water breaching the dam above the rice fields. Windows had been shattered and water damage had been severe.

When her mother had come home after the Season in Charleston she had complained bitterly about the damage to the furniture. For years thereafter, she had claimed that the stench of rotting vegetation left by the storm had somehow gotten into the wood of the house, where it remained to nauseate her whenever she entered those rooms. Almost her last words before leaving the plantation forever had been how glad she was never to have to smell that odor again.

The black stallion shifted from one hip to the other and Fancy swayed easily in the saddle. The horizon definitely seemed to be darkening, but not alarmingly so. Satisfied, she tugged at the reins, turning the horse's head back around, and continued her inspection.

"Maitresse, you must eat more. You have scarcely touched your food." Amos bent over her at the table.

She shook her head wearily. "It's too hot to eat. I'm just not hungry." Even as she spoke, she realized she told the truth rather than making up some excuse. She really did not feel hungry in the slightest.

"But, maitresse . . ."

"Amos, the food is good. I have tasted some of every dish. My compliments to Mattie." Laying her napkin beside her plate, she pushed back her chair.

Unhappily, Amos watched her leave. From the shadow of the doorway, Holy Dulcibella too stared at her, her face enigmatic as a sphinx.

Although the hour was late and she had ridden since dawn, Fancy did not go to her room. Instead, she lighted the reading lamps in the library and sat down to work at her father's desk.

Hearing the clock strike midnight, she leaned back in the chair and massaged her neck muscles, stiff from being held in one position for so long. Slowly, she rose and wandered through the dark, silent house to open the front door. The bright moonlight made a light unnecessary thereafter.

Thrusting her hands into the pockets of her father's trousers, she walked down the drive. Crickets chirped and a great horned owl hooted dismally from one of the giant water oaks that marched in silent pairs down the slope.

She stopped to listen, a tight smile on her lips. The night spoke to her with a gentler voice than human beings did. She hunched her shoulders and walked on as the owl called again.

Her passing must have disturbed a mouse or a rabbit. She heard a faint rustle in the leaves and undergrowth. Then the flap of heavy wings. The owl had risen from its limb. The ears and eyes of the night raptor were more than a match for the dodges of the fleeing prey.

The huge silhouette sailed between her and the moon, dropping fast. A thud, a scuffle, then the flapping of heavy wings again. Hurriedly, she walked on, not wanting to carry the shadow in her mind and add its horror to her burden.

The dew damp upon her boots, she returned to the house and slipped upstairs. The moon was halfway across the sky and the morning breeze had sprung up. A lantern suddenly glowed in the cookshack at the back.

She had walked the night away. Miles and miles she had traversed. She was tired and numb, but not sleepy. The stairs creaked beneath her feet. She must have something done about them.

As she walked along the hall toward her room, another lamp came on, its sliver of light showing under Dulci's door. Fancy increased her speed, but too late.

The woman swung the door open. "Maitresse! Do you try to kill yourself?"

Turning reluctantly, Fancy blinked in the lamplight. "Please, Dulci, don't fuss. I didn't mean to disturb you. Go back to sleep. It's too early to get up yet."

"You mean too late, don't you?"

"I'm going to bed right now." Fancy shuffled her feet under her. Rather than meet the housekeeper's accusing stare, she threw a glance over her shoulder in the direction of her room.

"Praise God," the woman intoned. "But how long will you stay?"

"Until it's time to get up." Fancy backed away down the hall. "Go back to bed, Dulci. I'm sorry I disturbed you."

Alone in her room, she pulled off her boots and stretched out across the bed. She was tired and a dull ache had begun in the small of her back. Perhaps she would be able to fall asleep immediately. If she stirred around, bathing and changing, she might wake herself up again.

A couple of hours later she awoke to discover that she was not pregnant. The pain, the intense restlessness, had all been symptomatic of her monthly courses no longer delayed.

At the telltale stains, she cried bitterly, her head in her hands. At last drained of tears, she fell asleep sprawled across the bed. When she awoke twelve hours later, she found that Dulci had moved her body into a more comfortable position and covered her with a light cotton blanket.

With a sort of stillness in her brain, Fancy slid her hand down between her hipbones, across her stomach. There had never been anything there but false hope. She must learn to put it aside.

A faint sound drew her attention to the door. Holy Dulcibella stuck her head around the edge. "You are awake?" she called softly.

"Yes, Dulci. Prepare me a bath. I'll come down to supper."

"Praise God," the woman murmured as she closed the door and hurried away.

Moving numbly, Fancy tossed back the covers and stood up. She would dress and go down as if nothing had happened. For nothing really had. Mentally, she told herself she was not surprised, nor even disappointed.

Chapter Seven

Ferris MacCullough shifted himself in the saddle. As stinging sweat trickled down into his eyebrows, he plucked off his hat and wiped his forehead on the sleeve of his shirt. "'Tis almost ready, Miz Gillard. Another few days, a week, and we'll—ever' man-jack of us—be in the fields."

She nodded shortly, her eyes too scanning the tobacco, now standing six feet high. Her long-sleeved white shirt was drenched with sweat deep under the armpits. Beneath her broad-brimmed hat, the kerchief bound around her hair was likewise soaked. "It's a wonderful crop, Mr. MacCullough."

He shot her a cynical glance before replacing his hat. "Any crop 'd look good if a body 'd never seen one before."

Her right hand clenched around the riding crop, then relaxed against her thigh. "So you have reminded me on more than one occasion, Mr. MacCullough," she replied, a dangerous softness in her voice. "I think you might do well to forego that comment."

He set his jaw to stubbornly ignore her warning. "Best be ridin' on, if we're t' see it all before the midday." He reined his gelding around and spurred the beast along the narrow trail.

Glaring after him, Fancy touched her spurred heels to her own horse's flanks. The black hunter plunged forward with a snort. Not only was his temper bad in the mornings, but he had a particular personality trait that irritated MacCullough almost as much as it pleased Fancy. He would not let another horse get ahead of him.

In less than a minute, MacCullough's sturdy gelding was overtaken and shouldered roughly aside on the narrow trail through the tobacco. The overseer muttered irritably about damage to the crop, but she had paid no attention. At last with a resigned sigh, he slowed his mount for the black horse to forge ahead.

"Have the work parties finished chopping all the firewood?" she asked over her shoulder.

"They'll finish tomorrow," MacCullough replied sourly.

While waiting for the leaves to ripen, hands were put to work chopping and piling cords of firewood hauled from the woods where trees had been selected, felled, and stacked the year before. The aged hardwood burned with a hot flame necessary to send the heat through the long metal flues in the curing barns. After the tobacco was harvested, another crop of trees would be felled.

Next to the dock below the house was the warehouse that stored the great hogsheads, now empty and waiting for their next crop. The tobacco that had been aged in them had already been shipped to Charleston for sale.

The whole process represented a yearly cycle of work that complemented the rice cycle so that the farm could produce two crops. If one failed, the other could still be counted on.

Following her out of the field on the river road,

MacCullough pulled his mount. "If you're through with your tour, I'd best be gettin' on about m' business." His sneering tone implied that she had required his escort on a pleasure junket, as one might tour a grand estate as a leisure-time activity. Barely touching his hat with the tip of his crop, he reined his mount aside and headed it down toward the dock.

She stared at his stiff back, her eyes hot and angry. For every day of the last four weeks, MacCullough had fought her. At first he had uttered outright insults and threats. These had given way to dire warnings and personal slurs. Gradually, the warnings had disappeared and the slurs had been reduced to sarcastic generalizations.

She would be rid of him in an instant had he not been the man her father had hired just before his death. Even that sentimental fact would not have kept his job given his attitude had not MacCullough known the business of England's Fancy. To replace him would be foolish, if not impossible. In his middle forties, he had at least a dozen years before he would be training a successor. For a couple of years at least, she could swallow her pride and learn from him.

Her morning ride over, she raised her crop in ironic salute before touching it lightly to the hunter's flank. He lifted into a rolling canter, his best gait, which cooled her as they swept up the lane to the house.

At the stables she dismounted and led the horse to the trough. When she raised her hands toward his head to unbuckle the cheek strap and pull the bit from his mouth, he laid back his ears and snorted a warning.

"Stop that," she snapped. "Black devil! When this summer is over, I swear I'll put you to pulling a plow."

As if he understood her threat, the stallion put his head meekly into her hands and allowed her to relieve him of the bridle. Then he dipped his nose into the clear

115

water and drank noisily. Leaning against the trough while she waited, Fancy pulled her hat and scarf off together and dipped one end into the water to pat it on her face and neck.

A minute, two, and she pulled the horse back. Without further display, he accepted the bit she put back between his teeth, waiting patiently till she buckled the cheek strap and swung up. Replacing her hat and pulling the end of her scarf through her belt, she cantered out of the yard and down toward the river.

Without thought as to direction, she rode for another two hours. For a while, she moved among the men chopping and stacking wood. When a drag was piled high, she rode beside the black teamster as he jogged along on foot at the side of the mules. At the furnaces, she sat on her horse for a quarter of an hour, listening attentively while MacCullough directed repairs to the bricks.

When he scowled for the tenth time, she turned and rode away down to the river. In the shade of the huge cypress trees, a trio of small black boys fished for their dinners.

She sat beside them for a while, listening to their chatter until suddenly her eyes filled with tears and she climbed back on the tireless horse and rode away.

Physically exhausted at five in the afternoon, she returned at last to the stable where she gave her mount over to the grooms and walked to the house.

Holy Dulcibella greeted her with a tall glass of cool water. "So, maitresse, you are close to death from starvation or from sunstroke?"

"Just thirst, Dulci," she smiled wanly. "And you have saved me." She handed back the empty glass.

"Your bath is ready," the housekeeper said, unsmiling.

"Then I shall be fully restored."

In the bedroom, Fancy stood before the glass to strip off her filthy clothes. Holy Dulcibella came up behind her to take her by the arm. The huge yellow stone in her turban flashed as the housekeeper shook her head. "Maitresse, look at yourself."

Fancy turned her head away. "I don't think it's necessary," she said dully.

"You look at yourself, before God. Your mother would scream and throw up her hands."

At first glance, Fancy found herself hard to recognize. The luxuriant red hair, once a deep auburn, now showed streaks of palest blond. Her gold eyes stared out of a tanned face with tiny wrinkles etched deeply into the corners of her eyes. Her cheekbones were clearly defined by the faint hollow beneath them. Her chin had a certain sharpness to it.

The soft round body of a month ago was gone entirely. The generous heavy breasts were smaller and harder. The rounded belly had flattened, the stretch marks of her pregnancies no more than silver lines. Her hipbones jutted out sharply above the long tapering legs. The thighs were much the same size, only now the flesh was smooth. The four weeks in the saddle had developed and hardened the long muscles. The calves, too, were firm and the ankles impossibly slender.

Her waist could be spanned by a man's two hands. *But I have no one to span it.* "I've lost some weight," she agreed out loud. At the same time, a faint flush rose in her cheeks. Her heart began to beat a little faster with hope that could not be suppressed. Hunter might love her now if he could only see her.

Holy Dulcibella gathered up the discarded clothing. "Not eating, not sleeping, working and sweating in the hot sun, does that to a man or a woman," came her sad soft comment.

Fancy shrugged as she settled into the slippery bath

117

with a sigh. Hunter was miles away, probably on the other side of the Atlantic by now—with Jessica Rutledge.

When she climbed from the bath, Holy Dulcibella was there to offer her a soft cotton sheet. Later in a fine batiste dressing gown, Fancy drank a cup of tea sweetened with new honey from the comb.

Holy Dulcibella pulled a dress from her wardrobe. "Will you wear this for dinner, maitresse?"

Fancy did not bother to glance at the garment. "I suppose so."

The housekeeper pressed her seamed lips tightly together. Carefully, she spread the dress on the bed, then turned and folded her arms. "One month I watch you now, maitresse. At first you were merely sad. Now you try to kill yourself."

Fancy shook her head wearily, but Holy Dulcibella continued solemnly. "Though you try by denying your body rest and food, it is from the seed of Great Edward. He was a strong man, too. You are his blood. Therefore, you are doomed to failure. You will find yourself still alive at the end of this summer. You cannot kill yourself."

The cup rattled in the saucer. "Is that what I'm trying to do, Dulci?"

"When first you return from Charleston, you ride each day but not so much. You eat good food. Rest. Now you do not eat. You ride until you are exhausted."

Fancy shrugged. "Ah, but I am not exhausted." She took another sip of tea. "Once I was. I could exhaust myself just by going out for an early morning ride with that swine MacCullough. Now I ride twelve hours and could ride farther."

"You are a small woman. You must rest. You do not

sleep at night. Do you think I do not hear you rise and walk?"

Fancy smiled. "It's too hot to walk during the day."

"Your workers fear for you. I fear for you. We all pray for God's strength to you. You are not trying to fight the demon."

"Nonsense. You're all wrong. I made a vow to fight a battle with myself. I have fought and won. My figure is much the same as when I married."

"Your body will never be the same. You are a woman. Not a girl. Look at your body. You try to starve it. What have you eaten today?"

"I don't remember."

"I remember. Nothing. No breakfast. No lunch."

"Then I shall eat a good dinner. I don't want to get sick."

"Do you not?"

"No." Fancy shook her head definitely.

"I think you do not eat more than a few bites for the last two weeks."

Fancy waved her hand dismissively. "You're imagining things."

"No. God knows I do not imagine. You were careful what you ate when you came home. I was not worried about you. Now you are not careful."

Fancy was silent for a moment. When she spoke, her voice broke and quavered. "There is no longer any reason to be careful."

Holy Dulcibella stared. Her brow knotted in puzzlement, then cleared. "Ah, maitresse, did you have hope?"

Fancy dropped her head to hide the pain in her eyes. "Only a faint one, Dulci, but it was all I had. Now I have nothing."

The old woman clasped the bent shoulders in her hands and hugged the girl hard. "Ah, my maitresse.

Sweet baby. I think you should know that there is only one son for many generations."

"What?"

"Great Edward's father was an only child. Great Edward had no brothers, no sisters. Your father was the only child of Lucilla. You are the only child of your father."

"And Alex is the only living child of my body."

"I think it is the way of things."

"And he has been taken away from me." The pain in the voice was like a knife.

"He will return. I promise you."

"If he is able. I know the dangers of the sea. Father told me as a child the stories of shipwrecks, of storms, of bad food, of little water."

"Not for the captain's son."

"If a ship sinks, they all go down together—cabin boy and captain's son." Fancy stood abruptly. "Help me on with that dress. Then go and tell Amos to serve dinner. Tell him to open a bottle of wine. I have been alone a month now. I have survived. It's time for a celebration."

By the clock it was dawn when she dressed, but no light streaked the summer sky. An awful fear in her, she pulled on her clothes and ran for the stable.

"Saddle the black horse!"

"But, maitresse . . ." The head groom had never questioned her commands. "You cannot ride today. There will be a storm."

"Of course, there'll be a storm. That's why I must ride. Everyone must work. Even you. As soon as he's saddled, you and your helpers must report to Mr. MacCullough. Everyone must cut tobacco today."

"But, maitresse . . ."

120

She slashed the crop against the hitching post. "Must I strike you? Will you continue to argue until I beat you?"

He backed away a couple of steps, then spun and lunged into the stable, shouting for the boys.

A solitary gust of wind snatched her hat from her head and sent it cartwheeling across the yard. She did not bother to retrieve it. Instead, she faced the east, watching the gray clouds move in the dark sky.

The black horse came out of the stall like a demon. Neighing a challenge, he reared to the length of his lead lines, pawing the air.

The younger groom swore passionately as he stumbled back and fell sprawling almost at Fancy's feet. Throwing her a sullen look, he climbed to his feet and hurried over to the hitching post. With great difficulty, the two men managed to saddle the excited beast.

Only when she had settled herself firmly in the saddle did Fancy nod to the grooms to unfasten the lathered horse. When he felt himself free, he clamped his jaws on the bit and reared straight up.

Fancy flung herself forward on his back, counter-balancing her weight.

He came down with a jarring thud, both legs straight, and buck-jumped twice. Fancy caught one glimpse of the grooms' awed faces, then she brought her crop down with all her might on the black rump and drove her heels into his flanks.

With a furious squeal, he plunged out of the stable yard. Fancy did not allow him to stop his headlong gallop until he had run the full length of the road and back. Only then did she guide him into the fields.

"What in hell d' y' think your doin' here?" MacCullough roared as she approached. The gusts of wind from the approaching storm flattened his bristly

121

beard. He looked anxiously over her shoulder at the clouds boiling toward them.

"I've come to help."

"Be gone, damn you. You're no help. There's a bloody great storm comin'. I don't have time to play escort t' a fool."

"Don't call me a fool, MacCullough."

At the tone of her voice, he stepped back. Then tried again in a milder tone. "We're cuttin' here. Ye'll get in the way. Men're workin' wi' knives. Ye'll get yerself hurt."

"I can scarcely be in the way up here on the back of my horse." Fancy struggled to keep her voice even. "Please continue."

His rage boiled up in him until he lost all control. "Nae," he shouted. "Not until ye leave." He swung his crop under the nose of the stallion, who reared and backed into the row of tobacco, trampling several of the plants. "Ye see. That damned horse'll ruin—"

"No more than you, striding toward me across the rows."

He cursed then, a foul word that Fancy had never heard before. The next intelligible sentence came out as a growl. "A woman dinna belong in the field where men are cutting."

"A man's leg or arm is no more proof against a knife than a woman's. I'm the owner here. I'll take the chances."

"I canna get the men t' work properly in front of ye," he growled.

She looked pointedly at the crop. "If that means that you cannot whip them, then I shall surely stay."

His face, already livid with anger, darkened until Fancy feared he might burst a blood vessel. "I dinna use the whip unless 'tis absolutely necessary." He strode over to the nearest black man and pulled the

122

thick cotton shirt down from the heavily muscled shoulder. "Not a mark on him. I'm nae a monster."

"Then, for God's sake, why?"

He looked wildly around him, then came toward her again, his face contorted. Alarmed, she tightened her grip on the reins. Was he going to attack her?

He came to a halt with his shoulder against the horse's neck, his bearded chin thrust out pugnaciously. Again, the quick glance around, then his answer in a low growl. "I willna work with a woman. 'Tis bad enough to work *for* one." His face twisted in a combination of rage and shame, fearful and at the same time pathetic to behold. "Do ye ken me, Miz Gillard. I willna work *with* a woman. 'Tis unmanly."

Fancy stared down into his angry face for a full minute. Then, without a word, she reined the horse aside and rode away. Spots of color bloomed in her cheeks as she sought to keep her anger under control.

That evening, she sent for him. He came with his shoulders hunched pugnaciously, his beard bristling.

She regarded him silently for a moment from behind the mahogany desk Edward England had brought from Madagascar. "I have called you in to effect a compromise, Mr. MacCullough. You will not have to see me again." His shoulders relaxed fractionally and he shifted uneasily. "To spare you any embarrassment, you will divide your work party and we'll work in two different fields."

"Nae," MacCullough protested viciously. "I'll nae split up my men."

"I think you will. We can get twice as much done with two overseers."

"Nae! I willna let a woman do my work. Besides, ye might be hurt."

The golden eyes glittered angrily. "Mr. MacCullough, you will not tell me what I will not do again. *I will.* I will do exactly as I choose and no one— no one—will tell me 'nae.'" She leaned forward, her hands spread out on the desk in front of her. They were deeply tanned now, a strong contrast to the pristine whiteness of Richard England's old-fashioned lace cuffed shirt. She seldom thought about her own clothing anymore. Her father's things had been brought down, pressed, and altered for her. "Furthermore, I will not be told to 'go away' on my own plantation. If your masculine pride is damaged by working beside a woman, you may quit this evening and walk away. However, if you stay, you will obey me."

His chest swelled. He rocked back on his heels. "There's nae a man about that feels any different from me."

"That may be true, but I can certainly see for myself, Mr. MacCullough. I had understood that jobs were hard to come by with the war ending and so many men coming back and needing employment. Surely, somewhere in Colleton County there would be a good man needing employment."

"Ye wouldn't!" His beard fairly vibrated with righteous wrath. "Ye're bluffin'. Ye've nae got the time."

She shrugged. "Charleston is but a day's ride away."

"Mr. Gillard . . ."

"Do you see him?" she interrupted coldly.

"Wha? . . ."

She motioned toward the door, the lace and fine cotton swinging gently. "Call him in to push me from behind this desk."

"He hired me," the man insisted doggedly.

124

"In point of fact, my father, Richard England, hired you. You have taken orders from my husband for several years now, but he has gone. For a year," she added, swallowing hard.

"Aye, so he told me." He hunched his shoulders even deeper. His eyes dropped fractionally.

She stared at him. "You knew."

He shuffled from one foot to the other. His hands balled into fists at his sides; then he locked them behind his back. "Aye."

She stared at him, swallowing this bit of information for contemplation at another time. "And you approved?"

He clamped his lips together until they disappeared in his beard.

"Mr. MacCullough . . ." she began, shaking her head.

"Nae!" he blurted shortly. "I dinna approve. A man should stick by his decisions. I made my choice years ago. Decided I wasna for marriage. But a man should stick by his decisions. I dinna 'prove his takin' the boy and leavin'."

"I thank you for that, Mr. MacCullough."

He nodded shortly. The silence grew between them. He cleared his throat. "But that doesna mean that I approve your workin' in the fields."

"And what if he does not return?"

"Well, then ye'll get yerself another man."

She clasped her hands on the desk in front of her. She needed this man. She knew it. The talk about hiring someone else in Colleton County or in Charleston had been just so much talk. This man was already privy to her personal life. A bit more could not hurt. "Ah, but, Mr. MacCullough, I am myself no longer 'for marriage.'"

125

His eyes narrowed, his brows drawing together in a frown.

She stared into them, struggling to keep her voice level. "Since my husband told you so much about his plans, surely he told you why he was leaving me."

"He wanted to take the boy to sea."

"That was one of the reasons." *And Jessica Rutledge was another.* "But the other stemmed from the fact that I can never have another child." She watched the flush rise in his cheeks despite the dark freckles. Such things were never discussed between a married woman and an old bachelor. "What man would want a woman who could no longer perform the function for which nature intended her?" Her eyes were liquid gold in the lamplight, her voice hoarse with emotion.

His own face sagged with honest pity. "Nae, ma'am. Ye're judgin' yerself too short. Why, any man would be glad to be a husband to ye. Men want a bonny lass like yerself to be a helpmate, to walk beside them." His voice trailed away, but the heavy flush remained as the sense of his words dawned on him.

She regarded him steadily, a tiny quizzical smile on her face.

He brought his arms around to his sides and drew himself up to attention. His eyes met hers with calm acceptance. "I'll be amicable for you to work another field, ma'am. And"—he swallowed hard, as if the admission galled him—"glad of the help."

"Thank you, Mr. MacCullough."

When he had gone, she could no longer ignore the cold, hard knot swelled in her belly. All around her she was discovering betrayal. Her mother, her stepfather, her employees, probably her friends as well. Had everyone along the eastern seaboard conspired together to help Hunter leave her?

126

Bitterness gnawed at her. Her body trembled as she rose from the desk and made her way outside. No moon tonight. Far distant thunder rumbled, and heat lightning flashed eerily amidst the thick piles of clouds.

She thrust her hands into her pockets and began to walk.

Chapter Eight

Omnipresent thunder rumbled to the south and the sky turned purple at midday. To the north marched gray thunderheads, with huge shafts of water slanting downward out of them. Throughout the gray, steamy day the men labored frantically, cutting and tying the big bright leaves.

Riding constantly among them, MacCullough alternately encouraged and cursed them to work faster. His placid gelding trotted back and forth down the rows as the overseer supervised the operation, from the gathering to the transporting of the bundles to the curing sheds. Very occasionally, MacCullough would stop when thunder rumbled particularly near. Then, hands on hips, he would scowl ferociously at it. He did not waste his breath on the weather.

Fancy oversaw a crew that worked the upper slope between the house and the river on the north side. She was nearer to the curing sheds and could oversee the whole. She accompanied each cartload of bundles down the hill, then galloped back as the unloading was finished.

Whether the men slackened or worked well for her, she could not tell. The threatening storms made her so nervous that all the workers seemed to be barely moving. In the early afternoon, she was ready to scream with frustration when one young black man collapsed in the smothering heat. As if by common consent, the rest of the crew stopped working to watch what she would do.

Immediately, she slid down from her horse to direct a pair of comrades to stretch him out under the shade of the cart. Then, desperate to save the crop that had become a symbol of survival, she snatched up the curved knife that had fallen from his hand and began to work in his place.

The workers close by stared at her in disbelief. Then, one by one, they returned to their jobs. The last to return was the worker who had collapsed. The water that his comrades had poured over him still drenching his body, he staggered to his feet, wiped the sweat out of his eyes, and approached her. At first she shook her head, but his black eyes flashed as he held out his hand. With a nod, she relinquished the knife and climbed back on the horse.

The crew increased their pace as a result. Admiration for the mistress of England's Fancy moved them to strip most of the mature leaves from the section before MacCullough came around the hill and saw them.

The Scotsman took off his hat and watched, mouth agape, as the mistress of the plantation rode among the sweating men, carrying heavy waterbags across her saddle and ladling water into their mouths and over their heads. After a few minutes, he shook his head and rode down.

"'Tis enough for today," he called from the end of the row where she worked. She did not hear him. The crew exchanged surreptitious glances but did not stop at his command.

MacCullough scowled. "Enough, men. Come out of

there. There's food and drink for all."

Fancy wiped the stinging sweat from her forehead. Dazedly, she stared at MacCullough's shape, unable to recognize her overseer in the gathering dusk.

Again the silence and the waiting.

"Go on, men," MacCullough called testily. "I'll take care of her. Can y' not see she's too tired to know what she's doing?"

As if finally convinced, the men began to move away slowly, their dark bodies fading into the growing blackness. Gently, the young black man whose place she had taken lifted the waterbags from the saddle. She frowned down at him, shaking her head. "I'm all right." Her voice startled her with its hollowness. "Really. Don't take that away. I'm fine."

"Rest, maitresse." The deep voice of the young man reassured her. "We work again tomorrow."

"But the storm . . . the tobacco . . ." she croaked.

MacCullough reined the gelding closer. "Come now, Miz Gillard. 'Tis all we can do. The dark has caught us. We've done all we can tonight."

Even as he spoke, lightning limned the thunderheads to the south and east.

"The storm . . ."

"'Tis in God's hands."

Holy Dulcibella put her to bed without a bath, because for the first time since Hunter had left her, Fancy collapsed from weariness.

Sometime after midnight the rain hit. It fell in drops so big they struck the jalousies like pebbles. With a cry of pure anguish, Fancy sat up in bed. The tobacco. The tobacco that remained in the field. As if the rain struck her own body, she cringed. Eyes bright with tears, she pulled the covers higher and curled into a ball.

131

By dawn the wind was a howling banshee and the black loam of England's Fancy ran into the rushing river. The house timbers groaned constantly. A lighted candle was out of the question, for even the lamps flickered fitfully as the wind sought out every chink in the walls.

Fancy dressed herself and opened the front door, but the wind jerked it from her hand and slammed it into the wall. The rain slanted into the hall, drenching her skirt and driving her back.

Amos hurried forward to throw his weight against it and close it.

Holy Dulcibella came halfway down the stairs. "You can do nothing, maitresse. When the storm wind blows, men can only take shelter."

Her words reminded Fancy of her people cowering in their cabins not far from the curing sheds and the dock. Anguish over her lost crop changed to fear for them. "Where will they find shelter?" If England's Fancy, built of ship's timbers, would creak and groan, what of the knocked-together cabins?

She could not see through the driving rain; a few feet beyond the columns the world became a gray sheet of water. Over the roar of the storm, she looked up into Holy Dulcibella's piercing eyes. "I must get down there. They must all come here."

"You cannot leave this house."

"Oh, no, maitresse." Amos added his arguments to the housekeeper's. "You be blown away. Nobody stand out there."

"I'll go out the back, down the hill through the field. That way—"

"You have lost your mind."

"You be killed, maitresse."

Unheeding of their protests, Fancy darted away. Instinctively, she knew she was right when she could open the back door and step out onto the porch. If she kept in the lee of the house and of the hill, she could make her way to MacCullough's house. He would go with her and help her lead the men and their families back to the comparative safety.

One step off the porch and the rain hit her like a blow across her back and head. She staggered, bowed, unable to stand upright. Never in her wildest dreams had she imagined such force as primal nature unleashed. Feeling it against her made Fancy wonder, in the part of her mind not occupied with keeping from falling into the mire, how even Great Edward's house could stand against it.

Her clothing was instantly soaked. Each gasp for breath sucked in more water than air. Then she plunged in among the lashing, whipping tobacco plants. Like tentacles, their writhing stalks clutched at her ankles. She fell and mud splashed in her face, almost drowning her.

Up again. A few strides more. Then the branches of a falling limb scraped across her back, ripping her clothing and flinging her sideways. She did not stop to think that she would have been killed instantly if the bole rather than the leaves and twigs had struck her head. Her whole body was concentrated on pushing herself out of the clinging mud. And up again. Was she sobbing or only gasping for breath?

She could not return to her house. The power of will kept her moving. Somewhere ahead of her was MacCullough's house. Somewhere in the whirling, drowning world.

Even as it loomed out of the gray curtain, she banged her shin on the bottom step already covered by running water. She was wading! The land near the dock must be completely under water.

"Oh, God!" she screamed. "MacCullough!" She

133

lunged up the steps on hands and knees. Pounding on the panels and twisting at the doorknob, she burst into the room even before he could open it.

He slammed the door shut against the roaring tempest. "Almighty God! Miz Gillard!"

Weightless and disoriented, she tried to wipe the rain-soaked hair from her eyes. "I've come . . ." She wheezed, then sucked air into her lungs. "We must . . . get to the cabins . . . bring the people . . . back to the house."

He started in amazed disbelief. "Impossible."

She shook her head adamantly. Drops of water flew everywhere. "No. It's not impossible." Now that she was out of the driving rain, Fancy's knees began to wobble. She slumped back against the wall. "I made it here and that's impossible."

"But . . ."

His opposition angered her. Every minute they delayed, people could be dying. "The river is rising. Don't you understand? Your steps are already under water. You could be swimming for your life in a very few minutes."

"If the water is up to my steps, then 'tis too late," he declared.

"No." She found her voice then and yelled at him. "Those are my people. We can't let them drown."

Even as she spoke, the house gave a great groan. The foundation shifted and the floor tilted beneath her feet. Only MacCullough's hands clutching her arms kept her from being upset. The panes of window glass cracked and splintered. The howling wind rushed in.

"Almighty God," the Scotsman breathed.

"We must get to them," she shouted, tugging at his arm.

He shook his shaggy head. "No chance. We'll be damned lucky to save ourselves."

134

The house slid again. Timbers cracked and nails spanged. Glass shattered in another room. The door burst open, driven by the demon wind.

MacCullough caught her by the arm. Together they plunged out onto the crumbling porch. When she would have jumped immediately into the maelstrom that covered the third step, he tugged her to the right. "Higher ground," he shouted.

The wind and rain snatched the words from his mouth, but Fancy could do nothing more than follow where he led. Without MacCullough's strength, the ground would have been cut from beneath her by the water rushing down the slope and by the force of the gale.

After an eternity of slipping and falling, of being pelted by rain and slashed by disintegrating vegetation, they gained the lee of England's Fancy and felt their way along to the porch.

While MacCullough pounded on the door, Fancy slumped back against the wall, staring with anguished eyes at the gray curtain of water plunging down before her eyes. Sick with horror, she pictured her men and their families swept away to drown. Tears began in earnest, their paths undetectable on her wet cheeks.

Dimly, she was aware of Holy Dulcibella wrapping a heavy cotton sheet around her and leading her into the dark house, which creaked and groaned like the timbers of a ship. "Maitresse, come. It is in God's hands now. And He is good. He brought you back safe and sound."

Her failure to lead her people to safety had wrung the spirit from her exhausted body. The month of disillusionment and disappointment ending with the disaster of the hurricane drained the last of her strength. Once inside the house, she went down in a sodden heap. So total was her collapse that the

135

housekeeper was dragged to her knees beside her.

"Maitresse!"

Arms akimbo, MacCullough glared down into Fancy's unconscious face. "Women!" he sneered. "So I told her. I warned her, but she wouldna be warned. She had no business to try to do a man's work. This fool attempt—"

Holy Dulcibella motioned to Amos, who had to edge round the overseer to kneel at Fancy's side. "You are the one who is an ungrateful fool." The dark woman rose and advanced imperiously with eyes narrowed. "Would you have gotten out of your house and come to safety if not for the bravery of this one? Feeling as you do, I wonder you dragged her back with you. You were more likely to flee and leave her to try to save her people alone."

He flushed angrily. "I would have gone alone," he declared obstinately, "but 'twas already too late. The whole hill is awash. The river must be up thirty, maybe forty feet. And rising."

"Dulci . . ."

"My baby." The black woman spun. Amos had helped Fancy to her feet.

"Don't say anything more to MacCullough. He was right. I was too late."

"Maitresse. You tried. . . ."

"*Tried* is not good enough. I failed." She walked out of Amos's supporting hands and tottered to the foot of the staircase. "You are welcome, Mr. MacCullough. Amos, get him some dry clothing from Mr. Gillard's closet."

"I thank you kindly," MacCullough responded, inclining his head.

She did not even look at him. "I'm going to lie down, Dulci. This has been—" She choked over her words. A shudder racked her body. Hand gripping the railing as if she would pull herself up, she started up the stairs. "The wind . . . and rain . . ."

The water began to recede around noon the next day, leaving the entire plantation denuded of standing vegetation. Both sides of the river, as far as the eye could see, were wrecked. Trees a century old lay uprooted and half buried by drowned tobacco plants. What had been gently rolling ground was cratered and eroded by the rush of the water. The docks, the curing barns, the tool sheds, the storehouses and, most important, the workers' cabins were all swept away. The overseer's house canted off its foundation, a lopsided wreck. One half of the stable had lost its roof.

Fancy found her father's old jackboots. With the toes stuffed with stockings, they would fit, albeit uncomfortably. Most important, they came up around her thighs and would afford her some protection in the mire.

"You'll be findin' more than y' bargained for if a water moccasin winds itself around your ankle," MacCullough warned angrily.

Throwing him a disgusted glance, Fancy stepped out into the steamy hell. At the stables she found several of her workers, including the young man who had collapsed the day before. Fearfully, they came out of one of the stalls exposed by the torn roof.

Fancy's old mare, whose stall they had sheltered in, was nowhere to be seen.

Instead of inquiring as to the fate of the beast, Fancy managed a wan smile. "First, go up to the house," she commanded them. "Amos will give you food and fresh water to drink. When you've finished, come down to the river."

They bowed humbly and slogged off through the

clinging mud.

At the sound of her voice, the black hunter thrust his head over the stall and whickered in recognition. "So you survived, did you? The devil didn't want you?" With tears in her eyes, she put her hand on the black muzzle.

For once, the horse did not draw back. Seeking comfort in her familiar scent, he nudged against her hand and snuffled. He had torn his line loose from the eyebolt in the side of the stall and had kicked holes in the back, but somehow the structure had survived both his efforts and the hurricane.

Leading him out of the stall, Fancy mounted him bareback and let him pick his way through the hock-deep mud.

A hundred yards down the slope from the stable, she came upon the first bodies. A man, his black skin bleached and gray-looking, lay on his side, his arms around a naked child. They had evidently sought shelter in a culvert that had collapsed, half burying them in the mud and trapping them for the rising water.

A few yards farther down she came across two more victims. Clearly, they had been making for the stables. If she had risen earlier . . . If she had insisted that they quarter in the stables in the face of the storm . . . If . . .

Her stomach heaved. She clutched at the mane of her horse and vomited to the side. By the time MacCullough caught up with her, she had gotten herself under control. Except for a greenish tinge around her mouth, she was composed.

"Have you ever seen anything this bad?" she asked.

"No." His own voice was a low, strangled growl.

She glanced swiftly to the side and saw he was struggling for control as much as she. "What's to be done?"

"Burial. Swift. Only I'm afeared we've not got

138

enough livin' to bury the dead."

"And . . ."

"We'll be lucky to come out of this alive ourselves. We've no water and food. The storehouses 're washed away. The water's polluted."

"The wells?"

"Filled with silt and Lord knows what else . . . Every drop of water anybody drinks will have t' be boilt or we'll all die of fever." He looked bleakly around him. "And all the wood's too wet to burn."

"We'll use furniture."

"Miz Gillard . . ."

The look she threw him stilled his protest. "Not one person more shall die here," she vowed.

"So you fared as everyone else did." Reeves Tarleton looked unutterably weary, his face pinched around the mouth, his forehead knitted into a perpetual frown. "The tragedy of the century, so far as Colleton County is concerned."

Fancy nodded. "If the house had not been set on the top of the hill, we would have lost it, too."

"Sad. Sad." The banker stared downward at his clasped hands. "The Chalmettes, twenty miles south of you. Their house was built closer to the river. It washed away. All were drowned. All. Five children." He swallowed hard. "Wiped out."

She waited, unable to say anything. Knowing that if she spoke, the sorrow at her neighbors' loss, added to her own devastation, would strip her of her control.

"So . . ." he said at last.

"I need capital, Mr. Tarleton. The house is intact. Indeed, it sustained miraculously little damage. But the seeds for new crops were lost. We must begin to plant immediately. The rice seedlings were all washed away.

139

But with the ground so wet, we don't need seedlings. We can broadcast the crop in the old way. It can be done in a couple of days by the men I have left. It won't be more than a few weeks late. Then the workers' quarters have to be rebuilt. Right now they're living in the stable. The dock . . ."

She stopped as he held up his hand. "I haven't money of that amount to lend, Mrs. Gillard. You must understand everyone needs money as badly or worse than you do."

She stared at him, aghast. "How much can you lend me?"

He would not meet her eyes. "Perhaps a hundred dollars."

"A hundred dollars?!"

"Every bank in this part of South Carolina is in the same condition."

"But I have to buy more than a hundred dollars worth of food and medicine to take back with me." She leaned forward, her gloved hand grasping the edge of his desk. "You don't seem to understand, Mr. Tarleton. We have absolutely nothing . . . nothing to eat except what is in the pantry and cupboard of the great house. To feed fifty-eight people."

"I can't let you have more, Mrs. Gillard. I can't make a loan beyond that unless I can see that there is a chance of repayment."

"A chance of repayment! . . . The rice crop will be planted immediately. In five months, possibly four given the soaked condition of the ground, the rice will be ready to harvest and sell."

The banker cleared his throat. "Mrs. Gillard," he began gently, "you are a delicate and gentle lady. You can't expect to—"

She rose abruptly. "Am I to understand that you are able to loan me only a pittance because I am a woman?

140

Do you mean that if I were a man, you would loan me more?"

Tarleton rose too, his hands clasped unctuously. "Mrs. Gillard, you have no idea what lies ahead of you. You are to be commended for your Christian concern for your people. However, the task that lies ahead of all of us is monumental."

"It can be no more monumental for me than for any other grower."

"But they are experienced. They have always farmed."

"I am experienced. I have always farmed." Her response was not strictly true, but she knew more than Hunter, and he had farmed the place for ten years. "I have my father's own overseer, Ferris MacCullough, who will actually handle much of the physical labor."

The banker shook his head. "May I suggest that you bind over your workers to other growers in your area and—"

"You won't advance me even a thousand dollars?"

He hesitated, remembering her father. For the sake of his friendship with Richard England, he should do all he could to help his daughter. But she was so small. She could not have weighed over ninety-five pounds. The golden eyes were rimmed with dark circles from lack of rest and sleep. He would be doing her a favor to refuse. "I cannot see my way clear—"

She thrust out her chin. "Then I must withdraw all the money from my account."

He blinked then. "But . . . England's account is one of the oldest in the bank."

"I need that money. I would've liked to leave it in as collateral against the crop loan, but under these circumstances . . ."

"But . . ."

She pulled her bankbook from her purse. "I believe

141

we have some six thousand dollars in the account."

He did sit down then, his face thunderstruck. "Why, no, Mrs. Gillard. Mr. Gillard took five thousand from it to put into his latest venture."

"What?"

"He withdrew five thousand dollars. . . ."

"That money was the money from the sale of last year's tobacco," she all but screamed. "How could you let him take it?"

Tarleton leaned forward huffily. "It was his money, Mrs. Gillard."

"No, sir. It belonged to England's Fancy."

"And he owns England's Fancy."

She was so angry she could barely talk. "He—he does not. Besides, he has deserted it."

"A man on his way to being rich may use his capital to expand his investments. I talked with him about this trading venture. He had made arrangements with Shepperton's Shipping Lines of Charleston to purchase trade goods and transport aboard their new merchantman, the *Carolina*. I can assure you—"

Fancy's eyes blazed. "Damn you," she snarled, shocking the man into silence. "Damn you and damn him. He took my money and left me, and you let him."

"Mrs. Gillard . . ."

She slapped her gloved hand down on the top of the banker's desk. "Don't call me that again. Don't ever call me that again. I am Caroline England. And you have given my money away to a thieving philanderer."

"But . . ."

She drew a deep, angry breath. "Give me the remainder of the money in the account," she demanded.

"I assure you, Mrs. Gillard, that the money is safer here."

"It is not safer here," she sneered. "You would give it away to whoever came in with a proposition for a 'new profitable venture.' But you will not give me money to finance a rice crop on land that has grown rice successfully for a hundred years."

"Mr. Gillard is your husband. He could not have foreseen that a hurricane would strike with such devastation."

"Damn Mr. Gillard! And damn you, sir. This discussion is closed."

"You will move everyone into the great house, Mr. MacCullough."

"Miz Gillard, the stables—"

"The stables are for the horses. I have purchased two things, and two things only, with the money in the account. Food and rice seed. You will organize the planting of it. Sow it over every bit of wet bottom land."

"The tobacco land . . ."

"We'll have to wait for next year for tobacco. Now we must eat. And so must many of our neighbors. England's Fancy has always had bumper rice crops while others have not. They'll buy our rice from us, on loan for lumber and workers."

"When the rice is harvested," MacCullough supplied sourly. *"If* it's harvested."

"Oh, it'll be harvested, Mr. MacCullough. You'll see to it with all the workers we have left, plus any that our neighbors, who are less determined than we, may wish to loan to us."

He looked as if he wanted to disagree further, then shrugged. "I suppose you'll be with me, doggin' my footsteps," he growled unhappily.

"No, Mr. MacCullough. I'm going to Boston to get my money back from Josiah Shepperton. I know he supported, if not encouraged, Hunter in this desertion. He must have known that Hunter would use my money. I'm going to inform him and my mother of my need. If need be, I'll beg, but they *will* give me the money I need to rebuild."

MacCullough shook his head. "It was his money," he countered. "I think you've bitten off more than you can chew. You'd be smarter to take the banker's advice and loan your own workers out."

Fancy drew in a furious breath. "Mr. MacCullough, do you like your job?"

He flushed, then finally admitted slowly, "It's a good job."

"You expect to remain here as overseer until you retire, and then you expect to stay in a house on this plantation and supervise a young man who will take your place, don't you?"

"Yes, ma'am."

"Then, Mr. MacCullough, I suggest you fight for this land. It will not support you if you do not fight for it."

"When Mr. Gillard comes back, he'll—"

She made a cutting motion with her hand. "The rice needs to be planted now while the ground is soaked. The rotting tobacco plants will make good fertilizer."

He shook his head stubbornly.

She regarded him with such obvious contempt that he flushed. "You're letting prejudice against me blind you. You're a fool."

"I'm not a fool," he denied sullenly. "A man is a fool to fight when there is no chance."

"A man is a fool who quits before he even tries. That's what you're doing because you don't like me, Mr. MacCullough. For the past month, you've done

144

everything to hinder me and nothing to help me. You steadfastly refuse to see that I'm fighting for England's Fancy with every breath I draw."

"Miz Gillard . . ."

She turned her back on him. "If the rice is not planted when I get back, don't be here."

Chapter Nine

The captain of the *Carcasonne* shook his head over the raw table wine. *"Merde, Chasseur,* we were lucky to escape with our lives."

"Surely you exaggerate, *mon brave.*"

"Mais non." The man punctuated his denial with a stab of his index finger. "Those hurricanes sometimes rise out of the water faster than a man can think. I was in Charleston harbor when it began to blow. *Dieu!* I hoisted sail immediately. Two members of the crew were away, but I did not wait. The hold was only three-quarters full." He shrugged. "But better three-quarters than all of nothing."

"But you don't know whether the storm turned inland?"

The captain of the *Carcasonne* looked shrewdly at the man facing him. Clearly, the American was more than casually curious. *"Oui,* I do not know. I do not know that the sun will rise tomorrow or that the sea will not dry up. But I can make a good guess that those things will be so."

Hunter Gillard hunched forward in his chair, making no effort to conceal the worry in his face. "Have any ships arrived since you?"

Again the Gallic shrug, this time accompanied by a gesture toward the harbor of Cherbourg. "You can go out and see for yourself, *mon ami,* if you are so anxious to know. But me . . . I will guess that no ships have come in from the Carolinas after me."

Hunter tossed a couple of francs onto the plank table. "Drink heartily and celebrate your good fortune on safe arrival."

"Merci bien." The captain smiled and nodded. "And, *mon ami,* I hope your worries are for nothing."

"So do I. So do I." Hunter hurried out of *La Mouette.*

Inquiries at the offices of Tourneaux Lines staggered him.

"A hurricane, indeed, M'sieur Gillard. We have just heard. Almost a month ago one damaged the harbor at Charleston."

Hunter clutched the edge of the desk. "Is there any news from the inland areas?"

"Unfortunately, there is little. But what there is is very bad. The entire tobacco crop was destroyed, just like that." The clerk snapped his fingers. "Many people drowned."

"My God."

"M'sieur Gillard!"

Hunter shook his head several times, trying to clear it of the frightening picture of England's Fancy set in the bend of a raging Edisto River. The fearful vulnerability of the place sickened him. The only man on the place was the Scotsman MacCullough, a curmudgeon of a man, no hero certainly. Neither Amos, the old butler, nor the grooms in the stable would be any help at all in an emergency. They had all been born and reared on the plantation.

"M'sieur Gillard." The clerk repeated the name gently. "I hope I have not given you bad news."

Hunter took a deep, steadying breath. "I'm afraid so. My home—" he swallowed, "my home is fifty miles from Charleston on the river."

The clerk made a clucking sound with his lips and teeth. *"Sacre Bleu!* And you so far away. My sympathies, m'sieur."

Hunter waved a hand tiredly. "Thank you."

"You will not go to Boston alone, maitresse. To travel so far alone is unsuitable for a young woman. Also, it is unsafe. I will go with you."

Fancy clasped the woman's dark, withered hands and hugged them against her. "Oh, Dulci, I'm so glad you said that. I wasn't looking forward to making the journey alone. And when I get there, who knows what sort of reception I'm going to get. If what I've heard is true, Mother and Josiah have been told lies about me."

Holy Dulcibella nodded. "He is a fool for believing such self-serving lies. And she is a fool for marrying a fool. Your father Richard was a fine man. When a woman has had the best, she should not look for a replacement."

Once Fancy would have agreed wholeheartedly with the housekeeper's estimate of men in general and her father in particular. Now, imbued with the bitterness of her recent experience, she was not so sure. "Perhaps Mother didn't share your opinion of my father."

The housekeeper scanned her charge with glittering eyes. "You have lost much faith, maitresse."

"Not to speak of much hope and much charity, Dulci. I don't think that any man could be the be-all and end-all for a woman. I used to hate and despise my mother. Now I just feel a sort of weary acceptance of what she did."

Holy Dulcibella looked totally affronted. "Richard

149

was Great Edward's son. He was a good and kind man. I reared him," she added with pardonable pride.

"I'm sorry, Dulci." Fancy instantly regretted what she had said. "I didn't mean to upset you."

By way of closing the subject, the old woman turned away and opened the door to the huge wardrobe. "What will you take with you, maitresse?"

"My old clothes," came the amused reply. "Nothing else fits." She opened the jewel box on the top of her dresser and stared at the contents. "And these."

"We must have money."

"No. I won't take a penny that needs to go for seed and food. If I need money, I'll sell some of these." She dropped the lid closed and patted the top.

"Maitresse . . ." the housekeeper chided.

"I don't care about the baubles Hunter gave me, Dulci. All I want is to get to Boston and get back my money. And damn him for forcing me to make the trip."

"But our next port of call was to be Portsmouth."

"I know, Jessica, but the news from South Carolina changes all that. I can't just sail on until I know that everything is all right."

"You're being foolish." Her voice rose shrilly. "That awful coast is always getting storms. When it isn't steaming hot, it's storming. But the houses down there have stood for hundreds of years. Spanish moss simply hangs off them. I'm sure that man exaggerated."

"If I had spoken with only one man, I might agree with you. But two. And one of them was a sea captain. He couldn't help but know where he was on the seacoast."

"Perhaps one told the other." Jessica Rutledge felt the nervous flutterings begin in her stomach. Above all things, Hunter must not be allowed to turn back. "I'll bet the captain reported that information to the clerk at Tourneaux. Then the clerk exaggerated it to you."

Hunter looked doubtful. "But the stories didn't match. The captain of the *Carcasonne* told of escaping before the storm struck full force. The clerk was bemoaning the destroyed tobacco crop."

Jessica bit her lip. "I'm sure you misunderstood the clerk. Probably he was guessing that the tobacco crop would be damaged by a storm. You know what pessimists these French are."

"Jessica, I must go home if there is trouble," Hunter pleaded.

She slipped her arms around his body to hug him close and smile up into his face. "Well, of course you must, sweetheart. I know that. But I just don't want to spoil our trip for nothing. Think how you'd feel if you sailed home as fast as you could and there had only been a minor storm."

He ran his hand through his dark hair. "Perhaps you're right."

She followed his hand with her own, smoothing where he ravaged, then kissed the tip of his nose. "I know I am." Tilting her head, she placed her mouth beneath his. For an instant he hovered above it. With a quick birdlike movement, she stretched up to brush her lips to his. When he did not respond, she tightened her arms. "Hunter, you mustn't be so serious. The captain of the ship should relax while the ship is safely at anchor." She pressed herself against him, letting him feel her breasts.

His chest heaved. He lowered his head and took her mouth then. His kiss was long and deep. Still, he could not rid himself of tension. Distracted by the creak of the wooden sign of the seagull, he put her aside.

"Hunter . . ." she whimpered.

"I've got to find out more, Jessica." He crossed to the window and stared out at the harbor. The forest of masts tilted back and forth as the ships rode the swells.

Wrapping her arms around her body, she stared moodily at his broad back. She must distract him. Make him forget. Time would blur this—if only she could gain a bit of time. "It's almost time for dinner, Hunter."

"I'm not hungry."

She gritted her teeth but managed to put a sweet smile in her voice. "No, I don't suppose you are, but Alex is. Don't forget, he's got an appetite as big as he is." Struggling to sound pleasant and, above all, normal, she seated herself at the small dressing table and began to smooth her hair.

At the mention of Alex, Hunter stiffened. "Suppose I've taken that boy away from his mother and he'll never see her again."

"Nonsense." She looked at him sternly in the mirror. "You're letting this prey upon your mind without cause. I still say that these people don't know one part of the United States from another. They could just as easily be talking about North Carolina or Georgia or Maryland." She drew on her gloves.

"Perhaps . . ."

"Perhaps we should go and get Alex and take him to dinner. Then tomorrow if you're still worried after a good night's sleep, you can seek out the captain of the *Carcasonne* and have him describe the storm to you. When you hear it while he's sober, you'll probably laugh behind your hand."

Hunter looked a bit more hopeful. "He *was* drinking."

"There, you see. Let me play valet for you." She held out his coat for him to slip his arms into.

*　　*　　*

"I'm sorry, ma'am. Shepperton Lines does not grant travel passes unless they are authorized by Mr. Shepperton or one of his managers." The clerk looked over the top of his glasses at Fancy.

"But I'm Mr. Shepperton's stepdaughter. There should be no problem at all."

"No, ma'am. I'm sure you're right." The clerk came out from behind the desk, rubbing his hands together nervously. "If you'll just pay a quick visit to the office two doors down the block, Mr. Wentworth will provide you with the authorization, I'm sure."

Fancy's heart sank, but she assumed her iciest demeanor. "Is that really necessary? I am Josiah Shepperton's daughter. That simple fact should be sufficient."

"It is. It is. But . . ."

"You do not infer that I'm lying about who I am?"

"Oh, no, miss. No, indeed." The clerk fairly jumped across the office and flung open the door. "If you'll just wait a minute, I'll run down the street and fetch Mr. Wentworth. Save you the trouble."

"Wait . . ." But he paid no heed to her call. "Damn!"

"What is it, maitresse?"

"Nothing. No, that's not so. It's Wentworth."

"You expect that this man will not be sympathetic."

"I know that this man will not be sympathetic. I said some beastly things to him just before I left Charleston." She shook her head. "This could be most unpleasant."

As she spoke, Wentworth came out of the office door. Head thrust forward, he strode down the street, followed by the clerk who skipped nervously along in his effort to keep up.

As he walked past the window, she retreated until the edge of the counter nudged her ribs. "Damn," she murmured.

He plunged into the office, his eyes alighting on her

153

immediately. "Ah, Mrs. Gillard." His mouth twisted into a malevolent sneer; his voice dripped sarcasm.

She pushed herself away from the desk. "Mr. Wentworth. I am sorry this young man summoned you. I know how very busy you must be, with the storm and everything. Were any of my father's ships damaged?"

"Your *father's* ships. So Josiah Shepperton is your father, is he? No. Not at all."

"I am so glad to hear it. Nevertheless, you must be very busy. I'm sure your young man can take care of me. There was no need to bother you." She smiled blindingly at the young clerk who edged along the wall to get back behind the counter.

He smiled back warily. Then his eyes darted to Wentworth's face and the smile disappeared.

Wentworth squared his heavy shoulders. "But I wouldn't think of someone of your importance being handled by just anyone. As you say, Josiah Shepperton is your father."

"Er . . . yes . . ."

"And I am his employee, here to assist you." The man made her a sweeping formal bow, but his demeanor belied the exaggerated politeness. "Please let me know how I may be of service."

Fancy's pride rebelled against the thought of humbling herself before this malevolent toad of a man. She lifted her chin imperceptibly. How she longed to spit in his eye and walk out. But the fate of England's Fancy and its imperiled survivors depended on her.

She cleared her throat. "Mr. Wentworth, you must know that plantations all over South Carolina are in desperate straits."

"Of course, the hurricane."

"Exactly. The hurricane blew away everything." On this, at least, they could agree. She made no attempt to conceal the emotion in her voice. "Everything on England's Fancy was destroyed except the house itself. Many, many people were killed."

"My condolences."

He sounded sincere. Encouraged, she leaned forward. "Mr. Wentworth, the fact is that I need to go to Boston immediately on the next available ship. Bank capital in this state is almost exhausted. The amount that they can lend any one person is so small."

"Regrettable."

"It is indeed." Fancy nodded at the same time she smiled a gentle smile. "And then I realized that I could do my own part to ease the situation by going to Boston and borrowing the money I needed from Josiah. I knew he would lend it to me without question."

"Doubtless you are right."

"So . . ."

"So . . ."

She did not remember him as being so obtuse. "I need to book passage on the next available ship for me and my maid."

Wentworth smiled thinly. "That will be no trouble, Mrs. Gillard." As a functionary might serve a queen, he turned. "Dick, what is our next vessel bound for Boston?"

Dick smiled a relieved smile. "The *Columbia* leaves on the morning tide, sir."

Wentworth nodded, then turned back with a deep frown. "But perhaps she would not be to your liking, Mrs. Gillard. She is one of our older ships, from the eighteenth century actually, an old flute."

"That will be quite satisfactory, Mr. Wentworth. We must leave immediately. Time is everything to me."

"Of course." He turned to Dick. "I believe the *Cambridge* is in port. What time does she leave?"

Dick's smile broadened. "The *Cambridge* leaves at

155

the end of the week."

"Ah. That would really be your best choice, Mrs. Gillard. She is a first-class merchantman, of the same category as the *Carolina*. Very fast. Even though the old *Columbia* leaves three days earlier, she'll not arrive in Boston till two days after the *Cambridge* docks."

"Then by all means let us take the *Cambridge*."

"Very good." Wentworth smiled. "And what is the price for the passage for the two of them? Those are the best accommodations, of course."

Startled, the clerk looked from one to the other. "Er . . . one hundred dollars."

"And for her maid?"

The young man raised his eyebrows. "Well, if she travels in the same class, the price is the same. If she travels . . . er . . . twenty dollars."

Wentworth turned triumphantly. "There you have it, Mrs. Gillard. Do you wish to pay for your maid to travel at the same price as you?"

Fancy felt the hot color rise in her cheeks. "Mr. Wentworth, I expect that you will allow me free passage on Shepperton Lines."

He crossed his arms over his barrel chest. "Now, why would I do that, Mrs. Gillard? I have had no such instructions from Mr. Shepperton. Perhaps you have a letter about you?"

Fancy shook her head.

He rocked back on his heels, an expression of triumphant malice in his eyes. "Then I'm afraid I could not clearly frank your tickets. As you have pointed out to me, I always follow instructions to the letter."

Fancy could feel her ears burning. The clerk made a smothered exclamation and hastily buried his face in the register. Holy Dulcibella took a step forward, but Fancy raised her hand. "Mr. Wentworth, do you understand that I have no money to make this passage

156

because I have used every cent I have to help my people?"

His implacable demeanor never faltered. "That is certainly laudable of you, Mrs. Gillard, but I have a business to run and it must turn a profit. Berths are now at a premium. With the threats of cholera and yellow jack everywhere, so many people are sending their families to relatives."

Fancy stared into his eyes. They glittered between the fleshy pouches above and below them. *He expects me to beg for my people. He wants me to. Damn him!* She ducked her head. "How much for passage on the *Columbia?*"

The clerk leaned over the counter. "Only seventy-five dollars, ma'am. And the maid can travel free."

"But we will arrive a day later."

"Er . . . two days. The old flute's slow, but she's sure."

Not budging an inch, Wentworth regarded her triumphantly.

She folded her hands tightly together before her. "Dulci, will you bring my jewel box from the coach?"

"Yes, maitresse." For once, the housekeeper-turned-traveling-companion did not protest. She bowed as obsequiously as if she were the servant of a queen. In the uncomfortable moments of waiting, Fancy stared through the window at the masts bobbing.

When Holy Dulcibella returned, she carried the ornate silver box in both hands. Coming to stand directly in front of Fancy, she extended it with slow ceremony. "As you requested, maitresse," she intoned. Her eyes were blank, her face without expression.

"My maid and I will both travel first class on the *Cambridge,* Mr. Wentworth." She opened the lid and pulled out a tiny drawer in the bottom of the chest.

A kaleidoscope of light and color flashed in the

157

afternoon sun, beaming in through the shop window. Without any sign of regret, she tossed the beautiful thing at Wentworth's chest.

Taken by surprise, the man nevertheless managed to catch the slashing fire. Fumbling, he finally sorted it out and held it up. Capturing and reflecting the light of the afternoon sun was a gold filigree necklace set with faceted red stones.

"Rubies, Mr. Wentworth. Ten of them in all. And here. Catch these, too. I want you to have an even dozen." With a grimace, she tossed him the matching earbobs.

He caught one, but the other fell to the floor. Again he fumbled as the toe of his boot struck it and sent it sliding against the baseboard of the counter. Huffing angrily, he scurried to retrieve it.

"I trust that those will cover the two-hundred-dollar fee."

He regarded her sourly. "More than adequately, Mrs. Gillard. Always supposing you have the right to sell them."

Her fury spilled over. Fast as lightning, she stepped close to him and fetched him a slap across the side of his face. "They are my wedding jewels, sir. And, I trust, they belong to no one but me. Oh, yes. These, at least, are mine."

His fist closed around the necklace and earbobs. "Then you are right to sell them, Mrs. Gillard, since your marriage is obviously over." With that last word, he turned to the embarrassed Dick. "Book them for two for the *Columbia*."

Fancy started forward with an angry gasp.

Wentworth slapped the earbobs into the hand. "I wouldn't want to overcharge you," he sneered. "The *Columbia* sails slower, but you'll be out of Charleston sooner."

"Damn you," Fancy hissed.

"Say no more, Mrs. Gillard, or you'll be taking the stagecoach to Boston—a most long and uncomfortable trip." With that final threat uttered, he thrust the ruby necklace into his pocket and slammed out.

"We sail with the morning tide, Alex."

"Where to, Daddy?"

"We're going home. There's been a storm and I think your mother might need help."

Jessica crossed her fingers, hoping for a protest, but Alex caught at his father's hand. "A storm? With thunder and lightning? Then let's go quick as ever we can. I miss her. And my pony. Do you think my pony is all right?"

Jessica put her hand on his shoulder. "But you haven't even seen London, Alex. Surely you remember how you wanted to see London Bridge?"

The little boy looked at his father. "I did want to see it."

"This is not the only voyage you'll ever make." Hunter brushed aside his son's faint protest with a distracted air.

Jessica Rutledge clenched her fists until her fingernails pressed deep into her palms. "This is foolishness."

Hunter refused to look at her. "I have no more time to discuss this. I've wasted too much time. Over forty-eight hours I've waited, but the news is incontrovertible. And all bad. I must get back. She doesn't even have sufficient funds in the bank. I invested heavily in the cargo for this venture."

Jessica put her hands on Alex's shoulders. "Why don't you go and get a sweet from the *concierge?* I'll bet she'll have a pastry for you."

"Shall I, Daddy?"

159

"That's a good idea."

When they were alone, Hunter held up his hand. "Jessica, I don't want to hear any objections. I've made up my mind on this. Fancy is my wife. I am sworn to protect her."

"And what about the promises you made to me?"

He shifted uncomfortably. "I still intend to keep them."

"You are going to her, giving up everything, wasting all this time and money, when you have no knowledge that anything is wrong."

"Nothing wrong. My God, woman. The port is full of reports. I've talked to over a dozen men in the last two days. The storm was terrible. And Fancy was alone on that damned plantation in the bend of the river."

"Exactly."

He gaped at her, trying to read her meaning. When it dawned, the color drained from beneath his dark skin, leaving it a muddy gray. "I'll not think about that."

"Perhaps you'd better. If the damage is as bad as all the reports have led you to believe, perhaps you have nothing to go back to."

"I'll not believe it."

"Do you want to take your son back to learn his mother is dead?"

He spun away from her, clapping the heel of his hand against his forehead. "Jessica," he croaked. "Don't say any more. If she's dead, he's going to find out sooner or later."

She came to him and took his arm. "Then let it be later," she urged, shaking him gently. "Continue the voyage as you've planned. By the time he returns, he'll have been weaned away from her. He'll be sorry, but the tie will be broken. He'll have become independent. He won't need her. If you take him back now and find her gone, he'll feel guilty. And you won't have accomplished anything."

With a violent movement, Hunter shook her off. "Be quiet!" he shouted. "Don't say another word! Not one more!"

"Hunter . . ."

"Not one more." He strode to the door. "Pack your things. We're going back. I'm not going to argue about it."

"For heaven's sake, Hunter. . . . I'm only thinking of what's best . . ."

The door slammed behind him with such force that her little bottles of cosmetics and perfumes jumped and rattled on her dressing table.

Chapter Ten

"Dulci," Fancy whispered out of the side of her mouth. "That man is staring at you."

The older woman sniffed indulgently. "Not at me. No, maitresse. He probably stares at you but does not want his captain to suspect."

Fancy glanced around again, her eyes skittering off the man and up into the rigging as if she were distracted by its squeaking. Quickly, they returned to scanning Charleston Harbor as the *Columbia* carried them on their way. "No," she insisted. "I'm certain. When you came aboard, he looked at you twice as if he couldn't believe his eyes. Since then, he's moved three times but always where he can get a better look at you."

"You will see you are wrong." Holy Dulcibella crossed her hands more firmly across her waist. Tightening her mouth into a single line, she turned and directed a freezing look in the direction of the seaman.

Instead of sidling away or even ducking his head over the length of line he was coiling, he cocked up his head, sunk between his bent shoulders. His faded blue eyes searched her features; at first he smiled hesitantly. Skin so weathered as to be indistinguishable from leather crinkled around his eyes.

Holy Dulcibella swayed. Her eyes widened, then the frown smoothed out between her brows.

The seaman's smile became a cheeky grin. He took a step forward and made a passable leg. One broad, calloused foot, almost black on the bottom with tar, pointed gracefully in front of him, presenting the muscular calf. At the same time, he swept the faded blue kerchief off his head and bowed. "M'lady."

To Fancy's amazement, Holy Dulcibella's tight mouth trembled, then softened. She put out both hands. "L—Lemuel," she whispered.

He tottered slightly as he straightened. "Yes, m'lady."

"Lemuel Jakes."

He nodded. "M'lady."

"Give me your hands, Lemuel."

He put out his gnarled, horny paws, and she grasped them and pulled them to her. As if touching were not enough, she moved closer until the two were standing with her skirts brushing around his knees. Through a mist of tears, she looked up into his face.

"M'lady, I'm filthy," he warned, a suggestion of a quiver in his deep voice.

Her thumbs moved over and over his hands, feeling the craters left by sharp edges, the callouses around the palms from the lines, the deep scar where the left little finger and ring finger were missing. She closed her eyes.

Fancy stirred uncomfortably in the presence of such tension, then politely turned away to study the tiny sprays of foam splattering off the tops of the waves.

"Lady England?"

A tear slipped from one corner of her eye to find its way through the furrows of her cheek. "Lemuel Jakes," she whispered again.

"Yes, m'lady."

"You have had hard times."

"'Tis the life of the sea, m'lady."

"You should have come with us."

He grinned then, breaking the moment between them. "I'm no landlubber."

She nodded, giving his hands one last caress. "So you sail on the *Columbia*. What position?"

"Able seaman, m'lady." He inclined his head.

She smiled. "You, an able seaman. What a waste."

"I am old, m'lady."

"Surely not." She took a deep breath and stepped back. "You must meet my maitresse."

He started. "You have a mistress. You?"

"We all grow old," she reminded him dryly. "Come. Maitresse."

He looked around quickly, but the captain was kneeling on the edge of the forward hold, his back to them.

Fancy turned back at the call. "Maitresse Caroline Fancy England." Holy Dulcibella pronounced the names with pride ringing in her voice and unceremoniously divesting Fancy of the name Gillard.

Lemuel Jakes started, then stared hard. "Fancy England," he whispered. "Fancy England." His face split into a grin. He put back his head and laughed richly. "M'lady." Again he made the gallant leg, so incongruous in the seaman's faded canvas knee britches and bare feet and calves.

"I beg to present Able Seaman Lemuel Jakes." Holy Dulcibella's face was softer than Fancy had ever seen it. "He sailed with your grandfather."

"My grandfather!" Fancy could not conceal her incredulity. "He knew my grandfather!"

"And served him well."

"But my grandfather has been dead for years."

"He died before you were born," she agreed, "but he was much older than Lemuel."

"I'll never forget him," Lemuel began. "I was not so very much older than your—"

Holy Dulcibella interrupted, "Lemuel, the captain is coming this way."

The old man nodded. "Then I'd best be about my business, but we'll have time to talk. This old flute fairly sails herself up the coast. Once we get underway, 'tis lyin' round the deck most of the time." He grinned. "Not a bad way to end my life."

Fancy stared after him as he moved on, checking the rigging for any loose knots. "I never before met a man who knew my grandfather," she murmured. "I think of him as belonging to another century. It seems as though everyone who knew him should be long dead and buried."

Holy Dulcibella shook her head. "He lived a long life, and he did not come to England's Fancy until he was in his middle years."

"It's hard to imagine."

The older woman smiled. "Someday you will be old and you will remember this conversation and marvel that you could not understand." Her eyes followed Lemuel's stooped form, tall despite his bent shoulders. "Pray God you live long and prosper as he did."

The *Columbia* sailed smoothly up the coast, stopping daily, unloading and loading cargo. As Lemuel had said, the crew of twelve men and the captain sailed her with a minimum of effort. At every port supplies were brought on board, so the food, while plain, was always fresh, the water clear and plentiful.

The lazy voyage over the warm blue ocean did much to repair Fancy's abused body. Only her troubled mind and spirit remained unrelieved as her sense of responsibility to the people of England's Fancy gnawed at her conscience. Too many people depended upon her for their very lives. Had she left them with enough money? Had they enough food? Was the rice crop planted and growing well?

Damn Hunter for taking almost the entire bank account! Face turned to the north, Fancy leaned against the rail for hours each day and willed the ship to move faster. Her face was tanned and her lips chapped, but the trouble in her mind would not allow her to stay in the shade of her cabin.

"She commands a crippled ship. Pray God she has the strength for it," Holy Dulcibella confided to Lemuel Jakes. "Just like her grandfather, England's Fancy is hers. Instead of leaving her a ship, he left her the land. Make no mistake, she commands it just as he commanded his. And all the people on it are her crew. Like a good captain, she would give the blood from her veins to care for them."

"She's Captain England's granddaughter then, for sure."

The old woman nodded. "All her life she was cosseted. She did not know what she was until recently. Suddenly the command was hers. She could have deserted, but she did not. She met adversity head-on. Now she has come to know what her heritage means."

He looked at her a long time. "And what does your heritage mean, Lady England?"

She shrugged. "I have put away that name. I am content. I sometimes think about what might have been, but then I pray and God removes the useless thoughts from my mind."

He stared at the slim figure leaning against the rail, as close to the bow of the ship as she could get. "But even she doesn't know. Lord England's granddaughter.

167

She thinks you're a servant."

Holy Dulcibella inclined her head. The gold glass setting in the pin of her kerchief flashed in the afternoon light. "You were ever a clever man, Lemuel. You did not need to be warned not to give away my secret."

"A person doesn't get to our age, m'lady, without having a whole bundle of secrets that're nobody's business."

The two were silent. The rigging creaked. The wind blew through Fancy's red hair, billowing the skirt of her gown and petticoats.

"We arrive in Boston safely, praise God."

He nodded. "You never had anything to worry about, m'lady."

"I never worry. I have lived my alloted threescore and ten. The rest are a gift from heaven."

"You're sure right about that."

"How long will the *Columbia* be in Boston?"

"Well, now, quite a spell. I'll be laying by above Skarlet's Tavern whilst the *Columbia*'s in drydock. I'd think about finding another berth, but truth to tell, I like this sailing up and down the coast. At the least sign of a blow, we run for port. It's like you say, m'lady. These years are a gift, so why not enjoy them?"

"If Almighty God planned this meeting, then perhaps he will grant me that I will see you again before we return to Charleston." Holy Dulcibella looked toward her charge, her eyes too scanning the slight figure. A troubled frown marred her forehead. "She must ask for money. To secure it may take many days. They may not want to give it to her."

Lemuel nodded sagely. "Wouldn't be surprised. Josiah Shepperton's not a generous man."

"Then I will send a message to you when I know our plans. To Skarlet's Tavern, did you say?"

"Behind Shepperton's shipyard at the end of Prince Street."

The missing trees were the things Hunter noticed first. Stately water oaks planted some fifty feet apart had flanked the road up to the main house. Three closest to the bank of the river were missing, the earth on which they stood crumbled away. Two had huge limbs broken out of them. One lay in the field, a portion of it still attached to the splintered trunk.

Alex knelt on the seat, leaning his head out the window. Suddenly, he gave a sharp exclamation and pulled back in. "Daddy, what happened to the dock? And my little boat?"

"It must have been blown away in the storm."

"My boat . . ."

"I'll get you a new boat, Alex," Hunter interrupted his son firmly. His own agitation was growing. Not only the dock and Alex's boat were missing, but the storehouses and the curing sheds as well. A frantic feeling possessed him; he had to bite his lips to keep from calling out to the driver to hurry. The horses, pushed to their limits since leaving Charleston, labored up the drive.

Beyond the row of trees, he could see that the sloping fields were neatly plowed, evidence that reclamation had already begun. Although he had forcibly rejected farming, he had been a planter long enough to recognize that the proper care had been instituted after the hurricane. That thought have him some reassurance. MacCullough was a good man.

Almost before the coach swayed to a halt, Hunter sprang from the cab. Catching his son under the armpits, he lifted the boy down and swung him up the porch steps in one smooth motion.

Amos opened it immediately. "Praise the Lord, you come home, Mr. Gillard. I sure am glad. I sure am. Mr. MacCullough, he's about run ragged." The old man appeared to have aged immeasurably in less than three months.

Stunned by his first impressions of the plantation, Hunter grasped the old man's trembling hand in an uncharacteristic gesture of concern. "MacCullough? Run ragged?" He entered the house, his nose immediately assailed by its musty odor. The hallway seemed darker than he remembered.

"Yes, sir. He's had to do just about everything since Miz Gillard left for Boston."

"My wife. My wife is not here?"

Alex's mouth began to quiver. "Mama's gone?"

Hunter put his hand on his son's shoulder and hugged the boy against his side. "Amos, Alex is tired and hungry. Would it be possible to have Mattie fix him a light supper? . . ."

Amos's eyes filled with tears. "Mattie's dead, Mr. Gillard."

Hunter passed his hand across his eyes. "Who is doing the cooking?" he asked in a choked voice.

"Mattie's dead?" Tears began to trickle down Alex's cheeks. He dug his fists into his eyes. "I want Mama. Can we go after Mama, Daddy?"

Hunter guided the little boy in the direction of the breakfast room. "Not tonight, Alex. We'll see about getting you something to eat and then a good night's sleep. Have someone make up his bed."

Amos shifted from one foot to the other. "It'll take a few minutes, Mr. Gillard. Miz Gillard got women and children stayin' in all the bedrooms except hers."

Noisily expelling a sigh, Hunter rolled his eyes toward the ceiling. "Women and children . . . Then we'll put him to sleep in Mrs. Gillard's bed after he has

170

a light meal."

Alex pulled away from his father's side and started for the stairs, his youthful voice thick with hurt and anger. "Someone better not be sleeping in my bed. Mama wouldn't put somebody in my room."

"Come back here," Hunter called. "You wouldn't want someone to have to sleep out in the cold when your bed wasn't being used." Reluctantly, the boy turned. Hunter looked wearily at Amos. "Can we at least get something to eat?"

Amos wrung his hands. "We don't got much, Mr. Gillard. Just some rice and flour and beans."

"Anything."

By the time Hunter had taken care of Alex, feeding and bundling the exhausted boy off to bed, Mac-Cullough had arrived from the fields. The Scotsman faced Gillard in the plantation library, where every night three men slept on pallets unrolled on the floor.

Feeling himself about at the end of his tether, Hunter seated himself behind the desk. "Sketch in what has happened, MacCullough. I can see the storm damage was extensive."

"'Tis a wonder any of us 're still alive." MacCullough shook his head at the memory. He had aged in just the couple of months since Hunter had left. His redoubled efforts had cost him ten pounds. Its loss showed in the lines on his face, in the loose wrinkled skin of his neck, and in the way his shoulders stooped. "The river rose and smashed everything in its path. We lost seventy-eight workers and family members. I'd probably be dead myself if Mrs. Gillard hadna come down the slope in the drivin' rain and wind and rousted me out of my house."

"Caroline came out in the storm?" Hunter leaned forward incredulously.

"Yes, sir. Soaked to the skin she was, with the wind

171

full of stuff. A thousand wonders she wasna knocked in the head and killed."

Hunter gulped. "But she wasn't injured?"

"No, sir. Just half drowned."

"Where is she now?"

"Gone to Boston to try to pry some money from her stepfather and mother. The bank wouldn't loan her a thing but a pittance. At that she got more than was in the account." Here he looked accusingly at Hunter. "She took everything she could come by and put it into food for the workers and rice seed."

Hunter pointedly ignored the man's accusation. "I can't believe this happened."

"'Tis the way of nature, Mr. Gillard," MacCullough sneered sourly. "She'll show her teeth every so often."

"Why are people staying in the house?"

"No time to rebuild the cabins yet. No lumber without money, y' ken. I was against it, but she told me to put all the hands in the house and what's left of the stables."

"All those people. Where? . . ."

MacCullough's expression became more dour than ever. "We lost more than half our people, Mr. Gillard. Swept into the river and drowned. I'm tellin' ye, man, it was hell."

Hunter wiped his hand across the lower half of his face as his imagination dealt with the picture Mac-Cullough painted. "But surely temporary quarters—"

"No one to construct them and no tools to construct them with. Don't y' ken what I've been sayin' to y'? Everything was swept away. We sowed the rice by hand."

Hunter slumped back in his chair. "Why wouldn't the bank loan her money for workers and tools? God knows we're good for it if anyone is."

MacCullough frowned. "Banker claimed he didna have any to loan." The Scotsman pursed his lips and studied his employer calculatingly.

"I can't believe that."

MacCullough thrust out his chin aggressively. "She didna, either. She said it was because he knew you werena interested in in the place anymore."

Hunter reddened. MacCullough's statement was no more than the truth. Every man with whom he associated had known of his dissatisfaction with the plantation. Many had known of his investments in trade goods. He had had no need to be secretive since Caroline had taken no interest in business.

"They were mistaken. I returned as soon as I heard of the hurricane," he defended himself mendaciously.

"Aye." MacCullough's chin did not drop one iota.

"I'm surprised that Mrs. Gillard was able to make that trip to Boston. Her health's been so precarious over the past couple of years that I wouldn't have expected her to find the strength."

MacCullough's mouth twitched. He cleared his throat noisily. "She had to have the money. As y' see, we're in dire straits. Needs must when the de'il drives."

"Of course." Hunter sat silent a moment. "I shall, of course, attend to the purchase of lumber and supplies in the morning. I don't have much more cash than she did, but I can certainly arrange a bank loan."

"That's good news, sir."

"And then I'll sail after her." Hunter smiled at the thought of seeing Caroline Fancy again. He had not missed her exactly, but she was his wife. Furthermore, her stepfather would probably not be willing to give her the money she needed. "She'll be lost in Boston," he added.

"Yes, sir." This time MacCullough made no attempt to conceal his mocking expression.

"Mr. Gillard, I can't tell you how amazed I am to see

173

you." Wentworth gaped incredulously at the man standing in the doorway.

"I heard of the hurricane and came home as fast as I could," Hunter answered. "I am given to understand that my wife and her maidservant booked passage on a ship."

Wentworth's forehead beaded with sweat, but he kept his face bland and unctuous. "Actually, that's true, although berths were few and far between. You must understand that everyone—absolutely everyone—was trying to send his wife and children out of Charleston until the mess gets cleaned up. There were no cabins—nothing—available. Even places on the decks were booked."

Hunter stared at the man. "Did she or did she not sail on a Shepperton Lines vessel?"

"She did. The *Columbia*, a respectable packet."

Hunter frowned. "The *Columbia* . . ."

Wentworth smirked. "She came in demanding complimentary passage on the *Cambridge* for herself and her maid, but I quickly disavowed her of that. Josiah Shepperton gave me no such instruction. Furthermore, I knew that every berth on the *Cambridge* would sell."

Aghast, Hunter eyed the man's obvious satisfaction. "And she had no money," he muttered.

"She didn't have money," Wentworth agreed, "but I made sure she put up security for her passage."

"Security?"

Fairly gloating, Wentworth crossed to the desk. "I have a duty to Shepperton's. My job is to run this branch of the line at a profit." He threw a triumphant glance over his shoulder. "You'll be pleased to vouch for me to Mr. Shepperton when I tell him that I make no exceptions to his rules."

"But under the circumstances . . ."

"I'm not inflexible. I just made sure that Shepperton's would eventually get the money." He pulled a set of keys from his pocket and bent to open the bottom drawer of his desk. Extracting a metal box, he turned a second key in its lock. "I had her leave this as security," he crowed, draping the necklace about his hand and dangling it in the sunlight.

Hunter stared at the flashing, glinting object, disgust and guilt warring within him for preeminence. He could not help but recognize the center piece in the set he had given Fancy. It had been his wedding gift to her. They had been joyously happy.

She had thrown herself into his arms and kissed him until she had almost overset him. That night, she had come to him naked except for his jewels at her ears and around her throat. With loving attention, she had undressed him and . . . Alex had been born almost nine months to the day thereafter. He closed his eyes against the sharp pang of memory.

"She'll pay for her passage right enough," Wentworth chuckled. He tossed the necklace carelessly into the air and caught it.

"How much was the price of her ticket?" Hunter's voice was hoarse.

"Seventy-five dollars for mistress and maid." He tossed it into the air again.

Like a striking snake, Hunter's hand shot out and snatched the necklace from the air. "Damn you! This is worth ten times that paltry sum. With the earbobs, there are an even dozen rubies in the set." He gulped in air. "Where are the earbobs?"

For the first time, Wentworth discerned that Gillard regarded him as something less than the clever fellow he thought himself to be. "I—I gave them back to her." He flushed. "The necklace was sufficient security."

"You are speaking of my wife." Hunter's black

175

brows came together in a ferocious scowl.

"Your wife"—Wentworth wet his lips as he cast a nervous glance at Gillard. "That is, I assume she is your wife at the present time—is a very rude person. She shouted and screamed and demanded in a most unladylike manner. My clerk and I were both shocked."

Self-condemnation made Hunter shudder. *I never heard her raise her voice . . . until the last day I saw her.* "For God's sake, man, more than half her workers and their families were lost in the hurricane. She shouldered the responsibility of their care. And her plantation, of course, was leveled."

"So was everyone's," Wentworth snapped self-righteously. "They didn't expect something for nothing."

"And you did not step forward with any help for them, I gather."

Wentworth choked. "That's not the way to turn a profit."

"But simple charity buys good will that turns into profits in the long run." Hunter sighed. The man was clearly impossible. "When did the *Columbia* dock in Boston?"

"At the end of last week, if they didn't have any delays."

Hunter thrust the necklace into his pocket. "Then I'll be sailing immediately."

Wentworth frowned. "But—but you're supposed to transport goods from England for trade in India. The *Carolina* is scheduled for a long voyage."

"And so she will continue it, but first I have to help my wife. A man's duty—"

"Mr. Shepperton gave you that ship for the long trade voyage. Not just to return home at the first sign of a storm."

176

Suddenly, Hunter could stand no more of the man's pettiness. "You're discharged, Mr. Wentworth."

The man's flush deepened until his skin was mottled with purple. "Discharged! You can't do that. I have done exactly what a good employee should do."

Hunter unconsciously echoed Fancy's accusation of several weeks ago. "You may be able to obey Mr. Shepperton's instructions to the letter, but you don't exercise the good judgment that a manager should."

"I won't leave," Wentworth declared obstinately. "You can't fire me. Only Mr. Shepperton can fire me."

Hunter carefully stored his wife's rubies in the breast pocket of his coat. "Be on the lookout for another job," he instructed coldly. "The *Carolina* will leave for Boston as soon as she can be provisioned. I intend to report everything that has happened here to Josiah."

Part II

Boston, 1815

Chapter Eleven

"Does Mrs. Shepperton expect you?" the long-nosed butler inquired coldly, his eyes taking in the out-of-date clothing of the young woman and the gold turban with the flashing yellow glass of the older one.

"No, she doesn't," Fancy explained patiently. "But I'm confident she'll see her daughter."

The butler looked skeptical. "Her daughter?"

"If you will please announce that Fancy England is here."

"Er . . . Fancy . . . England . . ."

"That's correct."

When the man would have closed the door and left them standing on the front stoop of the three-story house, Holy Dulcibella caught it with her hand. "My maitresse will wait inside," she declared pointedly.

"Really." The butler's response was icy, but he did not throw himself against the door and try to prevent their entering.

The dark hallway was dominated by a dark green velvet sofa. The openwork lyres that supported the mahogany arms exemplified the finest craftsmanship of Duncan Phyfe. The butler glanced at it and then at his unwelcome visitors, but neither woman made a

181

move to take a seat. Holy Dulcibella stood like a statue beside it while Fancy paced nervously up and down.

At length, the butler returned. His cold eyes scrutinized her carefully. An uncomfortable silence ensued, until Fancy could no longer bear the man's rudeness. "Checking to see if we fit her description?" she sneered.

One eyebrow flicked upward. "Mrs. Shepperton could not believe her daughter could possibly be here. It was only when I described you both that she would allow you to be brought to her."

"How very kind of you."

He flushed at the sarcasm in her voice. "If you'll follow me." He led the way up the stairs.

Blanche Shepperton sat by the window in her sitting room. At her daughter's entrance, she extended a white hand bare of rings. "Caroline." The two might have been apart only a few hours rather than for over five years.

Taking her cue from her mother, Fancy clasped the limp fingers and bent to touch her tanned cheek to her mother's white one. Only a touch. Then they both pulled back, surveying each other critically.

An uncomfortable silence lengthened, until finally the butler inquired, "Shall I serve tea, madam?"

"Of course, Canham." Blanche looked toward the butler. Her eyes encountered Holy Dulcibella, who had waited in the hall during the reunion. "Why are you here?" she gasped.

"I came with maitresse. Before God, she could not come alone."

Blanche frowned heavily. "Surely there was someone else who could have traveled with you, Caroline?"

Fancy took a deep breath. "There was no one else, Mother." She waited as her mother looked from one to the other, her annoyance growing. "When the butler returns, please have him show Dulci to her room. She can have a short rest before dinner. She is very tired."

"Of course."

Again an uncomfortable silence ensued, until the butler returned and crossed the room to open a pair of paneled doors. Skillfully, he operated the ropes and pulley mechanism concealed behind them. The dumbwaiter rose, bearing a heavily ornate silver tea service. He carried it across the room to the table beside Mrs. Shepperton. "Shall I pour, madam?"

"No, thank you, Canham. Show my daughter's maid to a room where she may rest . . . and see that she is served a light meal as well." The last was uttered grudgingly.

"Show her to the room next to mine," Fancy interposed.

"Josiah would never hear of that, Caroline."

"Then put my things in the room next to hers, wherever that might be."

Blanche tightened her lips. Her eyes narrowed as she stared from her daughter to the tall black woman. "Oh, very well. Put them in the guest suite in the third story."

"Very good, ma'am. If you'll come this way . . ."

When they were alone, Fancy watched while her mother served tea. Her memories of her mother had dimmed over the past five years until she was not sure she would have recognized her had she seen her on the street. Although the face was still beautiful and remarkably unlined, age had loosened the delicate skin beneath the cheekbones. Small jowls now hung down to mar the once-straight line of the jaw. The hair likewise was as thick and brown as ever, but, looking at it critically, Fancy wondered if her mother used something to darken it. "You're looking very well, Mother."

The hazel eyes met her daughter's as she passed her the cup of tea. After a moment, they slid upward and then down to the hand that lifted the teacup. "And you are looking as if you have been in the sun much too much. Apparently, you have not been wearing your veil and gloves. Your skin is quite sallow."

Fancy bent her head to conceal a little smile. "No, Mother, I haven't been wearing my veil and gloves."

"It's nothing to joke about, Caroline. Your skin will be ruined and then you won't have the slightest chance of—" She bit her lip.

"—of getting Hunter to come back?" Suddenly the conversation had turned serious. Fancy had started to lift her teacup to her lips. With studied care, she returned it to the saucer unsipped. "I don't think I had much chance of that anyway."

Blanche caught the tremor in the voice. She looked sharply at her daughter. "Men become restless about this age. He's just working off some excess energy."

"It requires tremendous energy to run England's Fancy."

Blanche gave a dismissing wave. "Oh, that old place. I daresay it does. Certainly it took every bit of energy your father could muster and then some. To the sorrow of us all, it drove him into an early grave."

"My father died of gangrene from a compound fracture of his leg."

"He wouldn't have broken the leg had he not been riding about those endless fields," Blanche insisted coldly. Then, hastily, she extended a silver plate of thinly sliced jelly roll. "Have one of these. They are exceptionally good. And don't let's quarrel over the past."

Fancy hesitated. "Thank you," she said at last. Delicately, she selected the sweet for her own plate. Conscious of her mother's inspection, she took a small bite. "Delicious."

"You look very different," Blanche said at last.

"I am very different."

"Your hair is well done, but the shade. I don't seem to remember—"

"My hair has fallen prey to the sun that you observed on my skin."

"Caroline. After all I've tried to teach you."

Fancy gave up all pretense of trying to eat and drink. She set the plate and cup firmly aside. "Mother, there was no choice. Someone had to do the work after Hunter left."

Blanche looked more uncomfortable. "Are we going to have a quarrel?"

"I asked Hunter that very same thing the morning that he left me."

The older woman dropped her eyes. Carefully, she raised her cup to her lips and drank. The silence grew.

Fancy took a deep breath. "The fact is, Mother, that I have been working in the fields since the day I returned from Charleston."

"You went to Charleston?"

"I followed him after he took my son. I could not believe that he had actually meant what he said. Instead, I convinced myself that he was only testing me. I thought to come after him, to assure him that he meant so much to me that I would leave my plantation with the crop in the field and sail with him. When I arrived, I found him having tea with a woman whose husband left her during the war to go back to England. It was she who accompanied him on his voyage."

The very terseness of Fancy's recital revealed the deep hurt she had suffered. Blanche shivered. "I know you have suffered. . . ." she began.

"Indeed, Mother. And that wasn't all. I couldn't believe what I discovered next."

"Caroline . . ."

"Please call me Fancy, Mother. I went to the

185

Shepperton Lines office naturally expecting to find aid and support from my own family, so to speak, my own blood kin."

"Daughter . . ."

"There I discovered that Hunter was taking the *Carolina*, one of the premier ships in the line, with the full approval of Josiah Shepperton himself. When I tried to protest that Josiah Shepperton had been deceived, I was insulted by the branch manager of the lines, who told me that everyone knew I was a hopeless crazy woman and that everyone knew Hunter was doing the right thing in taking my son away from me."

Blanche looked away from the blazing anger in Fancy's eyes. "We did what we thought was best for Alex."

"For Alex! You haven't seen Alex in five years. How could you possibly know what was best for him?"

"That is only your fault," Blanche insisted. "You've refused to travel and bring him to Boston for a visit."

"You could travel to Carolina," Fancy reminded her. "I have been to Boston to visit since you have been to see me."

Blanche crumpled her napkin in her lap, giving up all pretense of trying to drink her tea. "I can't stand the place."

"Not even to see your grandson or your daughter when she was ill?"

"You have to admit that your grief had been of unnatural duration. In that, Josiah and I felt that Hunter was right. Two years is too long to remain in such a depression."

"And, of course, the quickest way to bring me out of my depression is for my husband to leave me for another woman."

Blanche shook her head. "Neither Josiah nor I had any knowledge of this other woman." Closing her eyes, she pressed her hand to her forehead. "Josiah will have a fit when he finds out. You know how strict he is about everything. You have not seen how dull and drab everything is. I've managed to decorate this room as I want it." She looked around her with a little smile. "But the rest of the house . . . My dear, it's too dark and the furniture is too heavy for the rooms."

"Don't change the subject, Mother."

"Well, I really don't see what point there is in discussing . . . the other." To emphasize the point, she spread the napkin in her lap again and took up her cup and saucer.

"There is every point. Hunter would not have left me with such ease had not the power of Shepperton's been behind him."

"I'm sure you exaggerate."

"Be that as it may, I want you to intercede with Josiah for me."

Blanche splashed some tea into her saucer. "What?"

"I want you to pave the way for me to talk to Josiah."

The older woman set the saucer back on the table. Her hands closed round the arms of her chair. "Why?"

Faced with such palpable hostility, Fancy longed to sweep the tea tray to the floor and storm out. She could not afford such histrionics. Lawyer Aiken and Wentworth both had been unaffected by them. Now her whole future and the future of all her people depended on her ability to borrow money from Josiah Shepperton.

"Because I need the money for England's Fancy."

Blanche rose angrily. "That again."

"Mother, I know you hate the place, but it's all I have."

"You have a husband and son. In my opinion, if you hadn't clung to that wreck, he wouldn't have left you."

Fancy dug her nails into the palms of her hands in an

187

effort to control her temper. "Mother, will you intercede with me to Josiah?"

"I really don't think—"

Fancy rose, too. "Mother, you both owe me."

Blanche drew herself up haughtily. "That's not so."

"While Hunter was sailing away with his mistress in the ship you so kindly provided for him, he took the money out of the bank account."

Blanche gasped. "Surely you are mistaken."

"I am not mistaken. How could I be mistaken?"

"Well, perhaps—perhaps the banker lied to you?"

"He might not have thought I was competent, but he would not have lied to me. Other men were refusing me all over Colleton County and Charleston as well, but they all told me why they were refusing me. They had no reason to lie." Fancy clenched her hands into tight fists at her sides. "They had been told one and all that I was a poor, deranged feeble sort of female. Hunter portrayed himself as the wronged husband taking his poor little boy to sea away from the harmful influence of his mad wife." Her voice roughened and deepened as the memory of injustice shook her.

Blanche retreated behind the chair. "You are overtired, Caro . . . er . . . daughter."

"The name is Fancy. Fancy."

"I'm sure Canham has gotten your room prepared by this time. You can go and lie down before dinner."

"Will you intercede with Josiah?"

"No . . ." She wrung her hands, her eyes skittering wildly round the room to avoid meeting her daughter's. "Yes . . . all right."

"Promise, Mother."

"Yes. I promise." The tenseness went out of them both. Fancy flexed her fingers. Her mother came out from behind the chair. "Goodness! What a fuss you're making about all this! Hunter will go junketing around

188

with his little playmate for a while, then leave her somewhere and come back to you. They all do."

At the comment, Fancy's face twisted in what might have been a smile. Without comment, she moved toward the door. Hand on the metal knob, she paused. "Perhaps they all do," she mused. "And perhaps their wives are glad to see them. Certainly if their wives are left in the condition that I was left in, they must be glad the men returned to save them from starvation."

"Caroline, I'm sure you exaggerate."

"No, Mother, I don't exaggerate. I would literally be starving to death right now if I had not come here for help. What I need is money for the people I left behind me who *are* in danger of starving."

Blanche stared at her. In five years, her daughter had changed beyond all recognition. The dress might be ten years old and out of style, but the figure beneath it did not look womanly. Her walk, while graceful, did not sway like a woman's should. The face was almost too thin, the jaw and cheekbones chiseled. Privately, Blanche could see how Hunter might have looked elsewhere for beauty, but how could he have dared to use the excuse that her daughter was mad? "I'll speak to Josiah," she whispered. "Come down to supper tonight. Afterward, I'll retire and you can present your case."

"Thank you, Mother."

"This veal is overdone." Linen napkin clutched in his left hand, Josiah Shepperton indicated the offending portion with his right index finger.

"I'm sorry, sir," Canham murmured as he whisked the offending dish away. "I'll inform the cook."

Josiah dropped the napkin back across his lap, raising one bushy eyebrow in the direction of his wife while still speaking to the butler. "Tell her if this is the best she can do, she may as well start looking for another place of employment."

Face impassive, Canham inclined his head. "I'm sure she'll do better, Mr. Shepperton," he offered. "Everyone has an occasional failure."

"We shall see."

Fancy chewed her bit of veal in silence. It was delicious, tender, faintly pink. When the butler came to take her plate, she motioned him away.

Blanche, however, who had instantly laid down her fork, indicated that Canham should take her plate, too.

When the butler had closed the door behind him, Shepperton touched his fingers to the corners of his moustachios. A small man, almost completely bald on top with only a tiny fringe above his ears, he made up for his lack of hair with the luxuriant growth on his lip and chin. His color was high. The look he flashed his wife vibrated with self-satisfaction.

"Mr. Shepperton is a true gourmet," Blanche informed Fancy, staring pointedly at her daughter's plate. "His palate is invariably right in culinary matters."

"What a burden that must be," Fancy murmured. "The veal tastes excellent to me. Of course," she hastened to add, "I have been eating shipboard fare for almost a week. It's usually barely edible."

Josiah Shepperton frowned at his stepdaughter-in-law. "The veal was excessively overdone," he pronounced. "The fish also was dry. I decided to overlook it." He smiled sweetly to his wife, who nodded graciously in return. "But when the veal was intolerable, I couldn't keep silent any longer."

"Of course you could not," Blanche cooed. "You were quite right, Mr. Shepperton. I'll speak to the cook tomorrow morning first thing."

"Do so. Remind her that she'll get no raise in salary from me with dishes like that."

Fancy could not look at either one of them. *Tight-fisted old liar,* she thought. "My cook was drowned," she said.

"Caroline," Blanche muttered *sotto voce*.

Josiah gave his stepdaughter his attention for the first time that night. "My sympathies. Boating accident?"

"No. She was drowned when the Edisto River rose and swept away the cabin where she was living with her family."

"Ah. The hurricane," Josiah guessed more knowledgeably. "I've had several reports about that. Fortunately, none of the ships in the Shepperton Lines sustained more than superficial damage."

"That's good to hear," Fancy agreed.

"I hardly think the table is the place to discuss this," Blanche interposed hurriedly.

"Quite right," Josiah agreed. At that moment, Canham presented a silver tray. "Ah, a bombe. Now this looks good," he declared.

Fancy watched her mother, seeing Blanche lean forward anxiously, then subside when her husband pronounced it fit. Had her mother become so thoroughly cowed that she could not even express an opinion regarding food?

"Things pretty well torn up, were they?"

Fancy turned her attention to Josiah's question. "We lost over half of our workers, not to speak of livestock, buildings, the entire tobacco crop, most of the equipment. And everyone in the county was in the same condition as we were, so no one was in a position to help another."

He shot her a swift look but did not ask for further information. In that minute, she knew that he had

191

guessed what she had come for. Furthermore, he did not intend to grant her request. A sick feeling grew inside her. Carefully, she laid her spoon down on the plate beside the untouched ice cream.

In silence, Josiah ate every bite of the rich dessert and folded his napkin to signal the meal was at an end. Blanche smiled and put down her fork. At her signal, Canham came forward to clear away.

The minute that his place was cleared, the master of the house rose. Coming round the table, he put his hand on his wife's shoulder. "Much as I hate to leave such charming company, I must bid you both good evening. Several pressing business matters await me in my study."

Blanche smiled up at her husband. "You work too much, Mr. Shepperton."

"So you have often told me, Mrs. Shepperton. At the same time, I'm sure you'll want to spend some private time with your daughter on the first night of her visit."

For an agonized moment, Fancy was afraid her mother would not keep her promise. She pushed back her chair, ready to speak, when Blanche patted the hand that rested on her shoulder. "How very thoughtful of you, Mr. Shepperton. However, Caroline and I have had a good visit this afternoon, and she has told me some most alarming things about the branch manager of Shepperton Lines in Charleston."

Josiah's genial expression changed. He frowned at her, then at Fancy. "What things about the branch manager in Charleston?"

"Certainly nothing that could not wait until tomorrow, since you have business to take care of tonight. First things first, you always say. Whatever Caroline had to report will keep until another time."

Shepperton paused, studying his wife's face. His eyebrows drew together until they formed a single

192

shaggy line. Then his eyes shifted to his stepdaughter. He cleared his throat. "Perhaps you would like to join me in my study for a brief spate?" he suggested. "Perhaps both of you would like a bit of sherry?"

"Not I." Blanche shook her head positively. "I've had quite enough of Caroline's terrible stories of what the whole state of South Carolina has endured. And I have a busy day tomorrow. Mr. Freneau is reading some selections from his poetry to the Anthology Society tomorrow, and I must supervise the tea that will precede him."

Josiah nodded solicitously in Fancy's direction. "Perhaps you, too, are fatigued?"

She clenched her fist beneath the table. Suddenly, she was desperately afraid. After months of being denied by every man she encountered, what chance had she of getting his approval? And this man was her last hope. If she failed to convince him to give her what she needed, then she would not be the only one to suffer. Her people were depending on her. She swallowed hard.

Both Josiah and Blanche were staring at her; Josiah, skeptically, Blanche, anxiously.

By a dint of conscious effort, she unclenched her fist. "No, of course not, Mr. Shepperton. The *Columbia* was quite a comfortable ship." She folded her napkin with deliberate care and laid it beside her plate. "I think now would be a perfect time for us to talk."

Josiah's study exemplified Blanche Shepperton's complaints about the house in Tontine Crescent. An Oriental rug, its colors indigo and crimson, spread beneath Fancy's feet. Dark huge furniture and book-cases stuffed with dark leather-bound books loomed around her.

Gesturing toward a chair covered in oxblood leather, he poured them each a small glass of dark sherry. When they had each taken a sip, he seated himself behind his mahogony desk with a hint of a sigh. "Now, Caroline, to what do we owe this visit?"

She wrapped her fingers delicately around the Waterford crystal stem. "I'm sure you've heard reports of the hurricane."

He nodded. "From newspapers, from people who were in it, from my own captains."

"Then I won't waste your time with general reports." She met his eyes squarely. "In so much as a place can be destroyed, my plantation, England's Fancy, was almost totally swept away. More than half of my workers were killed; my outbuildings were swept away. My tobacco crop, partially harvested in the curing sheds, the rest in the fields, was a total loss."

Josiah shook his head, although his face never changed expression. "A storm can do great damage. I was fortunate that none of my fleet was trapped in the harbor. That's where the greatest damage usually occurs. If the captain can take a ship out to sea and run before the storm, he can usually get away with minimal damage."

"It's agony to sit and watch a storm blow in," she commented dryly. "You can't very well take your crop and your people and run away."

"That's the trouble with farming," he agreed. "All your eggs in one basket, so to speak. If you lose, then you lose everything. The gamble is too great."

"Sometimes even when the losses are covered, other factors intervene," Fancy supplied meaningfully.

"Other factors?"

"Yes. I had over five thousand dollars cash money in the bank. More than enough to have made repairs, paid for seed, handled all the expenses. But the money had disappeared when I needed it."

Josiah stared at her intense face, then sighed heavily.

"You are about to tell me something important, young lady. Get on with it."

She set the glass down on the small drum table beside her. "Very well, sir. My husband, Hunter Gillard, deserted me. Before you say anything, I insist that you know he did so with your support and approval. You authorized his captaincy of the *Carolina*. He took my son Alex on a trade voyage to last a year." She leaned forward in her chair. "Where do you imagine he got the money to buy the goods to trade?"

Josiah rolled his eyes toward the ceiling. "A man should be able to spend the money he has made with his own efforts. A new business venture is always at risk."

"To cripple an old successful business in a gamble with a new is the height of folly."

The thin lips twitched nervously. Josiah steepled his hands in front of his chest. "Your husband has every assurance of success," he said at last.

"He had better have, because he and his mistress will have nothing else to live on," Fancy spat.

The bristly eyebrows rose. "His mistress?"

"He sailed away with another man's wife."

Josiah leaned forward, his hands spread out placatingly. "My dear lady, surely you are mistaken."

She could not suppress a digusted sound. "I am not mistaken. Why does everyone think I have gone stone blind? I found them together, taking tea, my son playing on the floor in front of them and calling her 'Aunt Jessica.'"

The proper Bostonian flushed dark red. "But surely you have misinterpreted the situation. Undoubtedly, she was a widow whose services he had secured."

"She was not a widow," Fancy insisted. "She has a husband in England."

"Still, I'm sure she was hired to act as a sort of substitute for the lad's mother."

"Then why would he not take the child's real mother?" Fancy's voice rose. "I had come to Charleston for the express purpose of telling my husband that I would abandon my plantation and follow him wherever he wanted to go."

"I cannot believe—"

She lost her temper then. All her careful planning, all her earnest cautioning of herself flew away in a blaze of unreasoning fury. Cheeks flushed, eyes spitting sparks of golden fire, she sprang to her feet. "Why will you not believe?" she cried. "When I tell you what I saw, what Hunter made no effort to deny? Why will you not believe me?"

He drew back coldly in the face of her wrath. "Females often put the wrong interpretation on a man's business."

Chapter Twelve

"Damn him! Oh, damn him!" Fancy's rage could not be contained. Slamming the door behind her, she stormed into the center of the room.

Holy Dulcibella hurried from her own bedroom. "He has refused."

"He didn't have to." Fancy swung round, her skirts swirling, her fists clenched. Color suffused her skin, darkening the tan to pale bronze. The golden eyes blazed. "He just simply sat there making excuses for— for—" she refused to say his name, "that *man.*"

"Maitresse."

"Oh, God, Dulci . . ." Fancy pressed her clenched fists against her cheeks. "What am I going to do? Where can I go? I can't go back empty-handed. Those poor people." Whirling away, she blundered against a drum table, sending it crashing over on its side. "Damn." The word escaped on a half sob as she rubbed her thigh over the bruise.

"Maitresse!" Holy Dulcibella came after her and caught her by the shoulders. "Maitresse, before God, you must not take so much of this disaster upon yourself."

Fancy shook her head. "If I don't, then no one will.

Oh, Dulci, I've spent every cent. Absolutely every cent I have. I don't even have enough money to get us back to Charleston."

"Maitresse, surely your mother—"

"Oh, of course." Fancy shuddered under the other woman's hands. "She'll be happy to persuade that pompous male down there that he should give us a passage back to Charleston. She'll be glad to see the back of us. But that's not the point. I've failed."

Even as she spoke, the anger drained away. Holy Dulcibella could feel the thin shoulders slump. "Sit down, maitresse. You have exhausted yourself today. You should get a good night's sleep. In the morning—in God's own good time—things will be better."

"I don't think anything will ever be better again," Fancy murmured. With the anger, her strength had drained away. She could barely stagger to the chair and sink into it. Putting back her head, she closed her eyes. Her hands lay lifeless in her lap.

Holy Dulcibella bent to chafe them. "Maitresse, I'll go down to the kitchen and fix you a hot drink. Some hot milk will help you sleep."

"Dulci, don't bother anyone," Fancy protested. "I can't stand for everyone to know how much this has upset me."

The old woman grinned. "I tell them I fix it for myself. Old body can't sleep in a strange bed."

Her charge shook her head, but before she could protest further, the old woman was gone. Wearily, Fancy leaned back again, staring without seeing at the Watteau print hanging a couple of feet above the high dark wainscotting.

No longer was she simply playing at being mistress of England's Fancy. Instead, she confronted the very real possibility of failure. If she could not come home with money to rebuild and replant, people would starve.

They were literally depending on her for their very lives. The full weight of the awesome responsibility bore down upon her. Her abdominal muscles clenched as a burning pain began to grow in her stomach.

Shuddering, she resolved that before she would let them die, she would sell the plantation. Of course, she would get practically nothing for it. Furthermore, when she did so, she would jeopardize her own future apart from the plantation. Where would she go? What could she do? Offer her services as overseer for a large plantation? The idea was absurd. Yet, growing tobacco and rice were the only things she really understood.

Bleakly, she realized her own prospects were not as good as those of the workers on England's Fancy. At least she cared about them and assumed responsibility for them, whereas she had no one. She was a woman alone, with no way of making a living and no husband to make one for her.

Of one thing she was certain. She could not live with her mother in this horrible house. The room sprang back into focus. Dark-stained wainscotting divided the eight-foot walls directly in half. Above that stretched dull Wedgwood green wallpapers printed with gray Grecian columns linked with garlands of acanthus leaves. She closed her eyes briefly to shut out the sight. Then, clasping her hands tightly, she rose and paced off the length of the room. The heavy mahogany drum table still lay on its side. Shaking her head at her own clumsiness, she wrestled it upright.

Her jewel box had been set on it. Fortunately, the lock had held secure so the contents were not scattered across the floor, but a copper plate had been knocked askew from the bottom.

As she sought to press the plate back into place between the bindings, the corner of a piece of paper brushed her fingertips. Curiously, she drew it out. It was a single thick sheet of brown parchment, only a few inches square.

A message from the grave? The jewel box had belonged to her grandmother Lucilla who, according to the stories, had died after a protracted illness. Great Edward, then a handsome middle-aged widower, had handed his only child over to the care of Holy Dulcibella, herself only a young girl at the time.

What secret had Lucilla had that she had hidden it so carefully?

Fancy set the jewel box down and turned the scrap of parchment over. Both sides were blank. Shrugging, she would have tossed it aside, but the door opened.

Holy Dulcibella clutched at the tray she carried. The chocolate pot and cup and saucer clinked against each other as her hands began to shake. Across the space the two women stared at each other, one in puzzlement, the other in obvious concern. "So, maitresse, you have found it."

"Found it?"

"The jewel box has kept its secret for over half a century."

"A blank scrap of paper?"

The old woman stared at it silently.

Fancy looked at it again, rubbing it between her thumbs and fingers. One edge was a tiny bit thicker than the other three. "It's folded."

With infinite care, she managed to slip a fingernail between the corners. At first she thought it would not separate. When it did, the two halves broke instantly into two parts. Wonderingly, she laid them side by side. Although the ink was faded, the message was easily discernible.

Fancy read it twice. *"17° 15′ 48° 15′.* That's all?"

"There is more, maitresse," Holy Dulcibella insisted.

She set the tray down on the table. "What else do you see?"

"Five circles."

"And . . ."

"That's all. Just five circles."

"What do you see about them?"

Fancy was growing exasperated. "They're all the same."

"No. Look closely."

"No, they're all the same." Fancy bent lower until her face was only inches from the pieces. "You're not talking about the way the bottom of one of the circles has two lines of ink instead of one?"

"Does it look as if it were carelessly drawn?" the housekeeper asked, mild sarcasm in her tone.

Fancy flushed. "No."

"Then those two lines were meant to be there."

Fancy raised her eyes. The old woman's face looked ineffably sad. Two lines of pain split the high forehead beneath the yellow silk turban. "What is this all about, Dulci?"

"I can tell you some, but not all. Oh, I cannot think how much to tell."

Fancy stared in awe. She could never remember Holy Dulcibella uncertain about anything. The old woman's hands were actually trembling. "Why don't we sit down?" she suggested suddenly. For the first time, she came to the old woman's side and took her arm to help her to a chair. "Would you like some hot milk?"

"No." The monosyllable quavered slightly, but the next denial gathered strength. "No. I will tell you so much as you need to know. But, oh, maitresse, I fear it will do you no good."

Fancy dragged the footstool in front of the old

woman's chair and took both the withered hands in her own. "Tell me."

For a minute the old woman stared at the two scraps of paper in silence. At last she turned back to Fancy. Brown eyes so dark they were black bored deep into golden ones. "You know your grandfather was a pirate."

Fancy grinned. "Come on. You're not going to tell me this is a map to a treasure."

The thin lips twitched faintly in answer. "It is."

"Dulci," Fancy chided. "This is the nineteenth century. There haven't been any pirates in a hundred years."

"England's Fancy was bought and built with pirate silver."

"I know that, but surely—"

"Great Edward could not bring so much. He left more than twice that much behind to come back to in time of need."

Fancy's eyes grew thoughtful. "But he never needed it."

"No, he never needed it. He never returned to that part of the world again, although he promised faithfully."

"What part of the world?"

The dark eyes burned. "Madagascar."

"In Africa?"

The gold glass bauble flashed as Holy Dulcibella lifted her head proudly. "Madagascar is not in Africa. It stands alone in the middle of the ocean. It is the kingdom of Merina."

Fancy sat back in her chair, unable to conceal her grin. "And you think that this is a map to a treasure buried there."

"I know."

"Dulci, from all you've told me about Great Edward,

he wouldn't leave a treasure like that behind him."

The old woman tucked her head in stubborn silence.

"Maybe this is where he buried his treasure originally. But he came round and dug it up and built England's Fancy. Isn't that right?"

Holy Dulcibella shook her head. Rising so abruptly that she startled her listener, she stalked across the room. "It is of no importance anyway. The treasure is thousands of miles away where you cannot get it. Perhaps it is better that you believe what you want to believe than that you know that somewhere in the world is the treasure that could save you, but you cannot get to it."

"You may have noticed that Mr. Shepperton has not been home for dinner these last two days, Caroline—I mean, Fancy," Blanche began, her voice querulous. "I think you should know that it is most unusual for him to miss his dinner."

Fancy clasped her hands together in her lap. "Yes, I have noticed, Mother. I'm sure he is staying away so he will not have to speak with me." She smiled mirthlessly. "However, it must be a relief not to have him at the supper table, Mother. You can at least finish your food."

Blanche put down her fork abruptly. "Fancy, that remark is uncalled-for. Furthermore, his absence is not a reason for rejoicing. He is my husband. I want him to come home for dinner." She drew a lace handkerchief from the sleeve of her dress and pressed it to her quivering mouth.

"Of course you do, Mother. I'm sorry. I know it can't be easy for you to have an embarrassment like me around. Dulci and I will leave at the end of the week if he doesn't come home before then."

"If you had confided in me, I would have warned you not to tell him about . . . that woman. Mr. Shepperton hates to think he's made a mistake. And worse than that, he hates to think that he has helped a man to leave his wife." She leaned forward, her face all earnestness. "Mr. Shepperton believes firmly in the sanctity of the home. He's furious with himself and with your husband and—" She gave an uncomfortable little shrug.

"—and with me for telling him about the whole sordid business."

Blanche nodded.

"But he doesn't feel furious enough to want to loan me the money to save England's Fancy."

"My dear, Mr. Shepperton weighs everything carefully."

Fancy shook her head. "I'm surprised any of his ships ever set sail."

"But that's business."

"So is this, Mother. Oh, I admit that I'm here because I'm your daughter, but the part about loaning me the money would all be strictly business. If he would only let me talk to him on a business basis, I would sign a note and pay interest."

Her mother put a hand to her cheek. "How very masculine you sound!"

Fancy sighed. "Evidently I don't sound masculine enough. Do you realize that if I were a man, I could borrow it somewhere else? But no one will lend it to a woman."

Unable to comprehend why Fancy should consider that unfair, Blanche looked helplessly at her daughter. The silence between them grew.

Blanche suddenly straightened her shoulders with a determined air. "Would you like to go shopping, dear? I notice your wardrobe is sadly lacking in style."

Without waiting for an answer, she hurried on. "You know that's one of the reasons I was so glad to come here. I just couldn't stand to live the rest of my life in that backwater without a shop or even a dress book. Your father never understood."

Fancy tilted her head to one side and regarded her mother critically. "Did you ever care anything about my father, Mother?"

"Well, of course I did, dear. How can you doubt it? He was so handsome. All that beautiful red hair—darker than yours actually—and those flashing golden eyes."

"Why, Mother . . ."

"Oh, I know. You think that because I married Mr. Shepperton, I couldn't possibly have a romantic bone in my body. But let me tell you that . . . What is it, Canham?"

"A message from Mr. Shepperton, ma'am." The butler offered a folded piece of paper on a silver tray.

Blanche tore it open, read it through once, gasped, and read it through again. "How absolutely wonderful!" She smiled brightly at Fancy. "Josiah will be coming home for dinner tonight and bringing a guest."

"How delightful for you, Mother!"

"Yes, indeed. Delightful. That settles it, Caroline. We must go out this afternoon so I can buy my daughter something really suitable to wear tonight."

The shopping trip proved remarkably pleasant. Fancy had been to the dressmaker only once in over two years, and then her emotions were so shredded as to make the experience at best an onerous chore. Now the pleasure of buying a new dress to fit her new figure was undeniable.

"That amber is perfect for you," her mother decreed.

205

"How fortunate that Mistress Batesly had it made up rather than one of that unfortunate puce material! You wouldn't look good at all in puce."

Fancy was not absolutely sure about the suitability of the amber, the dress being the latest style from London, where the clothes were much lighter weight than those she was accustomed to. However, she was sure that puce would have been a terrible mistake with her red hair.

"What about the blue?" Mrs. Batesly suggested. "I can have it made up and delivered to your house by the middle of next week."

"I don't think so...."

"Do you like it, Caro—Fancy?"

"Yes, Mother, but..."

"Then I will pay for it."

"But I may not be here next week."

Blanche hastily bent to examine the material, feeling its weight between her thumb and finger. "Lovely stuff," she commented. "I can't imagine that you would not be in my house next week. And if for some reason you are not, then surely I can have the dress sent to you. You won't have dropped off the face of the globe."

Fancy tried again. "Mother, I came to borrow money to take back to the plantation with me. I shan't need new clothes back there. Particularly not Wedgwood blue wool."

"Nevertheless, allow me to indulge myself. I haven't had a chance to buy for anyone except myself since I married."

While the modiste's assistant packed the amber dress in tissue paper, Blanche made arrangements for the blue to be delivered.

Stepping out into Tremont Street, she turned suddenly to her daughter. "Why have you disliked me all these years?"

"I didn't dislike you." Fancy stared straight ahead. "I think we both agreed that we did not share the same interests."

"But I am your mother. You should have been guided by me rather than following in your father's footsteps. It's too cruel the way you've turned out." Blanche's face was contorted with real pain.

"Mother, let's not go over the past again. Look! There's a coffeehouse on the other side of the street. Shall we have some?"

Her mother sighed. "Of course, dear."

Inside, they were shown to a seat in the window. Fancy stirred cream into the dark brew. "I love England's Fancy," she said at last.

"And your father."

"And my father, but my father loved you, too."

"All I wanted was for Richard to get away from that wretched place."

"Mother, it isn't wretched."

"You don't remember it as I do. Nothing but heat. Steaming days and sultry nights. Put on a cotton dress at breakfast and it's wilted by noon. And mosquitos. I don't know why we didn't all die of yellow jack. And . . ."

Fancy tasted her coffee, grimaced, and stirred a bit of sugar into it. To herself, she mused how things never changed. She had heard the variations of the same recitation so many times that she knew several by heart. *Mosquitos, flies, the water moccasins that the flood carried right under the porch steps.*

"The fact of the matter is, Caroline, that I have spoken with Mr. Shepperton on your behalf."

Suddenly, Fancy was alert.

"He is of the opinion that he can find a buyer for the plantation. With it sold, the remainder should make a nice little nest egg for you to live decently and sensibly

207

here in Boston close to us."

"Mother . . ."

"I want you to hear me out."

"Very well."

"We both agree that your prospects will be infinitely better in Boston than in Charleston."

"Prospects for what?"

"For getting your husband to return to you as he should."

Fancy set her coffee cup down in the saucer with a snap. "Mother, this may come as a shock to you, but I don't want him to return to me."

Blanche Stoddart England Shepperton gaped at her daughter. "Not want him to return?"

"After what he said to me and did to me, of course not."

"But . . . surely . . ."

"Mother, until that hurricane carried off the tobacco crop, I was as happy as it was possible for me to be— considering that I was worried to death about my only son. I worked hard, but the men respected me and—"

"But you don't have to work." Blanche pounced upon her daughter's statement. "Don't you see? You won't have to work. You'll have a nest egg from the sale of that awful plantation. You'll be able to live comfortably here."

"You mean you'd invite me to your Anthology Society meetings and Josiah would come home on the evenings you had me over for dinner?"

Blanche looked very uncomfortable. "Well, perhaps not at first."

"Then when?"

Blanche hesitated. "When Hunter comes back to you."

"And suppose he doesn't?"

"Oh, but he will. All men get wild hares at this time

in life."

Fancy smiled broadly for the first time in the entire day. "That's the first time I've ever heard you and Dulci agree on anything."

"Agree with Dulci." Blanche's eyebrows rose an inch. Her nostrils dilated as if she smelled something bad.

"Right. Dulci said that he'd come back when he had enough of the sea. She didn't know about Jessica Rutledge at the time."

"Please don't mention that woman's name. I do not want to know her."

"Very well. Suppose that Hunter doesn't come back to me and my nest egg from England's Fancy is exhausted, then what do I do?" She stared out the window at the carriages passing up and down the busy street. "Would you help me arrange for a divorce so that I could remarry?"

At the mention of the word *divorce*, Blanche turned white as the linen tablecloth in front of her. Hastily, she pulled her lace handkerchief from her sleeve and began to frantically fan herself with it. "My dear. Oh, Caroline . . ."

"Please, Mother, my name is Fancy."

"Fancy, then, although that's a horrible name. So unsuitable. It suggests all the wrong things. You can't consider a divorce. You simply mustn't. It simply isn't done. Hunter *will* return to you. Mr. Shepperton will see to that."

"What kind of hell are you planning to subject me to?" Fancy's voice rose sharply. Several patrons of the shop looked around as they overheard the word *hell*. "What happiness can I find separated from everything that I love, with a husband who hates me and who had to be forced to return to me?"

"But it wouldn't be like that, I'm sure. He would take

pity on you."

"Mother!" Flinging down her napkin, Fancy half rose from her chair. "I don't want pity. I want Josiah Shepperton to loan me enough money to make repairs and provide food until the rice crop comes in."

"Is there really treasure on the island of Madagascar, Dulci?"

"Before God, maitresse." The old woman nodded her head. Her eyes gleamed in the lamplight as she brushed Fancy's hair. "It is a great treasure."

"But even if we got there . . . I'm assuming the numbers on the map are not latitude and longitude. How would we get to the treasure?"

"The king of the island is an honorable man. He would help you."

"Dulci, this all sounds too ridiculous for words. Like—like a Gothic tale by Charles Brockden Brown."

"I know nothing of Mr. Brown but, before God, I know that the treasure is on Madagascar and that the king will help us get it."

Fancy stared at the mirror, seeing not herself and her maid reflected there, but rather the ocean stretching out, blue and boundless, for thousands of miles. "It's hopeless," she whispered. "We don't even have enough money for passage home. How could we hope to book passage to Madagascar, in case there was a ship that sails from Boston to Madagascar?"

Holy Dulcibella, too, closed her eyes. "I don't know, maitresse. That is why I didn't tell you the secret of the box. How could you hope to use the map?"

The clock on the mantel chimed the hour, breaking the women out of their reverie.

Heaving a bitter sigh, Fancy met Holy Dulcibella's eyes in the mirror. "I'm sure you were right to do so.

The thought of it only makes me more unhappy and angry. Hurry and finish my hair. I have to be extra presentable tonight. Josiah's bringing home a guest."

With a final pat, the older woman stepped back. "I am finished, maitresse."

Turning sideways to the standing mirror, Fancy sucked in her stomach and stared at herself critically. "This dress really shows off my figure. I'm glad Mother bought it for me." She plucked at the hemline. "Although it does show a lot of ankle, don't you think?"

"You have pretty, slender ankles. If that is the style, then why not show them?"

Fancy hugged her. "You aren't the least bit like an old woman, Dulci. Nothing ever shocks you."

"No. One should never be shocked by what other people do. They are like monkeys. They constantly find new ways to do old things." With that, Holy Dulcibella sailed across the room and opened the door for Fancy. "Be pleasant tonight, and perhaps tomorrow he will give you the money you need. A woman can often get her way if she plays the woman for the man."

"I'll try."

As she came down the stairs, she could hear the deep rumble of voices from the drawing room. Josiah's guest was a male, as was to be expected. As she approached the door, she heard her mother's lighter tones, excited, laughing. Smiling, Fancy lifted her chin as she crossed the threshold. "Sorry to be late."

Josiah grinned broadly at her from his place by the mantel. Her mother's expression was likewise happy, although she glanced nervously at the man on the sofa. At Fancy's words, the man rose to face her.

"Hello, Angel."

Chapter Thirteen

"Hunter!" Fancy fell back a step, caught at the door facing, but missed.

He sprang forward to catch her arm and steady her. Eager black eyes slid from her face down to her body clad in the new amber gown. Gradually, his look of amazement kindled into a warm possessiveness.

She stumbled for only a second, then she caught her balance and tried to pull away. "What are you doing here?"

At the coldness of her question, his gaze flicked back up. He blinked at the hostility in her face. She was not reacting at all as he had expected. Slowly, he released her. "I heard about the hurricane. I came home as soon as possible, but you had already left. What a terrible time you must have had!"

She nodded her head in acknowledgment of his sympathy. At the same time her eyes searched his face, unable to take in the fact that he dared to be standing there in her mother's drawing room, holding her arm and talking to her as if nothing had happened.

She knew herself to be a different person entirely. Why did he look just the same? So tall, so strikingly handsome, his skin the color of teak from his hours on the deck of the *Carolina*. He smiled down at her, his teeth incredibly white. Her heart turned over in her chest and a hot ache began deep inside her as all the desperate love she had poured over this man made her weak with wanting. But only for an instant.

"Isn't this a wonderful surprise, Caroline?" Blanche hurried to her side, her hands fluttering a bit anxiously on Fancy's other arm. "Shall we all sit back down? Dinner will be a little late, Canham has just informed us. So you're not late at all."

Fancy stared at her mother and caught the pleading look in her eyes. "Why, yes, I suppose that would be—"

Blanche gave a relieved laugh. "Mr. Shepperton, why don't you offer Caroline a sherry? The shock . . . that is, the surprise—"

"The very thing." Josiah bustled over to pour the required drink, then came to her, a broad, self-satisfied smirk on his face.

Avoiding Hunter's eyes, Fancy lifted the sherry to her lips with both hands.

Blanche's nervous little laugh again broke the awkward silence. "Well, then, let's all sit down," she repeated. "Standing here by the door won't hurry Cook along."

Josiah nodded. "Right you are. That woman really must be given a sharp reprimand. I want you to see to it, Mrs. Shepperton. Why just this week you remember the veal was overdone. And now dinner is late. Much more of this and she'll have to be let go." He led the way back to the mantel where he stationed himself, his back to the empty hearth.

Blanche hurried to perch nervously on the edge of her favorite chair. Her eyes flickered from her daughter's face to her son-in-law's and back again.

A far-off roaring in her ears, Fancy preceded Hunter to the sofa, the only other piece of furniture in the arrangement before the mantel. Carefully, feeling infinitely fragile, she seated herself close to the arm. A couple of seconds later, she felt Hunter's weight as he dropped down beside her.

She cleared her throat. "Where is Alex?"

"In bed," Blanche said. "The dear boy was exhausted and a trifle pettish, I would say."

"Is he sick?" Fancy asked anxiously.

"Not at all. Just a little upset." Hunter supplied the information when Blanche hesitated awkwardly. "Poor little fellow was very disappointed when we got back to the plantation and his mother wasn't there." He gave a scowl of disapproval, at the same time willing his wife to meet his eyes. She was certainly not acting like his wife as he remembered her. He could not get over the change in her.

"When did you arrive?"

"Only a couple of days after you left, according to MacCullough. He had things well in hand." His eyes traveled up the slender arm. He noted, with amazement, the color of her skin. All the women he had ever known had kept out of the sun to protect their white complexions. Yet here she sat, unconcerned, in violation of one of the most sacrosanct tenets of beauty. Moreover, far from being replulsed, he found himself wanting to kiss that golden throat and run his hands through her sun-kissed hair.

"Had they all enough to eat?"

He frowned again, not wanting to talk about the situation in South Carolina. "I took care of purchasing food and supplies for rebuilding the quarters down by the river. Everyone will be fine. They should be out of the house by now."

"They don't have to hurry."

He misinterpreted her meaning. "No, I agree. The thing to do is sell the plantation. You've done the right

215

thing by coming here. Now that I'm in business with Josiah"—he smiled at Shepperton, who nodded and smiled back—"Boston will be our home."

At his smug assumption, her head snapped up. At the same time, she avoided her mother's pleading stare. "Oh, really. I don't—"

Canham bowed obsequiously from the doorway. "Dinner is served."

Blanche rose hastily. "Oh, very good. I'm sure we're all hungry."

"Yes, indeed," Josiah seconded her enthusiasm. "Caroline, my dear." Bowing, he crooked his arm before her.

"Thank you, Mr. Shepperton."

Hunter rose, too, but had to step back as Josiah led his stepdaughter out. Then he graciously offered his arm to Blanche. As they followed the first couple into the dining room, he could not take his eyes off Fancy as she swayed ahead of him. Her waist was incredibly slender, while her back and shoulders were held proudly erect. Again he found himself scarcely able to recognize the pitiful creature he had left only a few short months ago.

"The voyage to France was successful then?" Josiah wanted to know over the first course.

"Eminently," Hunter declared, his eyes seeking Fancy's to share the news with her. "Had we not been forced to return home, I cannot see that anything would have interfered with a most successful voyage. The ship is sound, the captain and crew among the finest."

"Good. Good."

"How wonderful that Hunter's new venture is working out so well!" Blanche trilled.

He leaned across his plate, his face intent as he spoke. "You needn't be concerned, however, Caroline

216

Fancy. I shall certainly wait until you're settled suitably before continuing."

Neither looking in his direction nor responding, she signaled to Canham to take away her appetizer. Her stepfather frowned at her, but she smiled faintly and took a sip of water.

"Mr. Shepperton, you haven't even noticed our new gowns," Blanche chided shrilly.

Josiah blinked at his wife, then studied her dutifully. "Very nice, Mrs. Shepperton. And you, Caroline, look quite lovely. Your mother has chosen with her usual good taste."

"Thank you," she murmured.

"I agree," Hunter added, the tiniest hint of desperation in his voice. *Why would she not look at him?* "The dress becomes you in every way."

Her eyelids flashed up. "My mother bought it for me today so that I'd be suitably attired to meet the guest that was coming to dinner. If I had known there was no guest, I wouldn't have allowed it. I have no money to pay for it."

He flushed then, uncomfortable before her righteous indignation. "I—I humbly apologize for leaving you so short, madam. I did not take into consideration such a terrible act of God as a hurricane."

"The banker told me as much," she replied caustically.

Blanche signaled hastily to Canham to serve the next course at the same time she bestowed the anxious benison, "Well, all's well that ends well."

For several seconds, Fancy struggled to master her temper. Her whole body felt on fire with anger. She took a deep, controlling breath and reached again for her water glass. "Have you seen Alex, Mother?"

"Well, yes." The question had the effect of dampening Blanche's enthusiasm. "I mean, Mr. Shepperton sent me the message that Hunter was coming. We agreed that it would be a lovely surprise for you. So his father"—she gave a little flirt to her fingers—"sneaked him in the house. But he's just fine, all tucked in upstairs and sleeping like an angel."

"I see."

"After dinner we'll go up and see him together," Hunter promised. "He's grown some, even in just these couple of months."

Had it really only been two months? "I would expect him to." Canham presented a platter at her left. She glanced at the fish in dill sauce, then shook her head.

The dinner limped on as course after course came by. For form's sake, Fancy took an occasional helping that she barely tasted.

At last, when the dessert was carried away untouched, Blanche was almost in tears. "Caroline, you'll be sick if you don't eat something."

"Mother, you don't need to worry about me. I'll be fine. Have you finished?"

Blanche glanced at Josiah, who had been frowning for the last ten minutes. "If you gentlemen will excuse us, we'll retire and leave you to your brandy and cigars."

He cleared his throat noisily. "Mrs. Shepperton . . ." But before he could voice an objection, Fancy flung down the napkin at her place and pushed back her chair in one motion.

Canham hurried forward too late to do more than catch the back of it before she hurried away from the table.

Both gentlemen climbed to their feet as the butler held Blanche's chair, but Fancy was already out the door. Blanche caught up with her daughter on the landing of the second floor. "Caroline . . ."

"The name is Fancy, Mother." Her teeth were

clenched so tightly together that she could barely be understood.

Blanche drew back her hand instantly. "F—Fancy, did I do wrong?"

"Mother!"

"But I thought when you saw how fast he'd come for you . . ."

"He's been in town at least twenty-four hours and didn't even consider how much I would have liked to see my son."

Blanche's hand flew to her mouth. "Oh, Ca—I mean, Fancy, I apologize for the three of us. I truly never thought about that."

"No, Mother. You never would. But Hunter should have. Now, will you please have the goodness to tell me. Where is my child?"

"In the room next to Josiah's, further along the hall."

Fancy almost ran to the door. Cautiously, she opened it. The light spilled into the room. The figure in the bed stirred restlessly, then sat up. "Mama!"

"Sweetheart." She flew to him, her arms extended to gather him in. He flung his arms around her neck and hugged her tightly.

"Mama, I missed you."

"I missed you, sweetheart. Oh, Alex. Are you all right? Grandmother told me you were upset."

"My tummy hurt, but now it's all better."

She pushed him away from her and took his face between her hands. By the light from the door, she could see him. His cheeks felt smooth and warm and vibrantly alive between her hands. With a tiny laugh, she kissed his cheeks and forehead. "Oh, Alex. You've been out in the sun."

"I've been out every day except when it stormed. Then I had to stay in the cabin."

"Oh, Alex." She shivered, hugging him again,

rocking him back and forth, silent tears slipping down her cheeks. She had schooled herself to accept not seeing him or holding him for a year. Now with him in her arms, she felt whole again.

He laid his head on her shoulder, his forehead warm against the side of her neck. At last, he made a sniffling sound. "My pony and my little boat were gone."

She ran her hand over the back of his head. "The storm was terrible, darling."

"But my pony..." His voice was hoarse and quavery.

"I know."

His arms tightened around her neck. She could feel his tears. "If I had been there, I could have saved him."

"Oh, no, darling. You mustn't blame yourself. You couldn't have stood up in it. It would have knocked you down and swept you away, too."

"Daddy..."

She stiffened. Hunter's shadow covered them, then loomed up the wall as he came nearer. His hand, warm and strong, closed over her shoulder. Involuntarily, she clutched at Alex.

"Ouch, Mama."

"I'm sorry." Instantly, she loosened her hold.

"Are you two glad to see each other?"

Alex pulled away and sat back on the bed. "Daddy, Mama was telling me that I couldn't have stood up in the storm. But I bet I could."

"I doubt that you could, Alex. Remember the time the storm hit us at sea? You couldn't even stand up in the cabin."

"I got sick."

"That's right."

"But at least I didn't throw up. Aunt Jessica was supposed to be staying with me, but she threw up and cried for Daddy." He grinned a faintly malicious grin at

220

the memory of his superiority.

Fancy's hands clenched into tight fists.

"Alex! I think you'd better lie down and go back to sleep," Hunter suggested quickly. "You'll be able to spend all day tomorrow with your mother and tell her about all the things you've learned."

Obediently, the boy slid down in bed and Fancy covered him up. Her skin felt tight where the tears were beginning to dry on her cheeks. Deliberately, she refrained from wiping at them with her fingertips. She had an inordinate desire to conceal even the slightest trace of weakness from Hunter. Her face in the shadows, she bent to kiss Alex's forehead and both cheeks. "Sleep tight, sweetheart," she crooned.

"Yes, Mama."

When she rose from the bed, Hunter was waiting to take her arm and lead her out into the lighted hallway.

He purposefully did not release her as he quietly closed the door. "Why didn't you wait, Angel?" he asked softly. "We could have gone up together."

"What did you need to see him for? You've seen him every day for the whole summer."

"He would have been happier to see us together."

"Would he?"

He sighed. "We have to talk."

"Do we?"

"Don't be childish," he snapped.

"Oh, forgive me. I didn't realize. But then you must be the authority on what is being childish. I'm not the one who sneaked into town and into the house and played 'surprise.'"

"Fancy, that was your parents' idea."

"My stepfather's, you mean. You've upset him and made him feel guilty, Hunter."

"I? . . ." Her husband shuffled his feet uneasily. "I don't see how. Any man, on hearing his wife was in danger, would have cut short his voyage and raced home."

"Oh, that's not what is upsetting him."

"What then?"

"You don't really have to ask. Mr. Shepperton is a proper Bostonian."

Hunter stepped back. "You told him what you imagined, then?"

"I told him what I saw and know to be true."

He made a dismissive gesture with his hand. "You've misinterpreted the whole thing."

"How terrible for 'Aunt Jessica.'"

"Fancy . . ."

"Hunter, I'm terribly tired. I assume Alex has gone back to sleep, so I won't disturb him again tonight. If you will excuse me . . ."

"Excuse you? . . ." His irritation turned to incredulity.

"Yes. I don't intend to go back downstairs tonight." She had not gone more than a few steps before he came after her.

His hands were not gentle on her upper arms as he positioned her to face him. "Stop that, Fancy. We need to talk."

Her eyes blazed furiously. "Not tonight!"

He stared at her for a long moment. Reluctantly, he released her. As he stepped back, he drew a deep breath. "All right. When?"

"Tomorrow." She dropped her head to regard the pattern of the hall runner. "But not early. I'll want to have breakfast with Alex in peace."

"For heaven's sake, Angel. I'm your husband and you son's father. Not some nosy stranger."

"And then I'll want to take him for a walk, to see the sights of Boston."

"We could do that together."

"Yes, I suppose we could, but then we couldn't talk."

He stared at her. Throughout the entire exchange, her expression had not varied. It remained cold and still, her eyes hard, her mouth compressed. He wanted to grasp her by the shoulders and shake her until her teeth rattled. How could she be so stubborn? He raised his hands. "I've sailed all over the Atlantic Ocean to get to you."

Instantly, she stepped back out of his reach. "You sailed clear across the Atlantic Ocean to get away from me." Before he could frame a response, she turned on her heel and marched down the hall and into her room.

"Tell me about Lemuel Jakes."

"What do you want to know, maitresse?"

"Who was he before he became an able seaman aboard the *Columbia*?"

Holy Dulcibella hugged her arms across her meager chest. "He was an able seaman with your grandfather."

"And that's all?"

"Holy God created one of his finest works in Lemuel Jakes," the black woman pronounced piously. "He was the youngest of the crew when the *Fancy* met the *Lyme Regis* in the Mozambique Channel."

Fancy nodded. "So he was once a pirate."

Holy Dulcibella shrugged. "Your plantation that you would do anything to save was bought with pirate silver."

"And if it is to be saved, then it must be with pirate silver."

"Maitresse . . ."

"I want you to get word to Lemuel Jakes. I must meet him in secret. We will plan how to go to the island of Madagascar."

"But, maitresse, surely your stepfather . . ."

223

She shook her head disgustedly. "He considers that he has done his duty. Both he and my mother have reunited my husband and me."

The old woman made a clicking sound with her tongue. "The secret was well kept. I heard only after you went down to dinner that the little boy was in the house."

"They planned to surprise me." Fancy's bitterness was a tangible thing. "No one even considered how much I would want to see my son. Evidently, my son didn't want to see me very much, either." She began to pace, wringing her hands. "Hunter has made the grand offer to sell my plantation and set me up here in a house in Boston while he sails where and when he will as my stepfather's partner."

Holy Dulcibella said nothing. Her eyes followed Fancy back and forth.

"If I am to save England's Fancy and have a home to live in with dignity and security, I'm going to have to save it myself."

"But, maitresse, you would have a home with your husband. You and he would live together here in Boston. He would not dare to take a mistress if he wants to keep your stepfather's favor."

"Dulci," Fancy chided, "you sound like my stepmother. Next, you'll be telling me I don't have to work."

"Many women would be happy not to have to work."

"I like to work. What's more, I will not be bought and paid for. I will not be kept—especially by a man who doesn't want to keep me. If my husband has to be blackmailed to remain married to me, then I won't be married to him anymore."

"You loved him very much."

"He killed that love," Fancy sneered.

"Did he?"

"Oh, I admit I felt his kisses. I would not be a woman if I didn't feel them." She paused in her pacing. Holy Dulcibella saw her shiver and hug her arms tightly round herself. "I miss the touching and the being together. I miss the ecstasy. I thought we were happy." Her voice trembled.

"If you love him, perhaps you should go back to him and let him play the man for you again. Eventually, he will give up this other woman. She has no future with him. She is like a toy. He will tire of playing with her and throw her away."

"You're not convincing me. Your words make him sound worse and worse."

Holy Dulcibella shrugged. "You must be very sure of yourself. To summon Lemuel Jakes, to find a ship, to sail thousands of miles into another ocean . . . These things are not accomplished easily. And once begun, they cannot be easily abandoned."

Fancy caught the withered hands, testaments to the age of the woman who spanned three generations of Englands. "Dulci, I realize all that you say. And I don't ask you if you are willing to sail thousands of miles into another ocean. I know you're not able. I'm not asking you to go along. I understand how you feel about my going. But please don't fight me. Help me. I know you know where to find Lemuel Jakes."

"Lemuel is old like me. He is happy sailing up and down the coast on the *Columbia*."

"I'm not going to ask Lemuel Jakes to go with me. I only need someone who will speak to a captain for me. Someone who won't take advantage of my ignorance." Her grasp tightened. "Please, Dulci. Please."

The former housekeeper twisted her hands out of Fancy's earnest grasp and stepped back. "Maitresse, before God, you are talking like a wild woman."

225

Fancy clenched her fists. "Before God, Holy Dulcibella, I must find a way to save my home and my people. If you won't help me, then I'll find Jakes somehow myself. If *he* won't help me, then surely someone along the harbor will help me."

"You could be comfortable here," the old woman reminded her.

Fancy shook her head. "I'll never be comfortable here, not with Hunter Gillard. He destroyed any peace and comfort I'll ever feel around him. I'll never be able to trust myself to him again. Never." Bitter tears spilled from the golden eyes. "I doubt that I'll ever be able to trust anyone again."

"You say that now, but . . ."

"For God's sake, Dulci. Will you help me? I want to go home."

The old woman drew a deep breath. "Maitresse, I received you into my hands when you were born. I have never denied you. I will help you."

"Where is Lemuel Jakes staying?"

"At Skarlet's Tavern at the end of Prince Street."

"Can we get a message to him?"

"I can go out tomorrow and find him."

"You, Dulci?"

The old woman grinned. "You think me too old, maitresse. But you are wrong. I will go. Praise God. I have come this far. I shall go farther. I did not think to see Madagascar again, but now I think I see His hand in this."

Fancy stared at her. She looked like a woman transformed. Dark fires flickered in the deep brown eyes. Her mouth quirked in a smile. The straight back seemed impossibly straighter. "I didn't mean to involve you in this to the point where you might be in danger, Dulci."

"What is danger to the very old, maitresse? Danger

226

brings death. And death is a constant companion. Why fear him? I will see Lemuel tomorrow."

A tap at the door snapped both women's heads around. Fancy raised her clenched fist against her mouth.

"Caroline," her mother called her through the door.

"Go on to bed," Fancy hissed. "You need your rest. I'll talk to her." She put her hands around the old woman's shoulders and hugged her.

"Caro—Fancy?"

"What is it, Mother?"

"May I come in?"

"Mother, it's very late."

"Nonsense, it's quite early."

"Then, Mother, I don't want to talk. I have to think."

For almost a minute, nothing more was heard from behind the heavy door, then her mother's voice came again. "Fancy, I know you've been hurt. But I think you ought to be practical about this. This really is the best for everyone concerned."

Only a couple of feet from the door, Fancy clenched her fists and let her breath escape in a soft hiss.

There was another short silence. "Good night, Fancy. Remember we love you."

Chapter Fourteen

Fancy stared at herself in the mirror. Mauve shadows, the inevitable results of sleeplessness, made her eyes look bigger in her thin face. Angrily, she tossed her head. So he would know that she had not slept! She would study his face closely. Perhaps he too had not slept well.

"I'll wear the blue wool, Dulci."

The maid frowned. "But, maitresse, you have lost so much weight. It will not fit nearly so well as the dark green broadcloth."

Fancy shook her head decisively as Dulci held out the garment. "Besides being eight years out of style, the dark green broadcloth is cotton. I really don't have a choice. I'll have to wear the blue wool. It's heavier, and I'll need the weight when Alex and I go for a walk down the Mall." She glanced toward the window. Although the draperies had been opened, the absence of morning sun made the room even darker than usual. Fall was coming early to Massachusetts. She shivered. "How can anyone seriously consider living here, knowing that he could live in South Carolina?"

A heavy frown line drawn between her black eyebrows, Holy Dulcibella held the blue dress for

Fancy to step into. The reflection in the full-length mirror was unprepossessing. "Perhaps a few pins at the seams under the arms, maitresse . . ." she suggested doubtfully.

Fancy looked at herself. The dress did hang like a sack. The Empire style was only successful if it tucked in smartly under the breasts. Turning sideways, she heaved an impatient sigh. How her outlook had changed since Hunter had left her to shift for herself! Once she had been vitally interested in what she wore, concerned about how garments fitted and about what their lines did for her figure.

How she paced the floor with ill-controlled frustration while Holy Dulcibella went for the pincushion. She wanted to be at the breakfast table when her son came down. When finally her maid returned, Fancy had to force herself to stand patiently, arms out from her body, to allow the short side seams to be taken in with straight pins.

"Angel." Hunter waited for her at the foot of the stairs, his long brown fingers curled round the pineapple carving on the newel post.

She let her hand slide down the bannister as she descended, intending to take it off before she reached him; but he mounted the first two risers to meet her, taking her fingers in his to guide her down.

"Good morning." His breath was warm against her ear as he kissed her cheek.

She flinched.

"Angel," he chided, his tone faintly pleading.

"Hunter." She smiled faintly. *He did have circles under his eyes.*

"Alex isn't up yet, but I thought we might have

breakfast together before he—"

"I would rather wait to eat with my son."

He ignored her frosty tone. "Then let's wait in here." He opened the door to the parlor. "We can hear him when he comes down the stairs. Alex isn't capable of coming down stairs quietly."

At that comment, her smile broadened. "He's even a noisy sleeper."

"So I found out. Gallops all night, and groans and moans and takes on." He chuckled. "He almost ran us all crazy the first days out on board ship. I couldn't believe how much energy he had."

"He's always been so active, so healthy. Never days of being sick the way some children are. If he had something wrong with him, he always threw it over and fussed to get up the next day. I never could keep him in bed." Her eyes were warm, her mouth curved in a smile at her memories.

Hunter smiled down at her. He tightened his fingers, drawing her gently toward him.

"Mama! Daddy! Are you waiting for me? I'm hungry as a shark." Alex's sturdy shoes clumped and clattered as he hurried down the stairs. Four steps from the bottom, he launched himself outward into his father's arms. "Catch me," he whooped.

"You young heathen!" Hunter laughed as he dragged his son's thin, wiry body in against his chest in a bear hug. "Settle down and behave yourself. You're in your grandmother's house, not back on the *Carolina*."

He set his son on his feet and the two turned to Fancy. Both were laughing, their dark complexions and shining eyes so beautiful to her that she had to press her fist hard against her chest to contain the pain. Why had Hunter hurt her so badly? Why had he so

231

cruelly destroyed her peace?

"Aren't you hungry too, Mama?" Alex held out his hand.

She took it. Her face betrayed her strain to Hunter, who sobered instantly. "Yes, dearest, I am."

"Then come on! Let's go eat!" Alex charged forward between his parents, making a show of dragging them along.

"How wonderful you three look together! I'm so happy I could cry." The voice came from the top of the stairs. As Alex shouted, "Good morning, Grandmother," Blanche flicked her omnipresent lacy handkerchief from the sleeve of her gown, dabbing at first one cheek and then the other. "Good morning, Alex."

"Come on down and let's have breakfast. I'm starving."

"You three go ahead. I'm coming."

Between Blanche's questions and Alex's excited descriptions of his voyage, the talk around the table maintained the atmosphere of a happy family visit to Grandmother's house. No one would have known that the mother and father had not traveled there together with their son. Only the slight reluctance on the part of the mother to take part in the conversation, and the uneasy way that the father kept casting sidelong glances in her direction when he thought she was not watching, would have betrayed any uneasiness to the casual observer.

Finally, Blanche laid her napkin beside her plate. "Alex, I would like you to spend the day with me," she announced grandly.

"Mother . . ." Fancy protested.

"Please, Fancy. Indulge me in this. I haven't seen my grandson in years. Mr. Shepperton and I planned this before he left for work. There are many things here in Boston that I know he will enjoy. I have planned to

232

drive him in the carriage down to Shepperton's Offices. Josiah and I will then take him for a walk along the Long Wharf—with proper escort, of course. I know Alex has been on a ship, but he still should have an opportunity to see how his grandfather makes his living. We'll have lunch at Julien's Restorator and then—"

"Mother," Fancy interrupted, "I wanted to take Alex for a walk on the Common."

Hunter put his hand on her arm. "You can do that later. Let his grandmother have him for the morning."

Alex jumped to his feet and hurried to pull out Blanche's chair. "I want to go with Grandmother. I want to see all the ships."

Fancy's golden eyes accused her husband, even as she nodded to her son. Then, putting on a bright smile, she held out her hand. "Please give me a kiss before you leave, Alex."

"Mama," he groaned. However, a quick glance at his father made him close his mouth tightly. "All right, Mama." With dragging steps, he came back to her chair. She put her arm around him and hugged him against her as he gave her a quick peck on the forehead.

Fancy smiled. "Have a good time, Alex."

"Thanks." Then he was gone, his shoes thudding in his grandmother's wake.

When the dining room door closed, Hunter rose and moved behind Fancy. Hastily, keeping the chair between them, she too stood and pivoted to face him. "Keep your distance," she warned.

He smiled engagingly. "You don't have to be so determined to make this unpleasant."

"I don't have to work very hard."

"Don't fight me, Angel." He reached for her hands, but she put them behind her.

"Don't touch me until you say what you have to say."

233

"And then may I touch you?"

She shook her head. "I can't promise anything."

In silence, he held out his hand, his dark gaze compelling her to put hers into it. "I still love you, Angel. I don't think I ever stopped."

His words were painfully seductive. She inclined her head and allowed him to lead her into Josiah's study. With the door closed behind them, Hunter turned her to face him. Gently, with exquisite care, he raised her face. "My beautiful angel." He bent to brush her lips with his.

Mesmerized, drowning in the sensual habits of ten years standing, she allowed him to kiss her. Only when he drew back with a self-satisfied smile could she force herself to break the spell.

With a jerky motion, she looked away from his dear, beautiful face, her eyes mistily trying to focus on the row of titles behind the glass of the bookshelves. A whole row of volumes were bound in red and black leather with gold lettering, but the titles blurred.

He released his hold on her arms and stepped back, hands outspread as if in accession to her wishes. Unfortunately, the triumph in the curve of his lips, the lift of his eyebrow, the heightened color in his face, all gave him away.

Fancy saw them and lifted her chin. "What have we to talk about?"

His black eyes ran over her body. "You're beautful. I've never seen a woman's skin tanned like a man's. It's beautiful." He put out his hand.

She longed to flinch away but resisted. If she were going to be her own person rather than some submissive wretch, she would have to steel herself to his touch.

His fingers, infinitely gentle, touched her cheek, sliding up her temple and into her hair. "I think the color is richer than I remember. All that gold . . ."

She shuddered. "My skin was ruined working in the fields. Did Jessica manage to keep her skin white during the voyage?"

His hand dropped away abruptly. "I want you to put all thoughts of her out of your mind."

"How can I?" she flung at him. "Where did you leave her? At the hotel down the street?"

"Jessica Rutledge has no bearing on our relationship."

"Did you spend the night with her?"

"I stayed in this house in the room next to yours." She felt the heat rising in her cheeks.

He saw the color come with it. "Does it excite you to think of us only a few feet apart? You could have had me in bed beside you with only a whisper if you had only spoken."

"Hunter! This does no good."

"Of course it does. You come alive for me. You always have."

"Then why did you leave me?"

He hesitated. "A man has to be free."

The words sobered them both, her more than him. "Even though he has vowed to love and protect?"

He turned away, running his hand around the back of his neck. "I never wanted to be a farmer. It drives me crazy to be stuck day after day doing the same thing."

"I've never known anything more monotonous or confining than sailing up here on the *Columbia*," she countered.

He shrugged. "I never wanted to stay in one place."

"And you did want to be an adulterer?"

"Believe me, Caroline Fancy, had you been more of a wife to me, I wouldn't have turned to Jessica. Can't you see? She and I were just two lost souls who found each other."

Fancy's stomach almost rebelled. The high color drained away as swiftly as it had come. "Yes, I see. That certainly explains why you left. But why did you come back?"

He gaped at her. "Because you needed me."

She shook her head. "I need money to put England's Fancy back in order. You took the money that would have tided the plantation over in an emergency and put it into your venture and your—" She bit her tongue, suppressing the word *mistress*.

"I'm truly sorry about that. I never imagined. I couldn't have known about the hurricane."

"Every growing thing depends on the weather. And the weather can kill. You've been in storms at sea."

He shrugged helplessly. "I made a mistake. Can't you forgive me?"

She thought about it a minute. To her knowledge, no one had actually died on the plantation because of a shortage of funds. By sacrificing her furniture, they had boiled enough water for everyone to have plenty to drink. Food had been poor, but in sufficient quantities. She released her breath in a deep sigh. "Yes, I can forgive you."

He reached out for her then. But she stepped back out of his arms. "I forgive you, Hunter. Now you may be on your way."

"But, Fancy, we need to make plans."

"Very well. I'll appreciate your telling Josiah to loan me some money. If he can loan you a new ship, he should be able to loan me some money. I need to get back to South Carolina as soon as possible with just about everything—food, clothing, lumber, tools, seed."

He stared at her openmouthed. "Sweetheart, you're forgetting. That's all settled. We'll sell the plantation and everything on it. You won't have to work there anymore. You need never go back there again."

"But I want to go back there again."

"Nonsense. We'll live here in Boston." His old arrogance had returned.

She shivered. "I don't like Boston. I love South Carolina, where it's warm and green and beautiful. I love England's Fancy."

"Nonsense. Just think about it practically. I'll buy you a house close to your mother." He did not see the annoyed expression in her eyes. "You can furnish it any way you like. Alex can grow up around the shipyards as is his heritage. Josiah will offer me a partnership in time, and eventually it'll all come to Alex."

"Hunter Gillard, you're not listening to me. I won't live in Boston."

"Fancy, you'll grow to love it. Your mother will introduce you to society."

"The Anthology Society," she scoffed.

He shrugged. "It'll be good for you to see how other women live."

"Hunter, it might interest you to know that I've worked like a man for the last two months. I've seen how men live and I infinitely prefer that to the useless, unhappy existence that my mother has here in Josiah Shepperton's house."

He was annoyed in his turn. "Be serious."

"I am serious."

"Your mother has everything a woman could possibly want."

"She can't even call him by his first name. She addresses him as if he were a stranger. She can't even express a preference in food. She has to watch Josiah to see what he eats before she can eat it."

"I'm sure you're exaggerating."

She threw him a hot look. "Watch her tonight at the table. You'll see for yourself."

"But he wouldn't—"

"He would."

Baffled by her arguments, Hunter struggled to formulate a new plan. By this time, he had expected her to fall weeping into his arms, thanking him profusely for returning to her and relieving her of her many burdens. Indeed, he had not expected to have this argument at all. When he had stood up in her mother's parlor last night, he had expected her to fly into his arms laughing and crying for joy.

Certainly, by the time she had seen Alex and thought about her situation all night, she should have come smiling down the stairs and into his arms this morning. He had noticed the dark circles under her eyes. Now he scowled at her stubbornness; his dark brows drew together.

In the awkward silence that grew between them, Fancy seated herself in a huge chair of oxblood leather. She looked frail and very, very young in her pale blue wool dress, and somehow smaller than when he had married her. "What did you do to yourself?" he asked suddenly.

"I rode your black devil of a horse through the fields every day. At first MacCullough didn't like it at all. He didn't want to work for a woman. He said I'd shame him. But after we had a talk, he liked me well enough."

Hunter watched her face closely during her narration. The tone might have accused him of neglect. It might have carried a certain element of childlike pride. It did neither. It was a simple story, told matter-of-factly, expecting neither apology nor censure. It made him uncomfortable.

"You won't ever have to do that again," he promised, for the first time uncertain as to what her reaction might be.

She lifted her chin a notch. "Do you have some money to loan me?"

238

Then he did frown. "What for?"

"To buy food, clothing, lumber, equipment, and seed. That's, of course, the ideal. The rice crop is in the field and I spent all that was left in the bank account on food."

"Surely, you could have—"

She shook her head. "I did everything I could. No one willing to help me could help me. And those who could weren't willing. For now, my workers can continue to live in the house and what's left of the stable."

"Was that really necessary, Angel?"

She stared at him in horror. "Of course it was. They couldn't live out on a riverbank in the mud. And they couldn't drink the water without boiling it first. They would have died of fever. I'm sure by now the wood has dried out enough to build fires, so they won't have to continue to burn the furniture."

"I regret that I wasn't there when you needed me. Can you ever forgive me?"

The golden eyes appraised him. Even the look from her eyes was different. It was hard, calculating. No, not hard and calculating; he realized it was honest. She shrugged. "I already have."

"Fancy, I know you're angry because I wasn't there."

"No, I'm not. You couldn't have done anything more than any of us did. The house stood firm. Thank God! Even Mr. MacCullough's cottage was blown off its foundations."

"How can you even dream of going back there?"

"It's my home. It's all I have."

He exploded in exasperation. "You have me—and your son."

"So you say. But what about the cargo waiting in Boston Harbor? You're not finished with your trading venture."

"No, I'm not," he agreed. "I should have made

arrangements for you before I left. That's why this whole tragedy happened. I should have sold the plantation and brought you North. Then you would have been protected."

"You couldn't have sold the plantation. It belongs to me."

"Well, arranged for you to sell it," he amended. "I just thought you'd be happier there."

"I will be."

"But I can't leave you in such danger."

"I'll manage. Believe me, all I need is some money."

He shook his head. "I gave MacCullough every cent I could spare."

"How much?"

His head snapped up. "What?"

"How much money did you give them?"

He looked incensed. "That's none of your concern."

"Damn it!" she burst out. "It is my concern. You left me just a little over a thousand dollars in the bank account. I spent it all, plus another hundred Reeves Tarleton at the Colleton County Bank would let me have as a sort of pity loan. How much more did you contribute?"

Her frank discussion of money upset him further. "Fancy, this isn't the sort of thing a woman should be talking about."

"Damn you, Hunter. How much?"

He cleared his throat. "Two hundred and fifty."

"Two hundred and fifty is better than nothing," she replied, the bitterness and anger still evident in her voice.

"And I arranged for a loan at the bank of a thousand more."

She gave a little mirthless chuckle. "I was sure that Mr. Tarleton had more to lend than a hundred."

"He has undoubtedly been able to borrow funds

from other banks." Perversely, Hunter felt a need to defend the banker.

"Has Mr. MacCullough planted the rice?"

"Yes, he had to sow it by hand."

"But he did it."

"Yes."

Hunter ran his hand through his hair in frustration. "Angel," he exclaimed, "I can't seem to make you understand. You don't have to worry about any of that anymore. I've taken care of the worst of it."

"The worst of it, yes. And I thank you, but what about rebuilding and replacing? It will take thousands, not just hundreds."

He loomed over her, his face scowling. "You don't have to worry about it," he repeated as if she were not quite bright. "I'll sell the plantation and we'll buy a house up here. You'll be my wife just as you've always been. Alex can go to school here in Boston if you don't want to go to sea anymore."

"And what about Jessica Rutledge?"

He dismissed her with an arrogant gesture. "I've already told you to put her out of your mind."

"How can I? You haven't put her out of yours."

He ground his teeth together in frustration as he pulled her out of the big leather chair. "Damn it. A wife should be more complacent."

They were standing toe to toe now. His arrogance enraged her. "I was complacent," she almost shouted, "until you made it impossible for me to be. Just remember, Hunter Gillard, you're the one who left me. You hurt me so badly that I'll never heal."

"I made a mistake."

She wondered how she could stand before him with her eyes dry and her chin up. Inside, she felt as if she were dying. "And I have no way of telling when you'll make another one."

"Fancy!" he thundered. "You're my wife."

"Hunter . . ."

He caught her by the shoulders and shook her hard. "Let me love you, Angel. Forget the past." His arms went round her and he pulled her into his embrace. His mouth came down on hers.

Despite her resolution to remain cool, she gave a great shudder. Desire, tamped down for so long, burst inside her. Her belly ached with it. The blood of her veins heated with it.

One arm went all the way around her body until his fingertips could touch the swell of her breast beneath her arm. His other hand went into her hair, holding her to him to receive his kiss.

With the last semblance of sanity, she tried to pull away. One arm came up between his body and hers and pushed against his shoulder.

"Damn!" He jumped back suddenly. "Damn! Something stabbed me."

Swaying unsteadily after his unexpected release, she stared dumbly at the two dots of blood welling from the palm of his hand.

He rubbed his good hand over the other as if he could not believe his eyes. The spots smeared, but two more immediately welled up to take their places. "What in hell!"

She pressed her hand against the side of her body under her arm. "The pins," she informed him with a rueful laugh.

"Pins!"

"Yes, straight pins. Dulci had to take my dress in at the side seams. I've lost so much weight it didn't fit anymore."

His gaze flickered from the tiny wounds to the seams in the fabric. "How much did she have to take in?"

"Quite a bit. There's not a lot of me left."

He ran his tongue over his lower lip. Suddenly, he wanted to see that beautiful spare body. Wanted to see it and kiss it. Wanted to run his hands over it and bury himself to the hilt in it.

He took a step toward her but she backed away until her hand was on the doorknob behind her. "I think we've said all that can be said for now, Hunter. You need to go get that taken care of. You'll drip blood on Josiah's Oriental carpet."

"Damn Josiah and damn the Oriental carpet!"

"Hunter," she chided as she backed out the door, "you shouldn't say such things about your boss. Especially not in his house."

"Fancy . . ."

Angrily, she slammed the door and hurried up the stairs.

Chapter Fifteen

"Grandfather told me the names of all the ships on the Long Wharf," Alex told Fancy proudly.

Concealing her shock that Josiah would allow Alex to call him Grandfather, she smiled with a show of eagerness. "And what were they?"

"There were three schooners and six merchantmen and a couple of old flutes and—"

"I thought you meant the names of the ships."

"Mama." The young voice was heavy with scorn. "Don't you know anything? That's really not so important as what kind they are and how much weight they carry. He told me that a merchantman like my daddy's ship can carry seven hundred tons of cargo. It's the biggest ship in the sea-lanes." He stomped along beside his mother, his chest puffed out, his gait rolling from side to side in a fair imitation of a captain's on the quarterdeck.

"So you enjoyed yourself along the Long Wharf."

"I like ships. All kinds. Next year Daddy says I can go on a voyage with a different captain. I'll be a real cabin boy. And then later I can be a 'prentice."

She seated herself on a bench beneath the branches of a scarlet oak. A rather hesitant sun had finally made an appearance that day to warm the air. Shadows and patches of light moved over her skirt as a breeze ruffled the leaves.

When she patted the seat beside her, Alex shook his head. Instead, he stood in front of her with his legs spread wide, his arms akimbo. His face wore an obstinate, wary air.

She cleared her throat of the lump that began to grow in it. "I was rather hoping you'd want to come home to England's Fancy with me. You must be getting homesick for the plantation and all your friends. The first thing we'll do when we get to Charleston is buy you a new pony, and then you can ride everywhere with me."

"Grandmother told me that she and Grandfather could afford to buy a pony for me to ride before I go back to sea. Besides, Grandmother said you wouldn't be going back to South Carolina," he informed her.

A hollow sensation began to grow in the pit of her stomach. Her mother and stepfather had already foreseen the pony as her strongest inducement. She tried to smile. "But we have to go back to South Carolina, Alex. England's Fancy is yours and mine and I love it. Someday it'll be all yours. We can't live here in Boston."

He thrust out his bottom lip angrily. "Why not? Daddy and I are going to live here, and Grandmother and Grandfather. We want you to stay here with us. Besides, Daddy says that England's Fancy's just an old patch of dirt that nobody wants."

She thought her heart would break. Mustering her courage, she assumed her best authoritarian tone. "I want you to come to South Carolina with me, Alex."

His black brows drew together in a scowl all too reminiscent of his father's. "I'm going to be a cabin boy and then a 'prentice."

246

Silently, she damned Hunter for giving his own son such false information. "You'll find it much different when your father isn't on board to protect you. A captain can whip one of his men if the man disobeys him. Sailors get all sorts of diseases. Their gums bleed and their teeth fall out. They're cold and wet most of the time. It's a hard, filthy life."

"You just say that 'cause you're a girl. I'll be a man. I'm almost grown anyway. The cabin boy on the *Carolina* was only eight." He looked around him restlessly. "Can we go back to Grandmother's house? I need to be excused."

A dark bank of gray clouds was scudding in from the east. In another minute the sun would be gone. Perhaps the walk along the Mall had not been a good idea. Perhaps she should have taken him somewhere to enjoy something, but what? She could not compete with the ships docked to load and unload on the Long Wharf.

"Mama . . ." he prodded.

"Yes. All right, Alex." She had to use the armrest to push herself up from the bench. The three or four hundred yards back to Winter Street seemed inestimably farther now that she had nothing to look forward to.

"Can I run on ahead, Mama? I gotta go real bad."

"Yes, run on if you're sure you can find the way."

"Mama, it's only three turns."

"Go on." She might as well have saved her breath. He had dashed off before he had finished his own sentence. In less than a minute, the trees and shrubs of the Mall hid him from her view. She was alone and coldly miserable. Hunter had won.

"It all depends on how bad you want to sail to

247

Madagascar . . . and how soon you want to go."
Lemuel Jakes regarded Fancy skeptically.

"It's not a question of whether or not I want to go or
when," Fancy replied. "It's a case of must and soon as
possible."

"Why?" The old man stared at her, taking her
measure, missing nothing. Not the clear, steady gaze
from the gold eyes, the stern line of the delicate jaw, the
proud carriage of the slight form. Nor did he miss the
unhappiness that had grooved deep lines in the
beautiful face.

"If I'm to save anything of my birthright, I have to
have that treasure."

"The treasure's been buried over fifty years, m'lady.
You probably don't stand a chance of getting it."

"Because it's already been found?"

Chuckling, he shook his old head. The chuckle
ended in a raspy cough. "Oh, no. Not by a damn sight.
Not Great Edward's treasure. No, it wouldn't have
been found. He wasn't a fool. Not him. The only thing
might be the treasure's been buried so long that the
markers are gone. Land changes. And it was buried
deep."

"I won't be easily discouraged."

"You'd best not be. I'm telling you again, the
chances are not real good." He lifted the tankard of ale
to his lips and drank a long draught. Out of the corner
of his eye, he continued his scrutiny.

She sat at ease, her forearms resting on the raw,
stained planking, unmindful or uncaring that she
might stain the sleeves of her coat. Her small strong
hand curled round the base of her vessel. Although she
was not drinking now, she had taken a sip without
grimacing. She looked out of place among the rough
seamen, as well she might, but she did not look
uncomfortable.

A pair of rowdies began to argue loudly. Instead of jumping and shying in alarm, she merely regarded them with thin amusement. Even though she had prudently chosen the darkest corner of Skarlet's Tavern for their meeting, she did not despise or fear the men in it.

"You've a rich man for a stepfather and a trader for a husband," Jakes pointed out.

"My husband isn't going to help me," she stated flatly. "If I don't get the money, he'll sell my land and use the money for his own ventures."

"But he'd take care of you . . ."

She stared bleakly at the scene in the taproom. None of the confusion registered in her brain. "I can't be sure of that. He left me once and sailed off with another woman. It was a salutary experience. I was left totally alone and virtually helpless. Only one man would help me, and I had to threaten him with dismissal."

Lemuel Jakes let the breath him out from between his teeth. He stared long and soberly at the beautiful sad face.

She blinked. Suddenly, the taproom came back into focus. She shook her head. "I can't ever entrust myself to him again. If I let him do away with England's Fancy in South Carolina, I'll be living by his whim here in Boston. I'll have nothing that I can call mine. And I could very well end up with nothing at all. No land, no husband, no money, no son. I won't submit to that without a fight. I'll do anything I have to do to keep it from happening."

"You may sail to Madagascar and find nothing."

"Then I'll turn around and sail back to South Carolina to fight with whatever weapons I can muster. But I will fight." She lifted her tankard and drained the bitter ale without a shudder.

Jakes cupped his gnarled hands around his own

tankard. "I believe you would. Being Great Edward's granddaughter, you couldn't do less. But why come to me?"

"Because you're the only one I know who can help me. Holy Dulcibella trusts you. Her friends are my friends."

He ducked his head lower. When he spoke, his voice was gruff. "I'm an old man."

"But you aren't dead and you weren't always an able seaman. Dulci told me that."

"I couldn't . . ."

"There must be dozens of sailors on the shore here in Boston." She looked to him for confirmation.

"Aye, there are. The wars are over. Everywhere. Here. In France. In South America. Many a seafaring man doesn't know when his next berth is going out."

"Then you could recruit a crew—a good crew—for a venture such as this. We could take a small vessel."

"Take?"

She lifted her chin. Her eyes gleamed in the light from the hurricane lanterns. "My stepfather loaned my husband a ship to leave me on. I intend that he will loan me one to take me to Madagascar."

Lemuel Jakes pushed back his chair. His shaggy head wagged from side to side as his faded blue eyes widened in amazement. "That's piracy," he objected.

"Yes, it is."

"You could be hanged. We could all be hanged."

"I doubt that my mother will allow my stepfather to do that. Particularly if I merely borrow the vessel. I intend to leave a note to that effect. One that he'll find when we're well out to sea."

Jakes grinned in wonder. "And what vessel might you have in mind?"

"Well, the reason you are on the shore right now is because the *Columbia* is in drydock. You said she was

250

being overhauled. And she only requires a crew of a dozen."

Jakes shook his head. "The *Columbia's* too old. She'd never make it around the Cape of Good Hope. It's a hell of a place, m'lady. Better call it the Cape of Bad Storms. Waves so high . . ."

"I have just survived a hurricane that killed nearly eighty people. They were my own people, too. Don't try to frighten me with storms."

He threw up his arms. "Damn it, m'lady, we're not talking about sailing down the coast to Carolina. Nor even to the Caribbees. We're talking halfway around the world. Twelve thousand miles or more. We're going to cross the Atlantic and sail into the Indian Ocean. There's a whole big continent between here and there. The *Columbia's* being overhauled, not rebuilt. Her day is over."

She did not changed expression. "If not the *Columbia,* what then?"

"M'lady . . ."

"Mr. Jakes, are you not game for this voyage?"

He heaved a deep sigh. "Mayhap I am. A sailor never gets over wanting to return to the sea. But I may not be man enough for it."

"Holy Dulcibella says—"

His eyes narrowed suspiciously. "Lady . . . er . . . Dulci . . . Is she the one who's pushing for this?"

"She will go with me. Wherever I go, she goes."

He smiled then. "M'lady, we're both nearly four score years."

"Get some younger men to sail with us."

"We'll be making them guilty of piracy."

"I'll take the blame for them all. Don't tell them that I'm not entitled to the ship. What they don't know they can't be held responsible for. They will be innocent of any wrongdoing. I'll swear to it."

He capitulated then. "We'll need some money for provisions."

"I'm not surprised at that." She rubbed the heel of her hand hard against her forehead. "Without money, a person is nearly helpless."

He waited silently, unable to offer either advice or comfort.

At length, she raised her head. Her eyes were fierce. "I'll get it somehow," she promised. "Make the arrangements. I'll pay the tradesmen somehow."

"What ship did you have in mind?"

"Something small and fast that requires a small crew."

"A schooner would be the best choice." His eyes flared with excitement. "A schooner . . ." he murmured.

"Do you have something in mind?"

"I might." Then his grizzled head collapsed between his shoulders. "Ah, this is too much. I must be out of my mind to be thinking as I am."

"We'll need arms, too. And charts."

"You're asking the impossible."

"If I get the money for provisions . . ."

Suddenly, he raised his head. His teeth flashed in an ironic smile. "Don't worry about money, m'lady. If we're going to steal a ship, we'll steal one equipped to sail."

A chill of anticipation ran up her spine. Her eyes began to glow. "You know of a ship, don't you?" she whispered.

"Mayhap I do."

"And a crew . . ."

"I can think of an even dozen right now."

"What do Dulci and I do?"

"Just wait. I'll send you a message. If you don't meet me when I say, I'll know you've changed your mind.

But if you come, we'll sail within the hour."

"I won't change my mind, Mr. Jakes."

His grin broke wide then. "Aye, aye, Cap'n England."

Hunter met her in the foyer as she was letting herself in. "Where have you been?"

Fear that all her plans would be discovered before they could be put into action rooted her to the spot.

"Where have you been?" he repeated, his voice stern.

"Out."

"Do you know what time it is?"

As if by appointment, the grandfather clock at the foot of the stairs bonged six times.

"Where have you been?" he repeated.

"Sh—shopping."

He looked significantly at her empty arms.

She presented her shoulder to him and lifted her chin. "I didn't buy anything. I found something I liked, but I didn't have the money."

Instantly, he relented. His arm slid round her shoulders familiarly. "Why didn't you come to me before you left? We could have gone together and I would have bought you whatever you wanted."

Once she would have leaned her head against his chest with such pleasure. Now she merely glanced up at him, then quickly down to begin to unbutton her jacket. She sternly suppressed her heartfelt sigh of relief. *He believed her.* At least he believed that she had been doing nothing more than exactly what she said . . . shopping.

Hugging her once, he stepped back. His hands remained at her shoulders to receive her wrap. "Angel," he murmured, his mouth against her ear, "stop being so childish."

"Childish." She tilted her head to the side to avoid the touch of his lips. "Childish."

She could hear rather than see his smile. "You know you've come to your senses, but you just don't want to admit it."

Walking out of his arms, she shook her head. "I'm not being childish."

He followed her. "I can understand your feelings. You're proud. You always were. Nobody likes to admit when he's made a mistake."

She started to speak, but he put his finger over her lips. His warm smile was tearing her heart out. "We're your family, Angel. And I'm your husband. It's all right to give over. You've got to give something to gain something."

The pain of what they had lost made tears well in her eyes. "Hunter . . ."

He dropped his hands to her waist. His thumbs could almost meet in the middle. He stared down at the effect, a pleased smile on his face. "I've been itching to put my hands on your beautiful body. It's perfect. Perfect. So slender. Just the right size."

"Let me go." Her voice carried no conviction.

"Shhh." He kissed her on the mouth. "Don't make a scene. You know you want this." His lips trailed across her jaw to her earlobe. "You know you're going crazy trying to keep away from me. That's why you've been out all afternoon, isn't it?" He bit her earlobe. "Isn't it?"

She smiled then, smiled despite the shivers of sensual pleasure that ran through her body. He had worked out an explanation for her absence. The truth of her meeting with Lemuel Jakes, the plans they had made together were too far beyond Hunter's ken. If she had told them, he would, in all probability, have merely doubted her sanity.

"Isn't it?" His tongue caressed the shell of her ear,

away. And then the palms of his hands felt like fire, burning her waist through the thin amber silk. "Shall we go down to dinner?" he murmured as he stepped back. "We mustn't keep your family waiting."

She must have replied. Or perhaps she did not. But he took her hand and led her in a daze to the door. Dulci marched ahead to open it. The draft of air from the hall felt like ice to Fancy's flaming cheeks. As they descended the stairs together, she looked at him. A step below her, he fairly blazed with triumph and arrogance. His black eyes glittered, and he swaggered.

He was pride personified.

She took a deep, steadying breath. How could he be so composed when she quivered with the force of his purposeful arousal of her senses? He seemed cool and unflustered, while she could barely think.

Suddenly she knew. The knowledge hit her in the face full force. It rocked her, teetering her backward on the riser. His fingers tightened their hold as he glanced at her with quick solicitude.

Jessica! Jessica Rutledge!

While she had been denied simple affection, not to speak of sexual release, for the last two months, he had wallowed in his mistress's bed. While she now fell prey to her own desperate needs, he easily banked his fires and waited, supremely pleased with his power to torture her.

His cruelty, whether premeditated or thoughtless, sickened her. Her pain must have shown clearly as she met his gaze.

"Angel?" he murmured uncertainly.

Instantly, she dropped her eyes to hide the anger that flooded her mind. She dared not give him the upper hand again. In that instant, she was certain of her course. If she drowned in the Atlantic or succumbed to whatever unknown terrors awaited her on Madagascar, she would be better off than to live a total dependent of her husband.

Shaping her stiff lips into a smile, she raised her face. "I'm hungrier than I imagined," she explained. "Don't let's linger too long in the parlor."

He grinned then, easily placing his own construction on her suggestion. "Of course not," he agreed. "We don't need to linger too long either in the parlor or"— he paused significantly, lifting her fingers to his lips— "in the dining room."

She shivered again. Anger, heat, sensual excitement that could only be the result of long deprivation, raced through her body.

His black eyes met hers. They had reached the door of the parlor. "Dear God, Angel. I'm on fire for you."

She lifted her chin, stretching her neck purposefully to expose the pulse beating wildly beneath the golden skin. Two could play the teasing game. "And I for you." It was no more than the truth, but it galled her to admit it.

Hunter groaned faintly, but at that moment Canham came down the hall. "Allow me, sir." He pulled open the sliding door and stepped back obsequiously.

"Thank you." Hunter tucked her hand into the crook of his arm and led her into the parlor.

"Ah, here they are. Right on time," Josiah boomed.

Dinner that night was like a masquerade for Fancy. Desperately, she kept her mask in place while her mother, stepfather, and husband ate and drank with high conviviality. As if their triumph over her had released their emotions, long suppressed by guilt and the unfortunate awkwardness of the situation, they fairly outdid themselves in conceiving elaborate plans.

Blanche proposed to give a dinner party at the end of

258

the week to introduce the reunited couple to Boston society. An impromptu list was devised with Josiah's smiling approval. Then Josiah discussed the various homes to be acquired in the neighborhood. A couple of desirable houses were available in Colonnade Row on Tremont Street, a development of Boston architect and selectman, Charles Bulfinch.

"Of course, they do not quite overlook the Common," Josiah explained. "But they are conveniently near to the offices and the Long Wharf. I know you'll want to be as near to your two men as possible, my dear." He gave Fancy a knowing smile that she returned, although her face had begun to ache.

"And only a bit farther from our house." Blanche leaned forward. "So convenient for us to be together, Caroline. My carriage can swing by to take you with me for shopping, for outings of all sorts, for the Anthology Society." She positively glowed with pleasure. "At last I'll get to know my daughter."

At the mention of the Anthology Society, Hunter shot his wife an appraising glance, but Fancy had herself under control again. Now that he was seated safely across the table, she was able to erect her personal defenses and think coherently. Her only chance was to play their game. She would lull any suspicions they might have and wait for Lemuel Jakes to send a message.

"You'll have to have a new dress," Blanche announced. "For the dinner party. It will have to be something special. We'll go tomorrow to get it."

"I shall take my wife shopping for the dress tomorrow," Hunter interposed. "Thank you, Blanche, but Fancy and I have some catching up to do, and what better way than to be alone together for several hours."

"But shopping, my dear boy? You'll hardly be alone together in the dress shops."

Hunter grinned his devil's grin. "Ah, but we'll be alone in the carriage between the shops."

"Oh," Blanche blushed, and Josiah frowned his disapproval of such free speech.

Fancy bent her head over her plate as if to conceal her embarrassment. In actuality, she wondered how even Hunter could fail to suspect that she would not gladly submit to this imprisonment. For in her mind, she could see the iron doors swinging shut before her. She would be housed and dressed and locked up on Tremont Street to fade away until no one remembered who she had been or that she even existed. In her lap she clenched her fist until her nails cut into her palm. *Hurry, Lemuel! Hurry!"*

"What about Alex?" she managed, her voice a little hoarse with the effort to speak normally.

"Alex will be happy here," Hunter assured her.

"Yes, but will he be here? He informed me that he was going back to sea with you when you returned to complete your voyage. Then the following year he was going to serve as a cabin boy for another captain."

Hunter looked a bit uncomfortable. "I haven't made any promises on that score."

"Evidently, he thinks you have. He seemed very sure of himself. After he serves as cabin boy, then he's going to be an apprentice."

Blanche frowned. "Surely he's just indulging in a boyish fantasy. I hardly think that's the thing for my grandson. He needs to be in school."

Josiah added his argument to hers. "He must have the proper education if he's to go to Harvard. One voyage is all very well and good, but one's enough."

Hunter shrugged. "The boy enjoyed the Atlantic crossing so much I hated to disillusion him. Of course I'll settle him down before the *Carolina* sails. In fact, he might be better served to stay with you here in Boston and not make the rest of the trip at all." He looked at Fancy for approval. "How would that suit you?"

She gritted her teeth behind her smiling lips. "Fine." She felt a stab of pity for Alex. He was in for a rude awakening now that Hunter believed he had gained her compliance and no longer needed her son for a pawn.

At long last, Canham served the dessert. Fancy gave up the pretense of eating, rightly guessing that Hunter would suppose she could wait no longer for the end of the meal.

"Join me for a cigar and brandy, Hunter, my boy," Josiah invited. "We can settle the problem of the house tonight. With your wife properly situated, you can sail within the month."

Hunter looked reluctantly at Fancy, who smiled sweetly. "How nice to have you taking care of me so thoroughly," she cooed. "Do you suppose we could drive down Tremont Street tomorrow, Mother? I could look at the outside . . . unless it's supposed to be a surprise."

"Good idea," Josiah commented, signaling for his wife to rise from the table. "Go on, you two. This is men's talk."

When his wife hesitated, he winked knowingly. "I won't keep him too long, Caroline, my dear."

Fancy bestowed a blinding smile on them both. "Thank you, Josiah."

Outside in the hall, Blanche caught her daughter's arm. "Please, Caroline, don't be upset. Josiah only means the best for everybody."

A little surprised at her mother's perception, Fancy patted the gentle hand before stepping out of reach. "I'm sure he does."

"Would you like a cup of tea in the parlor?" Blanche asked anxiously.

Chapter Sixteen

Fancy had brought only flannel nightgowns with her from South Carolina. Envisioning herself sleeping alone during cold autumn nights, she had not packed a single one of her lace-edged silk creations. So much for looking alluring. She closed the wardrobe drawer with more force than necessary. If he wanted an easy time, she would give him an easy time.

With hot, angry hands she stripped off the amber silk, the chemise and petticoat beneath it, her slippers and hose. Standing naked in front of the mirror, she pulled the pins from her hair and combed through it with shaking fingers, uncaring how she tugged at her scalp.

Lamps in sconces on either side of the mahogany fan mirror moulded her shape in shadows and light. She guessed he would think she was beautiful. Once his approval would have made her heady with pleasure. Now it came too late.

When her hair hung around her in a glimmering curtain that reached below her waist in back, she turned down all but one of the lamps in the room and padded to the bed.

Wear something easy to take off, he had said. Very

well. He would find her more cooperative than ever. And more eager. At the same time, he would be completely assured that she would never object to anything he did again. Climbing into bed, she piled the pillows behind her and divided her hair at the nape of her neck. With fingers that shook slightly, she smoothed and arranged it over her breasts. The light shone on the twin skeins and picked out the golden threads that the sun had bleached. They were one of the changes Hunter had noted about her.

At that moment, she heard his step. Her senses instantly leaped to life. She took a deep breath and clenched her fists in the bedclothes.

At the door, the footsteps hesitated. She could almost see him trying to decide whether to knock or to come in as he had done for years. She held her breath. Then the doorknob turned.

"Angel . . ."

"Come in, Hunter."

He slid around the edge of the door and leaned against it. His eyes lighted at the sight of her sitting up, waiting for him. A single light on the bedside table cast only soft illumination.

"Angel," he whispered again, his voice hoarse.

"I didn't have a beautiful gown." She inclined her head demurely and laced her fingers together in an attitude of prayer. "So I thought to help you, I'd wait for you without any clothes on at all."

He shuddered visibly. "Angel . . . Sweetheart . . ."

"Are you going to stand over there all night?"

"God, no."

As he crossed to the bed, he shed his coat and cravat. She watched him come, seeing the swell beneath his trousers. He dropped down beside her on the bed and bent to kiss her mouth.

His tongue, his lips, his hands, all adored her body as

his breathing quickened. With a faint groan, he pushed back the thick curtain of hair and gathered her breasts in both hands. As she arched up to him, he pressed them together to kiss and suckle each nipple in turn.

"Hunter," she gasped.

"Beautiful, warm woman," he crooned. He slid down farther in the bed, pushing the covers before him, circling his tongue in her navel.

Her hands clasped his head and she reveled in the feel of his hair waving over her fingers.

"Angel . . ." he whispered. "Angel . . ."

She shuddered. Even as she dug her heels into the mattress and lifted herself up, his tongue touched the soft auburn hair at the base of her belly. She closed her eyes in ecstasy.

Her sense of grievance, the pain he had dealt her, the fear that she lived with, the awesome burden of responsibility she had assumed, all faded. She was a woman with a man. A woman who needed the release a man could give her before she could go on with her life.

"What do you want, sweetheart? Shall I kiss you where you like to be kissed?"

"Yes!" she cried in answer to his question. "Oh, God, yes. Please."

"Part the way for me, Angel," he whispered, his breath hot on her belly.

At the beloved command so often given in the midst of their lovemaking, a part of her longed to cry out her love for him. The old Caroline Fancy would have given him that assurance with her whole heart. But the wounds he had dealt her had scarred that part of her too deeply.

She could not speak. Nevertheless, obediently, her fingers left his head and pulled aside the auburn curls. She was shivering now, out of control, her body throbbing and vibrating beneath him.

"That's right. That's beautiful. Beautiful," he praised. His breath now seared the ultra-sensitive pearl of flesh her slender fingers exposed.

"Hunter," she pleaded.

"Tell me. Tell me what you want."

"You. Oh, please."

"What do you want me to do to you?"

She shuddered again, her hips lifting. "Kiss me. *Kiss me.*"

"Perhaps I shouldn't just yet," he teased. "I'm not even undressed."

"Hunter . . ."

"My poor Angel. So hungry. So excited."

"Yes . . ." She was gasping now. Her face and chest flushed, a fine glow of perspiration on her body.

"Then I mustn't torture you anymore." His lips took her delicately, making her cry out in ecstasy. She had no farther to climb on the mountain of passion. But when the exquisite sensations exploded in a fountain of sparks, they did not fall to earth but shot out farther and farther into limitless space and time. She sobbed and writhed and begged mindlessly for him to stop—and not to stop.

The light died at last. Her body lay still. So still that it might have died. Every muscle, even her heart and the heavy muscle that moved her lungs, collapsed, their oxygen depleted, incapable of further tension.

When Fancy returned to consciousness, she imagined for a divine moment that the last three horrible months had never happened. Hunter was beside her, cradling her body in the warmth and safety of his. Her cheek rested against the velvet skin of his shoulder. Her arm lay draped across his chest, her hand curved around his neck. Beneath her palm his pulse beat strong and steady. The pain of loss and love shook her.

He felt her tremble. "Was that what you wanted?" he

266

murmured, his voice rumbling beneath her hand.

"Yes."

"Good. I'm glad I could give you what you wanted and needed."

"What about you?"

He kissed the pulsebeat in her temple. "Go to sleep."

"No, not until I kiss you here." She slid her body down in the bedclothes until her lips touched his chest. Her tongue touched his nipple, circled it. As her lips closed over it, she felt his body stiffen. Her fingers crept down to caress the insides of his strong thigh.

"I wanted to do that for you, Angel," he murmured, struggling for control and losing the battle. "You don't have to pay me back. Rest now. There'll be plenty of time for me when you wake up."

She smiled against his chest as it heaved. The muscles of his legs stiffened beneath her fingers. "Do you really want me to stop?"

"I . . . You don't have to . . ."

Her free hand slipped beneath his hip and pushed upward as she rubbed her belly against his.

"Angel," he breathed. His fingers threaded through the hair at her temples, spreading it over his chest with one hand while the other carried a lock to his lips. "Angel. Oh, Angel." Spontaneously, he began to move, to respond to her. His hands, his mouth, the contours of his body fitted themselves to hers. Like trained dancers who have practiced their art to perfection, they moved together.

She mounted him, her body ready again, her excitement almost as great as it had been only minutes before. He clutched her thighs and pulled her down tighter and harder than she could have melded herself. Tears welled from her eyes and spilled down her cheeks.

Instantly, his hands released her. He leaned upward.

"Oh, God. I'm sorry, Caroline Fancy. I didn't meant to hurt you. I—"

She sank forward, her hair a silken veil on either side of his face. "You didn't. You didn't. It's just so beautiful. You feel so good. I haven't had . . . It's been so long. . . ." Every phrase was a gasp that she punctuated by a kiss on his cheek, his chin, his mouth. "Oh, love, Hunter. I need you. Give me . . . Please."

He pressed his lips together against the swell of emotion and grasped her thighs again. Digging his heels into the bed, he bridged up with a shout of ecstasy. "Caroline Fancy! There's nobody like you. Absolutely nobody."

His strength threw her forward as his words jolted her back. At the same time, her senses exploded. The touch of his body, the taste of his mouth, the sound of his breathing, the scent of his skin, the sight of his dark impassioned face, all came together. Simultaneously, she knew incredible ecstasy of body and terrible agony of spirit.

When his breathing told her he was asleep, she carefully slipped from his arms. Moving over to the far side of the bed, she pulled the covers more closely around herself. The sheets were chilly where he had not warmed them, but she endured the feeling until her own body heat finally lulled her to sleep.

When she awoke the next morning, Hunter was gone. Remembering his words of the night before, she felt no surprise. He might know nobody like her, but he had certainly made a comparison. Once upon a time he would have remained at her side, perhaps awakening her impatiently with an arousing kiss to gather her into his arms and repeat their pleasure.

Bitterly, she wondered how Jessica Rutledge went

about pleasing him.

Her movements stiff, she threw back the covers and climbed to her feet. Her own cynicism made a sick taste in her mouth. He was so sure of her, so arrogantly certain all was forgiven and forgotten that he probably thought nothing of leaving her to wake up alone while he went on about his business.

She saw the future clearly if she chose to remain in Boston. She would be expected to be silent and uncomplaining of his treatment of her. She was no fool. He would do what he pleased the few hours that he stayed at home, then he would go away, without a word, to his job or his mistress.

With a shudder, she sank back down on the bed and wrapped her arms tightly around her ribcage, her heart thumping painfully inside it.

A discreet knock made her raise her head. In the mirror across the room from the bed, she caught sight of her white face and naked body. "Just a minute." She pushed herself up, steadied herself with a hand around the bedpost, then staggered to the clothespress for her robe. "Come in."

"Maitresse, you are awake. Your husband sent me to greet you and to ask you to join him for breakfast."

Unclenching her fist and veiling the expression in her eyes, Fancy smiled. "How thoughtful of him."

Holy Dulcibella was not fooled. "It was not good, maitresse?"

Covering her face with her hands, Fancy swung away. "It was heaven, Dulci. And hell."

The older woman put her hands around the fragile shoulders. "Oh, maitresse, God help you."

"My husband loved me, Dulci, richly and expertly, and told me there was no one like me. But I kept feeling all along that he was making comparisons." Her smile was bleak. "At first I was a charity case for him. He

269

treated me as if I were some poor, starving waif who hadn't had a meal in months." Angrily, she pulled away, denying herself the proffered comfort. "Well, he can give his meals elsewhere," she choked.

Holy Dulcibella dropped her hands. Her old face creased in pain. "My heart weeps for you, maitresse. Only the good God knows why his children sometimes suffer."

The figure before her straightened. "Don't weep, Dulci. I don't intend to weep over this. Tears won't accomplish a thing except make my eyes red." She smiled grimly at the other woman's mirror reflection. "Pick out a walking dress for me, Dulci. Hunter's going to take me shopping for a gown to wear to the party."

"Mama, you're late for breakfast," Alex informed her. "Daddy and I have almost finished."

"Then I'll just have tea." She signaled to the butler.

"Nonsense." Hunter shot a dark frown at his son. "We have plenty of time. Eat some eggs and some of the porridge."

She shook her head. "I couldn't. Just tea."

"You've lost enough weight," he chided.

She did not bother to reply. "What do you two intend to do today?" she asked instead.

Immediately, Alex jumped excitedly out of his chair. "See, Daddy. I told you Mama wouldn't care if you took me to the *Carolina*. Daddy was going to take me to the ship, Mama, but he said he couldn't because he had to take you shopping." The last sentence was an accusation.

"Do you need to go to the *Carolina*?" she asked Hunter politely.

He frowned again. "Sit down, Alex, and finish your breakfast. I don't have to go immediately, Caroline

Fancy. Later on this afternoon will do just as well. Probably better. I'm prepared to take you on this shopping trip. What was it you saw yesterday that you didn't have money enough to buy?"

She smiled then to cover resentment and the dull ache in her heart. "Nothing but silly things, Hunter. A pair of gloves and a matching parasol. I can't even remember where I saw them."

He looked at the dress she wore. The green broadcloth was slightly familiar. Still, it looked fine on her, with her bright red hair and golden tanned skin. For a minute he weighed the possibility of giving her some money and sending her on the shopping expedition alone. He hated to shop with women. Their endless inspections of patterns and materials bored him silly. And then the fittings were sometimes embarrassing, with the shopgirls running in and out and giggling at him.

He really did need to be at the ship. Since he had sold part of her cargo in France without loading more, he needed to find another cargo to trade in England, his next port of call. Francs needed to be converted into dollars for the purchase. Furthermore, he needed to pay a visit to Jessica.

He glanced hastily at his wife. She was watching him closely, her gold eyes fastened on his face. Something in the quiet, still look about her mouth made him straighten in his chair. The skin over his spine and the base of his neck prickled alarmingly. "We'll leave the *Carolina* for another time, Alex. Your mother and I have important things to do today."

"This material is newly arrived from France," Mrs. Bromfield explained proudly. "We can get all the very latest things now that Napoleon is gone and everything

271

has settled down."

"It's beautiful," Fancy sighed. She ran her hand over the rose-pink velvet. A heavy floral design was hand cut in its soft surface. The dressmaker draped a length of it across Fancy's shoulder. The color immediately brought out the gold in her skin as well as the delicate flush of her cheeks. Likewise, the color of her hair seemed more intense. The fabric would make up into an elegant gown.

"I want it fitted on my wife," Hunter interposed. "None of those high-waisted styles. She has the figure of a girl of twenty. I want to show it off."

Fancy smiled up at him, while the dressmaker flipped hastily through her fashion plates to find the requested style. "Indeed, sir. I know just the thing. This will be perfect for mistress's exquisite figure." She held out a plate from France. Instead of the very high Empire line, a wide fitted band was sewn below the breasts the width of the midriff. Attached to it was a gored skirt that fell to the ankles. The long expanse of velvet would be relieved by a scalloped row of fringe.

Hunter looked at it hastily. "Just the thing. Exactly right."

Fancy smiled a half smile. "Yes."

The dressmaker beamed. "If you'll step into the dressing room now, my girl will take your measurements."

Hunter pulled out his pocket watch. "Now that we've got you fixed up, would you mind if I left you? I really do need to get on to the shipping office. I've cargo to arrange for. You know I came back across the Atlantic with most of the same cargo that I started with and the rest of the hold empty."

Her expression did not change, but she placed her hand on his forearm and squeezed it gently. "Because you heard that a hurricane had struck and you wanted to help me. I'll always remember that you did. Go right

272

ahead. I'll walk home."

He stared at her, then his eyes dropped to her hand resting on the fine dove-gray broadcloth of his coat. Her touch warmed him. Still, he had business to attend to. "Nonsense. I can walk more easily than you. I'll leave the carriage here."

"Why not take it and send it back?"

"Good idea. You're sure you don't mind?"

"I'm sure." She removed her hand.

The lack of consequence of the conversation would have amused her had she not known that he was longing to be gone. Her remark about his coming home was nothing less than the truth. She would always remember that he had come when he thought her in danger.

Looking at him now shuffling his feet and fumbling his watch back into his waistcoat pocket, she wondered why he had done so. Perhaps he carried some sense of guilt; probably he had not rid himself of the habit of thinking of her as his possession.

"Well, if you're sure you'll be all right?"

"I'm sure," she repeated.

He looked down into her face, so still except for the half smile curving her lips. "Fancy, aren't you pleased with the dress?"

She inclined her head to veil her eyes.

"Fancy?" He put his fingers under her chin and lifted her face.

"It will be a lovely dress."

"The color is perfect." He smiled broadly. "I have a reason for wanting you to have it."

"A reason?"

"It's a surprise."

"A surprise? . . ."

The dressmaker came back into the room. "Mistress Shepperton?"

Hunter glanced at the woman over Fancy's shoulder.

"This is not Mistress Shepperton. This is her daughter and my wife, Mistress Gillard."

"Please pardon me. I naturally assumed—"

Fancy smiled reassuringly at the dressmaker. "Just one minute more, Mrs. Bromfield." She laid her hand on Hunter's lapel, rose on tiptoe, and brushed her lips against his cheek. Ignoring the dressmaker's tiny gasp, she smiled before stepping back. "When will I see you?"

He hesitated. "I probably shan't be home for dinner."

"Why not?"

He shrugged offhandedly. "Business. It takes a long time to make arrangements to load a ship."

"Then you intend to sail shortly?"

"Just as soon as I can get the business of settling you taken care of." He stepped back. "I'll send the carriage back after you."

"Thank you."

The bell on the shop door jingled delicately, the open door letting in a draft of chilly air, and he was gone.

"Mistress Gillard . . ."

She allowed herself to be led into the dressing room, where she stood like a statue while the assistant took her measurements with a tape measure and noted them with care. Only when the angry blush had faded from her cheeks did she fix the dressmaker with an imperious stare. "I have decided against the rose-pink velvet. Make me the same pattern off that bolt of black."

"Black, Mistress Gillard?"

"Black."

"I was afraid you'd forgotten me. I've been lonely . . . and cold. . . . Boston is such a cold, dreary place." Jessica Rutledge put her arms around Hunter's waist

274

and laid her head against his chest.

He chafed his hands up and down her arms to warm her. "I'm sorry you've had to be alone."

"When are we leaving?"

He slid his hands up to cup her shoulders. "Soon."

"When?"

"I have to purchase extra cargo and have it loaded on the ship."

"And attend a dinner party given by your mother-in-law to welcome you and your charming wife to Boston society."

"How did you find out about that?"

"The invitations have been delivered. Several dressmakers are hoping for large commissions from the dress sales. They've hired extra seamstresses to take care of the rush." Keeping her arms tight around his waist, Jessica tilted her head back. "You're returning to her again?" Her tone was accusatory.

Gently, he freed himself from her clasp and stepped back. "She's my wife, Jessica."

Tears formed in the soft eyes. "And I'm nothing and nobody."

"No, Jessica. You're special. Very special to me. But you have a husband, too. Don't forget him."

"I could easily forget him. I want to forget him." She seated herself in a small carved rosewood chair. A bleak light came through the windows, which were clouded with salt spray from the harbor.

For the first time, Hunter noticed dark circles under her eyes. "Have you been feeling ill?" he asked.

She turned a pathetic face up to him. "This place is too cold for me. I can't seem to get warm." Her skin was translucent pearl; pale traceries of blue veins showed across her temples. Her throat and hands were likewise milk-white.

How different from Fancy's golden skin! Jessica

275

really should get out more. Yet Jessica was the fashion. He smiled winningly as he knelt beside her. "Would you like to go out to dinner this evening?"

She brightened instantly. "Could we?"

He felt a spurt of guilt at keeping her cooped up in these small rooms. "Of course."

"To Julien's Restorator?"

"Well . . ." Even as he was shaking his head, she was rising.

"Oh, Hunter, it's so wonderful. . . ."

"Jessica, I don't even know if the restorator is open at this time in the afternoon. Wouldn't you rather eat downstairs?"

"No. I eat downstairs here three times a day. I've had everything that the woman knows how to cook. And I never want to see another piece of cod or a bowl of chowder. I can't stand the taste of either one now." She pulled her spencer from the wardrobe and held it out to him.

"Jessica . . ." He tried to interrupt her, but she chattered on.

"Perhaps after we eat we can go for a walk on the Common. I've heard it's very lovely, especially at this time of the year when the leaves are all turning." She hurried to the mirror and stooped to tie the ribbons of her bonnet.

"Perhaps we'd better just go out and eat," he interposed hastily. "If you're not feeling well . . ."

She turned around, a bright smile on her face. Her hands pulled the bright ribbon bows out on one side of her chin and perked them attractively. "I'm ready."

Hunter was led out on the street before he knew what he was about. Hastily, he adjusted the collar of his coat well up around his ears and pulled the brim of his top hat well down. Fortunately, unless he were to encounter Josiah directly, he stood little chance of being recognized.

Still, he had trouble relaxing to enjoy his dinner in the restorator, which was indeed open. Jessica talked and flirted gracefully. Seated beside him at a table in the farthest corner of the room, she made a show of coaxing him to eat delicacies that she selected from the various plates they were served.

Under her solicitous service, he warmed and expanded. A woman should always treat a man as she treated him. His wife was too often concerned with the weather and whether worms would damage the tobacco.

With pleasure, he watched Jessica's white hands gracefuly manipulate the silver tongs to lift a small cherry tart onto an orange and black porcelain dessert plate. With a bright smile, she set it in front of him.

Smiling back, he turned the side of his fork to break the flaky pastry, then slid the tines under the piece. The succulent fruit, the rich sugary syrup, and the buttery shell filled his mouth as Jessica filled his eyes. He could not doubt her husband had been the brute she described. Otherwise, why would he have left her?

"Are you sure we don't have time for a walk on the Common?"

"Of course, my dear." Hunter smiled. No one had noticed them here. The Common was a big place. They were less likely to be recognized there than here. He was being overly cautious.

"May I speak to you, Josiah?"

Fancy's direct request, accompanied by the use of his first name, surprised her stepfather. He glanced hastily at his wife, who shook her head blankly at his unspoken question. "Well . . ." he began, "since your husband's not here, I suppose I can fill in for him." He frowned. "A hard worker. He worked through the noon hour making arrangements for some of his cargo, then went out in the middle of the afternoon to make arrangements for some more. He's a good man. A very good man."

"I'm sure," Fancy replied with a wintry smile.

"Well, come into my study then, Caroline, and we'll see what can be bothering you so much that you can't wait for your husband to solve it for you."

Seated behind his desk, he flipped up the lid of his humidor, then frowned at her and closed it.

"Please smoke if you like, Josiah," Fancy urged. "My father always liked a good pipe after dinner."

He frowned at the mention of Fancy's father and leaned back in his chair. The humidor stayed firmly closed. "He did, did he?"

She concealed her amazement at the realization that Josiah Shepperton was jealous of his wife's first husband, now long dead. What had he heard about Richard England that made him resent the slightest comparison with him?

"I raise tobacco," she amended. "I love the smell of it. It's like home to me."

He nodded. His hands twitched and he glanced longingly at the box. However, he laced his fingers together over his waistcoat and leaned back with an air of patience.

She took a deep breath. "Josiah, I really don't want to stay here in Boston." When he leaned forward with a start, she raised her hand. "And I don't think anyone really wants me here."

"Nonsense."

"I'm not talking nonsense. I don't fit in with your ideas. My husband is going away soon to sea. Then you'll be stuck with me just a few streets from you. My mother will insist on having me over for dinner at least

278

one night a week. You'll have me constantly underfoot"—she leaned forward—"and you don't like me above half."

"My dear girl . . ."

"I'm not a girl. I'm a woman with a ten-year-old son. That son will also be around here. And ten-year-olds can be trouble. You've already heard his father say that he doesn't intend to take him with him for the rest of the voyage. That's because Hunter doesn't want to be bothered with the childish misbehavior and the discipline that has to accompany that."

Shepperton leaned back in his chair now, his brows drawn together in a single line. His jaw clenched.

"I'm making you the same proposition that I made to you when I first came here. Loan me five thousand dollars, make arrangements for me and my son to take passage on the next packet home, and we'll never bother you and your wife again." Her eyes were intensely gold in the lamplight. She had curved her hands around the arms of her chair until her knuckles whitened.

In silence, they regarded each other. He pursed his lips, then raised his hand to wipe it across the lower half of his face. With a long sigh, he shook his head. "No, my dear girl. You don't know what you're facing. I can't let you go."

"You can!"

"No. My wife would never forgive me. And besides, your husband would just come after you."

"She would and he wouldn't. Neither one of them cares as much as you think they do."

"You're bound to need our help in rearing your son."

"You'll be busy and Hunter will be gone."

"Exactly."

"But my mother didn't rear me," Fancy pointed out. "The servants did it. And there'll be plenty of them on

England's Fancy eager to 'take over the job of instructing Alex."

"You can't go back there. You don't know what you'll find."

"I know exactly what I'll find. I'll find my home and my friends. I'll find my way of life."

"A pretty lady like you alone." He shook his head. "No. No. I can't allow it. Your husband would—"

She clenched her fists in her lap. "Josiah, Hunter will be gone from here in a couple of weeks. You could arrange for me to go then. By the time he gets back, he'll have forgotten that he wanted me here in the first place. Besides, if he's sailing all over the world, he can make Charleston his home port just as easy as Boston."

He stroked his chin ruminatively. "There is some merit in what you say. If the plantation were in good repair . . ."

"If you'll loan me the five thousand dollars, I can return it to good repair."

"Five thousand dollars is a lot of money."

She clasped her hands. "Or if five thousand sounds like too much, what will you loan me?"

"My dear girl, it's not a question of money. It's a question of the suitability of what you intend. You must realize that what you want to do just isn't done." His jaw snapped to, biting off the last word.

She raised her hands to her cheeks, then dropped them limply into her lap. "Then you won't help me."

"My dear girl, you should discuss this with your husband. . . ."

"He doesn't have five thousand dollars," she reminded him. "He took my money to finance this voyage."

"He worked the plantation," Josiah declared adamantly. "Now he wants to sell it rather than pour more money into it. The plan sounds feasible to me. He will

280

cut his losses in that manner and set you and his son up very nicely while—"

"Damn you!"

His mouth dropped open.

"Damn you! He means to sell my plantation and give me a pittance so that he may do as he likes without any responsibility. And you are helping him." She sprang to her feet.

"Caroline, calm yourself!" Josiah admonished sternly.

"Oh, I'll calm myself," she grated. "I'll certainly calm myself, but not here." She marched to the door, then spun round and came back. "Just remember, Josiah Shepperton, that I asked you for help and you refused me."

"I only did what was for the best. For your own good." He rose and put his hands on the desk.

She clenched her fists between her breasts. "You don't have the right to decide what is for my own good. I'm not a child, nor am I my mother. Please allow me to know what is right for me."

"When you raise your voice as you are doing now, I doubt your sanity, madam."

She clenched her fists and fought for control. "When you play God, you have to expect a blasphemer now and then, sir." She marched to the door. "Good night, sir."

Chapter Seventeen

"Sweetheart, you're not dressed." Resplendent in dove-gray superfine coat, pale gray buckskin trousers, and white satin waistcoat shot with silver threads, Hunter paused in the doorway.

Fancy clasped the edges of her robe together at the neck and managed a calm smile from the mirror. "I'm running a bit late. I took too long in the bath, and now Dulci is trying something new with my hair. You go on down. I'll be there in time for the receiving line. I promise."

He frowned at the gleaming mass of red twisted into a simple knot at the top of her head, then at Holy Dulcibella, who hovered over Fancy, brush in hand. "Your hair looks fine to me," he remarked. Ignoring his implied criticism, the black woman delicately smoothed an imaginary stray hair back into the coiffure.

Fancy smiled at him over her shoulder. "Please indulge me, sweetheart. I've never been out in Boston society before. And Mother tells me that it's 'the only real society in America.'" Turning back to the mirror, she chuckled. "I didn't bother to argue with her about that."

As the housekeeper discreetly carried away the towel she had draped across Fancy's shoulders, Hunter came to stand behind his wife. Keeping his eyes locked with hers in the mirror, he bent to drop a kiss beneath her earlobe. "Very wise." He brushed his cheek against hers, his eyes smiling. "Put out your hand and close your eyes."

Obediently, she did as he bade. First, she felt the touch of his fist in her palm; then his fingers opened. She felt him slip something warm and metallic into her hand. She opened her eyes.

Her rubies gleamed and glittered in the lamplight. His wedding gift to her. The necklace and earbobs Wentworth had extorted from her for the passage to Boston. Her eyes flew to his face. "How did you get these?"

"I took them away from that insensitive swine."

"I'm sure he told you quite a story." She could not keep the bitterness out of her voice.

"Yes." Gently, he turned her round on the vanity stool. Closing her hands together over the jewels, he clasped his own hands over them. "Fancy, I swear to you I never meant for you to suffer from want."

Instantly, she dropped her eyes, unable to look at him. The amazement and disgust would be there for him to read. She had never imagined Hunter to be naive. Yet here he stood, apologizing to her when she was only one of the many responsibilities he had abandoned. Perhaps people had not actually died because of his desertion, but certainly their lives had become immeasurably harder because of if.

Of course, Hunter had not seen the change she had suffered in the months he had left her to run the plantation. To him she was still the spoiled, self-pitying wife. He believed her to have come here asking for charity for herself and for some archaic dream house called England's Fancy. He could not know how the house no longer meant to her what her people and her land did.

In that moment she could forgive him, but she could not change her plans. *Poor Hunter*. She wondered if he would ever realize what she had become.

"Fancy," he urged.

Gently withdrawing her hands from between his, she opened them to look at the jewels. Beautiful as they were, they represented the vanity of another woman. To her they meant nothing. "Thank you for returning them to me, Hunter."

"Can't you look at me, Angel?"

A sad smile on her face, she lifted it to him. Her eyelashes swept up.

He stared deep and long into the gold eyes. He no longer understood what was going on behind her eyes. Very little of the woman he had married remained. He missed the open emotion that he had once taken for granted.

Hunter sighed heavily. "Hurry and finish dressing." As if he administered a benediction, he pressed his lips to her forehead and held them there for a long moment. "Boston has never seen the like of you."

When the door closed behind him, Fancy rose and shrugged out of her robe, which had concealed the black silk undergarments. "Hurry, Dulci."

The housekeeper carried the gown from the wardrobe. Neither woman spoke as Fancy stepped into the black velvet and the maid fastened it at the back.

"Now the rubies."

"Maitresse . . ."

"There is nothing to say, Dulci. He doesn't understand at all. I know that now. What he said to me tonight proves it. He doesn't realize the people of England's Fancy will be in want unless I can somehow find enough money to rebuild and replant what was lost."

The black woman heaved a sigh. "Then I must tell you. I had hoped that you would find happiness tonight, but God has laid another path for you."

Fancy swung round. "Tell me what?"

"Lemuel Jakes has found a ship. It has been fully outfitted. Forgive us, O Lord. It is to sail at dawn on Monday, the captain being a good Christian who will take himself to church in the morning for services."

"When do we go?" Fancy's voice was barely a whisper.

"Lemuel says the ship is at Shepperton's dock."

Fancy could not repress a smile. "Shepperton's?"

"Only a watchman will be on board. The crew is ready. We will have many hours head start and—"

"What time are we to be there?"

"At three."

She shivered.

"Before God, maitresse, do not go if you—"

"Pack only what we can carry, Dulci."

"Yes, maitresse."

Fancy turned to survey herself in the cheval glass. The black velvet had been a good choice. It suited her mood as the rose-pink never would. "The rubies, Dulci."

High color brightened her cheeks as she stared at the reflection of the glittering center stone. When all was securely fastened, Holy Dulcibella handed her charge a black lace fan.

Fancy snapped it open and closed in front of her. "Perfect."

"Yes, maitresse."

Hand on the door, Fancy smiled. "Pack what we need and take it to your room, Dulci. I'm sure my husband will spend tonight here."

The woman looked worried. "And how shall I wake you, maitresse?"

"You needn't worry on that score. I won't fall asleep."

The receiving line had already formed at the foot of the staircase. Canham and a footman were helping the first guests off with their wraps.

Fancy was halfway down the stairs before Blanche glanced up. Her look of irritation faded instantly as she gaped at her daughter. Josiah and then Hunter followed her stare. Their expressions of dismay and dawning appreciation gratified Fancy to the depths of her soul.

Although black was usually reserved for widows, it was not exclusively so. The low cut of the bosom contrasted starkly with the faintly golden skin and flaming red hair. The tightness of the waist moulding the figure so provocatively announced to everyone that its wearer was not bereaved. No, the black dress itself was not a cause for comment. However, the elegant carriage of the figure and the serenity of the face were.

The two couples just arriving noted the focus of the receiving line and turned around. Likewise the butler and footman paused in their duties. In a pool of almost reverent silence, Fancy descended the stairs.

Then Hunter blinked. "Ah, Caroline. Mr. and Mrs. Perkins, may I present my somewhat tardy wife, Caroline Gillard."

The nearest gentleman bowed graciously. "No apology necessary, I assure you. I always tell Mrs. Perkins we have to be somewhere earlier than we have to be. Otherwise, we'd always be late." Thomas Handasyd Perkins chuckled and his wife giggled at their own private joke.

Hunter offered his arm to his wife as she reached the landing, and he led her to her place. "I thought you were going to get a pink dress," he muttered out of the side of his mouth.

She smiled blindingly at Mr. Perkins's brother James. "So nice to meet you," she trilled, ignoring Hunter's comment.

"Glad to meet you, my dear. And let me say how welcome your husband is in the China trade. There's always room for more in that market. We can't get the goods here fast enough."

"The Perkins brothers are merchants," Blanche told her when the two couples had passed into the parlor, where another footman waited to offer them cups of whiskey punch and ratafia.

"And their wives?"

"Members of the Anthology Society."

"How nice."

"Mr. and Mrs. Josiah Quincy," Canham intoned, "and Mrs. Quincy."

"Good you could come, dear Mrs. Quincy." Blanche pressed her cheek to the old lady's withered one.

"Mother was pleased to be included," Quincy replied as his mother nodded vaguely.

"The President of Harvard College," Blanche informed her son-in-law and daughter archly. "In Boston, to know the right people is everything. Be sure to mention Alex tonight. It's never too soon to start preparing the way. I have friends who consider that Harvard is superior to Oxford."

Fancy's smile slipped, but the others in the receiving line were smiling enough to make up for her breach. Now she could understand why her mother put up with Josiah Shepperton and his absolute domination of her. Blanche was in her element playing hostess to the rich and famous. She loved it and wanted nothing else than

288

this and the Anthology Society.

"Caroline." Blanche nudged her. "May I present John Phillips and his wife?"

"So pleased."

"Delighted."

"And the Most Reverend Jean Cheverus."

"Charmed."

"So pleased."

When all twenty guests had arrived, the two dozen couples sat or stood in two groups in the parlor. The men talked politics and trade near the sideboard, where a footman refilled their silver punch cups with a silver ladle. The ladies discussed the upcoming speaker at the Anthology Society, the weather, the latest fashion plates, and servants.

When Canham announced that dinner was served, Fancy could have dashed across the room and hugged him. Her joy was short-lived, however. Her dinner partner proved to be Joseph Coolidge, brother-in-law of the illustrous Charles Bulfinch. Mr. Coolidge admired all of Bulfinch's architectural and civic works and began to recount them, beginning with the houses on Franklin Crescent.

Remembering that this would be her last formal meal for months, Fancy forced herself to eat some of the soup, an endive cream concoction much too lemony for her taste.

While Canham was serving the hot salad of artichoke hearts and asparagus tips and Mr. Coolidge was pausing for breath, Fancy overheard James Perkins address Josiah. "So Mr. Madison has finally determined on a firm stance against these piratical swine."

"Not firm enough. Or at least he has not convinced the Congress of what will happen unless the Navy is sent into action."

"But he has issued letters of marque?" Perkins prodded

"Oh, yes. I have a set in my possession. But of course I must furnish the ship, captain, and crew to sail under them," Josiah grumbled.

His guest shook his head. "The Virginian is a fool. Surely as a planter, he must see that the life blood of this nation depends on keeping the sealanes free."

"Every planter in South Carolina certainly understands." Fancy spoke without thinking. "Our largest and most lucrative markets are European."

Both Perkins brothers turned in surprise. "That's true, I'm sure," James said kindly. "Your husband's business could be severely damaged if pirates are allowed to ravage as they did in the last century."

"My business, the business of England's Fancy," she replied. "I am the planter, sir."

At the note of pride and determination in her voice, the table grew quiet. Josiah Shepperton cleared his throat harshly.

Suddenly, Blanche laughed. "Now, Mr. Shepperton, you gentlemen are talking business that we ladies don't understand. And we agreed that table talk should be general." Her last words, uttered on a pleading note, were directed to her daughter.

"Right, Mrs. Shepperton. Gentlemen. Let's have no more talk of pirates and politics. Canham, enough of these vegetables. Let's have the fish."

More amused than angry, Fancy waited in a pool of silence for the cod fillets in olive-pimiento sauce. She refused to look in Hunter's direction, knowing he would be frowning at her intrusion upon men's conversation.

During the roast lamb in elderberry sauce, she glanced down the table to catch Hunter smothering a yawn, having given up trying to make conversation

290

with Josiah Quincy's mother. By that time he had forgotten her faux pas. When he caught her watching him, he instantly straightened and smiled as if he were enjoying himself immensely.

You liar, she thought. *You're every bit as bored with this as I am, but you'd condemn me to an endless lifetime of it without a second thought.* Rather than let him see her own boredom, she glanced down as the footman whisked away her plate and Canham set before her a wedge of rich rum pie.

She stared at it in disgust. How could anyone be expected to eat this after all the other food that had been served?

"Ah, my favorite," her dinner partner murmured. "Don't suppose you're accustomed to anything like this in South Carolina?"

She looked him straight in the eye for the first time during that interminable meal. "I can swear to you that I'm not, Mr. Coolidge."

Long before Blanche announced that the ladies would retire, Fancy had folded her napkin beside her plate and snapped open her fan. When at last the command came, her eyes met Hunter's as he rose to pull out old Mrs. Quincy's chair and to help her totter to her feet.

"I cannot tell you when I've had a more delightful companion for dinner," Mr. Coolidge declared as he helped Fancy out of her chair. "My wife—Charles's sister—has a musicale once a month. I shall certainly get her to add your name to her list."

Fancy snapped open her fan as she rose and swept it across her bosom. "You do that, Mr. Coolidge. I'll be so pleased to come. Just delighted. Just so long as it doesn't conflict with a meeting of the Anthology Society."

"Oh, it would never do that," he hastened to assure

her. "She'd never miss one of their meetings. Almost the same group of ladies attend them both, whether they're musical or not." He chuckled as if he had made a great joke.

She fluttered her fan. "Then I'm sure I'll see her there."

Blanche motioned to her at that moment, and she slipped by him and preceded her mother out of the dining room. "You must be more discreet, Caroline," Blanche whispered as they followed the other women into the parlor. "You'll have poor Felicity in tears."

"Good grief! Because I had to sit at the table with her husband?"

"Because you looked as if you were enjoying yourself too much."

"Believe me, Mother, I was not enjoying myself."

"I think it went very well indeed, Mrs. Shepperton," Josiah remarked to his wife. "Both your daughter and son-in-law made a hit with our friends. That dress was a good choice. When I heard pink, I was afraid the color might be too bright, but black was a good choice. Tones down some of her unfortunate coloring."

Blanche looked at her husband with real annoyance. "What do you mean 'unfortunate coloring?'"

"Well, my dear, you will admit her hair is terribly red."

Blanche bit her lip. "Caroline looked beautiful tonight."

"Pretty is as pretty does."

"Mr. Shepperton, what are you talking about?"

At his wife's curt tone, Josiah blinked. Suddenly, he realized that his musings had not set well with her. He cleared his throat. "Nothing at all, Mrs. Shepperton. I know you're pleased to have your daughter and grandson here with you."

"I am, Mr. Shepperton. I have missed seeing Alex grow up." She looked at her husband's stern face, thinking how she wished he would smile more often. Neither had Caroline smiled during the party. Of course, the conversation had been mostly about doings in Boston. She would, of necessity, feel left out for a while. But then she would get to know people.

Blanche dropped her eyes to stare at the three large diamonds in the white-gold ring on her left hand. They were beautiful gems. All her jewels were beautiful. And her house, while not decorated the way she would have preferred, was in the most exclusive part of town. Her position in Boston society as the wife of shipowner Josiah Shepperton was unassailable. And Caroline would inherit all that if she would just . . .

"Mrs. Shepperton, it is time that you and I retire. We don't want to be inattentive in church in the morning."

She looked up at her husband. So different from Richard. Why had she thought of Richard now? For weeks on end she would not think about him, so different from Josiah in every way. Kind, generous, handsome, laughing. Given to dropping kisses on her at odd moments, regardless of who might be watching. And a wildly passionate lover.

"Coming, Mrs. Shepperton?" Josiah held the door for her.

"Coming, Mr. Shepperton."

Holy Dulcibella was waiting to undress Fancy. "A man will meet us at the corner of Federal Street. His name is Otis Greene. I knew a man named Otis Greene many years ago, but he was older than I. This man could not be the same."

"Perhaps his son."

293

The old woman shook her head. "More likely his grandson or even great-grandson." She laid down the pins from Fancy's hair and picked up the brush.

"You've packed some clothing for us."

"Yes, but not too much to carry."

"Good. We don't want to burden Mr. Greene."

"I doubt if Otis Greene will carry them for us anyway. His father never would have."

At Fancy's quizzical look, the old woman continued, "The Otis Greene I knew had been a slave. After he escaped, he vowed he would carry no man's burden. God's peace to his troubled spirit. He would not bend again."

"You have known some strange people in your life, Dulci."

"Stranger than you can imagine, maitresse. I will wait for you to meet them rather than telling you about them."

"Angel . . ." Hunter knocked discreetly at the door.

"Just a minute, Hunter." She hurried her friend to the other door that led to the adjoining chamber. "Sleep, Dulci. Lie down immediately and rest. I will wake you when it's time to go."

"But, maitresse . . ."

"I won't sleep, I promise you. I'll come for you in three hours."

"Angel . . ."

"Just a moment." She hurried to the mirror. Standing before it, she loosened her robe to the waist and shook out her hair until it swirled around her in a rich cloud of rose-gold. "I'm coming, love," she called. Kicking off her slippers, she sped to the door. "Hunter."

"Why did you lock the door?" he began irritably, then stopped. His mouth widened into a grin. "Angel," he breathed.

"Come in, Hunter." She reached out with both hands to draw him into the room.

He kicked the door to with his heel as he allowed her to guide his arms around her. "Angel."

"I want you." One arm went round his neck to drag him down. Her mouth fastened on his, sucking and nibbling at his tongue when he gasped in surprised pleasure.

He could not speak. But his hands moved down from her waist over her buttocks, clasping her to him. She writhed against those hands, rising on tiptoe to fit herself against him until he could feel the division of her mount. Her movements spread her gown farther apart until her naked skin pressed against his clothed length.

"You must know how I've missed you," she whispered feverishly.

"No more than I have you."

His lie angered her. She broke away suddenly, tearing herself out of his arms and backing away from him.

"Angel." He did not notice her anger. His mind and senses totally enslaved, he stared at the long, narrow rectangle of bare skin. His eyes fastened on the exposed tangle of red curls at the bottom of her belly. "Angel, you . . . What's got into you? You've never . . ." He gulped.

"You're my husband, Hunter."

"Yes." Because his lust was becoming a steady throbbing ache, he tore his eyes away to her face, but the move brought little relief.

She purposefully slid her tongue with careful slowness across her lower lip. "Hunter," she murmured.

He moaned. Even as his hands fumbled for the buttons on his waistcoat, he could not keep his eyes from dropping down the smooth column of her throat into the valley between her breasts and into the hollow of her navel.

"Come here," she whispered.

He tottered forward. Unlike his, her fingers worked efficiently. His fine linen cravat was plucked free of its complicated bow. His waistcoat and shirt were unbuttoned and tossed aside. While he shuddered and groaned, she bent to take his nipple between her lips, kissing and nipping it until he cried out, not from pain, but from the exquisite sensation.

While her teeth pleasurably tortured the other nub of sensitive flesh, her hands unbuttoned the front of his buckskin trousers and peeled them down around his thighs. She shot a glance up at him, but his eyes were closed, his jaw set to endure. His hands were clenched into hard fists at his sides.

His manhood was beautiful. If anything, it was more beautiful than she remembered. From a thick nest of black hair it sprang, iron sheathed in chamois. She caressed it with her hands while he moaned and threw back his head.

"Lie down."

He blinked once, then turned, hampered by his clothing. She pushed, her hand flat against his chest, and he sprawled backward on her bed.

Putting one knee on the bed, she rose to hover over him while she kissed his mouth, his throat. Sucking his left nipple into her mouth, she paused to feel the race of his heart beneath her lips. Satisfaction and, with it, power pounded in her veins as she thrust her tongue into his navel, then trailed down to the engorged tip that lay on his belly. When she touched it with the tip of her tongue, he moaned.

A tiny chuckle escaped her lips as she kissed it and slid her mouth around it. "Angel . . ." he gasped.

"A minute more, Hunter." She stooped to pull his pumps off. His stockings followed. Then his buckskin trousers. He lay nude before her, shuddering, watching her from beneath his long lashes.

Smiling, she tossed her robe aside at the same time she kept the end of the sash in her hand.

"You'll never leave me again," she promised. Teeth clenched in a demonic smile, she climbed onto the bed and grasped his wrists. Pulling them above his head, she bound his hands together with the silk sash.

"Angel . . ."

"Don't call me Angel tonight, Hunter. Tonight you've roused the devil."

His hips twitched, but he made no protest as she pulled his hands up, looped the sash twice around the bedpost, and tied it with a slipknot. Her nails scratched gently down the delicate skin on the undersides of his arms through the black tufts of hair in his armpits.

Air hissed between his clenched teeth as his need and excitement increased.

Her nails continued their journey, leaving tiny tracks of whitened skin that turned pink an instant after she passed on.

He writhed, clenching his fists, tugging gently at the silk knots, anticipating that she would come to his nipples.

At the moment she touched them, her mouth closed lovingly over his erect manhood. Her tongue circled it as she scored his nipples with her nails. The combination of pleasure and pain wrung an agonized groan from him at the same moment he bucked his hips upward.

"Do you see why you'll never leave me again, Hunter?"

"God, yes." He ground his teeth, struggling to keep some measure of control. The fantasy of helplessness was unbearable. When he thought he would explode, she twisted round on the bed and rose over him. On her knees on either side of his hips, she guided him to her.

Wild with wanting her, he thrust up out of control. She neither cried out nor pulled back. Instead, she thrust down against him to fuse them together.

"Angel!" He did not know that he shouted, only that his whole body convulsed when she sheathed him inside her.

Chapter Eighteen

"I never thought it was possible to love a woman the way I love you." As Hunter uttered the words, his arms tightened around Fancy's shoulders, holding her to him as if he would never let her go. She could feel his heart beat and his chest heave as he drew in a deep breath of contentment.

She raised her head and smiled down into his face. "Did you enjoy being made love to?"

"Enjoy it? My God! Any more pleasure and I would have died of a heart attack."

"I'm glad you didn't. Alex needs a father."

Frowning at the serious tone of her voice, he ran his fingers through the long fall of red hair that lay across their shoulders. "He needs us both."

"Yes."

"What are you thinking?"

She hesitated.

"Tell me. We have no secrets."

One white shoulder lifted in a shrug of capitulation. "About England's Fancy."

His hands stilled. "Forget it."

"I can't. My people are there. They're my obligations. Almost every one of them was born on England's

Fancy. It's the only home they've ever known."

He patted her as if she were a child. "I've already told you. It will all be settled. You don't have to worry your beautiful head about it any longer. Before I sail, I'll dispatch instructions to the lawyer . . . what's his name?"

"Aiken."

"Right. He can handle the sale of the land and house. No need to worry about the people. I'll tell him to arrange the bill of sale so that everyone is guaranteed his place."

She crossed her forearms on his chest and pushed herself up. Her hair made a curtain around the two of them. It had the effect of cutting out some of the light and concealing her expression in shadow. "And what about me?"

He stared up incredulously. "What about you?"

"What am I to do with myself while you are away at sea? You do intend to return to the sea, don't you?"

"Just as soon as I can," he smiled, then hastily amended his response. "But not before I get you and Alex settled in a house. Your stepfather suggests—"

"Alex thinks he's going with you."

Hunter frowned, then grinned. "But you'll be pleased to know I'm leaving him right here. The sea's too rough a life for a boy. You were right."

"And you intend to leave us here together?"

"Alex can go to Harvard."

She forbore to point out the obvious—that Alex was only ten. Instead, she smiled sweetly. "And I can join the Anthology Society?"

"Exactly."

"And . . . Jessica?" She hesitated a long time before she pronounced the word, whispering it to disturb the momentary silence like an acorn plopping into a forest pool.

She could feel her husband tense beneath her. His eyes narrowed, the dark lashes hiding their inky depths.

He stirred restlessly. "Jessica is returning to England and her husband. You know you completely misinterpreted that situation. Jessica means nothing to me. She never did. I am simply helping her return to her husband."

Fancy stared at him incredulously. His tone of voice and serious aspect could only mean that he believed what he said. Poor Jessica was to be carelessly abandoned. He felt no obligation to his mistress. Her mother had been right after all. She dropped her head onto his chest to hide her amazement.

Thinking that she acquiesced to everything, Hunter sighed in pure pleasure. His wife's slender body moved so sweetly across his own. Angel was perfect. Perfect. He raised his head and dropped a light kiss on the top of her head.

Her next question made him uncomfortable again. "Jessica is with you still then?"

He dropped back on the pillow. "Well, naturally. I couldn't just abandon her in France. The poor woman didn't even speak the language."

"Naturally. And she'll be sailing with you when you leave."

"Angel." He spanked her bottom lightly. "Just leave it alone, please. I've already told you she means nothing to me. She was more a governess for Alex than anything."

"Very well, Hunter." She began to kiss his chest. Her fingers ruffled the pelt of dark hair. She would try one more time. With all his faults, she loved him so. "Hunter, I really want to return to South Carolina. Please take me back to England's Fancy." Her voice broke slightly.

He did not notice the quaver. "Ah, Angel, sweetheart . . ." Her lips and tongue were leaving fire trails on his chest. "You don't want to go back to that old patch of ground. Your stepfather has offered me a partnership. We'll build a new life right here in Boston." He shuddered as her hand closed over his hard flesh. It began to throb as his heartbeat quickened.

"Perhaps you're right," she whispered. "Only a fool would care for a patch of ground."

He did not understand her words. Mindlessly, he clutched the back of her head with his hands and guided her mouth to him.

The little clock on the mantel chimed once. Fancy lay on her stomach, her cheek pillowed on Hunter's chest, her eyes staring at the faint glint of gold as the pendulum swung back and forth. Moonlight filtering through the lace curtains bathed the room.

With a sigh, she ran her palms down his flanks. When he suddenly caught his breath in his sleep, she froze, but it evened again almost immediately. Slowly, she pushed up and off him. She hated to exchange the warm bed for the cold room. The floor was so icy to her bare feet that she had to clench her teeth to keep them from chattering.

Hunter stirred restlessly. One strong hand slid down his body, groping. Hurriedly, she covered it with her own at the same time she pulled the blankets up around his neck. When he quieted, she released his hand.

Resisting the impulse to press a final kiss on his cheek, she snatched up her robe from the floor and flung it around her. Crossing on bare tiptoes to her dressing table, she opened her jewel case and took out the rubies and a piece of folded paper. With shaking fingers, she stood it on the dresser where it could not be missed. For an instant more she clutched the rubies to her heart, then laid them with the letter.

With a final glance in the direction of the bed, she ran to the door of Holy Dulcibella's room and eased it open. Only when it was closed with equal care did she turn to find her companion waiting for her fully dressed.

A tiny shielded candle provided just enough light for Fancy to dress, too. Feverishly, she tugged on rough seaman's breeches and leather boots, a seaman's smock and heavy wool coat. She carelessly tucked her long hair up under a knit cap.

Holy Dulcibella pointed to two seaman's bags. "Lemuel Jakes sent these," she whispered. "I have packed very carefully, maitresse."

Fancy hugged her hard before holding the old woman at arm's length. "This trip is going to be long, Dulci. It could be dangerous. You don't have to go. I'm sure you could stay here with Mother. She'll need help to take care of Alex after Hunter leaves."

Black eyes glittered in the dark. "I want to go, maitresse. I thought I would die without ever seeing my homeland again. Now I think I will live. I long to return." In an uncharacteristic gesture, she lifted Fancy's hand to her cheek. "Take me home, child of Great Edward. It is your duty."

Fancy leaned forward and kissed the woman's other cheek. "Then say no more. I must do my duty." She lifted both bags by their webbing straps and settled them over her shoulders. "Lead the way."

The old woman did not waste time in useless protest. Holding the candle high, she opened the door into the hall.

*　　　*　　　*

303

Otis Greene stepped out of the dark doorway at the corner of Franklin and Federal Streets. He was the tallest man Fancy had ever seen. Fully seven and a half feet tall and very thin, he stood, his skin so black that he appeared to have no face at all in the darkness.

With a smothered scream, Fancy staggered back against the building. Dropping one bag off her shoulder, she slung the other bag at the gigantic figure.

It did not even stagger him. Instead, he caught it easily, as if she had tossed it to him on purpose. His voice rumbled out of his chest. "Do you come for Lemuel Jakes?"

"Yes," Holy Dulcibella replied, her voice unperturbed.

"Then we must hurry." He held out the bag to Fancy. "I will lead the way."

"Just a minute . . ."

But he was already turning.

"It is he," Holy Dulcibella confirmed. "No need to be worried, maitresse. It is the son of Otis Greene."

"Grandson," the man supplied.

"How is your grandfather?"

"He is not well. He wishes he could come."

"But he cannot."

"No."

The tall man led the way, sometimes walking through Boston's streets, sometimes ducking into alleys. Holy Dulcibella followed. Fuming silently, Fancy panted after them, feeling more like a beast of burden instead of the instigator of the expedition.

"The Long Wharf," the man announced after a time.

Fancy could see the moon glinting on the waters of Boston Harbor. "Which ship?" she panted.

"Almost to the end. We have another half mile to go."

Fancy groaned. The canvas bags of clothing were

not so light that she could carry them all night long at a rapid pace.

In the distance, she could hear a clock strike in a church tower. Its bell tolled three times.

"We must hurry." The rumbling voice carried a hint of urgency. He took Holy Dulcibella by the arm. "I will carry you."

"I can walk."

"Not fast enough." Without effort, he swung her up into his arms and started off at a lope. His long legs immediately outdistanced Fancy.

At last, when she thought she would sink to the ground from exhaustion, Otis Greene stopped. A shorter dark figure stepped out of the shadow of some huge crates.

"Lemuel Jakes," she panted, her voice dry and raspy from breathing through her mouth.

"Here, Mistress Fancy."

"Thank God."

He caught her arm and steadied her as she swayed, her heart pounding, sweat trickling down her back. "We must be quick, m'lady."

"I'm ready, Mr. Jakes."

He made a sweeping guesture with his arm and dark figures swarmed out of hiding places along the Wharf. "Are you for it, lads?"

From the dark came soft mutters of assent.

"Then let's board her."

Fancy kept herself at his left shoulder as they crept across the wharf and up to the gangplank of a black hulk, with two masts slanted back across the moon. "What is she?" she whispered.

"The new schooner *Cayuga*."

She stopped short. "*Cayuga*" begins with a *C*. Does this ship belong to Shepperton?"

"Right." He paused fractionally, as if waiting for

305

some objection.

Her teeth flashed in the dark. "How appropriate!"

The first man up the gangplank was Otis Greene. The nightwatch took one look at the gigantic figure and turned to flee. Greene's big hands reached out to close over the frightened man's face and mouth before he could utter a cry for help.

"Tie him up."

"Better if we knock him over the head."

"No." Fancy stepped forward. Her voice rang loud and clear. "We don't hurt anyone. Not even a knock on the head. He might be injured permanently. Tie him up and hide him among the piles of cargo on the wharf."

The men froze at the sound of her voice. "I didn't count on no females," one hissed.

"She's the reason we're goin'," Lemuel Jakes announced. "She's the captain. Fancy England's her name."

"England," came the giant's rumble. "My grandfather sailed with a man named England . . . after England set him free."

"She's his granddaughter."

"She oughta be home in bed with her husband," came another voice. "If she's got one."

"We're wasting time," Fancy interposed. "You two, tie the man up and hide his body. We need to push off from here before the clock strikes the half hour."

Nobody moved. "It's bad luck to sail with a woman aboard."

"Bilge, Johnny Wheatley, and y' know it."

The guard groaned behind Otis Greene's hand.

Sensing she must seize the initiative when the chance came, she swaggered forward, hands on hips. "Tie him up, Johnny Wheatley, and help carry him ashore. Then if you'd rather stay, be off with you. We sail for Madagascar as the tide goes out. You can have a share or you can stay ashore."

"Damn you, Lemuel Jakes," Johnny Wheatley snarled. "You've roused my hopes."

Lemuel shrugged. "Get a movin', lads. We've got to cast off and raise sail to catch the land wind. Can't stand jawin'. Beany, see m'lady below."

A smaller figure that Fancy had not noticed before detached himself from the rail. "Come, m'lady," a young voice piped.

"Not me," Fancy told him. "*This* lady must go below and rest."

"Two of 'em," Johnny Wheatley whined. "For Gawd's sake . . ."

"Aye," Lemuel snickered. "A regular petticoat navy."

Otis Greene removed his hand from the guard's mouth and stuffed a wad of canvas in it. A couple of quick twists of line and the man's hands and feet were bound. Greene stooped and lifted him over his shoulder. "Comin', Johnny?"

The objector stood alone on the deck. Everyone around him had fallen to with a will. Fancy moved beside Lemuel Jakes as if on a tether, hauling what he hauled. The deck of the schooner lifted under her feet as the bow hawser fell away.

Otis Greene stomped back up the gangplank. "Last chance," called the black man.

"Hell an' damnation." Wheatley cursed furiously as he put his shoulder beside Greene's to haul in the gangplank.

Dear Hunter,

Believe me when I tell you I wish with all my heart that I could remain at your side. But you don't want me at your side. You want me in Boston at the Anthology Society. Perhaps

307

I would even do that for you—at least for a time—if you could agree to help me save England's Fancy.

I know you think I'm insane to want to save what is mine. The land means nothing to you but unpleasant work. But what you cannot understand is that I *want* to work and watch things grow among my own people. I want to ride my horse across England's Fancy and see a sea of green growing things everywhere I look. Not a sea of vast barren blueness.

Why do I want to work when I could live a life of no responsibility as your wife here in Boston? I cannot help but remember that I was that kind of wife for ten years.

And you left me.

Hunter, I could never trust myself to you again. I wish things could be different. Still, believe me when I say, I love you.

Fancy

Hunter could not believe his eyes. He read the letter through the second time before his mind comprehended what she had written. Then his hand began to shake. He stared at the vibrating pages and then at his other hand from which the jewels dripped gold and ruby fire.

She had left him. For a patch of ground. And last night she had told him she would never leave him. No, that was not quite true. She had said he would never leave her.

Red rage stained his vision. He smashed the sheets of paper together between his fists. That bitch! She had planned this from the very beginning. From the moment he had arrived in Boston, she had planned her revenge. The story of wanting the plantation was just that—a story. She did not care about it. He was certain she wanted her revenge. She wanted to make him look foolish.

Her maid. She would know where Fancy had gone. She would know and she would tell. He would wring her scrawny neck if she did not tell him immediately.

Naked, he strode to the connecting door and flung it open. Fancy's robe lay across the neatly made bed where her maid had slept. Otherwise, the room might never have been occupied.

Her mother! She must know something about this. A woman wouldn't just disappear into the night without leaving word with her mother. Fancy owed her mother the courtesy of telling her where she would be.

Back he lunged into the room where they had spent the night. Dropping the jewels and the crumpled papers on the table, he pulled on sufficient clothing to satisfy decency. Then, snatching them up again, he hurried down the stairs.

"Where is she?"

Josiah Shepperton stood at the sideboard filling his plate with kippers. Blanche sat at the breakfast table, a teacup just raised to her lips. When Hunter burst into the dining room, she stared in amazement. Never had she seen her son-in-law in such a state. Without coat or vest, his rumpled shirt was unbuttoned to the waist, exposing a V of black curling hair. He was unshaven, his hair uncombed. At his question, Blanche set the teacup down with a clink.

He caught the movement. "So you do know."

Blanche's face crumpled. As surely as if her daughter had told her intention, Blanche knew what Caroline had done. "No, I don't."

Clearly, he did not believe her. "Tell me," he warned, coming around the table. Under her nose, he waved the

309

papers crumpled in his fist. "Tell me."

"I don't know where she is, but I assume you mean Caroline."

"Caroline?" Josiah set his plate down on the sideboard. "What's this?"

"She's gone," Hunter flung over his shoulder. "And you know where." His eyes never left Blanche's white face.

Slowly, she shook her head. "No. I don't know. I suspect she's gone back to South Carolina. To try and save her plantation."

"What? Nonsense." Josiah came round to put his hand on the back of his wife's chair. "What's he talking about?"

"I'm talking about this." Hunter thrust the paper at Josiah. "This ridiculous . . . this foolish . . ."

Josiah took it from him, smoothed the pages, and held it out at arm's length. "What's she talking about? Wanting to work among her own people? We're her people." He stared at his wife much as Hunter was doing, as if she too were somehow to blame.

Blanche dropped her eyes to her teacup. The liquid was exactly the right temperature. She would not waste it. Ignoring them both, she lifted it to her lips, tasting it delicately, finding it had been brewed exactly right.

"Mrs. Shepperton," Josiah said sternly. "We are waiting for an explanation of where your daughter has gone."

Blanche set the cup down. "I will tell you both again. I do not know. I suspect that she has gone back to South Carolina. It is, after all, her home, and her father's and grandfather's before her. That means a great deal to my daughter. She is not at all like me."

"But . . ." Hunter had to swallow hard. "She's left her son and . . . me."

310

"May I see the letter?"

"She doesn't say where she's going or when she's coming back," Josiah supplied as he passed the paper over.

Blanche smoothed the paper again. Carefully she read it, seeing in it what neither of them saw. With a sigh she laid it down. "I did not realize she was so unhappy" was all she said.

"Unhappy!"

"*Unhappy!*" Hunter spun around and stalked across the room. Doubling his fist, he smashed it into the door facing.

Blanche jumped and raised a trembling hand to her temple.

"I say, my boy. Steady there," Josiah cautioned.

"How could she be unhappy? I came back to her. Brought her son back to her. Put some money in the bank to tide that damned place over until it could be sold."

"She didn't want to sell it," Blanche murmured.

"But that's insane."

Josiah nodded slowly. "She really didn't want to sell it. Why, she came to me just the other day wanting me to loan her the money so she could put it back on its feet."

"She wanted you to loan her money?" Blanche looked at her husband expectantly. "And what did you tell her?"

"Well, I told her not to be foolish," he admitted. "What else was I to tell her? A woman alone like that. I told her to do what her husband told her."

"Oh, Mr. Shepperton . . ."

Hunter spun around. "Did a packet sail this morning?"

Thankful for the interruption of his wife, Josiah ran

311

a hand through his thinning hair. "No. Today is Sunday. Shepperton ships do not sail on Sunday from Boston."

"Then she's still in town. Somewhere." He started for the door.

"Perhaps you should get dressed more appropriately before you go looking for her," Josiah suggested. "Wouldn't do to have you catch a chill going out all unbuttoned."

Hunter paused at the door. When he turned, his face wore a thin smile. "She's playing a game," he declared. "She's somewhere out there waiting for me to find her. She's expecting that I'll change my mind about that patch of dirt."

Suddenly, Blanche could stand his attitude no longer. Abruptly, she rose from her seat. "Hunter, I don't think she's playing a game."

He ignored his mother-in-law. "I'll watch the packet tomorrow. When she tries to board with her maid, I'll drag her back here and make her see sense."

Canham opened the door, startled to find Gillard standing at it. "Pardon me, sir."

Hunter inclined his head and stepped back.

The butler entered. "A messenger, Mr. Shepperton. You're needed at the shipyards immediately."

Blanche swayed and clutched the table for support. "Oh, Caroline."

Josiah patted her shoulder. "Now, don't get excited. I'm sure it's nothing to do with your daughter. Something has come up. Probably a message from an arriving ship."

"I'll dress and accompany you," Hunter offered. "Since it's something unusual, perhaps I can be of service." Then he strode from the room.

Josiah put his arm around her shoulder. "I'm sorry that this happened on Sunday morning, Mrs. Shepperton. Perhaps I can meet you at the church. This shouldn't take long."

"I don't think I'm able to go to church." Blanche turned to him. "What did Caroline say to you the second time you refused her?"

Josiah sighed heavily. Really, this thing was too much. "She wanted me to loan her five thousand dollars so she and Alex could return to England's Fancy. Naturally, I refused."

"Why was she so determined to return?"

"Because . . . Really, Mrs. Shepperton, this is not the sort of thing you should know about . . ."

"Is it because she suspected that her husband intended to sail away with Jessica Rutledge?"

"Mrs. Shepperton, I'm surprised at you."

"Don't be. Perhaps you do not know that Hunter is paying for Jessica Rutledge to stay in a hotel near the waterfront. Do you also know that he was seen dining with her at Julien's Restorator just this week?"

To her surprise, Josiah dropped his eyes.

"You did know about that?" Blanche shook her head. "Why, Mr. Shepperton, I'm truly shocked. And you expect her to live on what he gives her with nothing that she can fall back on?"

"My dear Mrs. Shepperton, I expect that every man will do his duty."

"Mr. Shepperton, every man is not like you."

"Ready, Mr. Shepperton," Hunter called from the doorway.

"Ready sir." He patted his wife's shoulder again. "Please don't worry, Mrs. Shepperton. Everything will be all right. I'll take care of it."

She only looked at him gloomily.

"The *Cayuga* is missing!"

313

"Aye, sir. Sailed out of the harbor right under the noses of the South Shore Battery."

"Good lord! Where is the nightwatchman?"

"Outside, sir. His story doesn't make sense. We suspect he's been drinking."

Josiah looked at Hunter. "Bring him in. Bring him in. Let's hear it anyway."

The manager escorted the watchman into the inner office. The man was clearly nervous, clutching his cap in his hand and biting his lips. "This is Junius Bradford, Mr. Shepperton."

"Now, Junius, let's hear your story."

"Not much to tell, sir. They come swarming up the gangplank, about a dozen of them, led by a giant black man. About eight or nine feet tall he was. I started to run, but his great long arms reached out and hauled me in. I thought for sure they was going to kill me and throw me to the fishes, but they didn't."

"Why did you think they were going to kill you, Junius?"

"Because they was pirates, sir. Pirates. I know the way they works."

"Pirates in Boston Harbor, Junius . . ." Josiah's voice was a model of skepticism.

"They'd have slit my throat for sure, but for this woman."

"Woman!" Hunter lunged forward and caught the nightwatchman by the shoulder. "A woman, you say."

Junius nodded fiercely, almost tearing his cap to pieces in his nervousness. "She told them not to hurt me. They was all for knocking me over the head, but she wouldn't let them. Told them to tie me up and hide me under canvas on the wharf."

"And they obeyed her?" Josiah asked incredulously. "Did they call her by name?"

Junius nodded eagerly. "That they did. One of 'em

314

named her right enough, but it wasn't a real name. Probably made up. Like Blackbeard."

"Why do you say that?"

"Well, it wasn't a real name. Leastways, I never heard of it before. Fancy England, it was."

"Damn," Hunter breathed.

"Lord help us," Josiah intoned.

"I heard where they were bound, sir. That's another reason why I knew they were pirates."

Josiah slumped down at his desk.

"Tell us," Hunter commanded.

"Madagascar."

Part III

Madagascar, 1816

Chapter Nineteen

Hunter thrust his fist into the sky above Boston Harbor. "When I get my hands on her, she'll wish she'd never been born."

Josiah Shepperton merely shook his head dazedly. "She stole the *Cayuga*." he whispered. "She and a crew of men stole the *Cayuga*. How? Why? Where are they going?"

"Madagascar. Of course."

The older man put his hand to his aching forehead. "Why Madagascar? What could possibly have possessed her? This simply isn't done. A woman simply does not hire a crew of men . . . ,"

"Pirates."

"P—pirates."

"Her grandfather was a pirate. Probably she contacted some of his scurvy crew."

"But—but it's been more than half a century since—"

Hunter was thinking hard. "That old woman." He smacked his fist into his hand. "She's from Madagascar. I'll be damned if she's not the leader of this expedition."

"An old black woman"—Josiah tottered over and sat down on the end of a barrel—"stole my ship."

"I'll bring them back. *Carolina* can be ready—"

At this, Josiah roused. "Not with the *Carolina*. Oh, no, I'll not have another valuable ship going into danger. The *Carolina* is a merchantman and a merchantman she'll stay."

Hunter glared impotently at the empty berth beside the wharf and then at Josiah, who fumbled for a handkerchief from his pocket and wiped his forehead.

The *Cayuga* was a sweet little craft. Lemuel Jakes sang her praises daily, and Fancy listened and agreed with him. To be slicing through the waves at eleven knots under full sail, the rigging creaking rhythmically, was different from lumbering along in the old flute *Columbia*. For over two weeks the moderate to strong wind held, and the schooner ran east then south in the horse latitudes along the coast of Africa.

So favorable were the winds that the crew did little but lounge under the running rigging and play at dice.

"You really are more than an able seaman," Fancy marveled as Jakes sighted through the sextant and recorded their passage in the log.

The old man grinned a one-sided grin. "Aye, cap'n. I'm a first-rate boatswain."

"And more," Fancy replied. "You know more than hull and rigging. A boatswain's a rigger."

"Aye, so he is. You know that, do you? Coming to be a right knowledgeable seaman yourself."

From the first day, she had questioned everything she saw. Far from being offended as MacCullough had been on the plantation, Jakes seemed to take pleasure in answering. Nor did he care how close she stayed to him. Consequently, she was never more than a few feet away. There she had learned the names and duties of every member of the ship's crew. She had stood at his side, putting her hand on the various lines attached to the spars while he named each one and told her its purpose. Every sail had a name and a purpose, and she likewise learned them.

Her mind expanded under the instruction as she came to love the *Cayuga* and think of the ship as the crew did. Within days, she had begun to give the schooner human qualities and to listen to the wind in the rigging as if the vessel were talking.

Furthermore, Fancy knew she would be having a wonderful time if she were not obsessed with speed. Her mind turned over and over on the thought that they had to get to Madagascar, find the treasure, and return with it before Hunter could sell England's Fancy. Had he already put plans in motion to sell the plantation in a fit of anger at her desertion? Would she return to nothing and the whole venture be a waste and a loss?

When she thought of England's Fancy, fear seethed in her veins. When she thought of Hunter, she remembered their last night together. And she clasped her arms tightly around her. How he would hate her. And how she regretted her loss.

Swaying gently in her hammock, she realized that once more sleep had eluded her. With a sigh, she tipped herself out of the netting and climbed the ladder to the deck. The watch nodded to her. He was like the others, used to seeing her slender figure restlessly pacing the deck or leaning against the rail, far below in the bow. The warm winds blew in her face, and if she cried, they dried her tears for her.

The darkness and the stars were like the terrace beyond the ballroom in Charleston. Indeed they were the same stars. Young, incredibly handsome, his face tanned a deep walnut-brown, she had felt a stir as Hunter entered the room.

Behind her fan, she whispered to the daughter of her hostess.

"Why, Hunter Gillard, my dear. The youngest captain on the Shepperton Lines. Mama made certain his ship would be docked when she planned this party." The blond girl raised her own fan and fluttered it flirtatiously.

The man's dark eyes roved the dancers, slid past them, then returned. His mouth parted as if to speak even at such a distance.

Fancy closed her fan, then swept it open again as she could feel herself begin to blush.

"Why, I do believe he's coming this way!" the other girl chattered. "Mama will be so pleased."

He had presented himself before them, craved an introduction, danced first with the daughter of the hostess, then danced with her. When it was over, she stared helplessly up into his eyes.

"Would you like some fresh air?"

"Yes, please."

On the terrace, he put his hands on her shoulders. "I'm going to marry you," he said. "I know this may come as a shock to you. You may have to take a while to get used to the idea, but I know what I want. I've always known what I wanted."

"Oh, yes,"she agreed. His black hair blended into the night sky. Venus blazed in the sky over his right shoulder.

His lips descended on hers in the first kiss she had ever received. She knew she loved him in that instant and she had loved him beyond reason for more than ten years.

He had not wanted to leave the sea. He had even made one more voyage while she was pregnant with Alex. Then Richard England had died so tragically and unexpectedly of gangrene. Blanche had left and Fancy had been alone.

She sighed. *If I hadn't been so incredibly happy . . . If I had thought about him more as a person and not just as my husband . . .* But he had filled her world.

She had ignored his unhappiness. No one could possibly be discontented or restless if he filled the person he loved with such joy.

Then her baby daughter had died.

She dropped her head from the stars to stare into the dark water. The changes in her life had overwhelmed her. Surely Dulci was correct. Her life had been so perfect until that moment. When she found herself faced with adversity, she had not known how to handle it. Like a spoiled child, she had tried to wreak her grief on everyone around her instead of giving Hunter the love he needed.

The rigging creaked as a gust of wind struck it. "Squall in the east, Captain," called the steersman.

Clouds swept across the stars. Fresh cold water pelted the deck. Rather than go below, she lifted her face and arms to it, blinking as the drops struck her eyes. Swaying easily with the additional rocking of the vessel, she allowed it to sluice over her face and through her hair.

It washed away the sweat and the brine, but it could not wash away the home truths she had visited upon herself. She had wronged Hunter by not loving him in the right way. She dropped her head to her chest, letting the rain pelt the crown of her head and the back of her neck.

She had loved him in a wrong, selfish way. She admitted that, but oh, God, how she had loved him.

And I love him still!

Hunter paced angrily back and forth in front of the

Sheppertons. "Just give me that letter of marque. I'll bring her back. Every day that passes means we're wasting time. If you had done as I requested the day she sailed, I might have been able to catch her in the Atlantic."

Josiah leaned wearily back in his chair in the parlor. Blanche stood behind him, her hand resting on his shoulder, her face drawn with worry. While she feared for Fancy, she was more concerned about Josiah. The last two weeks had exhausted him. Not only had the newest addition to the Shepperton Lines been stolen, but he could not report the theft because of the family reputation. No one in Boston could be allowed to suspect that the stepdaughter of Josiah Shepperton might be a pirate.

Furthermore, when Blanche had looked at him with such reproach in her eyes, he had been upset. Caroline was the daughter of his wife. When his wife was upset, he was upset. He could not escape the dictums of his youth. Women were to be protected and nurtured. Worse, he could not rid himself of the feeling that he had driven his stepdaughter to her rash, dangerous action.

His very helplessness and frustration had kept him sleepless and without appetite. He regarded the pacing man with irritation. If Hunter had not led his wife to believe that she had been abandoned, none of this would have happened in the first place. His head moved in negation against the back of his chair. "You have the *Carolina* and her cargo to see to."

"Let the mate of the *Carolina* take her on to England. I can catch up to her as she heads outward bound."

Josiah shook his head. "When you came to me to propose this venture, I was skeptical. Now you seem ready to abandon it, and the money and time, with

324

no thought. . . ."

Hunter slammed his fist into the palm of his hand. "I fully intend to live up to my responsibilities. Nothing would make me abandon this project except the most dire emergency. But she is my wife. She's in danger. She must be brought back."

Josiah cleared his throat. "Are you sure you're the one to do it, Hunter? After all, you have no experience with a fighting ship."

"I can command the ship with a mate under me with fighting experience," Hunter replied arrogantly. "I shall, of course, defer to him in matters of battle strategy. I consider myself responsible for Caroline's defection. I should have suspected that she would be stubborn when it came to that piece of ground. The moment I have her safe again, I shall rid her of that responsibility forever."

Blanche drew in her breath sharply. "I would suggest that you give that careful thought."

He started. His mouth dropped open.

"She loves that land and house. And it's hers from her grandfather and her father. I've watched my daughter since she came here. When you returned, she was glad to see you and overjoyed to see Alex. But she quickly realized that neither of you intended to remain with her. All she wanted was to return to South Carolina. I think you should let her."

"And I agree," Josiah seconded. With a show of uncharacteristic intimacy, he put his hand over his wife's fingers where they lay on his shoulder. "No woman should have to assume the responsiblity for so large an estate, but—" he paused significantly, "once she has done so and worked so hard, she should not have to lose it against her will. She is, after all, entitled to make her choice."

Hunter gaped at the pair of them. So stern, so

325

conservative, so Puritan. For the first time, he saw disapproval in their faces. Like a blow, he saw himself as he was judged by others. In that instant, he came to grips with the idea that his actions might not be met with enthusiastic approval. He hunched his shoulders. "A woman should cleave to her husband," he muttered.

"I do not disagree with that," Josiah said shortly. "But a man should also cleave to his wife."

The silence that followed was charged.

"Give me the letter of marque," Hunter asked again, his voice and face impassive. "I will bring her back, and we will come to an agreement that will be to our mutual satisfactions."

"Where are we now?" Fancy asked Lemuel Jakes as she stared at the chart of the Atlantic north of the Equinoctial Line.

Lemuel Jakes pointed with one of the needles of his dividers at a spot only a bit east of zero meridian. The temperature had been increasing daily. Everyone slept on deck at night and by day lay under canvas stretched above the deck to ward off the blistering heat.

"We're almost to Africa."

"Aye, cap'n, Africa lies north of us right now. She'll be our first landfall."

"Landfall?"

"We'll stop to take on fresh water and fresh supplies."

Fancy frowned. "Can we do that? Will it be safe for us to dock in a harbor in a ship with a woman as captain and no papers? Don't they have harbor masters and such things?"

He grinned. "Aye, they do—in Marseilles and Portsmouth—but we'll be putting in to the coast of Guinea, the Ivory Coast."

326

"The Ivory Coast . . ." she murmured. "I didn't think there really was such a place."

"Oh, there's such a place."

"I've read about it. It's a place of fabulous wealth." Her eyes sparkled at the memory.

He shook his head. "That must have been written by someone who'd never been there. It's the nearest thing to hell you'll find on this earth. And we won't stay a minute longer than we have to."

She flashed him a worried look. They were, after all, only fourteen people in a stolen ship. "Why stop at all?"

"This voyage can be hard or it can be easy. I look at m'lady's maid. She's an old woman. She needs her comforts. Just like I'm an old man."

"But surely there must be someplace else."

"Cap'n England," he addressed her sternly, "on the coast of Africa, one place is just as bad as another. There's naught but desert and jungle from the Strait of Gibraltar to the Cape. And fresh water and fresh vegetables and meats will make this voyage sure that we'll all get around the cape without the scurvy."

She still frowned. "We're making good time. Perhaps another place on the coast . . ."

"This harbor has another advantage," he interrupted softly. "The draft of this schooner is no more than five feet. And the harbor is shallow. If anyone—an angry husband, for instance—were to follow us, let's say in a big brigantine, his ship'd run aground. He'd never be able to bring her in."

Fancy smiled thinly. "The Ivory Coast it is then."

"There she is, lads, the mouth of the Rio St. Andries. At the foot of the Red Cliffs." Lemuel Jakes lowered the spyglass and pointed to the landfall that became more and more distinct on the horizon.

For the most part, no one stirred. The hot, muggy air made breathing itself a chore. Only Fancy managed to drag herself from beneath the canvas shade. Making her way to the rail beside Jakes, she squinted through the blinding blue.

"The Red Cliffs, huh?"

He passed her the spyglass. "Latitude five degrees north, longitude five degrees east."

Steadying against the rail, she sighted with one eye shut tight. As she adjusted to the rhythmic rolling of the ship, Lemuel Jakes looked down at her, making no effort to conceal his pride and affection.

She bore little resemblance to the young lady he had first seen on board the *Columbia*. Gone were the woman's dresses, the careful hair arrangement. Like the rest of the crew, she went barefoot and wore only minimal clothing. Canvas trousers reached only to her bare knees, and a loose smock had its sleeves rolled to her upper arms. Her red hair, now sun-streaked, was tied with a black ribbon in an old-fashioned queue.

Sweat trickled from her temples. Her garments were drenched despite the moderate wind that carried them nearer and nearer to the Ivory Coast. Yet he had never once heard her complain. Now she kept the heavy spyglass focused on the horizon as she spoke. "Will we reach the mouth of the river by nightfall?"

"Oh, aye, Cap'n. And Druwyn lies on the western side. We'll get provisions there and fresh water."

"Will we go ashore?"

"Some of us will have to. I'll appoint Otis Greene to head the party. He'll do all the bargaining for us. We'll be in and out by noon tomorrow if all goes well. And you, Cap'n, will have to stay in the cabin while we're in port."

She lowered the glass in astonishment. "Why? Why can't I go with you?"

328

"Because you're a white woman. With your skin alone, you're worth your weight in gold. Add to that your hair." He put forth his hand to lift the skein of sun-gilded red. "And you'll have a prize than any slaver would be willing to pay hundreds of dollars for."

She looked mutinous. "I had hoped to go ashore in Africa."

"We're not going in for a sightseeing trip. Not in that hell, at any rate. Besides," he told her kindly, "Madagascar isn't so different from Africa."

She raised the glass again to her eye and stared as the *Cayuga* swept onward toward landfall.

Her silence did not satisfy him. He took the spyglass away from her eye. "Come farther out, Cap'n."

Together they walked to the bow and out of hearing of the men sprawled on deck. "Cap'n England, you mustn't think of doing anything foolish such as showing yourself. We're only a dozen. We wouldn't stand a chance of defending you. We'd be dead in a minute and you—" he shook his head, "you'd be worse than dead. You'd be a prisoner among people who don't even know about Jesus Christ, much less the Lord's commandments."

His faded blue eyes regarded her so solemnly that Fancy could not help but nod solemnly in return. "I promise, Lemuel."

He drew in a relieved breath. "Good. The minute that we get close enough to sight a human being through the glass, you go below."

"That soon."

"They've got spyglasses, too. Sailors have been trading here for centuries. That's why it's called the Ivory Coast. Farther on to the east is the Gold Coast and beyond that the Slave Coast."

She shivered. "Is that where Otis Greene's grand-

329

father came from?"

"He came from this side of the continent. You might ask him some time if you're of a mind to."

"Oh, I wouldn't dare."

"Never be scared by size, Cap'n. Otis is just a man."

The *Cayuga* dropped anchor in the river mouth. Even before the sails had been reefed in, the schooner was surrounded by black men in bumboats, clumsily maneuvering their crafts made from hollowed-out tree trunks and offering good for sale.

Fancy knelt behind leaded panes in the captain's cabin. Although the thick glass distorted her features, she had wound her braid around her head and stuffed it under a cap. Moreover, she was careful not to get too near the window, so that sharp eyes would detect a watcher. So much she did for Lemuel's sake, but her own natural curiosity would not allow her to forego staring at the shore line of Africa.

She watched as eight men, with big Otis Greene prominent in the bow of the boat, rowed away among the chattering natives. She had sought among her jewels for pieces of sufficient worth to be turned into capital. Lemuel had told her that fences for every kind of stolen booty made their headquarters behind the walls of the stockade that was Druwyn.

Once the jewels were turned into money, then bargains could be struck for provisions to be brought alongside. Arrangements could be made for the casks to be transported from the *Cayuga* to be filled from freshwater springs rather than from the river, which Lemuel contended was disease-laden.

At last, most of the bumboat men paddled away from the schooner, following the men in the boat. Wearily, Fancy stripped off everything except a simple cotton singlet and drawers, then collapsed back on the bunk. Her face and body were drenched in perspiration as the cabin temperature hovered near the one-hundred-degree mark.

She might have fallen asleep or even fainted, but when she knew herself again, the sun had moved down in the west. The cabin was hotter, if anything, than before, and the sounds coming from the deck above her head could only mean that the supplies were being loaded.

Even as she prayed that they would be away shortly and she could get out of the cabin, a muffled cry filtered through the heavy white oak door.

Another and then another brought her up and across the cabin. Mindful of Lemuel Jakes's stern warnings, she opened the door a crack.

In the dimness below deck, Johnny Wheatley struggled with a small naked black boy. At first Fancy thought that the sailor had caught a thief. She would have shut the door had the cry of fear and pain not come again. In any language, pain made the same sound.

It made her open the door wider. The sailor had hold of the boy around the waist, but instead of hustling him up the ladder and out of the cargo space, he forced the child to his knees.

Before her horrified eyes, the man unbuttoned his pants. She still could not fathom what he intended until he grabbed the back of the child's neck with one hand and ground his face to the deck. As the little buttocks were upended, the man went down on his knees.

"No!"

At her cry Wheatley froze, his flushed face darkened even more as malevolence contorted it. "Get the hell back in that cabin," he growled.

"Let that child go."

"Like hell I will. I paid for him."

"He couldn't have understood what you were paying him for."

"Lemuel Jakes told you to stay under cover," Wheatley sneered. "You'll get more than you bargained for if some of those black bucks see you."

"Let that child go, and I will."

"It's your fault. I seen you for so long I gotta have a little relief."

"There must be whores."

"Yeah. Poxy, the whole lot of 'em. Get back in that cabin and leave me be." He pressed himself down against the boy, who shrieked like a wounded animal.

Fancy could stand the sight no longer, and she dashed back into the cabin. Even as she pawed through the desk drawer, the boy screamed again. His scream ended in a gasping sob. At last she found the key to the small arms chest. Unlocking it, she snatched out one of the two pistols.

She was too late. As Fancy flung open the door of the captain's cabin and strode through, Wheatley climbed to his feet. His face wore a grin of ugly satisfaction as he hitched up his pants and buttoned the placket. The child lay curled on the floor, thin hands wrapped around his head, sobs racking his body.

"Swine!" she hissed.

Wheatley grinned them. "Best be goin' back in your hidey-hole before you end up in some slaver's caravan," he taunted.

"I'll see you punished for this," she swore.

"Not me, Cap'n England," he retorted sarcastically. "I paid this little pig and now I'm through with him." He nudged the child with his bare foot. "Up," he grunted.

The boy rolled over like a hurt dog, his legs and arms crossed over his soft underbelly. He did not look in

Fancy's direction. Instead, his dark hurt eyes followed where Wheatley pointed. Then, like an animal on all fours, the child scrambled away and crawled up the ladder.

Fancy gagged. "You're a monster," she whispered.

He flexed his heavy shoulders. "Mighty tough talk for a little gal alone."

She glanced upward, reassured by the sounds coming from the deck above. "I'm not alone."

Wheatley grinned mockingly. "Them're just niggers bringin' the stuff on board. Jakes and Greene are still over there greasin' palms. And I was just takin' a bit of time off. Course, if you're so concerned about brats, you could always—"

Fancy did not allow him to finish, as she thrust the pistol forward. "Get up and do your work, or you'll never move again."

Wheatley's grin flickered, then died. He stared at the pistol and then at her. The weapon never wavered, nor did her gaze. His own eyes seething with hatred, he backed toward the ladder. When he reached it, he turned and started to climb up into the bright sunlight.

Fancy lowered the barrel of the pistol as she moved after him toward the ladder.

Wheatley climbed, a black silhouette against the blinding white hot sky. And then he leaped.

She screamed as the weight of his heavy chest struck her head and his legs wrapped around her. Borne backward, she fell flat. Her buttocks struck the white oak deck, jarring her spine all the way to her brain. Then her shoulders hit and last the back of her head, with most of Wheatley's filthy odorous weight on top of her.

When the back of her head struck, bright streaks of color exploded across her vision. Stunned, unable to clench her fists, she sprawled, the pistol slipping from her grip.

Wheatley laughed as he sat back, his buttocks finding a rest somewhere around her waist, impeding her breathing. "That was sure stupid, gal. Stupid."

With deliberate violence, he ripped the top of her smock, baring her shoulders and breasts. She shrieked, but the sound was only a thin, high whimper. In delight, he bounced his buttocks at her waist, forcing the air out of her lungs. He seized her breasts, one in each filthy hand, and squeezed.

"Pretty flat, gal." He laughed, leaning forward until his face was less than a foot from her own. "I like my women with lots of meat on 'em. They can't get too fat for me if they've got big tits." He squeezed harder.

She shrieked again, the sound a little stronger, but he cut it off by covering her mouth. His fetid breath almost suffocated her and his beard scratched her horribly. Weakly, she beat at his shoulders, but her blows had no force.

"Keep on, gal, I ain't got me near enough. That little black pig didn't half take me off. I'll be up in no time."

"I'll kill you!" she gasped.

Thoroughly enjoying her helplessness, he bounced his buttocks against her stomach. His nails scratched her nipples. "Naw. You'll squeal for me just like he did." Cruelly, he pinched and twisted at her abused flesh.

"Bastard!" Tears flowed out of the corners of her eyes. She writhed in agony.

"Good, gal. Good. That feels good." This time Wheatley rotated his buttocks, pressing them hard against her soft middle. "Y'll have me up in no time." He leaned a little closer. "And then when I'm through, y'll roll over and crawl up that ladder just like the other little pig did."

She spat in his face at the same time she went for his

eyes with her nails. Cursing furiously, he slapped her as stipples of blood oozed from the shallow furrows. Then he laughed. "Not a little pig at all. A little cat. With claws." He sank his nails into her nipple.

With the strength of pain and desperation, she sucked air into her lungs and screamed. Instantly, one hard hand clutched her throat to cut off the sound.

Then, suddenly, he stiffened. Staring up at his hideous face through tears of pain, she watched his eyes glaze. His mouth gaped, and he slumped to one side.

A huge silhouette and then another blocked the sun. And then Lemuel Jakes was on one side of her, lifting her by the shoulder, and Otis Greene was putting his big bare foot against the side of Johnny Wheatley's body and pulling out the knife.

Hunter rolled his eyes toward the ceiling, praying for patience to end this embarrassing interlude. He was thoroughly sick of Jessica's sobbing.

"But she chose to go," she repeated for the tenth time. "Why must you follow her?"

"I've told you over and over. She's my wife. She's going into danger. She doesn't know what she's doing."

Jessica refused to be convinced. She pulled back away from him and looked up at him with drowned pansy-brown eyes. "She's keeping you from what you want to do," she mourned softly, her face a replica of martyred saints.

Instantly, Hunter stiffened, pushing away from her and shrugging his shoulders in an effort to adjust his disarranged garments. "She isn't," he denied. "I fully intend to resume my new enterprise as soon as she is brought home safe and sound. My God, Jessica! She is the mother of my son."

"Is that what you want?" She followed him and put

her arms around him from the back. "I can have a child for you, Hunter."

He took a deep breath. "What would your husband say, my dear? You do plan to return to him after all."

"But I don't have to."

He unclasped her hands from his midriff. "Then what is this all about? I thought you were eager to return to him and upset because I was not going to captain the *Carolina.*"

"Hunter!" The tears began to trickle again. "You are misunderstanding everything I say. You wanted me to leave my home in Charleston and come with you on your trip around the world. At the end of it, we were supposed to decide what we were going to do."

He sighed again. *Lord deliver men from the toils of women.* "Of course, my dear. And I still intend to. That's why I'm asking you to wait for me. Just wait here in Boston. I won't be long. Your every wish will be catered to. You won't have any expenses. Go out. Go shopping. I'll be only a few months."

"Months!"

"Weeks! Really weeks. I won't be long at all. You'll find things to do. My mother-in-law has a wonderful time every week at the Anthology Society meeting."

"Anthology? . . ." Jessica frowned. "I don't think . . ."

"Jessica . . ." He caught her hands. "If you'll just be patient, I promise I'll take you when I get this mess straightened out."

She smiled up at him then, a weak, watery little smile. "Kiss me, Hunter."

His heart melted then. She was so sweetly forgiving. Not at all like his wife. At the thought of Fancy, his jaw clenched.

"Oh, darling . . ." Jessica quickly brushed her fingers across the taut muscle. "Sweetheart, what is it?"

He smiled down at her. Catching her hand, he touched his lips to her palm. "Nothing. Nothing that concerns you at all." He drew her into his arms and kissed her tenderly and patiently.

She sighed into his mouth. "How long will you be gone?"

"Just a few weeks. If the winds are right, ten at the most."

"It will be such a long, long time."

"Yes. Too long." He pressed himself against her as his kiss deepened.

Chapter Twenty

"Tamatave," Holy Dulcibella breathed. With shining eyes, she drank in the sight of the cluster of primitive buildings pressed down by swathes of gray-green mist. Up the mountain behind them marched emerald-green trees growing so thickly together that they seemed all one.

Fancy looked at the town with frank disappointment. Like most seacoast towns in this area of the world, cannon bristled out of a primitive wooden stockade. Behind and around the fort and up the slope, she could see winding paths with grass-topped hovels lining them. But never in her life had she seen such a green forest. "What kinds of trees are those?"

"All kinds," Holy Dulcibella replied, eyes gleaming. "That is the jungle where the rain never ceases."

As if to punctuate her speech, lightning suddenly crackled out of a line of gray clouds hovering on the northern horizon. Distant thunder rolled as a warm, wet wind billowed the *Cayuga's* sails.

Lemuel Jakes came up behind the two women. "Ready to go ashore, Lady England." As both turned, he bowed low, making a leg in front of the black woman.

"Lemuel," she chided, glancing uncertainly at Fancy.

He shrugged unrepentantly. "'Tis time, m'lady, that she learns who you are."

Puzzled, Fancy looked from one to the other.

"Lemuel, please."

"Cap'n England," he addressed the younger woman. "May I present Holy Dulcibella, Lady England, widow of Edward, Lord England."

Fancy put her hand over her mouth. "My grandmother."

"I am your stepgrandmother," Holy Dulcibella hastened to add. "Lucilla was Richard's real mother."

"But my grandfather married you."

"Yes."

Fancy stood in silence. "I can't believe it."

"It's true all right," Lemuel Jakes insisted, his smile fading to solemnity. "I was a witness in the church in Tananarive the day they were married."

"My grandfather would not marry a slave."

Lemuel nodded. "He did not marry one. Instead, he married Holy Dulcibella of the house of Merina."

"I don't understand." She looked from one to the other, her face anguished.

Jakes shrugged. "When Great Edward came here, there was war among the families."

"There was always war among the families," Holy Dulcibella inserted.

"He stepped into it without knowing and became a prisoner of the—what were they?"

"Sakalava."

"Right. Of course, they couldn't hold him long. He made his escape with no trouble, and we burned the *kraal.*"

"What's a *kraal?*"

"The chief's stockade. A sort of a thornbush fort."

340

"The Sakalava were Swahili," Holy Dulcibella said contemptuously. "They had no thought but slaving and killing."

"Well, they got more than they bargained for that day," Jakes grinned. "So we broke into their slave pens and let everybody go. Except for a couple of scared young things." He looked significantly at the old woman.

"I was not afraid," she denied.

"You sure as hell looked like it."

"Perhaps just a little."

He smiled fondly then. "So it turns out these two little girls were more than just a couple of scared little girls. They were hostages to keep their father from attacking and wiping out the *kraal.*"

"They were nothing but a band of filthy slavers." The old woman's eyes were bright with indignation. Fancy stared at Holy Dulcibella as if she had never seen her before.

"So Edward gets big Otis Greene—not his grandson, you understand—to talk to them."

"Otis Greene was Watusi. We could speak together because many of the Merina peoples were Kaffir."

Lemuel Jakes was enjoying himself hugely and Fancy, despite her resentment, was alive with curiosity. "So Otis Greene finds out that these two little girls belong in the mountains to the west. In the kingdom of Merina."

"Our father's kingdom," Holy Dulcibella supplied.

"So somehow m'lady manages to convince Great Edward that it'd be to his advantage to take them home. Probably offered him a reward or something. Except by the time we got through climbing up into the mountain, Edward wasn't thinking about reward."

To Fancy's surprise, Holy Dulcibella smiled and tucked her head down.

"Anyway, by the time they get to Tananarive, they're holding hands and he's helping her over rocks and bringing her drinks and standing guard while she and her little sister sleep. When we get there, we get the royal treatment. The king has a celebration, gives gifts for the return of his daughters. We're all sitting pretty, lying around on divans and having pretty girls stuff us with dried fruits and nuts and other things." At this, he smiled wickedly at Holy Dulcibella.

"It is the custom," she murmured.

"And a charming custom it is. So, finally, it's time for us to leave and Edward's looking like he's going to his death, but he won't ask for you."

Fancy looked from one to the other incredulously. "He won't ask. Why not?"

"Figures he's a pirate and she's a king's daughter."

"But I do not care. One of my great grandfathers was a pirate," Holy Dulcibella declared.

Jakes laughed. "Probably more than one, m'lady."

"So when I saw that he would not speak, I spoke. We were married immediately in the church, and I came away with him."

"To America."

"A far distant land."

"My grandfather married a—a black woman." Fancy could not keep the horror from her voice.

Holy Dulcibella did not flinch. "I am Malay" was all she said.

Fancy faced the two of them, fists clenched, jaw set stubbornly. "I don't believe this. Something is not right here. If you were my grandfather's wife, why didn't you tell. You've lived as a servant for all these years after he died. You're a servant still." Fancy looked at Jake. "And you're a pirate."

"But I'm not a liar."

Unable to answer that, Fancy walked away, her ears

burning, her thoughts seething with what she had heard.

Holy Dulcibella stood straight as a statue. "Lemuel Jakes, you are a wicked man."

"She would have found out sooner or later."

"I do not think so."

He shrugged, his expression unrepentant. "You've bowed your head too long, my'lady."

The anchor splashed into the water and almost immediately thereafter, the boat was lowered from the davits.

Fancy went below for the copy she had made of the message from the jewel box. She had memorized it, having looked at it innumerable times in the weeks they had been under sail. *17° 15' 48° 15'* Just that and five circles, one with an extra line under it.

She tucked her hair up under her cap and donned her stockings and shoes. She was staring at the copy of the message when a knock at the door swung her around. Hastily, she jammed it into the pocket of her trousers. "Captain?"

"Coming, Lemuel."

She walked out proudly, her head up, expecting to lead the expedition with Lemuel Jakes at her shoulder. In some astonishment, she stared over the railing at the people in the bow of the boat. Otis Greene had taken his place first as if he owned the world.

Just behind him the resplendent figure of Holy Dulcibella caught and held her eye. Had Fancy not known that her former housekeeper, her maid, her confidant throughout her life, was seated in the boat, she would never have recognized her. Seated directly behind Otis Greene in the center of a single thwart, she fairly glittered in the sunlight.

The head was still erect, clothed in the gold silk turban with its gold glass ornament. The figure beneath, however, was no longer clad in sensible black. Instead, a sari of tissue of gold was wrapped around a dress of deep indigo. Behind her sat Beany, the cabin boy, holding a long-handled silk parasol across his knees, ready to raise it over her head when she should be lifted from the boat.

Face red with resentment, Fancy climbed down into the stern of the boat and sat among the men. Lemuel Jakes climbed down behind her and took the tiller. "Now, lads," he called, "row gently. It's the princess we're taking home."

Their passage through the town of Tamatave quickly took on the appearance of a royal progress.

At the first sight of Holy Dulcibella, a great humming began. The people began to gather, to point, and to chatter.

Fancy quickly realized they were pointing not so much at the magnificent figure that her former housekeeper cut as at her headdress.

"What's going on?" she whispered out of the side of her mouth to Lemuel Jakes as together they brought up the rear of the procession. "What are they pointing at?"

"The Second Sun."

Fancy frowned. "What? What is the Second Sun?"

Jakes grinned. "I forget you didn't want to hear the whole story. How do you think Lady England expected to identify herself after all these years? She couldn't just waltz in here and tell people she was a long lost princess of the house of Merina and expect them to believe her. So she's brought her identification with her."

"What, for heaven's sake?"

"That big yellow diamond that she wears in her turban."

Fancy stumbled so badly that she would have

pitched headfirst into the roadway had he not caught her arm. "That's a *diamond?*"

"Always has been."

"I thought it was glass."

Lemuel chuckled as he enjoyed the rich joke. "That's how she kept it safe. If she'd hidden it, someone might have found it. Servants don't have any privacy. So she hid the Second Sun right out in front of people all these years. So, of course, they never saw it. And you never saw it."

"You're right," Fancy admitted. "I saw it everyday. I just assumed it was a piece of glass."

"So did everyone else in America except her husband, your grandfather."

"He was my grandfather, but I'm sure he wasn't her husband. My grandfather would never—"

Lemuel whistled between his teeth. "You don't know what Great Edward was like. He never saw the color of a man's skin. All he saw was the worth of the person. You've been reared on that plantation among black slaves, and you've been taught to despise them and treat them like possessions. You're what your world made you. But your grandfather came from a world where a man could believe what he wanted to believe."

When Fancy would have said more, the procession in which she walked came to a halt. Down the streets from the highest house on the hill came a very black man. His bright green garments of fine cotton were draped around him and bound beneath his arms and at his waist with colorful sashes. A length of silk thrown over his shoulders was banded in gold tissue. Both ears were pierced by at least a half a dozen gold hoops beginning at the lobe and running up the side.

He, too, advanced beneath a wide green umbrella held by a young black man. Otis Greene stepped aside and made a low bow. The man stopped and, putting his hands with palms facing outward on either side of his head, bowed too. *"Andriana,"* he intoned. *"Andriana."*

Inclining her head slightly as befitted one of superior rank, Holy Dulcibella answered him in a flood of language Fancy had never heard before.

The old man bowed again, at the same time sweeping his arms back in a motion of welcome.

Otis Greene spoke then, his speech halting, carefully pronouncing one word at a time as he used a language he had never heard, much less spoken before.

The old man answered. Two young men immediately ran away up the hill and disappeared into the thick forest. A third one turned and strode away through the crowd.

"Might as well sit down," Lemuel Jakes informed Fancy. Suiting action to word, he dropped down in the brick-red street, knees pulled up, legs crossed at the ankle in front of him.

"But what's going on? Why are we just sitting around here?"

"This isn't Boston. It isn't even South Carolina. Things are a lot slower here."

"But in the hot sun? And it looks as though it's going to rain."

"That's what the umbrellas are for—for the important people."

"What did he call her?"

"Andriana?" Lemuel grinned as he pulled out a small square of sail and draped it over his bare head. *"Andriana,* as nearly as I can remember, means 'sovereign.'"

While Fancy gaped in astonishment, the old man clapped his hands, and a young black woman carried forward a chair made out of horns and cushioned with a colorful spotted hide. Setting it in the exact center of the road, she bowed with her hands out at shoulder height as the old man had done.

Acknowledging the seat with a gracious inclination of her head, Holy Dulcibella lowered herself into it. Grinning from ear to ear, Beany came forward to hold the umbrella above her head.

An hour passed and another. A heavy downpour, lasting only a matter of minutes, wet everything thoroughly. Instead of cooling everything off, however, it had the opposite effect. Sweat trickled down Fancy's back. Steamy heat rose out of the roadbed, blistering her bottom and the sides of her feet and ankles through her thin clothing.

At last, when she thought she would pass out, the rapid thud of bare feet jolted through her daze. Out of a side street ran eight young men. They moved rapidly and rhythmically in two columns. Between the two columns they carried a chair.

Heat exhaustion forgotten, Fancy sat up straight.

"Ah! A throne for the princess. Better begin to be impressed with your grandfather's choice, Cap'n," Lemuel Jakes warned snidely. "Great Edward's lady she was—and more."

"I can't believe this. It's like something out of the *Arabian Nights*," Fancy muttered.

"Not so far wrong," he continued inexorably. "The royal house of Merina is Malay. She's more eastern than African."

"How do you know so much?" Fancy gibed crossly.

"I didn't come with a set of prejudices built in," he replied. "And I was just a lad when I came here and saw it all. It impressed me like nothing in my life ever has since."

Fancy looked at him then, unable to doubt the sincerity she read in those faded blue eyes. He smiled

347

sadly at her. "You've got a lot of things to rise above, haven't you?"

At the head of the street, Holy Dulcibella was installed in royal state in the sedan chair. A cover of silk was stretched across the top of the frame and down the back. Then four of the young men picked it up together and began jogging up the hill. The other four fell in behind them, ready to take their places when the first four should tire.

Fancy and her crew had nothing to do but follow as best they might.

Three days later they entered Tananarive. Through the streets of a town of limestone rectangular buildings with straw roofs, they traveled and wound up and out still higher onto the plateau.

A forest of baobab loomed before them. Beside the trail on either side were heavy columns of limestone. Fancy stared at the top of them, then looked away, her face reddened with shock. Pairs of figures like large dolls surmounted each one. To a gently bred American lady, they were horrifying in the extreme. Both of the statues were naked. From one, the male member protruded grotesquely, while from the other protruded the female's obviously pregnant body.

"Lemuel," she whimpered.

"Nothing to be alarmed about," he panted. The crew, with the exception of Otis Greene, had fallen somewhat behind the procession, for the steamy heat enervated them all. "Those things are all over these mountains."

"They're awful."

"Just natural," he grinned.

Suddenly, more than two dozen men came jogging down the road toward them. At the sight of the long flint-topped spears, Fancy climbed to her feet. "What do they want?"

Lemuel shrugged. "We'll soon find out."

The leader went directly to Fancy and bowed, palms at shoulders. "You must come," he said in passable English.

Exhausted, bewildered, and not a little frightened, she would have backed away had not two others run forward and lifted her by her arms.

"Lemuel!" she cried.

"What's going on?" he demanded.

The leader bowed again. "The Sister Queen. The one who wears the Second Sun sent us for *raza.*"

"*Raza?*" Lemuel scratched his head. "*Raza!*" Suddenly, he put back his head and laughed.

"Lemuel," Fancy cried as she was pushed toward a small sedan chair, much less elegant but just as efficient as the one that had carried away Holy Dulcibella. "Lemuel, for God's sake, what's happening? Don't let them take me away from you."

"Go on, Cap'n," he chuckled. "You're *raza*. That means 'family.' You're the granddaughter of the Sister Queen." He was still laughing as Fancy was borne away.

King Radama I welcomed his aunt with great pleasure. She was a *fady,* a relic that would bring delight to his people. As the sister of his father, she represented his touch with the past.

The entire court bowed down before the magnificent Second Sun blazing in her turban. Older men rose and assured him that she was indeed his father's sister. Did she not bear a striking resemblance to Andriananmpoinimerina, his father? Her return was a signal from the gods to continue his efforts to unite all Malagasy.

349

"Sister Queen," he greeted her, palms upraised.

"Your Majesty." Holy Dulcibella bowed with her palms upraised also.

He stepped back and motioned to the men around him. "Forgive me. I had forgotten of your existence." At his gesture, courtiers stepped forward, one by one, to drape heavy silver chains around her neck.

As was her due, she accepted them. When a dozen had made their obeisance, she motioned Beany forward. The little boy stood like a small wooden statue to hold the rest of the chains. The ritual complete, she inclined her head. "You have no need to ask forgiveness. I accept your tribute out of love. But I had never intended to return. My life has been for more than half a century in another world."

"Still you are welcome, Sister Queen, my aunt."

Holy Dulcibella smiled graciously. "I would that you met my grandaughter, your niece."

"Is it possible?" His deep brown eyes lighted with pleasure. "You have brought more *raza.*"

"Yes, my nephew. But wait until you see her to decide whether you want to claim her. She is strange *raza.*"

And so Fancy was brought before King Radama I, seated on his throne of silver. "Put me down." Whether at her command or at the command of someone else, her porters did indeed set her down in the center of the court.

Embarrassed and uncomfortable, she climbed out of the chair. All around her were men and women strangely but beautifully dressed in silks draped like Grecian togas, their ears gleaming with gold hoops, silver chains ornamenting their necks.

She stood in their midst in sun-faded sailor's smock and trousers, a cap covering her hair, mud-spattered stockings and shoes on her feet. And suddenly, she was so tired she wanted to cry.

"My nephew, my king," Holy Dulcibella said, extending her hand, "may I present my granddaughter, your niece, your *raza*, Fancy England."

The king stared at her, a deep frown creasing his forehead. "She is very slender," he remarked uncertainly. "And she has no hair."

"She has covered her hair to protect herself from men," his aunt explained. "Maitresse, you may remove your cap. Here you are safe."

She might have been granting permission, but Fancy recognized that the permit was really a command. Hastily, she reached up and snatched off the cap. The thick red braid tumbled down.

Radama blinked. "The color . . ." he began hesitantly.

"Her grandfather's legacy," Holy Dulcibella reminded him.

"Ah, yes. The *Tantara* speaks of the man with hair the color of the earth."

Fancy swayed where she stood. Instead of being in a position of superiority, which she had somehow expected, she found herself little more than a curiosity in the eyes of the court.

"You must eat and rest," Radama said. He clapped his hands.

Two young women came forward and presented themselves before him. He spoke to them rapidly. They bowed, then turned to Fancy. With motions, they indicated that she was to follow them.

Terrified, she looked toward Holy Dulcibella. "Go with them, my granddaughter. They will show you every hospitality."

Fancy was led away to a small room bare of furniture

except for a chair and small low table. When she was seated, one of the two women brought in a tray of food, set in on the table, and left. Beef and rice, a selection of strange fruits, and a cup of thick coffee were the sum total of the fare. The room in which they had placed the tray was windowless and lighted only by a tiny kerosene lamp.

Nervously, Fancy began to eat. But with every bite, her fear that she had been imprisoned grew. What would become of her crew if she had been taken captive? The eleven brave men who had signed on the *Cayuga* were in danger if she was in danger.

She tried to swallow, but the food stuck in her throat. Had she led them into danger? Massaging her temples with both hands, she tried to still her fears. Surely, Dulci—her Dulci—wouldn't let her be imprisoned. But Dulci was different. Suddenly, she was no longer a housekeeper, but the wife of Fancy's own grandfather and the aunt of a king.

When a knock finally sounded, she realized she had been sitting staring at nothing. Wearily, she pulled herself to her feet and opened the door.

"You are finished?" the woman asked in accented English.

"Yes."

"Good." While one covered the remains of the food and took the tray away, the other said, "You will come now and bathe. Then you will feel better. The Sister Queen has said that you are to have audience with the *Andriana* when you are prepared."

Fancy followed her to a large room with huge rectangular windows overlooking the forest of baobabs. To her surprise, it was beautifully appointed with different styles of furniture. A magnificently carved Spanish bed heavily covered with gold leaf dominated the room. In a small alcove discreetly partitioned off by

352

an Oriental screen was a French enamel slipper bath. Kashmiri carpet of finest silk and wool brushed her bare feet. "I don't understand," she whispered.

The girl bowed deeply, obviously upset. "You are displeased?"

"It's so beautiful. Why was I taken to that prison cell to eat?"

The girl shook her head in astonishment. "But that was not a cell. A member of the *raza* must always have the proper respect. You must always have total privacy when you eat. The *Andriana* has commanded that you be entertained even as he and his aunt are treated."

"Oh, of course," Fancy murmured hastily. "I just didn't understand the custom."

The girl smiled in relief. "Please ask if you do not understand. We are to serve you as we serve the *Andriana*. Now your bath is waiting."

"You speak English very well," Fancy complimented her as she stripped off the soiled, frayed smock and trousers.

The woman smiled shyly. "Many of us here learn English as well as French, so Merina may trade with merchants that pass through by our island in their tall ships."

Relaxing in the cool bath, Fancy was sure she could have gone to sleep had not the two plied her with questions about the ocean and America. "Malagasy is not a primitive country," the one insisted. "Europeans and Americans have traded with us for three hundred years."

Their words reassured Fancy that her men were being taken care of. Still, she recognized faint niggling thoughts of when they could get on their way to finding the treasure.

At last, wrapped in a long muslin towel, she sat before a silver-backed mirror to have her hair dried and

353

brushed until it shone and stood out around her head and shoulders like a cape. Then one of the women brought a pale blue dress and a rose silk sari, edged with gold tissue. "For the *raza* of the king."

So she walked into audience chamber, head held high, to receive the courtesy and deference such a position carried.

Chapter Twenty-One

A drop of blood beaded the point of Fernando del Cabo's dagger, but the Sakalava's face betrayed no emotion. "Don't try to hold me up for more, you black pig," the Portuguese gritted. "You tell me what you have to tell. Then I decide how much it's worth."

"You kill me, you never know what I have to tell." The thick lips barely moved. Except for a long sash wrapped round his loins and knotted below his navel, the man was naked. His belly caved in below his lean ribs. His knees were knobby, and every muscle of his thighs and calves stood out with almost painful definition.

"Speak up, damn you." Del Cabo jabbed the point a little deeper.

"American ship come Tamatave."

The Portuguese eased the dagger away from the man's throat. "That's more like it. What about this American ship?"

The Sakalava hastily stepped out of reach before he held up two fingers. "Two pieces of silver," he demanded.

Del Cabo cursed the man and his ancestry, consigning them all to hell as he dragged the two coins out of his purse.

Grinning faintly at the threatening speech, the spy knotted them into the corner of sash about his loins. "American ship bring *raza* of Radama."

"So? That's all you have to say. And you think that's worth two *cuatro reales*. You're crazy! I'll cut your black throat." Del Cabo started forward. The Sakalava did not give ground. "One is Sister Queen of Radama. She wears the Second Sun."

"The Second Sun?" The mention of the fabled diamond brought del Cabo up short. His eyebrows shot up. He shook his hoary head. "Who wears the Second Sun?"

"The Sister Queen of Radama. She had returned from across the sea. Her name is Holy Dulcibella, Lady England. With her comes her granddaughter."

"Lady England, did you say?" del Cabo whistled through stained and broken teeth. Memories stirred, tales of the old days of Madagascar when Dutch flutes lumbered through the Mozambique Channel and a man with a fast sloop could make a fortune. In those days, the names of pirates had been on everyone's lips. Names like Tews and Teach, Bartholomew Roberts and Calico Jack Rackham—and the gentleman pirate Edward England. He had thought them all long dead violently—in storm, in skirmish, and at the hands of the king's justice. "You sure? You wouldn't be lyin', would you?"

"Why lie?"

Del Cabo stared significantly at the knot in the spy's sash but did not comment. "Where'd she come from?" he demanded.

"America," the spy replied complacently.

"North or South?"

The spy shrugged. "Who knows? They come here now."

"Most of 'em end up in South America," del Cabo remarked.

While the pirate stared at the floor, his forehead wrinkled, his mouth twitching, the spy folded his arms. A slender line of blood that had oozed a couple of inches down the side of his throat began to dry, but he made no move to wipe it away.

For several moments del Cabo stood rapt. At last he spoke. "So they've come back. I don't give a damn if they've come back just for the hell of it. They can sail off the edge of the world for all I care. But if they've come for something more, I wanta know what. You go find out what they've come for."

"They go to Radama."

"No news there. Where else would they go?" Del Cabo threw the man a disgusted look.

Again the spy was silent, waiting.

Del Cabo looked speculative. "I've heard lots of tales of the old days. Tales of treasure. Lots of tales. Lots of treasures."

The Sakalava shrugged. "For another silver piece I would go to Tananarive. Listen. Learn. And return."

"Damn thieving pig. You go and listen and learn, and then I'll pay you."

The spy folded his arms across his chest but did not move.

"Damn your whoreson hide!" Del Cabo exploded into another round of invective. When it was over, he pulled another silver coin from his purse and flipped it at the man. The Sakalava caught it in midair, turned silently, and left.

"Edward England's wife," del Cabo mused. He ran his hand absently over the sheath that held his dagger.

"Maitresse, Radama is the *Andriana*. Thank the

good God he has been pleased to recognize me and you and offer us his hospitality. You must be a little patient." Holy Dulcibella clasped her hands together. Her mouth was set in an effort to conceal her irritation.

Fancy shook her head stubbornly. "I've got to get that treasure and get out of here as soon as possible."

The old woman's face twisted in pain. "You are angry to be around me," she said softly.

Fancy refused to meet her eyes. "Of course not," she denied too heartily. "You're forgetting that I came here in the first place in desperation to save England's Fancy. I can't sit around and have my hair brushed while my home and my people are in jeopardy."

"I am sure Radama will provide an expedition," Holy Dulcibella began. "But to hurry away when we have only just arrived would be insulting."

Fancy looked out the windows into the grove of baobab. "You need not come with me, you know."

The old woman hunched her shoulders as if she had been struck a blow. Pain contorted her face. When she spoke, her voice was raspy. "You—you no longer want me."

Fancy could not think of what to say. The silence extended between them.

Holy Dulcibella released her breath in a long sigh, then drew herself up proudly. "Very well then, I shall speak to Radama tomorrow." The silken garments swished softly as she left the room.

Fancy bit her lip. A bright flush rose in her cheeks as she clasped her arms tightly around her body. She should call after Holy Dulcibella. She should apologize. Only by virtue of her presence had Fancy been treated with every courtesy in the Merina court.

Nevertheless, she was furious at the idea that a black woman—a servant—claimed to be her grandmother— admittedly, stepgrandmother. If word of this relationship ever reached Charleston, or worse, Boston, the reputation of the family was doomed.

Fancy shuddered. Perhaps it would be best for all if Holy Dulcibella stayed here in the court of Radama rather than returned to America. She was an old woman anyway. She probably would not be able to survive the long journey home.

Even as she thought those thoughts, Fancy felt her resentment mix with shame.

Later in the afternoon, she walked alone among the tall smooth-barked baobabs. Lemuel Jakes came striding toward her. "You're coming with me, Mistress Gillard," he announced without preliminaries.

She misread his haste. "Are we leaving?"

"Leaving? Aye, we're leaving. We're going down to the church of Nossa Senhora da Cunha in Tananarive."

"Why? . . ." Then the reason dawned upon her. "Oh, no!" Like a recalicitrant child, she pulled back against his arm, digging her heels into the soft red earth on the forest floor.

He swung round to face her. Gone was the affable old man with the faded blue eyes who had been tutor, mentor, and father for the past months. The affability had been replaced by anger and contempt. "Oh, yes, Mistress Gillard."

"Don't call me that!"

"Why not? You're acting like Mistress Gillard, the spoiled useless wife of a half-hearted planter from South Carolina. She never had a thought beyond her own little hole in the world."

"That's not true."

"The hell it's not. Lady England said you were pampered, but I figured you could learn. You were doing right well on the trip here. I was proud as punch of you. Then you disappoint me like this and I find out I'm wrong. When I found your grandmother just now, do you know what she was doing? She was crying. She ought to be happy as a bird. And she was crying." His face worked. Angrily he mopped at his own eyes. "I've never seen her cry. And I've seen her through worse things than this."

"Lemuel." Fancy caught at him with both hands and tried to stop him. "Please. Let's not stay here any longer. Let's just get the treasure and leave."

"Always supposin' there is a treasure," he jeered. "If not, then what? Even if you find it, you'll have lost everything because you'll have lost the one person in the world that loves you—your grandmother."

Fancy swallowed hard. "She's not—"

His calloused hand manacled her wrist. "Don't say any more. Just come with me and keep your mouth shut. You're going to see the truth in the priest's own handwriting and your grandfather's. And then you're going to beg pardon of one of the finest ladies who ever lived."

"She is not my grandfather's widow."

"You'll soon find out," he growled.

The candles and incense could not altogether conceal the odor of mold from inside the church. Fancy wrinkled her nose but said nothing. She had stopped pulling back and now waited docilely while Lemuel spoke to the priest.

At last, the cleric in black robes nodded. "Come this way," he said in French.

Behind the altar, he pulled two huge leather-bound books from a huge chest. "Did the marriage take place between a Malagasy and a European?"

"Yes, an Englishman."

"And the date?"

Lemuel scratched his head. "Seventeen fifty-two or fifty-three. I disremember when. Long about Christmas time."

The cleric carried the smaller of the two books into an antechamber. "You must look then. I will leave you."

"No. Wait." The old sailor shuffled his feet. "Can't you look it up for us. I mean—"

The priest shook his head. "I have a call. Another minute and you would have missed me. I must go. You are welcome to search so long as you need or want." With a polite bow, he was gone.

Lemuel looked helplessly at Fancy.

"Well," she said sarcastically, "go ahead. I'm waiting."

"I can't," he muttered.

"Can't what?"

"Can't read."

Her mouth dropped open. "But you can read the maps. You write."

"The maps are pictures," he said desperately. "I can write my name. I can write my numbers. But the rest of it, I never learned."

"Then let's go."

"No." He caught her arm. "Damn it all—beg pardon—you can't turn away from this."

She shook his arm off. "I can," she declared flatly.

He clenched his jaw, the faded blue eyes sparking flames. "If you don't look up the names, I'll not take another step to find that treasure."

Toe to toe, they faced each other. Fancy's anger was a palpable thing. "How could you?"

"Easy."

"You really are a pirate."

"Now you're getting the picture. And in one of those books you'll see the proof of a pirate's marriage." He pointed to the dusty volumes. "Get on with it."

Fancy folded her arms. "I believe you," she said sullenly.

He looked at her through slitted eyes. "No, you don't. Not until you see it in black and white. And then you're going to commit this little bit to memory." He took her by the shoulder, not ungently but firmly, and led her to the slanted refectory table.

Reluctantly, she opened the volume.

She had only to turn a few pages before she came across the entry. *"Edward Fitzjohn, Lord England et Holy Dulcibella, 5th Decembre, anno domine 1752."* The ink had faded to a soft brown, but it was thoroughly legible.

Lemuel Jakes bent over the pages, squinting and sighting as best his old eyes could. Then he turned to face her.

Tears glistened in her eyes. Angrily, she wiped one away with the tips of her fingers before it could brim over. "So, she's my grandmother."

"Yes." When she remained stubbornly silent, he threw up his hands. "Oh, she's your grandmother, all right . . . if you're stupid enough to want to make that distinction."

"She's a servant."

He took her by the shoulders. "No, she's been pretending to be a servant to spare you and your father embarrassment. But what do you bet your mother knew?"

Fancy's head tilted back. Her eyes widened. "My mother?"

"From what you've said, she couldn't wait to get as far away from England's Fancy as possible. And she didn't exactly welcome the two of you with open arms in Boston."

"No . . . No, she didn't," she quavered. "In fact, she made some snide comment to Dulci." Suddenly, a whole host of things began to fall into place. Richard England's continual deferring to Holy Dulcibella. The separate quarters from the other servants. The clothing somber, yet made out of the very finest materials. Her mother's antipathy. The older servants' awe and respect. "Did everyone know but me?"

Lemuel Jakes shook his head. "I doubt it. Probably a few knew, a few more suspected, a lot forgot. It's not important."

"Not important?"

He put his arms around her shoulders and led her out into the sanctuary. "The only thing important about it is that while your grandfather was a bloody pirate with a price on his head, your grandmother is the aunt of a king. You have to decide who you're going to be proud of."

The churchyard was silent, the small undressed gravestones peeking their heads above the tall green grass. Fancy could feel her shame ebbing away. "When you put it that way, I don't really have much of a choice, do I?" she whispered.

He nodded his head. "Just don't hurt her any more. If it pleases you to forget when you go back to America, then you can and none of us will ever tell. But don't hurt her any more while you're here."

Impulsively, she threw her arms around his chest and hugged him hard. "You're so kind."

He chuckled as he patted her back awkwardly. "Me! I'm a bloodthirsty pirate."

*   *   *

363

Under full sail, the brigantine *Cassandra* swept into the channel between Isle Ste. Marie and the coast of Madagascar.

Hunter trained his spyglass on Baldridge's immense castle on the hill overlooking the harbor. "So that's the stronghold," he mused.

The mate at his side nodded. "One of 'em, at least. But it's not the only one by a long shot."

"But it's the oldest."

"Maybe." The man spat laconically over the railing.

Hunter lowered the glass. "Well, is it or isn't it?"

"It may be the oldest, but it's deserted. Most ships don't come around the back of Madagascar. They go through the Mozambique Channel on the western side. There's fresh water at Johanna Island. That's why pirates have taken over the town of Diego Soarez, so they can sail out quick and catch 'em sailing out. We oughta be on the western side."

"Nevertheless, we'll circle this island first. If we find nothing, we'll head on into Ranter Bay. I'm convinced that's where we'll find what we're looking for. The man who ran the pirate operations in Ranter Bay had a wife named Holy Eleanora."

The first mate chewed his tobacco reflectively. "Don't know nothin' about that."

"I have it on the best authority. And one of the women we're here to find is named Holy Dulcibella."

"We'd take a prize on the west coast," the mate grumbled. "Most likely two or three."

"We're not after just any prize. Our first objective is the *Cayuga*."

Without sighting a ship nor any sign of life, the *Cassandra* made a sweep around the island.

"I tell you, we're in the wrong place," the mate reiterated.

Wishing the man in Jericho, Hunter stamped below. Pouring himself a tot of brandy, he bent over his chart to study the bays and inlets. To the north lay Ranter Bay, the Baye d'Antongil of the old pirate maps. It would be his next stop. And he was almost certain that she would be there.

The clue came from a set of journals recounting the history of piracy in the eighteenth century. John Plantain, a man who traded with pirates and fenced their stolen goods in the previous century, had built a headquarters at Ranter Bay. Hunter had been sure that it had been Fancy's destination in the *Cayuga,* when he had read that Plantain's wife had been named Holy Eleanora because she could recite the Lord's Prayer, the Creed, and the Ten Commandments. He would bet his life that she was the kin, perhaps even the mother of his wife's servant.

When he found them . . . When he found Caroline, he had fantasized what he would do to her. For a month, his anger at her desertion had fueled him. He had planned to bind her hand and foot, throw her over his shoulder, and carry her aboard. He would take her directly to the storage closet aft and imprison her.

After a suitable number of hours, when she was thoroughly thirsty and hungry and frightened, he would have her brought to him. She would be trembling, weeping, begging for mercy. Sometimes she would still have her hands bound behind her. Sometimes not. But either way, she would sink to her knees and beg him to forgive her, to be merciful.

He would chastise her, of course. Not physically. But he would tell her, in no uncertain terms, that he would not tolerate her unwomanlike behavior any longer. She would behave as a proper wife. None of this nonsense about running off to Madagascar.

He ran his hand through his long black hair. It had not been cut in several months and hung well below the collar of his white cotton shirt. A sprinkling of gray showed at the temples. Lines incised deeply at the corners of his mouth.

He would not give in to her pleas until she told him why she had come to Madagascar. Why in the name of all that was holy had she come to this, the most god forsaken place in the seven seas? Steaming hot it was. Disease-ridden. Infested with brigands of every race and nationality, if the stories he had heard and read were true.

When she fell to her knees, he would not be moved— immediately. He would not tell her that he intended to let her return to England's Fancy. No, he would let her worry about that for a while. It would serve her right. Then when she asked him nicely on bended knee, he would grant her request. And she could thank him properly. She would come up off her knees sweetly into his arms. She would press her golden body against his. The long red hair would be down around her shoulders, and he would bury his hands in it and tilt her face back. . . .

A flash of lightning brightened the cabin. Thunder boomed malevolently. He felt the *Cassandra* lunge to the side as the storm wind struck the sails. With a sigh, he caught up the spyglass and climbed back to the deck. The heavy warm rain struck his face. In front of the wheelbox, he gave the order for the brigantine to head north. His next port would be Ranter Bay. He was sure he would find Fancy there.

His reconnoitering of the waters around Isle Ste. Marie had reassured him that the place was all but deserted. Except for the fortress on the hill, it might never have seen the hand of civilized man. Jungle growth rose from the red sands of the beach. Dimly, through the rain and mist, he could see a few hovels clustered together at the foot of the hill below the fortress.

Under full sail, the *Cassandra* moved up the coast. At the mouth of Ranter Bay, he dropped anchor in a torrential downpour. Still he was cautious. The crew stood on alert, the eight six-pounders bristling. Ranter Bay was a tight, confined area. He would not run the risk of an encounter with a hostile ship in such close quarters, where luck might make him lose.

"Ma'am, a Mrs. Rutledge asks to see you. She says it is urgent."

Blanche froze. The silk thread, wound thrice around her needle for the French knot, slipped from the point. Without bothering to recover it, she pushed the needle into the ecru linen and laid the embroidery aside. "I'll see her in the drawing room, Canham."

"Very good, ma'am."

So as not to appear overly anxious, Blanche thoroughly checked her appearance in the cheval glass, then changed her white linen collar and cuffs for a set of lace ones. At last, when she was assured that her appearance was unexceptionable, and that she had kept her caller waiting long enough to work herself into a nervous state, she descended the stairs.

With her light brown hair, blue eyes, and regular features, Jessical Rutledge was exactly what Blanche had expected. Pretty and submissive, Blanche guessed her to be, with just the right air of helpless fragility to appeal to a man like Hunter, who fancied himself of a heroic mold.

"Mrs. Rutledge," Blanche addressed her coldly.

"Mrs. Shepperton." Jessica rose carefully.

Blanche's eyes widened. "Mrs. Rutledge." Her voice rose on the final syllable.

The woman pressed her gloved hand to her abdomen. She started to speak, swallowed painfully, then finally brought out the words. "I don't know what to do."

Blanche cleared her throat as she felt heat rise in her cheeks. "I can assume then that—that the baby is my son-in-law's."

"Y—yes. Can you tell me when he'll be back?"

Blanche shook her head, at the same time motioning the young woman back to her chair. "I have no idea."

A snubbing sob escaped Jessica as she bent her head to fumble for her handkerchief. "He's gone to bring her back, hasn't he?" Jessica's voice was desperate and at the same time accusatory, as if all this were somehow Blanche's fault.

Fancy's mother stiffened. "Of course, you foolish woman. How could you think he would leave his wife permanently?"

The frail shoulders slumped. "But she didn't love him. He told me so."

"What else would you expect him to say to you? I have this wife who loves me to distraction, but I want to play with someone else for a while."

Jessica uttered a low wail and covered her ears with her hands.

Blanche took a deep breath and raised her voice. "She loves him to distraction. For myself, I think she must be exhausted much of the time from the strength of her emotions."

"But . . . she only wanted him to farm her land," Jessica whispered.

"She has been farming her land herself since he left

368

her. She has found that she doesn't need him for that reason at all."

"But he told me . . ."

"And, of course, you believed him. What do you suppose he told my daughter about you? If he would lie to her, his wife of ten years and the mother of his son, surely you must realize that he would lie to you."

Jessica clutched her arms tightly about her and rocked back and forth. Her despairing tears gradually ceased.

When she finally fell silent, Blanche spoke as calmly as possible. "What do you want to do?"

"What can I do?" Jessica rasped.

"My daughter told me you were married. That you had a husband in England. Can you return to him?"

The question started a new round of tears, which lasted of much shorter duration. "Not as I am," Jessica gulped.

The silence grew in the room. Blanche clenched her hands over the arms of the chair. A shocking idea was taking shape in her brain. "Perhaps after the baby is born?" she began tentatively.

"He'd never accept another man's child."

"What if . . . you left the baby here?"

"Here? Leave my own child in America and return to England?" Wide-eyed, Jessica began to shake her head. "I could never do that. Never. Never. My own baby."

"But you can have other babies," Blanche pointed out reasonably.

"No. Oh, no. Never."

Blanche stared at her silently, then drew herself up haughtily. "What do you intend to do here in Boston, Mrs. Rutledge?"

Jessica's defiance collapsed. "I don't know. I can't

think. I was so hoping you would know when Hunter will return."

Blanche looked toward the window. The garden looked particularly bleak with the trees denuded of their leaves. "He might never return," she sighed coldly. "I shouldn't be surprised if when he finds my daughter, they return immediately to South Carolina."

The younger woman sank back against the chair, her eyes closed. "What am I going to do?"

"You must do whatever you think best," Blanche paused, "for everyone."

Jessica's mouth quivered. "What would happen to my baby?" she whispered at last.

"I would take care of it," Blanche answered quickly. As she uttered the fatal words, she could feel cold sweat pop out on her forehead. She took a deep breath. "I would be responsible for its care. I and my husband." She almost choked over the word.

"You! Why?"

"For the sake of my daughter's marriage," Blanche replied cryptically.

"I'll have to think about this."

Blanche nodded. "I think that you should."

Jessica rose carefully, pulling the folds of her cape around her for maximum concealment.

Blanche rose, too, to walk beside her.

At the door, Jessica paused. "Are you sure that you have no idea when he'll be returning?"

The older woman tightened her lips. "You can check with the shipping lines if you do not believe me."

Jessica shook her head. "No, I believe you. He never really meant to divorce her, anyway. He—he was just—"

For the first time, Blanche allowed her hand to touch

the younger woman's shoulder. "He was just restless. And you were there."

When the door closed behind Jessica, Blanche turned back into the room, her whole body trembling. What had she done? What would her husband say? She had her own life, secure, tranquil, contented. Damn Hunter! Damn him and damn Fancy for being so stubborn.

Just like her father! Unbidden came the image of Richard England, red-haired, golden-eyed, laughing. She shivered.

Canham interrupted her thoughts. "May I bring you some tea, ma'am?"

She started, thankful to be torn out of her painful reverie. "Thank you, yes. I'll have it upstairs."

"So, my niece, my aunt tells me you have a special request."

"Your Majesty, your kindness is too great. I have already stayed here as your guest for a week." Fancy smiled at the lean, ascetic face of Holy Dulcibella's nephew. The family characteristics bred true. Or perhaps the dignity inherent in them both made them look and sound so much alike.

Her approach to the throne had been marked by open stares. The contrast she herself made to the rest of the court was so startling that she could do nothing discreetly. She wore a green silk sari wrapped and draped over a long dress of unbleached cotton. The effect was very pretty, but many women wore more beautiful ensembles. Her hair made the difference. Like rippling waves of copper, it hung soft as silk to well below her waist in back.

All around them members of the court loitered and gossiped. The audience was private and of a family nature. No one appeared to listen, yet no one standing near could help but overhear. Radama's voice was deep. He was somewhat uncomfortable with English, so he chose his words with great care, pronouncing each one with great distinction.

"You have brought the Sister Queen back for a long overdue visit. Your wish is my command."

Fancy cleared her throat and took a deep breath. "I have come for that which is mine. . . . And only mine," she hastened to add.

"Then it shall be given to you, if it is in my power. You have only to ask."

"My grandfather, the *husband* of your Sister Queen"—she emphasized the word for Holy Dulcibella's benefit—"buried some of his wealth on this island before he left with your aunt for America." Fancy watched Radama's face closely, convinced that if he had found the treasure and used it for his own, his face would betray him.

But he showed nothing. Nothing at all. Only pleasant interest and concern shone from his dark brown eyes. "Do you know where?"

She hesitated. Suddenly, the members of the court seemed inordinately quiet. The very walls might have ears. Could a stranger, perhaps a thief, be listening behind the jalousied windows? Who might be waiting outside the door for an audience? "I—I—" She took a deep breath. "I have a map. Not exactly a map. Just a pair of latitude and longitude figures and a drawing."

"What you seek might not be there after so many years. It might have been found by someone else," Radama pointed out reasonably.

"I know this."

"Yet you have come halfway round the world for it. The journey is long and arduous. It has remained hidden for more than half a century. Why do you come now?"

Again she hesitated. If this man were like the others, he would dismiss her cause as impossible for a woman to attain. "My people depend upon me," she said at last.

Radama glanced at his aunt, who sat silent and impassive watching her granddaughter. "Are they not your people too, Sister Queen?"

The old woman inclined her head. "In a sense they are. Yet as the wife of Great Edward, I was not responsible for his people. In America, the wife is the treasure to be guarded as much as the land."

"I do not see." Radama looked questioningly at Fancy.

"The son of Great Edward. Praise God, the boy Richard grew to beautiful, healthy manhood. When Edward England died, Richard England took his lands."

"And this Richard had no children?" Radama guessed.

"He had no sons. I am his daughter."

"Then he had a daughter. I do not see the problem. How long has Richard been dead?"

"Ten years—almost eleven."

"And you have ruled his land as *Andriana?*"

Fancy braced herself. Should she lie? She decided against it. "I have not ruled the land until this last year. I married and my husband ruled for me. I have a son who will some day rule."

"Then what? . . ."

"My husband deserted me. But I came immediately to ruling in my own right." She smiled at Holy Dulcibella. "I did not do badly. My grandmother was guiding me."

The old woman's stiff posture broke. She dropped her eyes to her hands, clasped tightly in her lap to still her trembling.

Fancy felt tears prick at the backs of her own eyes. "But a hurricane came. A gigantic storm that killed many of my people, wiped out most of my buildings, and destroyed my tobacco."

"You grew tobacco?"

"And rice."

Radama smiled. "Then you are a farmer like me. I grow rice and cloves. You need have no fear. I will give you the wealth you require. You have brought my Sister Queen, my *raza,* who is also my *fady.* You do not need to go on an arduous journey. I will give you silver chains."

Fancy clasped her hands. "My uncle, I thank you from the bottom of my heart. I would accept with pleasure, if the wealth were for me alone. But I have brought with me eleven men. They are friends and sons of friends of Great Edward. I have promised them their share in return for their taking me. Before this voyage, I did not know how to sail a ship."

Radama smiled, his austere face suddenly quite beautiful. "I admire you. You are a woman with great responsibilities. But that is not surprising. The *raza* are born for this. Is it not so, Sister Queen?"

Holy Dulcibella nodded proudly. "Praise God, who gives them the strength to carry their burdens with dignity and grace." Her eyes sparkled with tears as she stared at Fancy.

Radama resumed the posture of a king on his throne. "We shall outfit an expedition to escort our niece to find her treasure. She shall have the royal protection of the house of Merina, as is her due as *raza.*"

Fancy could not help but think of Lemuel Jakes as

374

she accepted the aid. Members of the court bowed to her, despite her white skin. A king gladly accepted her as his niece, although she was of a different race. And the odd thing about the whole experience was that she found herself proud to be *raza* with the house of Merina.

Chapter Twenty-Two

"Three silver pieces," the Sakalava demanded.

"Goddamn you!" del Cabo cursed flatly. Black eyes glittering, he stared malevolently at the skeletal black man. He licked his lips. "You've got something that's worth plenty and you know it."

The spy permitted his lips to move in a faint smirk.

"And you want three silver pieces."

The man did not move.

Cursing again, del Cabo pulled his leather purse from inside his pants. Shaking three *cuatro reales* out into his hand, he weighed them before slapping them down on the table in front of him. "Here, damn you. It better be good."

"Radama send men with granddaughter of Sister Queen, she who wears the Second Sun."

"Ah-ha!"

"There is a treasure. The location is directions—latitude and longitude"—he pronounced the words very carefully—"and a drawing. The granddaughter knows."

"Now why would a granddaughter know and not the grandmother?"

The spy shrugged. "The granddaughter is blood of

the pirate," he supplied as if that explained it all. "More. She is *volamena*."

"*Volamena*. Red silver?"

The spy nodded, his icy impassivity thawing slightly. "Hair red, long." He made motions with his hands in an effort to describe the length.

"So, he left the directions to the treasure to his granddaughter rather than his wife." Del Cabo shrugged, losing interest. Any reasons that the Sakalava might have invented around the red hair were just so much superstition. "Who cares? But the treasure of Edward England . . . Now that'd be a prize worth taking."

"It will be very hard. The *Andriana* sends many men to help his Sister Queen."

"Damn. I'll have to think about this. When do they leave?"

"They had not said when I came to you."

"Then get back there and find out."

"One silver piece."

"Hell, no. That ain't hard to find out at all. You can just stand around in a whorehouse and get that information."

"Silver piece to pay whore," the man insisted.

"Damned thief!"

The spy left with his *cuatro real,* and del Cabo remained seated at the table. Wearily, he wiped his hand across the bottom of his face. The good old days were just about over. It he could lay his hands on just one good prize, he would quit the bloody business.

Now that the war with America was over, the British fleet was harrying the west coast of Madagascar, escorting their merchant ships in and out from the Comoros and Joanna Island in particular. Moreover, the last ship he had taken had been a disappointment. Cinnamon and cloves. Hell, what was he going to do with spices? It took too long to turn that kind of cargo into money. And then the fences took more than half.

He rose, cursing his stiff leg. When it rained now, he could barely walk. A piece of shrapnel had done severe damage to his thigh, but the clumsy fool who had cut it out had done more. Del Cabo grimaced at the thought of the great bloody hole left in the muscle. It had never healed over. After all was said and done, it might have been better to have let the fool go ahead and cut it off. Except then he'd probably have bled to death.

One more prize. The treasure of Edward England. Damn! He poured himself a stiff tot of rum, downed it, and ran his hand through his gray locks. The treasure of Edward England.

"Captain del Cabo! Captain del Cabo!"

He turned sourly.

"Ship in the bay! Ship in the bay!"

"Hell!" Del Cabo limped up the steps to the top of his house. Throwing open the shutters at the end of the gable, he sighted through the spyglass mounted on a tripod for the purpose. "A Yankee brigantine."

The rain was too heavy for him to pick up many of the details, but for sure the *Cassandra* was not a merchant ship. "What in hell does she want?"

"A couple of ships in the harbor, but neither one is the *Cayuga*, Captain Gillard," the mate informed him. "Guessed wrong again."

"She could have hidden her somewhere in another bay or inlet. One that we missed. I'm going ashore to ask questions."

"But, Captain . . ."

"Yes, Mr. Yates . . ."

The mate strove to be patient. "Captain, these are pirate waters, for all the pirates favor the other side of the island. We don't know whose ships those are. But they're sloops, sir. Their drafts are half what ours are."

"I'm fully aware of the differences between sloops and brigantines. But I must find the *Cayuga*. As I've said, I've reason to believe my wife was making for this port. For this reason, we passed up several ports farther south of here and came here directly."

"Yes, sir, but . . ."

"Of course, she may have come and gone. In which case, we need to know where. We may have passed her somewhere in mid ocean. She may be behind us. In which case, we may wait around for a few days."

"Aye, Captain."

"Mr. Yates, we have eight six-pounders and a crew of fifty. More than enough to take on a sloop and win."

The mate spat a stream of tobacco over the side and stared glumly after Gillard as he gave orders for the second mate to lower the boat.

"Can you make out the name of the vessel?" Gillard asked the mate as the crew rowed by the first of the anchored sloops.

"*El Galanteador*," came the reply.

"A Spanish sloop then."

"The name's Spanish."

"Does anyone on board speak Spanish?"

"No, sir."

Gillard shook his head. "Too bad. We might have a problem getting information if the man doesn't speak the language."

"Somebody around'll likely speak English. Most do in this part of the world."

In silence, they rowed past the other, a slightly smaller craft wih the name *Vazimba* painted on her side.

"What does that mean?"

"Haven't the foggiest notion, Captain, but I'll bet it wasn't the name she set sail with."

"Captain Hunter Gillard of the brigantine *Cassandra*." Hunter introduced himself.

The man behind the table smirked. "Captain Fernando del Cabo of the sloop *El Galanteador*." His tone was sarcastic. "To what do I owe the pleasure of this visit to my humble town, Captain?"

"I'm in pursuit of a particular ship, the *Cayuga*, stolen from Shepperton Lines of Boston. We want her back."

"The *Cayuga*?" Del Cabo started.

"Yes." Hunter was instantly on the alert. "You've seen her?"

"No, but there are many schooners in this area. Many bays and inlets. The seacoast of the island is rotten with them. Many river mouths. Many places where a schooner could hide."

"How did you know the *Cayuga* was a schooner?"

Del Cabo's face darkened. His black eyes glittered with dislike, then he raised his eyebrows and shrugged. "Ah, so you caught me, Captain. A little joke. I never like to give information before I know what it is worth, you understand?"

Hunter's face did not change. "Then you do know where she is?"

In pretended innocence, del Cabo's eyes widened. "No. Me? No. I don't know. Not now. I heard about her. A storm. Very sad."

"She was wrecked?" Hunter felt a shaft of pain so acute that it staggered him.

The reaction was not lost on del Cabo. "What is this to you? More than a ship?"

"My wife."

Del Cabo sat up straighter. "Your wife is aboard the *Cayuga?*"

"Was she wrecked?"

The Portuguese seemed to be turning over something in his mind. "I will take you to the place," he began slowly, "but I must have money for my trouble. You understand?"

Hunter's control broke. "Damn you! You're lying through your teeth." He sprang across the table, grabbing del Cabo by the front of his shirt. "Tell me the truth. Where have you heard of the *Cayuga?*"

Del Cabo's expression was murderous, but Hunter's was icy with fury. "Tell me, damn you!"

"She landed south of here."

The grip on the shirt eased.

"South of here?"

"At Tamatave."

Dimly, Hunter remembered the small harbor, a few masts rising in the air. He had guessed it was a fishing village. "Why there?"

Del Cabo shrugged free and made an elaborate pretense of straightening his clothing and dusting himself off. "How the hell should I know? I just heard about her coming in."

"And the people on board?"

Del Cabo shrugged. "I don't know any more than I've told you. They didn't have anything worth stealing, so . . ." He spread his hands.

"Are they still there?"

"As far as I know."

"Tamatave? South of here." Hunter did not wait for del Cabo to reconfirm the information. He strode out the door.

The sound of the door to the street slamming galvanized the Portuguese into action. Pushing himself

382

out of his chair and leaning out the window, he shouted down into the courtyard at the back of the house. "Hey, you! Mali! Sound the alarm! Roust those bastards out of their cribs. We're going to take that brigantine. Quick! Before she gets out of the harbor."

Before he had ducked back in, a tall bare-breasted woman, with skin so black it was almost blue, yanked on the rope of a huge bronze bell that swung from a yoke in the middle of the courtyard. The first notes had no sooner sounded than Ranter Bay came alive, as men abandoned whatever they were doing and answered the call.

"Something's happening, Captain," the second mate yelled. "We'd better get the hell out of here."

"You're right."

Down the muddy lane they dashed. The rowers were waiting at the shingle.

"Shove off!" Hunter yelled when they came in sight. "Shove off!"

Once in the boat and rowing for the brigantine, Hunter stared through the spyglass at activity on the shore. "They're launching their own boats."

The mate kept the course true with the tiller. "They'll never catch us, Captain. We've got too much of a head start on them. Row, lads. Put your backs into it."

Using a cane, del Cabo hurried out onto the small dock. Desite his bad leg, his movements were practiced and efficient. He wasted no time in starting after them. Instead, he directed the men into the boats tied there.

Balanced on a thwart, Hunter steadied the spyglass and watched. "They aren't trying to catch us in the rowboats," he reported. "They're making for the sloops." A cold feeling began in his stomach as he remembered Yates's words. "Row, lads. We've got to get under way before they do. Otherwise they'll outmaneuver us." Silently, he prayed that Yates had kept good watch on board the *Cassandra*.

The rain stopped as suddenly as it started. Beneath a blinding sun, steam rose from the water of the bay. The men's skins were bathed in perspiration, their faces red with effort. Even as the distance to the *Cassandra* lessened, Hunter could hear the squeak of lines across the water as the rigging was run up on *El Galanteador*.

Then the boat bumped against the side of the *Cassandra*. Hunter and the second mate leaped for the lines to haul the boat aboard. "Up the ladders, men," he called.

The crew shipped their oars and scrambled up the sides. "Get us under way, Mr. Yates!" Hunter shouted.

"Aye, sir." The first mate shouted orders to the crew to haul on the rigging with a will.

Hunter leaped for the deck as the boat was swung up and settled in the davits. "Gun crews, at the ready!"

Even as he spoke, *El Galanteador* began to heel. Her spanker caught the wind and the light sloop began a tight turn, its sails already moving it steadily in the still waters.

The untrained gun crew of the brigantine stared at the captain and then at the powder and shot. One man picked up a power cartridge and hesitantly stuffed it into the cannon's mouth.

Hunter stared at him, amazed. "Cartridge, wadding, and ball. Damn it!" he yelled.

At that instant, an explosion from *El Galanteador* startled them all.

"My God. They're attacking," one man yelled. His voice was lost in the whistle of the ball as it came plowing through the headsails, damaging the bowsprit and missing the gunner's head by inches.

Yates swung the wheel. "Turn her into the breeze," he yelled. "Stud sails, lads."

"Aye, sir."

The *Cassandra* was moving at last, but *El Galanteador* had already swept by her, firing her four six-pounders broadside as fast as the pirate crew could reload. Pieces of iron whizzed through the air, shredding the sails and splintering wood. One of the *Cassandra*'s six-pounders was knocked out on the first round. Its crew lay moaning, stunned, and dead around it.

"Captain . . ."

A man hauling at the fore-topsail went down with blood spouting from his mouth and a piece of shrapnel in the side of his neck. Hunter leaped into his place.

The pirate sloop came swinging round to make another pass, but by this time the brigantine was under way. "Well done, Yates," Hunter had time to call as he directed the four guns on the starboard side.

The first mate nodded shortly. His mouth was set in a tight line as he spoke in the ear of the young man at the helm.

"Fire!" Hunter shouted.

Four of the six-pounders spouted flame at the same moment that the oncoming sloop fired.

The balls and scraps of iron tore through the rigging again and over the heads of the men, but no masts were hit and the fore-topsails filled with wind. As the two ships passed, Hunter could see that his shots had caused some damage. Two pieces of the rail had been shot away and splintered wood littered the deck where one of the pirates writhed in agony.

"Shall we head for the open sea, Captain?"

Hunter followed the course of the sloop. She was turning, coming back for a third run. The other sloop had not moved. No crew had boarded her. *El Galanteador* was alone in her battle. "Bring her around!" he shouted. "We'll engage."

"But, Captain . . ."

Hunter turned to the gun crews. "All right, boys, now you know how it's done. You can do it better this time. Load up."

The men steadied. This time they managed to load all seven of the undamaged guns and stand ready.

Rolling his eyes heavenward, Yates added his weight to the helmsman's to bring the ship around. The lines creaked and the sails luffed, then filled again. The *Cassandra* gained speed.

This time the sloop veered away at the last minute to avoid a broadside. Firing as she turned, her shot tore through the jibs, severing the lines on one. The canvas collapsed, but the seven guns of the *Cassandra* spoke in unison, catching the stern of the sloop.

El Galanteador staggered. When she righted herself, she did not come round but continued on a course, running away from the battle toward the south side of the bay.

"After her," Hunter yelled. "We've got her now."

A cheer went up from the gun crews at the sight of the ship obviously trying to escape.

"Aye, Captain."

The gun crews reloaded, eager now, their success shining through their smoke-blackened faces. The sloop was running. They were about to win their first victory at sea.

Behind them near the dock, unnoticed, the second sloop sprang to life. The crew crouching behind the rails of the *Vazimba* raised her sails. Within seconds, she had cast free of her moorings and caught the breeze in her sails.

She came sweeping after the brigantine, all sails full, her guns loaded, her gunners ready with slow matches in their hands. At its helm, her hair like a black aureola, stood the black woman Mali, who had sounded the call for del Cabo. No longer bare to the waist, she had crisscrossed a length of red silk over her full breasts and bound it tightly between.

"Captain!" Yates sprang down from the wheelbox to the main deck. Desperately, he caught at Hunter's arm. "Captain! He's headin' in for shore and we don't know these waters. Could be they're too shallow for the *Cassandra*."

Realizing Yates spoke the truth, Hunter nodded. "Give the order to pull sail. We'll come around and broadside him one more time, then—"

"Sail ho!" came the cry from the crow's nest. "Aft, Captain. Aft! She's bearing down hard."

Hunter and Yates whirled simultaneously to face the second pirate ship. At the same instant, the *Cassandra* ran aground. Her prow sliced into the bottom of Ranter Bay, throwing the men on her decks off their feet. A sickening grinding noise came from beneath them, the masts whipped, and stays snapped like pistol shots.

"Hard astern!" Hunter managed to shout to the helmsman, but the man, too, had been thrown down. The wheel spun, the rudder flapped. The studding sails, still full of wind, drove her deeper into the mud of the bottom.

Yates managed to climb to his hands and knees. Blood trickled from his forehead where his head had struck the deck. Through half-blind eyes, he watched the *Vazimba* execute a neat turn and present her broadside. The black woman's arm slashed down, the cutlass she carried glinting in the sunlight. At her signal, the guns opened up, sleeting the *Cassandra*'s deck with bits of iron. One struck Yates between the eyes, killing him instantly.

As if a concerted chorus, Hunter heard the screams of his men. As some pieces of the iron struck the *Cassandra*'s railings, the splinters themselves became

387

lethal weapons flying through the air, tearing flesh wherever they struck. The standing rigging on the starboard side was severed. Lines and blocks whipped through the demoralized crews as more taut stays for the masts spanged loose.

Climbing to his feet, Hunter lunged for a cannon to return fire when something struck him hard in the middle of the back. Knocked flat on the deck again, he fell across Yates's legs. Without breath in his lungs or strength in his limbs, he nevertheless tried to rise. His body refused to obey him.

The second mate came running. "Captain, shall I run up the white flag?"

Hunter rolled over, or tried to. The lines of communication seemed to be down between his head and his legs. "No," he groaned. "Man the cannons. Blast the sons of bitches out of the water!"

"But, Captain. We've only got four cannon left."

From somewhere within himself, Hunter managed to find strength. Feebly, he pushed himself up to a sitting position, his head swimming dizzily. The deck was a shambles. Men moaned and writhed or lay still, their bodies at unnatural angles. Blood, fresh and shining an awful red, streamed from their bodies as their hearts overcharged with adrenaline still pumped frantically.

"Captain!" The voice from the crow's nest was a shriek of terror. "The other sloop. The other sloop!"

Still unable to feel his body below the waist, Hunter caught hold of the second mate's shoulder. "Up!" he grated. "Lift me up."

The man slipped his own shoulder into Hunter's armpit and heaved. Shattering pain made Hunter scream, but he did not lose consciousness. Through eyes stinging with burning powder, he saw that *El Galanteador* had turned and was bearing down upon them. He managed to twist around. The *Vazimba*, too, had finished her run and was turning.

"My God, Captain," the second mate cried. "They'll have us in a cross fire."

"Yes," Hunter moaned. The sky was darkening for him. The bright sunlight was fading, and he could only see shadows now when he needed to see most clearly. "Strike the colors," he whispered.

When his full weight hit the second mate's shoulder, the man let him fall. "Run up the white flag, mates," he yelled. "We'll see if we can keep alive for another hour or two."

He staggered across Hunter's prone body to drop down on his knees beside the first mate's. "Ah, Yates," he groaned. "What a bloody mess."

Mali preened, tossing her head from side to side. Fancy's ruby earbobs dangled from her ears. Against the blue-black skin of her chest, the gold and ruby necklace gleamed and beamed fire. Her black eyes laughed as del Cabo raised his beaker of rum in tribute to her.

They clinked beakers and drank it down. Then the Portuguese counted the gold from the strongbox taken from the captain's cabin of the *Cassandra*. True, it was only a small amount. And the single set of jewels was the only one, but the battle had cost them practically nothing. Furthermore, the brigantine had not been badly damaged. She could be pulled off the bar and floated with minimal repairs.

"A new ship," del Cabo laughed. "A brand-new ship. Why some of the white oak still has its leaves."

Mali said nothing. She merely tipped up her beaker of rum and counted the rubies about her throat. Smiling, she watched del Cabo's glee. She could feel

389

her breasts tightening beneath the red silk. Soon she would take it off and sit bare-breasted in front of him. He would turn to her then and drive his body into hers, pleasing her over and over.

Del Cabo took another swig of rum. "But the greatest treasure is still to come, sweet Mali." He laughed again.

She watched him rise and limp to the window. "Bring the captain up," he bawled.

"Why keep him?" she asked throatily. Del Cabo was hard as metal when he had made a kill. "He'll never join us. Better to kill him. We should have thrown his body over the side."

"Ah, no. My sweet, bloodthirsty wench." The Portuguese poured himself more rum. "He's worth more alive. Much, much more."

The thud and shuffle of feet sounded on the stairs. Two men dragged the barely conscious Hunter in between them. From the front, he appeared unhurt. Evidence of the hard-fought battle was only in his face and clothing, blackened with powder smoke. In the doorway, they paused with him. He blinked at the light. His long black hair straggled across his forehead.

"Drop him," came the brutal command.

They did so and stomped out.

Face down on the floor, Hunter presented a much different picture. At the back of his waist, a piece of iron had torn a huge gash. He was bloody from the bottom of his ribcage to the top of his thigh.

Mali looked at him speculatively. "He's dying."

Del Cabo limped forward and prodded the man's cheek with the tip of his cane. "Don't die, you stupid Yankee. I need you alive for the time being." When Hunter did not move, he limped to the window again. "Get the doctor," he called. He limped back to stand over Hunter's prone body. "Don't you die," he cautioned. "I need you alive."

Mali reached for the knot between her breasts. "Why?" She rose with lazy grace from behind the table and stalked around toward del Cabo. "Why?" The tight crimson silk fell off one shoulder.

Del Cabo turned. "Because . . ." He saw her then.

Her breast was full, the nipple hard as stone and pointing. The skin was blue-black, the color of ebony. The golden filigree of the necklace glimmered in the light. The crimson silk that bound the other breast caught and echoed the color of the rubies.

Del Cabo grunted as if he had been punched in the gut.

When she was only an arm's length from him, Mali stopped. "We must hurry before the doctor comes." Deliberately, she raised her arms and pushed her long fingers into her black hair, lifting it farther outward from the scalp. If light was reflected off the necklace, it died in her hair, black as the eternal darkness of the bottom of sea.

With her arms raised, he could smell her, sharp and acrid, woman triumphant. The tufts of curly hair in her armpits glistened.

He could not control himself. Suddenly, he was hard and hurting. Flinging the cane aside, he undid the buttons of his pants. His member thrust forward hard as metal. "Come," he motioned to her.

But she shook her head. Her hand closed round him, jerking him hard toward the table.

"Damn you, Mali. You slut," he groaned.

Her face might have been carved in ebony. Her hard buttocks found a perch at the edge of the table. In one swift movement, she spread her legs and guided him into her. She was hot and ready for his thrust.

"Damn you," he groaned again.

She was a little taller than he, so he could not reach

391

her mouth unless she allowed it She did not. Instead, she arched impossibly, pointing her hard breast up to the roof. Her palms were flat behind her head as she bridged up higher.

"Damn you," he sobbed, his breath coming hard. "Damn you." He bit her nipple. The pain made her clutch him. Her long legs whipped round him. She locked her ankles and dragged him into her. The ring of muscle around his manhood tightened, giving him incredible pleasure.

His teeth savaged up the side of her armpit and bit her again.

Her scream was high and ecstatic. Then the violence exploded within them and swept them away.

Chapter Twenty-Three

The pain smote him in the back. Its talons ripped at his flesh and radiated from the point of impact to all parts of his body. Even the tips of his fingers ached as they twitched involuntarily on the filthy floor. He managed only a grating moan before he lost consciousness again.

Rough hands held his shoulders. "Steady, boys," came a slurred voice. "Hold him steady."

Pressure on his shoulders, pressure on his buttocks. Then an agony so awful that his throat splintered from his scream.

The next time he stayed awake longer. He lay on his face still, his head turned to the side. He drew a tentative breath; the odors of dust and moldy straw filled his nostrils. He sneezed.

The contraction of his muscles pained him, but the pain was bearable. Groaning, he pulled one hand up beside his shoulder and gingerly pushed himself till he lay on his side.

"He's moving. Call del Cabo."

Hunter opened his eyes. Smoky lantern-light gave

little illumination to the room. He blinked. A silhouette moved just to the right of the point of light.

The black woman who had commanded the second pirate ship bent over him. "Are you awake?" She slapped his cheek lightly. "Wake up." She slapped him again. "You're not badly hurt. Del Cabo has plans for you."

"Water," he whispered. His throat hurt where he had screamed.

Supporting his head, she lifted a tin cup to his lips.

He drank eagerly, then lay still on his side. His mind dived into despair, remembering the loss of the *Cassandra*. "Where am I?"

"Maroantsetra." The corners of her mouth lifted. "Now do you know where you are, Yankee?"

His eyes were closing, but he blinked them open. "My crew?"

"You'd better worry about yourself."

"Is he awake?" Del Cabo limped into the room.

"Barely."

The pirate bent over him, blocking the light. "Tell me the name of your wife, Captain."

At the mention of his wife, Hunter rallied. "Fancy? What do you want with her?" Alarm roused him as nothing else would have. He raised himself up on one elbow. "Damn you. You won't touch her."

Del Cabo leered at him. "You talk big for a man lying in the straw with his back torn open. How do you think you're going to keep me from touching her?"

Hunter fell back on the pallet. The dust rose around his head. He coughed and sneezed wrenchingly.

Del Cabo laughed. "Fancy, huh? Is that her real name?"

Hunter shook his head. ". . . never tell you her real name."

The pirate bent closer. "I don't need to know her real

394

name if I know the name you call her by, idiot. I only have to tell her that the man who calls her Fancy is lying wounded, and she'll come right to my hand. Women are like that."

The light was growing dim. Hunter found he was so tired he could not keep his eyes open. "She's not." He could barely force the word out between his lips. "She's . . . hard."

Whatever del Cabo might have answered was lost to him. He slipped off into unconsciousness.

The next time he awoke, the room was full of light. Cautiously, he looked around. Apparently, he was alone. He strained his ears to listen. Noises filtered through the window from the street outside, but he heard nothing from beyond the door.

Experimentally, he felt for the dull ache situated at his waist on the left side. He was bandaged around his middle with a pad on that particular area. Was that his only wound? He tested his limbs, finding them in generally good working order.

Judging by the oppressive warmth of the room, the day must be well along. He licked his dry lips. Where were his men? Yates he knew was dead, and undoubtedly some of the gun crew as well. Had the others fought after he had been knocked unconscious? Had they laid down their arms? His last order had been to surrender.

The disaster he had foolishly brought upon himself and his crew appalled him. Clenching his fists, he flung his arm over his eyes. The movement sent a shaft of pain up his side from the wound. Although he flinched and halted the swing of his arm, he found the pain was bearable.

It faded into insignificance beside the flailing of his

conscience. So many men dead, a fine ship destroyed or in pirate hands. His fault. He had to find his crew. If they were still alive, they could not be far from where he lay. He must get them out of this fix. Lying here moaning about what had been done would not free them.

Putting the *Cassandra*'s fate firmly aside, he cautiously pushed himself up to a sitting position. The room was small and bare, hardly more than a cubicle with a window looking out over the bay. He lay on a pallet of straw, by the smell of it. A lantern stood on the floor beside him.

Tentatively, he arched his back. Again the flaming pain, but he did not give in to it this time. Instead, he lifted his head and gazed around him. He wondered what had hit him and how badly he was wounded. Not too badly, judging by how well he was moving. At best, he might have a small cut and a huge bruise.

With one hand braced against the wall, he managed to get his feet under him and to rise. His head swam, but he kept his back and legs firmly braced until the dizziness abated. Sweat popped out on his forehead, but he wiped it away and pushed off.

The window looked out on a lush green square of a courtyard, with a bell hanging from a yoke in the center of it. The alarm bell, undoubtedly. He and Yates had heard it as they dashed down the street.

"Yates," he whispered. The mate had complained of this venture from the time Hunter had ordered the heading around the eastern side of the island. And if Ranter Bay had been his death trap, Hunter had been his killer.

Hunter clenched his fists as more waves of dizziness threatened to send him tumbling to the floor. Bracing himself, he leaned his head back against the rough wall. In his mind he heard the cry of the lookout and whirled to see the second sloop bearing down on them.

A callow youth, a mere cadet, would not have forgotten a second enemy sloop at his back. Yet he had. As if the possibility of a crew for it did not exist, he had hared off after the first one. The whole thing had been over almost before it had begun. He could hardly say he had been in a fight. The quick, clever sloops and their treacherous captains had played games with him, trapping the *Cassandra* in the shallows as if he—her captain—were the merest babe. Or the greatest fool! What had del Cabo called him? Idiot?

Fancy had to take part of the blame for this. His desire to punish her had clouded his judgment. She was selfish and willful, irresponsible too. If she had remained safe at home in Boston, taking care of her son as she should have, he would have been able to go on with his planned voyage aboard the *Carolina*.

He shook his head. He was not even thinking clearly. She had defied him in the first place. Obstinately, she had wanted to return to that damned piece of land in South Carolina. But what was she doing here in Madagascar? It made no sense at all. When he got his hands on her . . .

Discouraged, he staggered back across the narrow room to the pallet and lowered himself jerkily. The wound in his back was clawing at him now. Would it become infected? Would he die here? What would become of his crew? His thoughts turned back to them. Somehow he must get back to them and lead them out of this death trap. He prayed they had not already been killed

He should have listened to Yates. With far more experience than he, the mate had warned him repeatedly. When the *Cayuga* had not been there, he had been anxious to save face, to prove that this trip to Ranter Bay had not been a waste of time. So he had sailed after the Portugeuse sloop into unknown waters. The brigantine was lost to him and Yates was dead, as well as several of his crew. He was a complete and utter fool.

He thought about his wife again. Fancy . . . Del Cabo had wanted to know her name. What had he wanted to know for? If that swine hurt her . . . He opened his eyes to stare round him at the bleak room.

With despair came weakness. His head lolled back against the rough wall. Black spots swam in front of his eyes. He slumped over on the pallet, twisting his injured side. The pain shocked him out of the faint for a minute. He fell to cursing weakly, impotently. He could do nothing. He had only brought problems down upon his crew and perhaps her. He prayed that she would not be caught unawares as he had been.

Fancy looked up as a servant bowed in a gaunt black man, naked except for a sash wrapped round and round his loins.

"Two pieces of silver." The Sakalava held up the appropriate number of fingers.

"What do I give you these two pieces for?" Fancy asked reasonably.

"I tell you about your husband."

"My husband?" A cold fist suddenly clenched inside Fancy's stomach. She swallowed hard. "My husband is in Boston with my son."

"No. In Malagasy."

"You're lying."

The Sakalava shook his head. "I do not lie. Two silver pieces and I tell you more."

"I don't want to know any more. I don't know why you're here, but you'd better get out before I call for help."

"I do not lie," the man protested.

Fancy strode to the door. "Lemuel," she called, "this man doesn't belong here."

"I do not lie," the Sakalava whined. The interview was not going as he had expected at all.

"My husband is a merchant captain," Fancy informed him smugly. "He wouldn't be on Madagascar." She calculated quickly. "Probably right now he's in the Mediterranean."

"No. Here."

"Let's go, bucko," Lemuel Jakes called to the man. "The lady doesn't have any money to give you and she doesn't believe your lies."

"Your name is Fancy," the spy tried again desperately.

Fractionally, she hesitated, then shook her head. "You could have learned that somewhere else."

"No, he tell me."

"Otis," Lemuel called. "We've a little matter here that needs some attention."

The Sakalava stared up and up as the figure of Otis Greene filled the doorway. Then he cast his eyes desperately in Fancy's direction. Abandoning all hopes of getting any payment, he tried to deliver the message as he had it. "Your husband's ship—"

"The *Carolina* is in the Mediterranean," she interrupted him.

"No. Del Cabo has your husband."

"Never heard of him." Lemuel jerked his head in the direction of the door, and Otis Greene put his hands on the Sakalava's shoulders and dragged the man out.

Fancy frowned. "I don't understand what that was all about."

"Probably somebody wanting to go on the expedition," Jakes suggested. "Maybe he thought he could be a guide."

"He said Hunter was on Madagascar."

Jakes's eyebrows rose. "Do you believe him?"

"Not really. I can't imagine that I would mean so much to Hunter that he would follow me. I'm sure he was angry when he woke up and found me gone, but I can't believe that he would abandon his new venture to come after me." Her voice trailed away on a bitter note. She walked to the window and leaned her head against the frame.

Lemuel Jakes came to stand beside her, staring out over the same landscape. He thrust his hands into the hip pockets of his trousers. The posture had the effect of hunching him over more than ever. He looked old and very, very tired.

She felt her eyes fill with tears. "When can we go, Lemuel? I want to get out of this place before something terrible happens to one of us."

"Aye, Captain." Sighing heavily, he placed one hand comfortingly on her shoulder.

She patted it in her turn. "We have to leave tomorrow. I'll talk to Radama tonight. If he can't see his way clear to send an escort, we'll go alone. I'll explain to him that too many people are awaiting the results of this trip for me to delay any longer. People are going to be in want very soon at home."

"And what if it's a wild-goose chase, Captain?"

She bowed her head. "Then I'll just have to hurry home to try something else."

He shook his head wonderingly in the face of her determination.

"And, Lemuel, I want you to know that no matter what happens, I don't consider this trip a waste of time. If I hadn't made it, I'd never have known you and Otis and Beany and the rest. I'd never have sailed the seas my grandfather loved. And I'd never have come to know my grandmother. I want you to remember that."

"Aye, Captain," he agreed soberly.

"So what'd she say? Is she coming here for her precious husband?"

The Sakalava braced himself for the fury he knew was sure to follow. "She no care about her husband. She no listen."

"What?"

"She no care."

Del Cabo rose from behind the table. "What the hell?"

"She no care."

He snatched his knife from its sheath. "If you're lying to me, I'll rip your heart out and feed it to you."

"I no lie."

Throwing the spy one last malevolent stare, del Cabo limped up the stairs to the room where Hunter was imprisoned. "Your wife doesn't care a damn about you," he accused without preamble.

Seated on the pallet, his back against the wall, Hunter managed a wry grin. "I'm not surprised to hear it. She stole the ship she's sailing and left me in Boston."

"She's got to care about you."

Hunter shrugged. "Looks like your luck's run out."

"No," del Cabo snarled. "Your luck's run out." He stabbed his knife at Hunter's throat.

But Hunter was too quick. He caught the pirate's wrist in both his hands and twisted the man off balance. Del Cabo fell with a heavy thud. His curses filled the air as Hunter wrestled him for the knife.

The end was never in doubt. Vulnerable and weakened by the loss of blood, Hunter could not hold on. Del Cabo punched him savagely in the side. Hunter cried out. His grip failed and del Cabo rolled away, coming up on one knee with the knife extended.

From across the room, he glared at Hunter who lay limp, his face bathed in perspiration, his chest heaving as he fought the pain.

"You're gonna pay," del Cabo grated, climbing unsteadily to his feet, his bad leg threatening to buckle under him. Edging along the wall to the door, he slid round the jamb and slammed it behind him.

In minutes he was back, accompanied by two black men. As if Hunter were already dead, they picked him up by his shoulders and knees.

"Throw this pig to the pigs!" del Cabo ordered. "But don't kill him. I think maybe we still might get his wife to notice him if he looks bad enough."

"You gave me this necklace, damn you," Mali objected, her hands pressed against her throat to protect the rubies. "It's part of my share."

"You can have it back," del Cabo promised angrily. "I don't think his woman believes that we really have her husband prisoner. That Sakalava bastard probably tried to make a little money on the side and she thought he was lying to her. She needs proof that her husband's really here. And she'll recognize this necklace."

"You don't even know that it's her necklace."

"Let's see what he says about it, then."

"No." She backed away.

"Slut! You can keep the earbobs. And when we have the treasure and she's dead, you can take it off her body." He came on, arms outspread to prevent her slipping by him.

She kept shaking her head. "Del Cabo, you bastard. You gave me this necklace."

"And I'm taking it back."

"No!" She feinted right, then leaped left.

He whirled and fastened his hand in the inky mesh of hair, then twisted. Her cry was drowned in his laugh as he brought her to her knees.

Then his knife was at her throat. "Unfasten the necklace, Mali. Unfasten it, slut, or I'll take it off without unfastening it."

Furious and terrified at the same time, she nevertheless raised her hands and fumbled with the catch.

"Quicker." He worried her head back and forth. The knife point sliced across her throat, leaving a bright red trail in the blackness of her skin.

She screamed, gasped, writhed. The necklace came free.

"Drop it," he commanded.

"Don't kill me, Fernando."

"Why not?"

"I—I'll be good."

"You'll do what I say." It was not a question.

"Yes . . ."

He scratched her again. "You don't say that like you mean it."

"*Yes*. Yes. Yes."

He took the knife away from her throat. "Turn round."

Still on her knees, she edged round on the floor until she was facing him, her mouth level with his belly.

His hand, still twisted in her hair, forced her head back. When she hissed in pain his response was to tighten his hold until her eyes slanted upward, the whites a shocking contrast to the black skin. Her white teeth, too, were exposed in a feral snarl.

Far from fearing her hatred, he merely laughed. "Open it up, Mali, and show me how much you love me."

Obedient, she unbuttoned his trousers.

His hardened manhood thrust out at her lips. He

laughed exultantly. "By God, more 'n half a century old and I'm still a bull."

He rubbed himself back and forth across her mouth, then yanked her head back. "Find that necklace," he chuckled.

Gasping in pain she patted the tips of her trembling fingers around on the floor until she found it.

"Now wrap it around me a couple of times. It'll seem more like you gave it to me 'cause you wanted me to have it."

She was gaining control over the pain; her face became an ebony mask. "I want you to have it," she moaned, knowing her part now. Knowing what was coming.

He stared into her eyes, reading her deep hatred there as well as the passion his torture had aroused. "Sure you do. Every now and then a woman gets to thinking she's more than she is. That's when she needs a man to put her in her place." He pronounced the last sentence with a shudder as he guided himself into her mouth.

On a platform atop the walls of a stockade pen, two men paused, staring for a moment at the filthy upturned faces of the surviving members of the crew of the *Cassandra*. Dark faces impassive, as if they did not hear the insults and jeers of their prisoners, they flung their burden into the mire below. The crew first scattered, then gathered round to peer at the still figure.

"It's Captain Gillard!"

"God. Get him out of that mess!"

The stockade walls were ten feet high and slick. The surviving crew of the *Cassandra* shared the enclosure with more than a dozen grunting pigs that rooted hock-deep in soupy mud. Hunter had been dropped brutally from the top of the wall into the deepest part of the wallow.

Two of the gunners struggled forward and dragged him up onto a relatively dry section of the enclosure that the men had claimed for themselves.

The pigs that had run, squealing in alarm, now returned with grunts of indignation.

"Captain." The second mate shook Hunter's shoulder.

"Here's blood," one of the gunners called as he held up the mud-stained hand he had used to lift Hunter.

Helpless to improvise a bandage, they gathered around him. Filth covered them all. Though they were shaded by the walls of the stockade from the direct rays of the sun, the heat had enervated them all.

At last Hunter stirred, groaning.

"Captain." His eyelids flickered. "Captain. It's Rawlins."

He stared into the eyes of his second mate. "Is—is everyone all right?"

Rawlins glanced up at his fellows. "Some of us are bunged up a bit, sir, but nobody's badly wounded. How about yourself?"

"Fine . . ." Hunter's voice was faint. "Where are we?"

"A pigsty, sir."

He groaned. His bloodshot eyes roamed the grimy faces forming a circle above him. "We've got to get out."

"Yes, sir." Rawlins looked around at his mates skeptically. "And then where?"

"We take back our ship or one of theirs and blow this whole nest out of the water." He sat up with their help and, for the first time, looked down at himself.

"They dropped you in the wallow, sir."

He shuddered. "Yes, well, I wasn't too clean to begin with."

"You're bleeding, sir," the gunner informed him, "and we don't have anything to clean it or make a bandage out of."

"Leave it." Hunter managed a shrug. "I'm beginning to think that's not much more than a scratch. It's sore as the very devil, but I wouldn't be able to move if it were deep."

The gunner looked grimly at his hand, then wiped it surreptitiously on the side of his pants.

"Tell me what happened."

Rawlins swallowed. "When we surrendered, they boarded us immediately. Took all the weapons and anything else they could find of value. Your strongbox, sir."

Hunter nodded.

"They threw the dead overboard"—the second mate ducked his head—"and the badly wounded."

One man fell to cursing and stalked away to slam his fist against one of the poles of the stockade.

"Musgrave lost his brother, sir," Rawlins explained. "He's taking it mighty hard."

Hunter felt the familiar wave of despair sweep over him. Resolutely, he fought back its numbing tide. "What do they intend to do with us?"

Rawlins shrugged. "They want us to turn pirate, sir."

"What?"

"They seem to think that after a few days we'll decide that that's the best course. Then we'll be let out to sail with them on board the *Cassandra*. We'll be with them when they take a ship. Once we've done it, we'll be branded pirates and be hanged if we try to go home to America."

Hunter sat silent for a minute. "That's utter nonsense."

"Yes, sir."

"So do it."

"Sir?"

"That's the way out. With enough of us loose, we'll take back our ship or one of theirs. That way we stand a chance. Here we don't." Hunter's voice strengthened. "It'll take a few days. But one by one, we'll tell them we've decided to join them. Then when most of us are free, we'll unite and strike."

"But, sir . . ."

"They're probably right. We can't last long here." He looked around him. Sweat poured from their faces. Their eyes were sunk back in their heads. Some wore makeshift bandages. "In a matter of days, we'll get so weak that we can't fight. Then we'll either do as they say or die. They don't much care."

Rawlins sank back on his heals. "No, sir."

"The trick is to fool them. Pretend to go along with their idea before we get so weak we can't help ourselves."

The men looked at each other doubtfully and then back at him. His own condition was more desperate than any of theirs. Rawlins spoke at last. "You're right, sir. Pirate it is."

Chapter Twenty-Four

"Maitresse, I wish you would not go. Let the men go and find the treasure and return with it. Radama's men will ensure that they return."

Fancy tightened the belt of braided sisal around her slim middle and adjusted the scabbard of the dagger on her hip. The frightened, pampered child-woman who had been deserted by her husband ten months ago was gone forever. In her place stood a self-confident, independent creature who would not hesitate to dare the devil.

She did not even look the same. Her dark auburn hair had been bleached by the sun to a streaked burnished copper. Her golden skin was no longer the carefully pampered skin of the self-indulgent. Tiny lines gathered at the corners of her eyes, incised there as she strained too long at the far horizon from the deck of the schooner.

Balancing easily, she slipped her feet into leather boots and bent to pull them up over her knees. "Dulci, I'm not afraid that they won't return or that they'll steal part of the treasure. I trust Lemuel Jakes completely. At any time during this voyage, he could have thrown us both overboard and sailed there with the map."

"But, maitresse . . ."

Without glancing in the mirror, Fancy tied a rolled kerchief around her brow to absorb the perspiration she knew she would shed on the long trip. "I simply want to go with them. This is my grandfather's treasure. I think he meant it for me."

Holy Dulcibella looked at her granddaughter lovingly. "He would be very, very proud of you, maitresse."

"I wish you wouldn't call me maitresse. The Sister Queen of Merina shouldn't have a maitresse."

The old woman smiled. "I have called you that for so long it is like my pet name for you."

"Please call me Fancy. You're the only one I know who'll use the name I want to be called by. Hunter and my mother won't use it at all. And Alex calls me Mama."

Holy Dulcibella dropped her eyes to her wrinkled hands where they lay gracefully at ease in her lap. "I do not think I can call you Fancy. The word would sound too strange."

Fancy put her arm around her shoulders and bent to kiss her cheek. "Please try."

The old woman caught her hands and held them. "If you really want me to."

"I really do."

"God will go with you. He will protect you. But I beg you to be careful."

"I will. I have to come back safe and rich, so we can go home to South Carolina." Fancy straightened and looked down into the wise eyes, glistening now with tears. "Will I have to go home alone?" she asked softly.

"Do you want to?"

"No."

"I am not really comfortable here as the Sister Queen. Perhaps it is part of my own heritage that wars against too much of this formality."

Fancy frowned in puzzlement.

"My grandfather, too, was a pirate."

Fancy laughed then. "You'll have to tell me all about him when I get back." Giving Holy Dulcibella's hands a final squeeze, she stepped back. "You'd better come home with me. We're two of a kind."

The first night when the expedition made camp, Lemuel Jakes entered Fancy's tent and laid out a pair of maps on the small dining table.

With a muffled groan, he lowered himself to a camp stool. Fancy looked at him sharply. He looked tired to death, his eyes sunk back in his head and dark-circled. "Are you all right?"

"I've sweated myself dry today, and I'm not much for traveling on land. I'll pick up after a day or two." He dismissed her concern with a wave of his hand. "I've laid the oldest chart that I've got over the new map of Madagascar that Radama gave us," he explained.

Fancy bent over him, eager to understand what they might explain to her.

He heaved a great sigh as he massaged his forehead with his hand. "They don't mesh by half, you understand. This is awful tricky business, Captain. I don't know if we'll find anything when we get there. We could be miles off. But if blind luck has any bearing on this, then *17° 15′ 48° 15′* is on the eastern shore of Lake Alaotra."

"That's good, then, isn't it? At least we won't have to

411

search in one direction."

He shook his head glumly. "Might be bad. Could be that if they've had a rainy season, then the lake might be way up. Maybe what we want is under water."

Fancy shrugged. "We'll never know until we try to find it." She studied the map intently, then laid the piece of paper with its figures over the spot where the latitude and longitude came together. "I wonder what the five circles represent."

"Maybe holes in the ground. Maybe trees, though I sort of doubt it. Trees don't last. Maybe rocks. Maybe caves. Maybe mountains." Lemuel picked up the piece of paper and stared at it with a malevolence unnatural for him. "Looking at this, I can tell that Great Edward intended to come back for it himself. He knew what these were, and the latitude and longitude were just to get him within a few miles of the place."

"One circle has a line under it," Fancy observed, staring down at it over his shoulder.

"That's where the treasure is for sure," Lemuel agreed. "But even that doesn't tell us anything. If there're five caves, then how do we pick the other four? How do we know which one is the one that has the treasure? These circles are in a circle. It's going to take a damned miracle for us to find the treasure."

They looked hopelessly into each other's eyes. At last Fancy spoke. "It's a miracle we've come this far. Maybe our luck will hold till the end."

Heaving a great sigh, he rolled the charts and replaced them in their tube. "At least nobody'll know where we're going until in the morning."

Fancy grinned at him before her mouth widened into a yawn that she covered without apology. "I can appreciate that. I always felt that the walls had ears back in Radama's palace. Too much of our business had to be conducted out in front of the court. Too many people knew it."

"Like that native that came with that message about your husband."

Fancy snorted her disbelief. "Hunter's not even in this part of the world."

"What if he were?"

Her mouth tightened into a sober line. "Then I'd be scared to death. The only reason he'd have to come after me would be to half kill me—if I were lucky. Then he'd drag me back to Boston and divorce me, or lock me up in some insane asylum."

"You think that's all he'd want?" Jakes eyed her slender figure. Since the sisal belt tied in the loose clothing, her breasts thrust out smartly above a waist of incredible slimness. If he were a young man, he knew why he would have followed her—to the ends of the earth if necessary.

"What else? I stole the *Cayuga*. I deceived him into thinking I was going to stay there in Boston like a proper housewife. And I—"

"What?"

She bit her lip. Her eyes sparkled with mischief. "I . . . ahem . . . went to bed with him and then left him." A bright red blush suffused her cheeks. "I must be going crazy. I can't believe I just said that to you. You must think I'm terrible."

Lemuel Jakes shook his head. "I've heard worse confessions, believe me." He rose with difficulty, groping for the center pole of the tent to catch his balance.

"Lemuel, are you sure you're all right?"

"Just need a good night's sleep," he assured her gruffly as he thrust the chart under his arm. "Good night, Cap'n."

413

After she had tied the flap of her tent closed, Fancy lay down on the pallet. The hot night around her was full of strange sounds that she could not identify. Before it was over, the rain would probably fall not once but twice or three times. Tomorrow an escort provided her by a king would lead the way for her. How amazing to think that she, Fancy England, should be lying on the ground on top of a desert plateau rising high above a dense jungle. She should have been fearful of the things that were about her, but all she could think of was how lucky she was. . . .

To have friends like her grandmother, Holy Dulcibella, and Lemuel Jakes. To be a cousin of King Radama I of Merina. To be here on the other side of the world hunting for treasure buried more than half a century ago. To have a grandfather whom people still referred to as Great Edward.

If Hunter were here with her . . . She stared upward into the perfect darkness. She missed him. Tired as she was from the twenty-five miles they had traveled that day she still could not sleep. If she were at home on England's Fancy and not in the wilds of Madagascar, she would have risen and walked out into the night.

He was her only love, and no matter how he might have hurt her, she still ached for him. His handsome face with its strong jaw, the dimple that appeared and disappeared in the side of his cheek. The deeply tanned skin. The tall hard body with its long straight legs. The black eyes with long black lashes and the thick black hair.

Unconsciously, she flexed her fingers, wishing that he were there. How long had she been hungry? How long since she had lain wantonly atop his body, the tips of her breasts within easy reach of his lips, her fingers threaded through his mane, urging him to kiss her, to suckle her, to drive her mad with desire?

"Hunter!" She said his name out loud, at the same time closing her eyes to shut out the empty darkness. "Oh, Hunter."

"She comes this way for three days," the Sakalava reported. "I talk with one of the drivers of the carts. He tell me they go to Lake Alaotra."

Del Cabo grinned. "Then we'll meet them there."

"Two pieces of silver."

Instantly, del Cabo's affability disappeared. "When we get the treasure—not before."

"No, now."

"Thief," the Portuguese snarled. "We're going after the greatest treasure in the world and you're begging for pennies. You'll get your share."

"No, now."

The pirate lunged from behind the desk and grabbed the man by the scruff of the neck. "Get out of here with your begging. Damn you! You'll get your pay when the rest of us do." He forced the protesting man out onto the landing of the second-floor room, where he held him effortlessly at the head of the stairs. "You give me any more lip about wanting to be paid and you'll pick yourself up from the bottom. Hear me?"

"Yes," the man managed to gasp.

"By God, you'd better hear me. Otherwise, you'll end up dead." Giving the slighter man another violent shake, del Cabo released him. The Sakalava staggered in terror, windmilling his arms. The pirate laughed nastily as the man's skinny backbone collided with the newel post at the head of the stairs. The spy caught at it in time to save himself from a bad fall.

"Now get out of here. We'll come as soon as I can

organize a little surprise for the woman."

"What are you planning?" Mali rose naked from the bed as del Cabo limped into the bedroom. Her mouth was swollen; a tiny crack of broken skin showed angry red at the corner of her lips.

"Ring the bell. We're going overland to Lake Alaotra."

Mali hesitated. "Everybody?"

"Of course, everybody."

"Some of those sailors from the *Cassandra* have joined us. But I don't trust them. They might decide to change sides when they see Radama's men."

"I'll take care of that. Ring the bell!"

Reluctantly, she wrapped a sari round her body and padded down into the courtyard. At the sound of the bell, the men, almost two hundred strong, assembled beside the dock.

"Follow me!" del Cabo called.

Shoving and muttering among themselves, they followed him to the prison stockade. There, mounting the ladder, he called down to the remaining men in the mire below. "Captain Gillard!"

Hunter stared up at him, shading with his hand the sun that blazed behind del Cabo.

"Captain Gillard, how do you like your prison?"

"It's all the same to me, if I'm in here with them or out there with you. Pigs are pigs."

Surprisingly, del Cabo did not take offense. He merely laughed nastily. "Brave words, Captain. Brave words." He turned to the assembled men. "We're after a prize, men. But we won't take it on the sea. Instead, we'll take it from the land. More gold and silver than we could get from a hundred ships."

416

The muttering grew and the men stirred, looking at del Cabo and then at each other.

"A woman has come here from America. A Yankee woman. With a treasure map. The treasure map of Edward England."

As if a bolt of lightning had struck him, Hunter froze. At last he knew why Fancy had left him.

Beyond the walls of the stockade, the muttering grew. One of the younger pirates yelled, "Who the hell is Edward England?"

Del Cabo laughed. "Ah, right. You wouldn't know, would you? You're too young. Edward England was an English m'lord, he was. Turned pirate a hundred years ago. Roamed these waters under the black flag. Took the greatest prizes in his ship the *Fancy*. Took and sank the pride of Spain and Portugal, he did. And England, too. He wasn't too particular." Del Cabo laughed and the men laughed too, enjoying the joke and slapping each other on the back.

"Finally, one voyage he set out and didn't come back. And nobody ever knew what happened to him . . . until now." Del Cabo paused for effect.

"What the hell happened?" the young pirate yelled. "Don't make a bloody bedtime story outer it."

"He took part of his treasure with him to America and left the rest behind. Right here on Madagascar. And it's been here all these years just waitin' for us. Think of it, men. So much treasure that he couldn't carry it all on one ship. So much treasure that he made a map and left it to his granddaughter to come and find."

"A map. A map." The words ran through the horde of men like a storm wind.

"And we're going to get it from her." He held up his hands then as the noise grew until it was in danger of

417

drowning him out. "We're going to make her give it to us."

"How we gonna do that?" the young pirate sneered.

"You're gonna show her your ugly face, and she's gonna drop it and run," another man yelled.

"We're going to make her pay for her husband's life, with it," del Cabo thundered.

"Her husband!?"

"Captain Gillard."

In a nightmare, Hunter saw the rope ladder lowered and two brawny men spring down into the stockade. His futile resistance was brushed aside. A noose was slipped over his shoulders and under his armpits, and he was hauled painfully and unceremoniously to the top, where rough hands set him on his feet and turned him to face the crowd. Half unconscious from the hideous pain the rough handling had caused, he swayed on his feet being held erect by the men who had drawn him up.

"Phew—ee—ee!" someone cried. "Better wash him up, Captain del Cabo. Ain't no woman want anything that looks and smells like that."

"Maybe his face," del Cabo agreed, laughing. "The rain'll take care of that. She'll be willing to pay quicker if she thinks he's had a bad time."

Hunter, who had finally managed to draw a full breath, doubled his fists together and jabbed his elbow into the stomach of the man beside him. The man's breath whooshed out as he fell over the back of the stockade and into the wallow below. As the crowd below the platform howled, Hunter leaped for del Cabo's throat.

Taken by surprise, the pirate captain could not avoid the fate of his fellow. Hunter's fist rammed into his face, driving him backward as well, off the top of the

418

stockade, and into the midst of the terrified pigs.

When Hunter would have turned, he was struck from behind by the butt of a dagger wielded by the third man. The pain of the blow exploded in his head and he knew nothing more.

Blessed rain beating on the back of his head, cleansing away the muck from the pigsty, brought him back to consciousness. Painfully, he lifted his head to find himself tied erect to a pole on the back of an oxcart. The driver whipped up a team of dark gray zebus that loped down the road at a fast clip. For only a few minutes, he was sharply conscious then pain in his head and his side, hunger, and bad treatment all took their toll.

Conscious only sporadically through the long day, he knew that the pirates jogged silently alongside and behind him, and that another oxcart was ahead of him carrying del Cabo and the black woman Mali. From time to time they stopped to rest. Once some kind soul held a leather bottle of rum to his lips. Greedily, he drank the fiery liquid, welcoming its restorative power however temporary.

Each time he tried to scan the faces of the pirates in hopes of catching sight of one of his own men, but they were nowhere to be seen.

Before nightfall, they stopped and began to build their cook fires. A man came to untie his hands and drive him at gunpoint into one of the circles of light. There del Cabo sat, his arm round the curvaceous Mali, a leather bottle of rum in his hands.

"Tomorrow we see your wife, Captain Gillard. What you think she's gonna say now?"

"She'll probably spit on the lot of you."

419

Del Cabo threw back his head and laughed. Then he sobered, as if he had never laughed in his life. "You better pray she don't. 'Cause if she does, we're going to cut you to pieces before her eyes." He took a drink from the bottle, then passed it to Mali. While the black woman drank, he looked at Hunter speculatively. "What you do to this woman that she hate you so much?"

"I—I left her for another woman."

"So. That shouldn't make no difference to her. That your business. You're the man. Tell me. Did you beat her enough?" He squeezed Mali's bare black breast for effect. "That's what a woman likes. Then she knows exactly where she stands."

Gillard regarded the black woman soberly. "I didn't beat her at all," he replied.

Del Cabo laughed. "Then that's your big mistake. Right, Mali?"

She did not answer. Her eyes did not leave the face of Gillard as she lifted del Cabo's hand from her breast and kissed it.

"See! You don't know how to treat a woman."

But Hunter, swaying on his feet, stared into the woman's black eyes and wondered at the hatred he saw there. "I suppose not."

"We're going to get up close to this little wife of yours and then we're going to wait. Wait until she finds the treasure. Then we're going to show her the necklace."

"Necklace?" Hunter had forgotten Fancy's rubies. He had brought them with him to put them on her again when all the past was behind them. As his wedding gift to her ten years ago, he had meant them as a renewal of their vows. Now they were in the hands of this monster to be used against Fancy. "I don't know what you're talking about," he lied.

Mali shot a quick look at del Cabo. "It's not his wife's necklace," she said. "Give it back to me."

"He lies," del Cabo said easily. "Didn't you see the look in his eyes when I mentioned it? It's here, all right."

"But . . ."

Del Cabo looked angrily at Gillard. "You cause more trouble for me, Yankee. Now you got Mali all upset. You tell her that necklace is your wife's."

"I don't know what you're talking about."

The pirate motioned to the guards who had brought Gillard into the circle. "Take him back and tie him away from the fire. Strip that shirt off him and let the mosquitos work on him tonight. I was going to give you something to eat, Yankee, and let you lie here where you won't get eaten alive. But now you made me mad. I don't like it when people lie to me." He made a slashing motion with his hand, and Hunter was dragged off into the night.

"Lake Alaotra," the guide announced with a sweep of his hand. The edge of the ridge dropped away abruptly. Below lay a long finger of blue-gray water partially concealed by low hanging clouds. To the far east, a bank of storm clouds relieved themselves of their contents before blowing on.

With the lush jungle vastness stretched out in front of them, the plateau on which they stood, though liberally sprinkled with palm trees, seemed barren and unfertile by comparison.

"Where are we now?" Fancy asked Lemuel Jakes.

With hands that shook, he took a reading with the sextant and consulted the chronometer. "Only a few minutes off, Captain."

Fancy looked over the edge of the plateau. "What does that mean?"

Lemuel Jakes lowered the instrument from his sweaty face. "It means that we could be standing right on top of the treasure or it could be two . . . three . . . four miles from here in any direction."

She closed her eyes. "What shall we do?"

"Well, Captain, don't guess there's anything to do but to climb down off this plateau. After we get to the bottom, then we slog through the jungle till we get to the lake. We might get lucky."

"If we only knew what we were looking for . . ."

As they made their way down through the sharp gray rocks, the growth thickened until Fancy really could not tell when they reached the bottom. The trees rose up around them and the jungle creepers grew across their paths. Exotic birds flitted from bow to bow overhead and strange white-faced monkeylike creatures with long ringed tails bounded from tree to tree chattering shrilly.

Every thread on Fancy's body was soaked with perspiration. Twice she had literally wrung out the kerchief that bound her brow. Still her own sweat stung her eyes until she could barely see. She began to feel as if she were drowning as her lungs labored to extract oxygen from the water-laden air.

Radama's men slashed and hacked their way through the forest, and only big Otis Greene from among the pirates was able to assist them. Looking at Lemuel Jakes, Fancy realized that the old man was in worse shape than she. At that point she called a halt, claiming that she could go no farther until she had rested.

Another hour through thick jungle with the hacking of long knives constantly in her ears, Fancy finally began to hear something else. The roar of a waterfall. "Listen, Lemuel," she whispered for his ears alone. "We're going to make it. Do you hear me? We're going to make it. The lake is just ahead. I can hear a waterfall. We'll make it. We'll get a boat there and sail until we come to the spot where the *17° 15′* meets *48° 15′*."

His face was pasty beneath the weathered seaman's tan. He wasted no breath in replying but clutched grimly at the vines as he staggered doggedly along in the wake of Radama's men. The ground grew spongy under their feet, then marshy. The very earth sucked at their feet till each step was a labor.

At long last, the man in the lead gave a hoarse shout.

Panting and gasping, Fancy held onto the vine beside Lemuel's head. "We've made it, Lemuel. We've made it."

"Aye, Captain," he whispered. Suddenly, he sank to his knees beside her and then fell over onto his side.

"Lemuel!" she cried. "Lemuel." She went down on her knees beside him. "Otis Greene! Otis!"

The black man came plunging back along the cleared trail.

She pressed her head to Lemuel's chest but could hear nothing. "Lemuel," she sobbed. She sat up and slapped his face lightly. His head rolled to the side. "Lemuel."

Coming at a run, Otis Greene slid down beside Fancy and pushed her aside. His big hands felt for the pulse in the side of his old friend's throat. A minute passed. Then another. Grimly, he shook his head.

"Oh, no."

"I'm sorry, Captain. He's dead."

"Oh, no." Curled into a tight ball of grief, Fancy

bowed her head over her knees. "Oh, no."

"Captain, he's dead," Otis repeated.

She raised her tear-streaked face. "He was walking along beside me just a minute before."

"His heart must have stopped. He was an old man. Near eighty years old."

"But . . ."

The black man rose and pulled her to her feet. "Come out by the lake, Captain. We've reached the shore of it. It's a little cooler. You can rest and we'll bury him."

"Oh, God."

He led the heartbroken woman to the edge of the lake. A mass of gray rocks, their sides covered by lichen, offered a relatively dry seat for her. She caught his hand as he turned to leave. "Don't bury him back in the jungle, Otis. Bring him out here in the light."

He nodded and was gone. All around her Radama's men had thrown themselves down and lay panting. Some had leaped into the lake to cool off in its waters. The waterfall she had heard for the last few minutes fell in spectacular glory from somewhere near the top of the plateau.

Heartbroken, she stared at it. From its advent, it fell onto a huge round gray shelf of table rock that jutted out into its path and diverted it to a second shelf some feet to the right. The second tipped the water back to the left. From the top of a third it ran over the lip onto a fourth, which threw it back to the right. Finally, it took a spectacular fall from the last stone, which ended in a splashing mist and rainbows at the head of the lake.

Her eyes traveled up and up. Far above the waterfall was the top of the plateau on which they had been standing when Lemuel took the sighting. *17° 15′ 48° 15′.*

She stared again at the waterfall. The ends of the huge shelf rocks were like great circles of granite thrust

424

out. . . . Great circles of granite. Five great circles of granite arranged themselves in a kind of circle . . . with a line drawn under the second one from the top.

The men returned with the old man's body, and she bowed her head over it. "Oh, Lemuel," she mourned. "We've found it. We've found it."

Chapter Twenty-Five

The gaunt spy seemed to appear out of nowhere. Fancy raised her head from her reverie to see him standing in the middle of the lush greenery of the jungle, where a minute before there had been no one.

"Old man die?" he asked.

Fancy started up in alarm, turning over the camp stool on which she sat. Fear shot through her. A curtain of green separated her from the sight of the men who were digging Lemuel Jakes's grave and making preparations to spend the night. Although all around her were the sounds of their activities, she felt peculiarly vulnerable. Without apparent difficulty the Malagasy had slipped into the very heart of the camp. Her voice broke in the middle of the sentence. "What are you doing here?"

"I bring message from Captain del Cabo."

"Who?"

"Del Cabo. He has your husband."

Angrily, she shook her head. "You're lying. My husband is in the middle of the Mediterranean. There is no work for you here in this camp. You'll have to leave."

"Del Cabo want to meet with you."

"Where is he?"

"Not far."

"Then he can come here to the camp."

"No, he say you must come to him. See husband." The Sakalava took a step toward her.

Instantly, she retreated. Her experience with Johnny Wheatley had taught her to be wary of men. "Get out of this camp."

"Del Cabo say to show you this." He fumbled in the end of the cloth wound round his loins. The hilt of a long knife was within a couple of inches of his hand.

"Otis!" she shouted. "Otis Greene."

"Wait. I show you." The spy pulled an object from a pouch in the end of the material.

"Captain . . ." The huge black man pushed through the curtain of undergrowth. Reacting instantly to the sight of the Sakalava, he grabbed the man's arm as it rose. A fierce twist and the spy screeched as the elbow joint crackled. The tendons at his wrist, punished by Otis's grip, released the object he had pulled from his clothing. It fell to the forest floor with a faint metallic clink. "What do you want me to do with him, Captain?"

She did not consider the question. Instead, she stared in disbelief at the small tangle of gold and red that lay in the leaf mold. Dropping to her knees, she lifted it carefully, holding it to the light and draping it over her hand. "Where did you get this?" she demanded hoarsely.

"Del Cabo," the spy groaned as Otis Greene relieved the pressure on his wrist an infinitesimal amount.

"Where did he get it?"

The spy took a deep breath. "Two silver pieces," he whined.

"Tell her," Otis growled. He punctuated his command by twisting the abused wrist.

"Ship's captain!" came the anguished cry. The pressure eased again. The Sakalava shot Fancy a pleading look. "I tell everything," he offered. "No ask for money."

Closing her shaking fingers around the necklace, she nodded to the big man to ease up on his captive.

Rubbing his arm and shoulder, the spy cast a malevolent glance at Otis. "I remember you," he promised.

"You're too dumb to remember anything," came the deep rejoinder.

"Talk," Fancy ordered, putting her hand on Otis's arm when he would have grabbed the man again.

The spy nodded. "Ship come into Ranter Bay. Big ship. Yankee ship." He narrowed his eyes as he tried to judge the impression he was making. "Maybe you pay when you hear story," he suggested.

"A Yankee ship? . . ." Fancy prodded.

The spy shrugged. "Captain comes ashore. He want to know who comes to Merina. Want to know about you. Del Cabo tell him he not know. Then captain go back to his own ship and attack del Cabo's ship."

"Why would he do that?" Fancy asked Otis Greene wonderingly.

The big man shrugged. "Take anything a lying scum like this has to say with a grain of salt."

"No lie," the man protested. "He make del Cabo very angry, so del Cabo take him prisoner. Want you to come for him. You, his wife?"

"What is he doing here in the first place? And why did he attack del Cabo?" Fancy still could not believe that there was not some mistake.

The spy half turned to go. "Come. I take you to del Cabo."

Otis Greene shook his head. "You're not taking her anywhere. If you've got her husband, then you bring him here."

"No. Del Cabo not bring him here. You come with me."

"I don't know what to do," Fancy murmured, wishing painfully for Lemuel Jakes.

"If there was a fight between two ships," Otis Greene suggested, "your husband might not be alive, Captain."

"He alive," the spy interposed. "He hurt. Del Cabo very angry."

Fancy felt a start of fear. "Perhaps I'd better go."

Otis Greene shook his head. "Not on your life, Captain." He turned to the spy. "Where is this del Cabo anyway? How do we know he's got the captain's husband? We don't have any proof except your word and a necklace. It might be the captain's necklace, but it might be one that looks a lot like it. As for you, I wouldn't trust you as far as I can throw you."

The Sakalava retreated hastily. "He at north end of lake. He wait."

"Well, tell him to show himself and the captain's husband. Then we might talk about some kind of reward if he's in good condition. But tell him we've got the palace guard from Tananarive, and they're well armed."

The spy looked as if he might say more, but Otis took a menacing step toward him. He vanished into the undergrowth as silently as he had come.

With a shudder, Fancy sank back on the stool and stared at the necklace. She shook her head. "None of this makes any sense."

Otis Greene snorted. "I got a suspicion that this character, del Cabo, knows what we're here for."

The light dawned on Fancy. "Of course. They know we're after Great Edward's treasure."

Otis nodded. "Probably everybody on the damned island knows. My guess is this del Cabo is a thief of some kind. Maybe a pirate. Recollect my granddaddy mentioning Ranter Bay. It's up at the north end of the island. Good shallow harbor."

If pirates were after them, Fancy wanted to be away faster than ever. The death of Lemuel Jakes was preying on her conscience. She could not bear to think someone else might be endangered. Swiftly, she calculated the dying afternoon light. "Can we get across the lake and up to the second stone before evening?"

"Not a chance."

"Then we'll do it first thing in the morning. As soon as there's enough light to see by."

Climbing upward over huge rocks slippery with spray and gray-green slime was a nightmare Fancy would remember as long as she lived. One of her men, a man of middle years named Putman, slipped and fell more than a dozen feet before his leg wedged between two rocks that held him from falling into the lake.

He was forced to hang helpless upside down for the better part of an hour while the first attempt to rescue him failed. The rocks were so slippery that finally the only solution was to lower Beany on a line of sisal, with another to tie around Putman's middle. Then the combined strength of several men finally pulled him loose. He was badly bruised, but the heavy canvas of his pants had saved his skin.

When he stood beside them on the ledge, they all looked at Fancy. Her face was pale but determined. Flashing a grim smile, she turned to the face of the escarpment and started up again.

At length, the band reached the underside of the second rock. The men of the *Cayuga* crouched behind their captain on a smaller ledge that slanted inward.

Amidst the tumble of rocks was an opening no more than two feet high and perhaps twice as wide. Fancy and Otis Greene put their hands on the edge of it and stared into impenetrable blackness A slot in living stone.

Fancy tentatively reached out her fingertips and ran them over the rough lip. It was damp and covered with the same green lichen that covered all the stones, but it was not wet despite the water that splashed onto the covering stone and poured down over one side. Smiling nervously, she threw a glance behind her at her men. "I'll need a lantern."

Silently Otis lighted the one they had brought for the purpose and handed it to her.

Without giving herself the time to think, Fancy set the lantern on the lip of stone and thrust her head through the opening. The light drove the darkness back only a few feet, but they were enough to see that the passage widened. Unfortunately, the light revealed inch-long scurrying creatures that hissed warningly at her. She could not quite smother a cry of revulsion.

"What is it?" Otis called.

"Cockroaches," she moaned.

"You're lucky," came the succinct comment.

The rock surface on which she crawled gave off a fetid odor. She gulped as her stomach threatened to give up its contents. She must not be sick and contribute to the unpleasantness. Reaching behind her, she dragged the lantern forward, then hunched another couple of feet.

"See anything?" Otis called anxously as the soles of her boots disappeared into the slot.

"Nothing yet." She swallowed convulsively, trying not to think of the weight of rock and water above her.

"Be careful."

The slot seemed to be getting narrower, but she

could not be certain. The heat, darkness, and odor could be making it only seem narrower. Wringing wet with perspiration, she could breathe only in panicky gasps. The distance she crawled could have been only a few yards, but it seemed to take her hours.

At last when she was sure her nerves would allow her to go no farther, when she was sure she would faint from breathing the oxygen-poor fetid air, she reached the edge of the stone. Cautiously, so as not to bump her head, she pushed herself up. Miraculously, the slot had widened above her head. She drew her legs up under her and reached her hand out in front of her into black space.

A quiver ran through her limbs. Breathlessness of an entirely different sort attacked her. A chamber of some sort lay ahead of her. Twelve thousand miles she had traveled to come to this place, a sweltering stone slot with a chamber at the end. Uttering a little prayer, Fancy extended the lantern into the open space beyond.

The light illuminated an uneven floor on which were stacked, in somewhat haphazard fashion, many small chests, each of a size such as one might might easily carry. "Thank you, oh Lord," she breathed.

Cautiously, holding the lantern before her, she slid down from the slot. The toes of her boots scraped the side of the nearest chest. Setting her light on the floor she went down on her knees in front of it. The metal hasp was locked in place but completely deteriorated with rust. Drawing her dagger from her belt, she thrust the point up under the latch. A light tap on the handle and the joint broke away from the hinge portion.

Her hands were suddenly clammy. At last she was to see what she had come halfway around the world for. Drawing in a deep breath and holding it, she pushed against the lid. At first it did not move. The fittings were rusted together.

She took another breath and pushed harder. Suddenly, one entire side of the chest broke away. In the interior exposed by the light of the lantern were large pouches blue with mildew. She lifted one gingerly. It was very heavy and it clinked. She loosed the drawstring and spread open its mouth.

Tarnished black coins fell out into her hand, a disappointing sight. With her dagger she scraped the edge of one. Letting her breath out in a sigh, she bent her head over the chest.

Silver!

"Thank you, God!" she whispered. "Thank you, God. And, Grandfather. Oh, Great Edward, thank you."

"You all right?" Otis Greene's voice came booming through the slot.

"Yes," she managed to reply.

"Find anything?" he asked hopefully.

She cleared her throat. "Yes, I found it. Oh, Otis. I found it. It's here. The treasure's here."

"She's found it, boys."

A general cheer went up.

Suddenly, she could stand the heat no longer. Drawing the string up tight and pushing it over her wrist, she climbed back onto the ledge. "I'm coming out," she called.

A few seconds later she was crouched on the ledge with them in the blessed light. Laughing a little hysterically, she opened the pouch again and poured its contents out on the stone while they gathered around. "Look."

"It's black!" Beany exclaimed in disappointment, but Otis Greene began to grin from ear to ear.

"Tarnish," he laughed, slapping the man beside him on the back. He picked one up and scraped at the edge of it as Fancy had done. "Lookee, Beany. It's solid silver. He tilted it so he could read it more easily. *"Dei Great Philippus."* He clapped the little boy on the back. "Pieces of eight, Beany. A whole sack of them. And more where that come from?" He looked inquiringly at Fancy.

Smiling, she nodded foolishly as the men picked up the coins and tested them as Otis had done. "Great Edward's treasure," she murmured. "At least a dozen chests of it."

The men began to chuckle and laugh in relief and wonder.

"The stash," Otis laughed, throwing back his big head. His white teeth flashed in pure delight.

"I don't understand."

"This is his stash. The sea's a rough mistress. Never put all your treasure on one ship. A big storm comes up, it springs a leak and down it goes. You've lost everything. The Spanish learned that to their sorrow."

"You mean he—"

"I mean he probably divided the treasure and hid half of it in these chests. If anything happened to the first ship, he had a stash to come back to. Small chests. Easy to carry away. Easy to hide."

"But the chests are rotten," she objected. "We'll probably have to pass the bags out. They seem in pretty good shape." She hefted the one she held to demonstrate.

"He never had to come back, did he?"

"Why, no," she agreed slowly. "He bought England's Fancy and settled down to becoming a tobacco farmer."

"With the Lady Holy Dulcibella and his son. He had everything anyone would want. No one's ever needed the stash. He looked at her significantly. "Until now."

"Until now," she agreed, her eyes shining. Suddenly,

she could see a plan to her grandfather's life. A plan that extended to his granddaughter as surely as if he had told it to her herself. A chill ran up her spine, and she shook herself to rid herself of the eerie feeling.

Otis noted her movement. "We'd better get a move on," he suggested.

She looked around her. "Yes, we'll have to work out some way to get them up to the top of the plateau." Her face was bleak as she thought of Lemuel Jakes. "I don't want to go down into that jungle again."

Putman was dispatched to tell the escort to move the camp back to the top of the plateau above the waterfall. The men then fell to with a will, only too happy to move where the sun was just as hot, but the air blew across their sweaty skins and cooled them somewhat. There a man could draw a breath without feeling he was drowning.

The crew of the *Cayuga* formed a chain, with big Otis Greene actually in the chamber itself, passing out the leather bags. Four men climbed to the top of the plateau above the falls. From there they lowered a line with a canvas sling attached. Fancy and Beany would then place half a dozen bags of silver in it and watch as the crew hauled them to the top.

Twenty-four times the sling came down the side of the escarpment and twenty-four times it returned, laden, to the top of the plateau. Finally, there was nothing left in the chamber but the wrecks of the chests.

"Captain, why don't you come back here and have a last look around, just to make sure I haven't missed anything?" Otis called.

Reluctantly, Fancy crept back through the slot. The process of dragging the bags through it as well as the bodies of the men crawling through it had swept it clean of its lichen and mold. Likewise, the smoky odor of the lantern had overpowered the fetid odor from the rock face.

Otis Greene had stripped down to a breechclout as he had labored in the chamber. Now he pulled on his trousers for decency's sake. "I wanted you to be sure that we got it all," he told her, his big voice unnaturally loud in the confined space. "You'll never have another chance."

"No," she whispered. "I'll never have another chance." She looked around her at the shambles of broken chests. Like empty cocoons they lay smashed by Otis's heavy hand. "It's sad," she whispered. "They've held their treasure for so long."

"No need to be sad, Captain. They wouldn't have held it much longer. Another eight or ten years and those chests would have fallen away just like you see them. Your grandfather must have meant to come back here sooner than fifty years."

"He found that he had enough," she told him again. "He bought England's Fancy and neither he nor Holy Dulcibella ever wanted for anything. Somehow I know, Otis. This treasure is mine."

Hunkering down beside the one she had broken open herself, she picked up a piece of the side. When she pressed the wood between her thumb and finger, it disintegrated. With a sigh and a half smile, she rose, wiping her hand on the side of her trousers.

It was time to go, yet still she stared around her at the empty chamber. Suddenly, light from the afternoon sun shone through the slot. The time was exactly right to illuminate the chamber even through the falling water. The rippling of the water cast variegated lights on her face, creating the effect of tears on her cheeks. "Why couldn't Lemuel be standing here beside us?"

Otis Greene slipped on his shirt and put a hand on

437

her shoulder. "Don't grieve about Lemuel, Captain."

She gave a dry sob, struggling, almost choking to keep her tears under control. "I brought him all this way to die. He was perfectly happy to sail along in the *Columbia*. He said he'd found a good berth to last him until . . . And now he's dead."

"No, Captain. He wasn't happy sailing on the *Columbia*. He was satisfied that he'd found a berth to last him the rest of his life. He didn't want to leave the sea, but he was too old to sail on any but an old scow. You gave him his chance to sail back across the Atlantic on a fleet ship navigated by him. He loved you like a daughter."

"He loved my grandmother."

"That he did. And he got to be with her again after all the years they'd been apart."

"If I hadn't insisted on this, they could have still been together and he would still be alive."

"Maybe so. Maybe not. His heart gave out. It was going to do that anyway. It could have done it on the *Columbia* as he reefed in a sail. And he wouldn't have been having such a hell of a good time."

Fancy looked up into his dark face. His eyes were shining with tears and truth. Even as the sun dropped away from the slot and the chamber darkened again, she found she sincerely believed him.

"I still wish he could go back with us."

"And do what?"

"Enjoy Great Edward's treasure."

Otis chuckled. "He was a seafaring man. No place to spend your money on the sea. He probably wouldn't have taken his share. He enjoyed the voyage, Captain. Being with you and your grandmother. That's what he was enjoying right up to the minute that he went, simple and easy. Here one minute and gone the next. Just the way we all want to go."

She bowed her head in silence.

"Say good-bye to it all," Otis advised, "and let's get out of here."

She looked around her one last time, then turned her back and crawled through the slot and out into the light. Using the sling line, she climbed up the side of the escarpment. On top of the plateau, she did not even look back at the lake and the jungle. She had come for treasure to save her people, and she had gotten what she came for.

Radama's guards had loaded the wagons for the trip back to Tananarive. Wearily, the master and crew of the *Cayuga* piled in on top of the bags of silver and settled down for the ride. The zebus plodded back along the trail they had traveled only twenty-four hours before. It had all been so easy and yet such a terrible price had been exacted.

The report of a musket shattered the night, extinguishing the normal sounds of the night creatures.

"Fancy England!"

She sat bolt upright on the cot inside the tent.

"Fancy England! You want your husband back in one piece, you better come and talk with me." The voice was male, hoarse and mocking.

Throwing back the flap of the little tent, she stood up as Otis Greene came running up to her.

"Get back inside the tent," he ordered. "We'll handle this."

"Nonsense. The captain's got to be on deck, not cowering in the cabin when danger threatens." Around her middle, she tied her belt and thrust the dagger into it.

"Fancy England, you better answer or he gets cut."

"Don't," Otis Greene counselled, but she shook

439

her head.

"Even if they don't have my husband, some poor man's going to get cut if I don't answer." She raised her voice. "I'm Fancy England! Who are you and what do you want?"

"Come out into the light!"

When she would have answered, Otis put his hand on her arm. "She stays right where she is. If you want to say something, you come to her." His deep voice rang across the plateau.

A long silence ensued, then again came the voice in its accented English. "We don't want to hurt her. We just want to talk."

"No! She stays here with us."

"What about her husband, Captain Gillard? If she wants to keep him in one piece, she better—"

"Captain England's husband is in the Mediterranean Sea," Otis returned, then his voice thundered out of his chest with such force that even Fancy jumped. "All right, men. Close in!"

Fancy could only guess that the palace guards had deployed themselves in the direction of the voice. Within minutes she heard shouts and a scuffle. A shot was followed by a cry of pain.

"Otis!" Fancy grabbed his arm. "I don't want anyone else hurt."

"*You* don't, Captain. But they don't give a damn."

More shouts, then an awful silence.

Suddenly the darkness gave way to a single tiny flame. It grew as it was touched to a pile of brush. Fancy could hear its crackling. The smoke drifted to her. Silhouettes flitted back and forth between her and it. Then a pair of lean zebus drew a primitive oxcart up beside it.

By the light of the wildly leaping flames, Fancy could make out the figure of a man standing in the cart. He appeared to be bent over, his arms behind him.

Two more figures, a man and a woman, joined the first in the wagon, so that the three were all clearly illuminated. The man came to the forefront, leaning forward over the rumps of the cattle. He grinned with devilish malevolence. "Hey, Fancy England," he bawled. "You don't care anything about your husband. You want to see him cut to pieces before your eyes. Call off these guards."

Behind him, the woman sank her fist into the tangled black mop of hair and jerked the unfortunate man up into a standing position.

"Hey, Fancy England. You see this face?" the man called.

Fancy shook her head in horror. "It's Hunter," she whispered.

Otis looked at the figure doubtfully. "How can you be sure from this distance?"

"I know him. It's my husband." Her words were without inflection. She might have been turned to stone.

"He looks dead," Otis observed, squinting through the dark. He raised his voice. "You got a dead man there," he scoffed.

In reply, Mali pulled a knife from her belt. Without letting go of Hunter's head, she brought the knife slashing across his chest. Red welled and dripped down behind her blade. Hunter might have been a corpse. He made no sign that he had even felt the torturing slash.

"Dead men don't bleed!" the woman shrilled.

Fancy clamped her fist to her mouth to suppress a cry. Fury welled in her. Her own hand went to the dagger at her belt. "I'll kill her," she vowed in a whisper.

Struck by her tone, the black man glanced down, amazed at the tiny figure beside him, then back at the scene.

441

"Come on out, Fancy England," the man yelled again. "You don't want us to hurt him again. He's in bad shape. You can see he's bleedin' bad."

"Captain, he's in a bad way. If he's not dead, he's probably so bad hurt he won't last long."

"Otis, I can't let this happen. Will you go out there with me?"

He nodded. "Sure, Captain. Me and the boys will back your play all the way."

Del Cabo stepped to the back of the oxcart and doubled his fist under Hunter's chin. By the leaping flames, he could see Hunter's eyes open. He grinned maliciously. "Don't have much to say with that piece of cork in your mouth, do you, Captain?" He stepped back to the end of his arm. "Hey, Mali," he yelled for effect. "Why don't you cut off his ear? He can't hear anyway when he's out like that."

Roughly, the black woman pushed Hunter's hair to the side. With the other hand, she lifted the knife.

"Otis . . ."

"Wait," the big man yelled.

Both pirates eased back, exchanging grins. "Looks like your lady love's coming for you after all, Captain," del Cabo jeered. "What'd I tell you, Mali? Women are like that."

The black eyes reflected the flames of the bonfire. No expression crossed the face. "Some women," he hastily amended.

Fancy approached the cart with Otis Greene trailing behind her. His expression was so disapproving that Fancy faltered for a moment. Then he shrugged faintly and lifted her over the tailgate of the cart.

The pirate captain swept her a mocking bow. "Fancy England . . ."

The cart tilted and he staggered slightly, his bad leg destroying his precarious balance. Otis Greene climbed

442

into the back of the wagon and stood behind Fancy with hands folded across his massive chest. "That's Captain England to you," he warned, "of the schooner *Cayuga*."

The pirate nodded sardonically. "Of course, Captain England. I am Captain del Cabo of the sloop *El Galanteador*."

Fancy said nothing. Ignoring the other occupants of the cart, she went to Hunter's side, lifting his chin to look into his face. "Hunter," she called softly. "Hunter, can you hear me?"

To her intense relief, the black eyes fluttered open, then widened. He grunted, twisting painfully in the lines that bound his swollen arms. Mali kept her knife pricking the skin between his ribs.

"Hunter," she repeated.

"Well, now, he can't talk, Captain. We got him stuffed up. No sense listening to him trying to talk us out of anything. He'd just be wasting his breath and ours."

She drew a deep breath. "What do you want to let him go?"

"Well, now, I'm glad you asked that."

"What do you want?"

"I understand you've been taking something from a cave under a rock back at Alaotra."

"Get to the point."

"We'll trade you him for what you got out of the cave."

"Go to hell," Otis snarled.

Del Cabo ignored him. "Is it a trade, Captain England?"

She stared into Hunter's pain-filled eyes. He managed to shake his head. Again the painful groaning sounds. But she really had no choice. "Yes," she whispered. "Just don't hurt him anymore."

443

Chapter Twenty-Six

"Hunter." She held his face between her hands.

His eyes bulged with the effort to speak to her. He could manage only a couple of negative grunts.

She swung on the black woman whom she had pushed away from him. "What've you done to him? Why can't he speak?"

Otis's voice, deeper and grimmer than she had ever heard, rumbled behind her. "The bitch probably corked him."

Almost frantic, she put her arm around Hunter's shoulders. His skin was unnaturally hot to the touch. "What? What happened? I don't understand."

"He's all right." Del Cabo stepped forward with a show of affability. He nodded to Mali, who shouldered Fancy aside.

"What are you going to do?" Before her horrified eyes, Mali pulled Hunter's jaw down. When he groaned heavily, Fancy would have sprung forward, but Otis caught and held her. "Stop! You're hurting him!"

"It's the only way, Captain," he murmured in her ear.

In agony herself, Fancy watched Mali pull her deadly knife again and stab it at something between Hunter's teeth. Fancy screamed, then screamed again as chunks of dark brownish-red substance fell from Hunter's mouth.

"They stuffed a hunk of cork in his mouth," Otis explained in her ear. "He couldn't spit it out, so gradually it expanded. It'll choke a man to death sometimes."

Del Cabo gave a deprecatory shrug. "Only if left in. We only wanted him quiet while we were approaching. We could not have him give away our position. He is a very brave man, Fancy . . ."

"*Captain* England. And don't you forget it," Otis interrupted the man's oily platitudes.

The pirate inclined his head in mocking deference. "*Captain* England."

The cork broke into pieces and Hunter was able to expel it. He hung his head, then wearily lifted it. "C—Caro . . ." he managed to whisper.

"There, you see. He's perfectly all right."

Fancy put her hand around his shoulders. "Release him."

Del Cabo hooked his thumbs into the wide leather belt around his thick waist. "A wagon for a wagon."

She turned to Otis Greene. "See to it."

He hesitated, then nodded. He took her arm. "Come, Captain."

"I'll stay with Hunter."

Otis looked at the avid faces of Mali and del Cabo. The leaping flames cast a bloodlike color upon their skins. "You come with me," he insisted in a tone that brooked no argument.

"Go . . ." Hunter managed to breathe.

She hung back stubbornly. "He must have something to drink. Now!"

Silently, Mali signaled to one of the pirates watching the scene in the cart with avid interest. The man passed his bota of raw wine up to her. When she would have aimed it at Hunter's mouth herself, Fancy took it away from her and held it to her husband's lips.

The eagerness with which he drank brought tears to her eyes. Regretting that she had nothing else to use, she pulled off the rolled kerchief she had bound around her forehead. Emptying some of the wine onto it, she used it to wipe his cheeks and mouth.

All the time she did him this small service, he stared down into her face, his black eyes enigmatic. She held the wine for him to drink again, and yet again.

"Very tender," del Cabo remarked maliciously. "What did I tell you, Mali? Women like to do these things for their men."

Hunter's black eyes flickered upward to the Portuguese's grinning countenance, then back to his wife. "Leave me." His vocal cords, tortured so long, had little resonance. The sound of his voice was painful to hear. "Get away from here and don't come back."

"Hunter!"

"You better shut your mouth, Captain."

"Take her away from here." Hunter's voice gathered strength. He looked directly at Otis Greene. "Take her away from here. Don't let her give up the treasure. She—"

Before he could say more and before anyone could act, Mali brought the hilt of her dagger slashing full force across the side of his face. His head snapped back against the post to which he was bound.

Two things happened simultaneously. Del Cabo turned to Otis Greene to shrug an excuse for the impetuosity of his lover, and Fancy, white and silent as the death angel, pulled her knife from the scabbard at her belt.

Instead of drawing the dagger back and bringing it down in time-honored tradition, she thrust forward with it like a small sword. Needle-pointed and slender,

447

a perfect weapon for a woman's small strength, it slid into Mali's body before the woman even had a chance to defend herself.

A guttural scream tore out of her throat as she plunged back from Fancy's dagger. The move tore it from her hip but did terrible damage as it scraped across the pelvic bone and tore out through the skin just above her thigh. Her shriek of agony was awful to hear. Blood sprayed over Fancy's hand and gushed down Mali's leg onto the rough boards of the cart.

The black woman collapsed a second later, screaming and writhing. Fancy stood over her, all emotion dead, relentlessly hovering should her adversary make another move to harm her and hers. Del Cabo sought to draw his sword, but Otis grabbed him and twisted his arm up behind him.

The entire episode might have been over had not del Cabo screamed an order. The pirates around the cart leaped for its sides. Swiftly, they overpowered Otis, who could not throw them out fast enough, and dragged him out and onto the ground.

Del Cabo staggered back, lost his balance, and fell to the floor of the cart. Several of his crew massed in front of him to form a circle around Fancy, who suddenly became aware of them. Fearfully, she backed away until she was pressed against Hunter's chest.

"Fancy," he whispered. His lips were in her hair. "Oh, my darling. Caroline Fancy. Get away. Run while you can."

"Stay back!" she warned them, sweeping the dagger in a semicircle before her. "Stay back!"

"Don't touch her." The roar came from Otis Greene, struggling on his back on the ground in the hands of four stalwarts. "Don't touch her."

The cart rocked as del Cabo struggled to his feet and pushed away from the corner where Otis had thrown him. "Stop. Stop!" He had to shout above Mali's hysterical crying.

The semicircle dissolved willingly enough. One man even vaulted from the cart, out of the reach of the wild woman who had brought down the fierce captain of the *Vazimba*.

Del Cabo steadied himself by grabbing the shoulder of one of the men who stood in front of him. "Captain England," he whined, limping forward, her title falling naturally from his lips. "Captain England. Calm yourself."

The wild light faded somewhat in Fancy's eyes. The men straightened out of their crouching positions and drew breath again.

Fancy, too, straightened away from Hunter, although she kept her left hand behind her, pressed against his thigh. "No one is to touch him again," she commanded. "No one. Do you hear?"

"Of course not, Captain England. No one will harm him. He will remain in this cart alone until the exchange is made."

Fancy glanced once more at the figure at her feet. "She's not to come near him."

With a snap of his fingers, del Cabo signaled to two of his men. They bent and lifted the wounded woman between them. Mali screamed pitifully and then went limp in their hands. "I do not think she is able to come near him," del Cabo remarked sarcastically.

While the men carefully passed Mali's body down, Fancy slipped behind Hunter's back and pricked away at the lines that bound him to the pole. The dagger point made short work of the knots. When they fell away, Hunter could not suppress a groan as he tried to move his arms, bound so long in one position. The circulation rushing back into his hands was so painful that tears started in his eyes.

449

"Hunter," she moaned as she massaged his right hand between hers.

"Caroline Fancy." He swayed where he stood. "Angel."

Thrusting her shoulder under his, she helped him to sit. With a tired sigh, he stretched out his legs in front of him and leaned his head back against the side of the cart.

She pushed his tangled black hair off his forehead with tender hands. "They won't hurt you anymore," she promised. "I'll have to leave you for a little while, but Otis and I will be back. Then you'll be free."

He caught at her wrist with useless fingers. "Don't give them what they want."

"Shhh." She rose up on her knees and pressed her lips to his forehead. "Otis," she called.

"Ready, Captain."

Hunter made another weak pass at her leg as she stepped over him, but his fingers were still too numb to hold her. "No."

The cart rocked as she jumped down into Otis's hands. She looked up into del Cabo's face. "Have him just as I left him, or my men and I won't leave a single one of you alive."

The bonfire had died down, so that only the embers glowed red. Her red hair seemed to be on fire and her eyes seemed to strike sparks. Del Cabo, who had passed unmoved through scenes of horror that would have made strong men blanch, felt a tremor run up his spine.

"Remember," she warned.

He nodded grimly.

"Come on, Otis. Let's get this damned business over with." She turned on her heel and hurried off into the night.

Del Cabo climbed awkwardly down out of the cart

450

and limped to Mali's side.

"She bleedin' like a pig, Captain," one of the men supplied. "We got nothing to stop it with."

"Use a brand."

"But, Captain, the pain . . ."

Del Cabo shrugged. "It's the only chance she's got."

In less than a minute, Mali's gurgling shriek tore through the night.

In the camp, Otis called to Putman, "It's the *Redoubt* and the *Argos* all over again."

"The *Redoubt* and the *Argos*?"

"Aye." He turned to Fancy. "Captain, why don't you rest yourself for a few minutes? You need to clean the blood off your hands."

At his words she looked down, seeing not only her hands but the legs of her canvas trousers for the first time. "My God." The darkness became impenetrable and she fell into Otis's arms.

Del Cabo hoisted a bag of silver and opened it. The black coins fell out into his hands. He weighed one, turning it over and over in the light of the fire, scraping at its edge with his knife. His eyes met Otis Greene's. "Pieces of eight." He put back his gray head and laughed.

The black man said nothing. The malevolence in his eyes spoke for him.

The pirate slipped the coins back in the bag and selected another bag from the second row. The first faint shades of dawn came stealing across the plateau. "You were a long time coming," he remarked conversationally.

Otis shrugged. "Captain England was resting."

"Mali's going to rest a long time," del Cabo grated. "She died." He pivoted angrily, his cane digging into the silver. "You hear that, Captain England? Mali's dead."

Fancy turned from the side of the cart where she had been assuring herself that Hunter was as she had left him. "She tortured my husband."

The pirate's glare was pure malevolence, but when she faced him without flinching, it faded and he turned back to the cart. Spreading the mouth of the second bag, he emptied several coins into his hand. "The treasure of Edward England," he chuckled.

Fancy motioned to Otis Greene. "Let's go." She swung up into the cart beside her husband. Otis Greene climbed over the front and lifted the zebu's reins. Slapping them against the animals' rumps, he gave a stentorian shout. The beasts threw their necks against the primitive yoke and the cart creaked forward.

"Hey," del Cabo called after them, "you better get off Madagascar quick, Captain Fancy England. I'm going to miss Mali. She was one hot woman. I bet you're hot, too. I bet you could scratch and bite just like she did, then purr like a little kitten. I bet—"

Otis Greene hit the bony rumps again and the oxcart gathered speed. The rumble of the wheels over the uneven terrain drowned out the Portuguese's obscenities.

Hunter's superb physical condition had begun to recover itself almost by the time they reached Tananarive. In the palace of Radama I, he had been greeted as the husband of *raza* and given the very best of care.

"What is this all about?" he demanded of his wife when his body had been bathed and massaged with warm oils and his wounds cared for by the *Andriana*'s own physician. He cut a resplendent figure in indigo silk vest and loose baggy trousers of the Far East. His black hair had been trimmed and combed, his face clean shaven.

"You are my husband," she replied coolly, seeking to disguise her instant reaction to his beauty and masculine allure. "Holy Dulcibella is Sister Queen and *fady* to Radama I. I am her granddaughter. . . ."

"You're what?"

"I am her granddaughter." Fancy adjusted the aquamarine silk sari on her shoulder. "She is the widow of Edward Fitzjohn, Lord England, my grandfather, and aunt of Radama I of the House of Merina. I am her granddaughter. . . ."

"You're no blood kin to her," he denied angrily.

"And if I were?"

"But you're not."

"But if I were?" Her gold eyes flashed dangerously.

He shrugged. "I—I suppose it wouldn't make any difference."

"Are you very sure?"

He swallowed. "I'm sure, Angel."

She smiled a wintry smile. "I don't suppose it really makes any difference. We'll be leaving here tomorrow anyway."

His surprise showed in his startled expression. She had not bothered to tell him of her decision, let alone consult him about it. "Just like that."

"Just like what? Nothing's changed really. I have to get back to South Carolina. Dulci and I had already planned that we would leave as soon as the treasure . . . that is, as soon as we had finished our business. She has no desire to linger for the rest of her life in her nephew's court. Her home is in South Carolina on England's Fancy, as is mine."

He bowed his head. "My ship is in Ranter Bay. And

my men are imprisoned there. I must go back there and set them free if I can."

"Otis Greene and I have been discussing that. We think we can sail up the coast and perhaps surprise them in the schooner. She only has a six-foot draft. With del Cabo the only captain of the pirates left alive, we might be able to pull the *Cassandra* off the bar and rescue your men at the same time. Then you can sail home to Boston."

He looked at her strangely. "Would you rather I went to Boston or came home to South Carolina?" he asked.

She turned her back on him. "Do whatever you wish. You have to make up your own mind."

"Which would you prefer, Caroline Fancy?" he asked softly.

She was trying not to tremble. "If you come home to South Carolina, or even if you make Charleston your home port, you have to do it because you want to. Not because of some sense of gratitude."

"I'd be dead if not for you." He put his hands on her shoulders.

She turned in his arms. "But that has nothing to do with whether you want to live with me or not." Her gold eyes searched his face, trying to read what was going on behind his enigmatic black eyes.

"Fancy . . ." He bent to kiss her.

The touch was like chain lightning. Passion suddenly flamed between them, fierce, burning, all-consuming. As swift as the fall of jungle downpour, their bodies flowed together, their arms went round each other, their mouths melded.

The room was silent except for the sound of their breathing intermingling as they clasped each other.

"This is not the way I intended this. It's not," he moaned. His hands slid over her body, clad in the thin

454

clinging cotton, slid beneath her silk sari to find her breasts. "I wanted to make love to you. To make it special. I . . . God, Fancy. Del Cabo told me at first that your ship had been wrecked. I thought I'd never see you again. I felt for a single minute as if the sun had died. Then I turned on the Portuguese bastard and made him admit that he'd lied."

"Hunter," she groaned, writhing beneath his eager hands. "Hunter."

"When I saw you coming out of the dark to rescue me, I knew I didn't have to live any longer. You were all right. You were alive. I could die happy. I really wanted you to turn around and leave me. Do you believe that?"

"But, Hunter, how could I leave you? You're my husband."

"I couldn't bear to have you save me. Couldn't bear for you to sacrifice your ambition for mine." He sank to his knees, then his head pressed against her stomach, his hot breath warming her skin through the thin layers of her garments. "Angel, give me a chance to get the silver back for you. It's your grandfather's gift to you. And you gave it for me. Let me get it back for you."

She was sobbing with desire. She had been so long without him, so long without the touch of any man. And so much horror had occurred. Death had been so close. And Hunter's life had been the same. . . .

She put her hands under the silk vest and pulled it down over his shoulders. At the same time, she went down on her knees, too. Her mouth found his nipple, nuzzled the black curls on his chest, begged with lips and tongue to arouse him so that he could deny her nothing.

He gasped with the ecstasy, then pushed impatiently at her skirt, gathering it around her waist. "Angel," he whispered. One hand came round to clasp her buttocks and the other slid between her thighs, his fingers rubbing the fevered, moist part of her.

"Oh, Hunter. Oh, dearest." Scalding tears welled in her eyes and trickled down her cheeks. He felt so good. So good.

The fine Oriental carpet received them. In one fluid motion, he parted her thighs and drove into her, to the hilt. The hard bone of his pelvis ground against hers. She cried out. He moved.

Then the coiled spring of her orgasm began, spinning out from the center of delight where his hard body had found its home. Outward, the ripples of sensation spread. Out and out they spread in almost unbearable pleasure, in ever-widening circles through her thighs to the very tips of her toes. Her heart thundered in her ears as the ripples of pleasure accelerated it.

"Angel!" His own desperate thrust achieved what he sought. He gave her the strength of his body and the pledge of his love.

"I'll get your silver back for you," he promised when his breathing allowed him to speak. "I swear I will. You'll never have to go haring off around the world into such desperate danger again. I swear." Was it only her imagination or did moisture dampen her dress where his face was pressed?

"Hunter," she ran her fingers through his hair. "Hunter. I love you."

"I love you, too," he replied hoarsely. His hands tightened at her waist, then relaxed.

She stared upward at the white plaster of the ceiling. *At least he was as eager for me this time as I for him. He has not been with Jessica.* It was enough for the moment. Her body felt female again for the first time in a very long time.

"How did we get so much luggage?" Fancy wanted to

know, looking at the heavy chests and bundles that were being loaded onto three oxcarts bound for Tamatave.

Otis Greene shrugged. "The Sister Queen cannot return to her homeland without many gifts from her nephew. Radama and she both realize that she will never see him again, but he wants her to remember him."

Fancy nodded. "He's asked me to return for a visit and bring my son. He says that Alex will add to the lustre of his *raza.*" She looked speculatively at Otis Greene. "Where will you be in a couple of years, Mr. Greene?"

He grinned at her. "I promise to keep in touch, Captain England. Only don't wait too long. You don't want to get out of practice. The sea's not for captains who don't sail her regularly."

She nodded her head.

The *Cayuga*'s sheets filled with a fair wind as she sailed out of the harbor at Tamatave. Holy Dulcibella stood on the aft deck, her smile gallant, her eyes brilliant with tears that streamed down her cheeks. The Second Sun flashed from the yellow silk turban.

Fancy put her arms around her grandmother's gaunt shoulders. "I love you," she murmured, planting a kiss on the wrinkled cheek.

"I know, maitresse. Your love is the thing that sustains me."

"I wish you could stay longer."

Holy Dulcibella shook her head. "I do not. The visit was enough. I saw my homeland again. I returned to my father's court. It was much changed. I was received with great courtesy, but it was not my home. My home is the same as yours—England's Fancy."

457

"Oh, Dulci. I've prayed every night that we don't come back too late."

"God's will be done, maitresse."

"I know. But all those people. Depending on me." She shuddered at the thought of them dying. Then she flung her head back. "With fair winds, we'll be home in the spring." She looked at Dulci peculiarly. "You know, I think we must have forgotten Christmas."

The old woman smiled. "I think we did forget."

"Forget what?" Hunter came up behind them.

"Christmas."

He frowned. "Yes, I think it was last month. I didn't even think about it when I wrote the day down in the log."

"I must start the log again," Fancy said. "The next captain of the *Cayuga* will have some interesting reading."

"I could do it for you," her husband offered, watching her closely.

"No. It's the captain's job."

He did not move. With Holy Dulcibella between them, they stared into each other's eyes. Then he inclined his head formally. "You're right. My mistake, Captain England."

"Not at all, Captain Gillard."

"Mouth of Ranter Bay dead ahead, Captain," Otis Greene announced. He handed the spyglass over to her. She looked through it, then passed it to Hunter, who had striven to conceal his impatience.

The warm rain had fallen periodically along the coast all morning, so the jungle was bathed in haze. The huge trees were separated from the sea by a gray band of steam. The break in the trees signaled the entrance to the bay.

"We cannot fight, Hunter," Fancy cautioned. "We are only twelve and have nothing to fight with."

"Right." He faced her, his wife, so diminutive that she could not weigh a hundred pounds. Yet she was the captain of this vessel. He must defer to her. "I propose that we go in but stay back away from Maroantsetra. That's the name of the pirate anchorage. We'll wait for nightfall, then I'll take the boat and reconnoiter. I can get ashore unnoticed and release my men. Then we'll be able to take one of the sloops. With any luck at all by morning, the sloop and the schooner together should be able to drag the *Cassandra* off the bottom.

"What if she's too badly damaged to be sailed?" Otis Greene inquired dryly.

Hunter shrugged. "Then I'll take the sloop and follow the schooner home. But I'm hoping that she's not. There was no report of damage."

"From what you've told, there wasn't time for any report."

Hunter glared at the black man. "Will you give me the boat, Captain England?"

"Yes, Captain Gillard, and go with you, too, if you need."

"No, I don't intend to put anyone else in danger. Wait for me."

"You need to give us a signal."

"I'll wave a lantern back and forth and up and down in the sign of the cross. When you see it, come to it."

In darkness so thick that it seemed impenetrable, Hunter slid a brace of pistols and a sword into his belt. "I'm ready."

The davits creaked as the small boat went down.

Fancy put her arms around him. "I wish you wouldn't go."

He held her tight, feeling her body against him. The dearest thing in the world to him, and he had forgotten how to appreciate her until he had almost lost her. He laid his cheek against the top of her head. The silence grew between them.

At last he put her away from him. "Angel, those men are my men. I have to rescue them if I can."

"But they may all be dead. You don't know what that monster has done since he came back here."

He caressed her cheek with his fingertips, then laid them on her lips. "You put yourself into danger to rescue your people, didn't you? And you don't know what you'll find when you get back from Madagascar. This may all have been for nothing. But still you tried. I can't go away without trying to rescue them. Surely you see that."

She stifled a sob, but he felt her effort. "Don't cry, Angel. I promise I'll be back as soon as I possibly can."

"Captain Gillard."

"Coming." He lowered himself into the boat. The oars slapped the water, and then he feathered them and rowed away.

Chapter Twenty-Seven

"Rawlins!"

A moment of silence, then a faint grunt reached Hunter's ears.

"Rawlins!" he called as loudly as he dared.

A stirring. A muttered conversation. Then Rawlins's voice came weakly out of the stockade. "Wha' d'y' want with 'im?"

"Rawlins, it's Captain Gillard. I've come to get you out." To suit his action to his words, Hunter looped the top rung of a rope ladder over the spikes at the top of the stockade and dropped it down. "Up you come, men."

"Captain Gillard!" The shufflings and stirrings grew louder. A pig gave an irritated grunt.

"Careful, men. Don't make too much noise. They don't have a clue that I'm around. We'll take them completely by surprise." Hunter assisted Rawlins over the top of the stockade and shook his hand as he gained his feet on the platform. "How many of our men joined?"

"None, sir . . . That is, four, but when the pirates came back from the jungle where they had taken you, they tossed our lads back in here with us. That del Cabo was mad as hell about something. Mad as hell!"

461

"His woman was killed," Hunter supplied the information. "Who among you managed to get outside the stockade?" He looked around him as more men scurried up the ladder and out onto the platform.

"Me, sir." A tall thin man raised his hand.

"Did you hear or see what was done with the *Cassandra?*"

The man hesitated before answering. "I'm not sure, sir. I heard on the way back through the jungle that del Cabo was going to drag her out of the mud and sail her, but then I was thrown back in here."

Hunter stared around him at the pale shapes of faces. "So she's still out there so far as anyone knows."

"Aye, sir."

"Then our job is to get her. To the docks, men. We'll take over one of their sloops and sail out to get the *Cassandra.* When we've got her, we'll come back in here and capture them all. Are you with me?"

"Why bother to take the sloop first, Captain?" one man growled. "Let's get 'em right now. While they're sleepin'. The murderin' swine. Just give me a chance."

"Ease off, Musgrave," Rawlins advised. "We've got to work together on this."

"We want them all," Hunter explained patiently. "Too many would escape if we tried what you suggest, Mr. Musgrave. They'd get away into the jungle and reform to rob and plunder again. Worse. That sort of thing could be dangerous. The alarm could be given at any moment. I'm sorry about your brother. Every man here understands the way you feel. Btt you've got to think of the common good."

Muttering and cursing, the man called Musgrave slipped back into the group of some three dozen men who had survived the attack.

"Let's go, men. And stick close together. W don't want to be separated if we can help it."

In a tight knot they padded between the rude dwellings in the direction of the dock. A tiny showe⁻ of rain wet their clothing, then drifted on. Nowhere was there a light to be seen. Nothing moved in the steamy night. Sounds of birds and small animals filtered from the jungle growth some distance beyond the *kraal* the pirates had erected around the village.

Hunter strained to see in the dark, guided more by the sound of water lapping against the shoreline than by shapes. Just as they reached the dock, the rolling clouds parted momentarily to allow a tiny sliver of moon to shine through.

Hunter raised his hand and called for a halt. One of the sloops, the *Vazimba*, swung at anchor only a few rods from the end of the dock.

"Who can swim?" he whispered.

"Me, sir."

"Me."

"I'll need half a dozen of you to follow me then." He handed over his two pistols. "Rawlins, cover us. Hold the dock. We'll bring her in when we're aboard."

"Yes, sir."

Hunter stripped off his shirt and footgear. Except for the dagger Fancy had given him, he was defenseless. "Quietly now, men." He slid into the warm waters.

Behind him, without so much as a splash, six men lowered themselves into the bay.

Watching from the end of the dock, Rawlins could barely make out their heads bobbing on the water. Then they disappeared entirely in the shadow cast by the hull.

Treading water, Hunter gave whispered instructions, then caught the anchor hawser and began to climb. In less than a minute, he reached the bobstays and swung himself up onto the bowsprit. On silent feet, he climbed down onto the deck. The whole operation had been executed so easily that he shook his head in amazement.

Behind him another man climbed down. Hunter motioned him to silence and to watch before he left the bow. A quick reconnoiter of the deck revealed no one. The brotherhood of Ranter Bay evidently lacked discipline.

Dropping a rope ladder over the side, he was soon joined by the swimmers in the water. "Now, men, raise the mainsail and we'll bring her in to the dock for the rest."

Wincing inwardly as the rigging creaked, he listened with every nerve alert. At any minute, someone might discover what they were about. But no lights appeared. The alarm bell in the courtyard behind del Cabo's house remained silent.

"Be under way in just a minute," one of the men reported. "It's great to have a deck under my feet again. I was sure I was going to die in that pigsty."

Hunter clapped him on the back. "We'll be home before you know it."

"Thanks to you, Captain Gillard."

"And thanks to my wife, Captain England. She's the one who set me free and brought me here."

"Your wife, sir?" The man's voice revealed his incredulity. "Captain England?"

"It's a long story."

The *Vazimba* slipped in beside the dock, and the men swarmed aboard her. Rawlins had already given preliminary orders while they stood on dock, so much of the business of getting under way was accomplished without commands.

"Where now, Captain?" the mate asked. "The *Cassandra*?"

"Right you are, Mr. Rawlins. We'll take this sloop down the bay a half a mile or so and wait until it's light enough to see. Then we'll locate the *Cassandra* and pull her off the bottom. Inform the men."

"Aye, aye, sir."

The Sakalava stirred from the shadows beside the dock. When the Yankee crew boarded the *Vazimba*, he calculated the gain to himself if he waked del Cabo and sold the information. Then discarded the idea.

Del Cabo would not pay him for the information. The pirate captain had spent the afternoon going through the house where he had lived since making Ranter Bay his headquarters. He had collected everything of value and loaded it aboard *El Galanteador*.

If the Yankees stayed in the stockaded pigsty or escaped, del Cabo would probably not care. He was more concerned about sailing the first thing in the morning for the shallows where the *Cassandra* was still aground. If he could get the big brigantine out of the mud, he would transfer the treasure again. If not, he would leave her. Either way, he would be gone from Ranter Bay today. The pirates were leaving, and the Sakalava would have to find another way of making a living.

He owed del Cabo no loyalty. As a result, he watched the Yankees hoist the sail and slip away in the darkness without a single regret. Tomorrow he would climb the plateau and make for Merina. Perhaps Radama I could use a good spy that spoke English,

Malagasy, and Portuguese.

At first light, del Cabo heaved himself up with a groan. He made an abortive motion toward the side of the bed next to the wall before he remembered that no one slept beside him. A weary curse broke from his lips as he drew the hand back and wiped it across his forehead. He flung the thin netting to one side and dragged himself to his feet.

Directly before him was the open window through which he stared blearily. At first the view did not register on his mind, still befogged with sleep and alcohol. He wiped his eyes again, then ran his tongue over the outside of his teeth. Only gradually did he realize what was wrong. The hair prickled on the back of his neck.

The harbor was still in gray light, but not so gray that he couldn't see one of the sloops was missing.

Cursing flatly but virulently, he pulled on his clothes with frantic haste. Down the stairs he limped and out into the courtyard. For the last time he rang the bell.

His men crept out of their huts, rubbing their eyes and generally shaking themselves awake. The guard at the stockade yawned and stretched. Almost as an afterthought, he peeked through a gap between the logs. With a sick feeling building in his stomach, he gaped in horror.

The pen was empty of all save pigs. Stumbling back, he all but fell in his haste to report the escape to the captain.

His first effort met with no success. Del Cabo had already limped onto the dock, where he oversaw the loading of *El Galanteador*. At the guard's approach, he turned.

"Captain del Cabo, the prisoners are loose."

Del Cabo did not waste time in furious recriminations. "They've got the *Vazimba*, then. Mali must not have hurt Captain Gillard nearly enough. Damn him! And that bitch of a wife."

"The cargo's loaded, Captain."

"Then cast off. They're probably waiting for us at the mouth of the bay." Without a backward glance, del Cabo took his place beside the helmsman of the sloop. "Look alert, men. With any luck, we'll get the Yankee brigantine out of mud and blow the *Vazimba* out of the water on our way out of here. But no matter what, we've got a fight on our hands."

"Row, lads, row." Hunter gasped as he strained against the oars. Both boats from the *Cassandra* and *Vazimba* were in the water, tow lines attached to the stern of the brigantine.

"She's not movin', Captain."

"She's got to." Hunter groaned with the effort.

Not a breeze stirred. The air the men breathed was laden with water. Suddenly, lightning streaked out of a bank of clouds to the south of them. A crackling rumble of thunder followed. A breeze slightly cooler than the air around them blew into their faces.

"Raise those sails," Hunter yelled to the men in the *Cassandra*.

"The storm," groaned Rawlins on the thwart beside him. "She's coming, Captain."

"I hope to God she lasts."

As the first drops of water hit their faces, the *Cassandra*'s sails filled with wind. Her rigging creaked. An ugly grating sound came from beneath the feet of the men on her deck.

467

"She's movin', Captain."

"Pull, men!"

The thunder sounded directly overhead.

"Stay . . . with . . . us," Hunter groaned, as if his command could keep the wind in their faces. His shoulders strained. The men sitting on the thwart behind him saw fresh blood stain the bandage about his waist.

"She's goin', Captain. She's goin'."

Both hawsers suddenly went slack at the same moment as the huge vessel floated free. A cheer went up from the men on the back of the *Cassandra* and on the *Vazimba*. The men in the boats tilted back their heads and drank in the last drops of the passing thunderstorm as it flew north across the bay.

"Why don't we see a signal, Otis?" Fancy lifted her spyglass to her eye for the tenth time. "It's almost dawn."

"He's a busy man, Captain. He's likely freed his crew and they're too busy trying to get away without alerting del Cabo what they're about. Then they'll want to try for the *Cassandra*."

She shook her head impatiently. "If the crew is free, that should be enough. It'll be a little crowded, but we can sail home all right aboard the *Cayuga*."

Otis looked down at her. "Come on now, Captain. You don't think your husband's going to be satisfied to let you rescue him and bring him home with his tail between his legs."

"Well . . ."

"He came after pirates, didn't he?"

"Actually, he came after me."

"But you don't count. He can't come home empty-handed. He's got to get that ship back, or bring one home with his crew more or less intact. He's got his own share of pride."

Fancy said nothing. Her lips pressed together in a stubborn line as she lifted the spyglass again to her eye.

Otis reached around her and took it out of her hand. "You can't see a thing, Captain. There's a storm blowin' in from across the bay. Besides, you've got to let him do what he needs to do. You're mighty hard competition for any man, you know. He wants to show you what he can do."

"Me? . . ." she scoffed.

"You." The black man smiled knowingly. "You're the one who took the plantation he deserted and ran it. You'd have been a success except for a hurricane that damn near killed you and destroyed it."

"That's right. I lost just about everything. So what's he got to prove?"

"He's got to prove that he's at least your equal. You didn't lie down and die. By the time he got back, you'd gotten the plantation in order again and were trying to make business deals behind his back. He expected you to fall into his arms, weeping with thankfulness."

When she turned to protest, he chuckled. "Lemuel told me all about you. I wouldn't have come unless I knew what kind of a captain I was going to sail under."

"Lemuel said you were all broke and out of work," she muttered.

"So we were, and so were you. But you were the one who had the guts to steal a ship and go for a treasure."

"I—I had to do it."

"Sure you did. But about your husband. He's come after you, and lost his ship and his men and damn near lost his life." Otis Greene chuckled as he leaned against the rail. "You even had to rescue him."

"He told me he didn't want me to give up the treasure for him. He said he would rather have died."

"I can sort of see how he feels. If what you say is true—if he really came after you—then he planned to rescue you, not the other way around."

"But . . ."

"Good God, Captain," Otis rumbled in exasperation. "He lost his ship. He's got to get her back, or he might as well stay here. He'd be through as a captain."

Fancy let a low whistle out from between her teeth. "I should have realized. I just didn't think. He borrowed the *Cassandra* from Josiah, who'd already loaned him the *Carolina*. That's why I didn't believe that he could possibly be in this part of the world. He abandoned a trading voyage to come home and see that I was all right."

"And you didn't fall weeping into his arms," Otis reminded her for the second time.

Fancy flushed, glad of the darkness. "I couldn't. . . . No . . . That is, he still had his mistress with him."

Otis shrugged. "She was just dead weight to him by that time. If he hadn't wanted you, he wouldn't have come back to you. You're the woman he wants. He's out there right now trying to prove himself to you."

A shiver ran up Fancy's spine as she clutched at the rail and stared into the darkness. Far to the south and west, lightning illuminated a mountain range of fast-moving thunderheads.

Del Cabo stared through the spyglass. The storm was upon him. Huge drops of rain pelted his head and shoulders, the sails, the deck, everything on *El Galanteador*. The soaking was unimportant, except for the fact that the storm impeded his visibility. He could not see the ship that he sought.

Cursing mildly, he drew his brows together and hunched his heavy shoulders against the rain.

The sloop drove on, making good headway. Then, as suddenly as it had begun, the storm abated. As the last drops fell, the heavy clouds parted. The sky behind them lightened to the gray of morning.

"Captain del Cabo!" the lookout shouted. "Sail ho."

Before he saw her, he knew what she was. The *Cassandra* hove majestically out of the mist, mainsails set, only a couple of hundred yards ahead. Del Cabo's reactions were instantaneous. "Hard aport! Bring her around, lads. We'll run for it. Catch the storm if we can."

His crew sprang to obey his command.

Aboard the *Cassandra*, similar commands were being given, but the crew responded slowly. Green as grass on their encounter with the pirates, they now feared to engage them a second time. Spirits broken, many of their comrades dead, they had no stomach for a battle. Though Rawlins urged and Hunter cursed, the crew obeyed every command with leaden reluctance.

El Galanteador swept in a wide arc and retreated like a wraith into the leaden clouds.

The *Cassandra* was not even fully under way in pursuit when Hunter spied the *Vazimba* behind and to the larboard, coming fast. While the crew of the brigantine gaped, the second pirate sloop swept by her with all sails set.

"Where the hell is that ship going?" Hunter thundered.

Rawlins frowned. "I'm afraid it might be Musgrave, sir. He's a bosun, you know, as well as a gunnery sergeant. The men have great respect for him. . . ."

471

"He's on the *Vazimba*!" Hunter exclaimed incredulously. His gaze flicked from the commandeered sloop to the gray wall of storm clouds that had swallowed *El Galanteador*. A chill of precognition ran up his spine. He could not tell how he knew, but he was certain that del Cabo did not intend to return to Maroansetra. Fancy's treasure—the treasure she had given as his ransom—was on board that ship.

"No doubt he had time to give instructions and assignments to the men while we were getting the *Cassandra* off the bottom," Rawlins was saying.

"Damn! Damn!" Hunter rounded on the crew. "Are you going to let your mates do your fighting for you?" he shouted. "Unreef the topgallants."

"Aye, sir."

El Galanteador caught the tail of the storm. It swept her with it toward the mouth of the bay. Del Cabo kept a weather eye to the rear. If he could reach the open sea, he did not doubt he could escape. His light sloop sailed by experienced men could easily lose the heavier brigantine with a green crew and possible damage by the bow.

"Sail off the portside, sir!"

Del Cabo whipped out his spyglass. "A schooner," he muttered. "A schooner in these waters." He snapped his fingers. "The *Cayuga*." White hot anger seared him. The bitch who had killed Mali and cost him the brigantine was within his grasp. Not that he had loved the black woman, but she had been stabbed before his eyes. He could not let the death go unavenged. One sweep, he promised himself. One broadside. He had the time. The brigantine was surely damaged by the bow. Her crew had responded like old women.

"Hard aport!" he shouted. "Man the guns!"

"Aye, sir."

"Mr. Musgrave, sir. We've outdistanced the captain," the seaman mentioned timidly.

"He can't sail any better than he can fight," came the sarcastic reply.

"But, sir . . ."

Musgrave did not so much as glance at the dissenter. "When we sight our target, men, we'll blow her out of the water." He lifted his fist in defiance. "That son of a bitch that threw my brother overboard to drown and kept me in a pigsty thinks he's going to get away." He threw back his head to shout a challenge to the crew. "What d' ye say, boys? Shall we catch him and bring him down ourselves?"

"Aye, Mr. Musgrave." A few of the men cheered loudly. Others looked at each other with a shrug.

"Man the forward guns," Musgrave called. The men jumped to obey him. After all, the mission was to rid the sea of pirates. "Steady as she goes." His angry eyes were trained to the gray wall of clouds. "When we get within range, at my command aim for his rudder."

"Aye, sir."

"Sail off the stern, sir. Comin' fast."

"The hell you say."

"It's a sloop, Captain. *The Vazimba*."

Del Cabo whipped up the spyglass. "Stay between her and the schooner. They don't dare fire for fear of hitting their friends. Steady as she goes. We'll blow the schooner out of the water and leave the survivors for the *Vazimba* to pick up."

"Aye, Captain."

"The *Cassandra*'s dragging, sir. She's damaged below the water line."

"Damn." Hunter could have died with frustration. What was happening behind the wall of clouds at the mouth of the bay? "Man the pumps. Let's keep up as much speed as we can."

Rawlins spoke at his elbow to the sailor who reported the damage. "Can the carpenter nail a piece of sail over the hole?"

"He's already done that, sir. But it's not that kind of a leak. Nothing's really busted. Just some of the molding's sprung loose from the forefoot. She needs to take it easy."

"Damn it, mister!" Hunter rounded on the man. "Do the best you can. We will not take it easy. The pirates are getting away."

The man cowered, then straightened with a doubtful look. "I'll do what I can, sir."

"Steady as she goes," Musgrave shouted. "Steady. Gunners ready?"

"Mr. Musgrave, we can't fire. She's less than a hundred yards from the schooner." The older man laid a restraining hand on the bosun's shoulder.

"What the hell difference does that make?"

"That schooner's the *Cayuga*. She's Josiah Shepperton's ship. We can't—"

But Musgrave raised his voice. "Lower your sights, men. Aim for the rudder at the waterline. *Fire!*"

The three forward guns of the *Vazimba* spoke together. One missed the target entirely, geysering

474

water over the deck of the helpless *Cayuga*. The second did minimal damage to the wheelbox, and the third tore a hole in the stern but barely grazed the white oak rudder.

El Galanteador shuddered and veered to the starboard. The sails luffed, then caught the wind again.

The crew of the *Vazimba* burst into a cheer that drowned Musgrave's command to reload.

El Galanteador's helmsman had been killed in the blast, the wheel partially blown away. Del Cabo grabbed the splintered spokes, forcing the ship to respond at the same time he bellowed orders. At his commands, the crew straightened the ship's course with the flying jib and spanker.

Aboard the *Cayuga* less than a hundred yards away, men scaled the rigging in a futile attempt to unfurl the sails and get the schooner under way and out of the line of fire. "Get below!" Otis Greene shouted to Fancy. "There's nothing we can do. A stray shot could hit us at any minute."

Shaking her head, she planted herself at the helmsman's shoulder, her arms locked behind her.

His lips peeled back from his teeth in a fierce snarl, del Cabo tacked and veered, seeking to duck behind the prow of the schooner.

At Musgrave's command, the *Vazimba* swung wide to follow *El Galanteador*. Suddenly, she was running parallel to her adversary.

"Starboard guns! Fire!" del Cabo screamed.

475

"Aim for the waterline!" Musgrave yelled. *"Fire!"* The port guns of the *Vazimba* spoke in unison with *El Galanteador*'s.

The *Vazimba* veered away, her decks raked by grapeshot. The screams and howls of the injured filled the air. Musgrave stared aghast at the bloody wound in the top of his thigh.

Aboard *El Galanteador*, the seasoned warrior del Cabo allowed himself a vicious grin before ordering the men below to man the pumps. Damaged below the waterline and already beginning to list to starboard, the sloop still could sweep the decks of the unarmed *Cayuga*. Instantly, his plan was made. "Grapeshot in the port guns. We'll take the schooner and escape in her."

"Captain!" A terrified screech whirled him around.

Out of the wall of gray clouds driven before the rushing wind and rain came the *Cassandra*. The big brigantine fairly lunged through the water toward the struggling vessels.

Del Cabo gaped. He could handle two ships, especially one unarmed one, but he could not handle three. His only chance was to run alongside the *Cayuga* and board her. This time Fancy England would be his hostage. He'd be damned if he'd let her go. "Steady as she goes, mates! Bring her in closer. Fire the starboard cannon. Give the bastard something to think about. His crew's scared of their own shadows."

"My God, Captain! Musgrave's been hit!" Rawlins pointed excitedly.

"But he got del Cabo. His ship's listing to starboard."

"Is he ready to surrender?" Rawlins asked.

Spyglass fixed to his eye, Hunter saw the sweep of del Cabo's arm. "Hard aport!" he bawled.

The *Cassandra* responded to the wheel just in time. The shots from del Cabo's ship sent geysers of water astern.

"Shall we fire in return, Captain?" Rawlins shouted.

"And risk hitting the *Cayuga?*" Hunter snarled. "Steady as she goes. Come at him on his starboard side. He can't get off a round at us from that side. His guns are pointed down into the water. Bring her on in. We'll board him."

"Board him?" Rawlins gasped. Hunter's black eyes stabbed into the hapless man. Then, "Aye, Captain! Prepare to board!" he bawled, swinging away.

Too late, del Cabo saw Hunter's intention. The distance between the two sloops narrowed, but slowly. Too slowly. Growling with frustration, the Portuguese realized he could not reach his prey before the *Cassandra* caught him.

"Every man for himself. We'll give the bastards the fight of their lives, lads!" he bellowed. "Remember, they're a bunch of scurvy cowards."

Heartened, the crew of *El Galanteador* drew their weapons or caught up lengths of tarred rope, pieces of chain, anything that might deliver a blow to knock a man unconscious or disable him until he could be heaved over the side.

With a splintering crunch, the two came together. Grappling hooks whistled through the air. Boarding ladders slid down across the intervening space. The

477

pirate crew waited grimly on a deck slanting beneath their feet.

"Follow me, men." Pistol in one hand, long-knife in the other, Hunter dropped back half the width of the deck, ran forward, and leaped. His foot slipped on the slanting deck, but he recovered himself as del Cabo aimed a pistol at him.

"You're a dead man, Captain."

But Hunter threw himself to one side, rolled, and came up as the ball buried itself in the deck a yard from him. "You had your chance, del Cabo. Order your men to surrender. Your ship is sinking under you. You're outnumbered."

Del Cabo raised his hands to shoulder height. "What you say may be true, Captain Gillard. And then again . . ." He grinned like a demon as one of his crew leaped upon Hunter from behind. A blow to the side of the head with a belaying pin sent him toppling.

From the deck of the *Cayuga*, Fancy screamed in horror.

Rawlins fired from the top of the ladder, and the pirate clutched at his chest and slumped against the rail. "Come on, men!" The mate waved them down with his pistol. "Don't let the captain do all the fighting for us." Several of the older members of the crew of the *Cassandra* swung down on lines from the spars, while others followed the mate down the ladders with knives drawn. Hastily, the pirates retreated up the slanting deck to gain the advantage of high ground from which to fight.

His head spinning from the glancing blow, Hunter nevertheless managed to struggle up to his knees and grasp the rigging as *El Galanteador* heeled farther over, despite the grappling hooks and lines.

His bad leg throwing him off balance, del Cabo fumbled as he sought frantically to reload his pistol. A bucket of coals on the deck spilled onto a downed sail blown away by the *Vazimba*'s volley.

Suddenly, there was a blinding explosion, and streaks of flaming canvas and debris spouted over pirates and crewmen alike. Gunpowder, spilled on the sail and on the deck, ignited.

"Fire!"

Hunter staggered to his feet. Tongues of flame ran up the rigging and across the deck. Another charge exploded, drowning out his shout to Rawlins. He waved frantically. "Get back. She's lost."

Those of the crew who had not come on board stopped at the rail. With weapons at the ready, they covered their shipmates below as they retreated for the ladders. Del Cabo, looking more than ever like a demon, his face black with smoke, threw up a protective arm before his face and made for one of the ladders.

Hunter leaped to intercept him. Catching the man by the shirtfront, he slammed his back against the railing. "The treasure," he yelled. "Is it aboard?"

Though the pirate's face streamed with tears from the smoke, his triumph was evident. "Too late for that, Captain Gillard. I'm afraid your wife's silver will be on the floor of the ocean in a matter of minutes."

"Damn you!" Hunter struck the man to the deck. "Volunteers!" he yelled.

A couple of men started forward when another blast stronger than any before rocked the vessel.

Del Cabo rolled over on one elbow. "The powder kegs." He laughed weakly. "The whole ship'll be gone in minutes."

"Where is the treasure, damn you?" Hunter stabbed his knife against the man's throat, drawing blood.

"My cabin," del Cabo grunted, gesturing with his hand. Then, as Hunter sprang away, the pirate crawled to his feet and made for the ladder. The rest of his crew were already swarming up the sides of the *Cassandra* to surrender.

"Captain Gillard! There's no chance."

Flames shot between the planks of the deck beneath Hunter's feet.

"We've got to cut the *Cassandra* free," Rawlins yelled. "The masts are tangled. She'll set us afire."

Hunter threw a horrified look upward. The slant of *El Galanteador* had crossed her spars with the brigantine's and the flames were climbing the tar-befouled rigging. He shook his head stubbornly. "I can't leave it. You don't understand."

"Captain . . ."

Two burly seamen caught him by the arms.

"Damn you! Let me go!"

Rawlins, his face grim, motioned with his arm. They dragged Gillard to the ladder and hauled him aboard the brigantine. No sooner had the lines been cast aside than *El Galanteador* settled by the bow. Another explosion. A rush of wind. And the sizzle of fire being smothered by water.

Hunter clutched the rail of the brigantine, his face a twisted mask of tragedy. The sight of the sinking ship should have brought such pleasure. Instead, pain clawed at his gut. Fancy's treasure—the treasure of Edward England—settled before his eyes. How could he face her?

Aboard the *Cayuga* less than a hundred yards away, Fancy shielded her face from the heat and clutched Otis Greene's arm. "She's sinking!" she cried.

Otis nodded. "When she caught fire, she was a goner."

"It seems a shame."

"He sure blew the bastards right out of the water, Captain. He's a good man, your husband."

"Yes, he is."

The *Vazimba* with Musgrave, wounded but gamely erect at the helm, came round the *Cassandra* in a wide circle, both crews cheering to each other.

"It was Musgrave's round that did it," Rawlins acknowledged excitedly. "His shots into her waterline gave us the advantage."

Ignoring the mate, Hunter clutched the railing, his knuckles white. All around him men were celebrating sweet victory over *El Galanteador*, while he swallowed the bitterness of the worst defeat in his life.

"Captain?" Rawlins queried hesitantly.

Before Hunter could answer, del Cabo sent up his raucous cheer from where he leaned against the rail near the bow. His visage blackened with smoke, his clothing singed, he limped down hand over hand toward Hunter. "So, Captain Gillard, you have sunk my ship."

Squaring his shoulders, Hunter turned.

Del Cabo rested his elbow on the rail, his bad leg threatening to buckle under him. His triumphant eyes left Hunter's face to scan the decks of the *Cayuga* as she moved alongside. He laughed, coughed smoke, and laughed again. "How are you going to apologize to your bitch of a wife, Captain?"

Hunter felt the words like a knife twist in his gut.

"The captain saved her life and her ship," Rawlins insisted stoutly, motioning to two seamen to take the pirate captive.

"But not her silver," del Cabo gloated. "Her grandfather's treasure that she paid for your damned

481

life with. It went down on *El Galanteador*." Del Cabo laughed again. Shrugging off the restraining hands of the crewmen, he limped to Hunter's side. "Hey, bitch!" he shouted.

The *Cayuga* maneuvered alongside the brigantine. Only a few yards of open water separated the railings of the two ships. Fancy stared up at the malovelent face from the schooner's slightly lower deck.

Del Cabo steadied himself on the rail. "Did you cheer when they blew my ship out the water, Fancy England?" Her name was an insult on his lips. "Did you cheer your brave husband when he made his kill?"

Otis Greene put his hand on her shoulder. "Come away, Captain. You don't have to listen to that jackass braying."

"I'm not a jackass, black man. I'm telling her the simple truth. She won't want to hear it, but it's the truth. You know what was on board my ship? It was your grandfather's treasure. Your bags of silver just went to the bottom of the ocean."

He threw back his head and laughed. "My God, I wish Mali was here. She'd laugh at you. She'd laugh. And laugh."

Hunter gestured with his hand. "Take him below," he commanded, his voice ragged. "Put him in irons. Him and his crew. They'll all hang in Boston." With dragging steps, he walked to the rail and stared down into his wife's face. Her eyes were clear, with only the faintest trace of moisture. Her face was stiff with the effort to conceal her emotions. He could not speak the words he longed to say across the intervening space. Not before the crews. Not with big Otis Greene hovering like a fiercely protective guardian angel.

They stared into each other's eyes for a full minute.

Then she managed a light shrug and a smile, as if none of it mattered at all.

Suddenly, he did not care who heard him or what they might construe about what he said. The moment was too important between him and his wife. "I love you, Angel," he called. "I've always loved you and I'll never stop."

"I love you, too, Hunter."

Chapter Twenty-Eight

On the deck of the *Cassandra*, Captain Hunter Gillard put his arms around Captain Fancy England and rested his cheek against the top of her head. The night was warm, the wind fair; the panorama of the southern hemisphere spread before them in a sky so clear it was midnight-blue rather than black. His lips moved against her hair. "Don't worry, Angel. Please don't."

"I'm not, Hunter."

He hugged her to him, the ineffable fragility of her body moving him. "I promise you," he vowed hoarsely, "the prize money for the *Vazimba* will more than cover the money that we've had to borrow, plus the money that I invested in the cargo for the *Carolina*. You'll be able to rebuild England's Fancy and—"

"I know, Hunter." She turned in his arms and put her hand to his lips. "Don't say any more. I began to make other plans when I gave del Cabo the treasure. You're more important than anything else in the world to me. That's what I've learned from all of this."

He closed his eyes to her beauty. His own guilt clawed and ripped at him at the same time that her sweet feminine form aroused him. His nerves sent conflicting commands to the muscles and tendons until he had to set his teeth against physical pain.

"What is it, Hunter? Are your wounds—?"

He shook his head. "No," he grated. "It's not that."

"Then what? . . ."

He took a deep breath and opened his eyes, staring over her head at the four bright stars of the Southern Cross, a beacon to every wandering mariner. "I can't believe how lucky I am to be holding you in my arms like this." He stared down into her face, seeing the starlight swim in her eyes. "By all rights, you should be damning me to hell instead of standing here so sweet and warm against me."

"Hunter, you're my husband. You abandoned your trading voyage when you heard about the hurricane. I couldn't allow—"

"You're very generous to forgive and forget. But I can't. I'll never be able to forget. My own selfishness has come so damned close to destroying everything you cherish."

She let her eyelids fall over her eyes, rather than let him see the quick tears. "I—I still have England's Fancy," she murmured.

"And you'll always have it," he promised fervently.

"As for the monetary worth of the treasure, it was an unknown quantity. It might have been less than I imagined," she tried to reassure him.

"Stop it," he commanded, taking her by the shoulders. "You never cared about the money. Any money will spend just as well to take care of your people. I know that. Do you think I'm utterly insensitive and a fool to boot?"

"No. I know you're not."

"I'm not so sure that I know that about myself. But I know why a tiny portion of you will always hate me." His face was a dark shadow, his eyes glittering out of it.

"Hunter . . . I don't hate you," she insisted.

He shook his head sadly. "You can't help but hate me a little bit for allowing the treasure of Great Edward England to go to the bottom of the Indian Ocean."

She shivered, for she had not thought him so perceptive. "It's only . . . It's . . ."

"It's the silver your grandfather buried half a century ago. It was kept safe beneath a waterfall for the rightful owner to return for it. You found it as if it called you to it, and then you gave it up for me." He let go of her shoulders and turned away. The very saying of it seemed to defeat him. His whole body slumped.

She stared after him, struggling to bring her conflicting emotions under control. He had said it and now she had to look at it. She took a deep breath.

She did not hate Hunter. The terrible rage she felt was directed at the greed and cruelty of del Cabo, and at the waste of the treasure that could have brought so much good to the people of England's Fancy, not to speak of the loyal crew of the *Cayuga*, cruising along in the starboard wake of the *Cassandra*. She smiled. "Hunter."

He had walked across the deck to the other railing, staring toward the south where they had rounded the Cape of Good Hope more than a week ago. She came up behind him and put her hand on his arm. "Hunter, forgive yourself. You didn't throw the treasure overboard. It wasn't even your fault that it went down. It was an accident. You tried to save it. You rescued your men and got the *Cassandra* off the bottom. You wiped out the pirates at Ranter Bay. You're bringing home a pirate sloop."

"I wouldn't have had to rescue my men or get the *Cassandra* off the bottom if I hadn't been such a damned fool in the first place."

She shook her head as she put her arms around him

and laid her head on his chest. "Forgive yourself, dearest."

He pressed his mouth against the top of her head, then looked at the sky. "You're different in so many ways."

"We both are."

They stood together for a long time, then he reached under her chin and tipped back her head. "I never loved you so much as I love you at this moment."

Standing on tiptoe, she said her next words against his lips. "I love you more."

"May I take you below and prove it?"

"Yes."

With perfect ease, they pulled off their clothing and walked into each other's arms. In the warm darkness of the cabin, their hands found each other's most sensitive points. Each bent on the selfless giving of pleasure, they worked in silence. Only sighs and faint gasps guided them—those, and the warmth and silken moistness of the skin they touched.

Hunter found his wife's body reduced to the very essence of womanliness, more beautiful than he could ever had imagined. Developed by the demanding labor she had performed, the firm muscles were nevertheless sheathed in silk. The nipples of her breasts rubbed through the curling hair of his chest. Groaning with the exquisite sensation, teeth set to still his shivering, he tried to stem the tide of his own pleasure while he served her.

As if she recognized his effort and would not allow it to succeed, she placed her mouth over his nipple and took it delicately between her teeth. The anticipation alone would have driven him quite mad, but when she nipped him a hoarse sound tore from his throat. He splayed his fingers around her buttocks and lifted her against him.

Her response was instant and hot. Her arms and legs, never so strong nor supple as a young bride, now wrapped round him and clasped him to her. Hot and moist, she lowered herself onto his shaft, at the same time arching away from him to offer her breasts for his lips.

"Angel," he whispered. "Angel." His mouth adored her; his tongue circled the nipple until it hardened.

Deliberately, she twisted on his staff and dragged him ever deeper into her with the strength of her legs. "Hunter."

"Such an insatiable lover you've become. So beautiful and demanding."

She moaned softly as he transferred his mouth to the other nipple. "I want you so much."

"And I want you," he growled, thrusting upward and then groaning as his lust sent painful ripples through his thighs.

"And you've always been able to get what you wanted or do what you wanted or be what you wanted." With each phrase, she clenched her buttocks, clasping and releasing him while he set his teeth.

"Wicked Angel," he grated. "You're driving me crazy." His hands slid from her buttocks up to her waist.

"Um-hmmm."

He thrust upward as he pushed her down.

She cried out as the shudders began at the center of pleasure and rippled out from that point. As the sensations spiraled, she fastened her mouth against his and strained him to her. It was her last conscious act.

As never before, he felt a part of her, joined to her, the source and the recipient of pleasure, of love, of life itself. *I'll love her till I die. Without her I'd have no purpose.*

He closed his eyes, wrapped her more securely in his

arms, and poured his life into her body.

The arrival of the brigantine *Cassandra* with the schooner *Cayuga* and the sloop *Vazimba* in Boston Harbor created a minor sensation on the Long Wharf. Josiah Shepperton himself dashed out of his office and practically ran the distance from Broad Street. He arrived, puffing and red in the face, in time to see the crew of the brigantine secure the last hawser and let down the gangplank.

"Hunter, my good man. Welcome home." He shook hands energetically, his smile wide and warm. It cooled somewhat when he turned to his stepdaughter. "And, Caroline. Welcome home."

"Thank you, Josiah. You'll be pleased to know the *Cayuga* is intact. Not a scratch on her."

"I am pleased. Very pleased." He managed to smile a bit more enthusiastically.

"The *Vazimba* is a pirate sloop," Hunter told him. "And we sank another. So we should collect prize money for two, plus the sloop naturally belongs to Shepperton's to do with as she will."

"Wonderful." His smile was almost as bright as before.

"The *Cassandra* is slightly damaged, having been in two seafights, but she sailed home from Madagascar with no problem. She's right and tight," Hunter declared heartily. "But you'll read all about everything in my report." He indicated the packet he carried in his left hand.

"Then come home. Come home now." Josiah paused, staring uncomfortably from one to the other. "Blanche has not been well. You've been gone so long, she's almost lost her mind."

"I'm sorry," Fancy murmured.

490

"And so you should be," he scolded. "Your mother's been so upset. For a long time she would hardly speak to me."

Fancy looked at him strangely. "Why shouldn't she speak to you?"

He clamped his lips together in a thin line. "You made good time, Hunter. Very good time. And brought home a sloop as well. Very good. Very good."

"How is Alex?"

"Growing like a weed. You'll have trouble recognizing him. He celebrated his eleventh birthday while you were away. He's not a little boy any longer."

Fancy nodded sadly. "No, he's not, but I want to hurry home and see him as soon as possible." She came a bit closer to Josiah, leaving Hunter to begin overseeing the docking of the *Vazimba*. "I want you to understand from the outset, Josiah. The men who accompanied me on this voyage are not in any way to blame. And I'd like you to find berths for them on Shepperton ships. A captain couldn't have more loyal crew members than they have been to me."

Shepperton looked doubtfully at the big black man at the helm of the *Cayuga* as she slipped into her place on the Long Wharf.

Fancy followed the direction of his stare. "Otis Greene is my first mate. He's one of the best. I was very fortunate in my choice."

Josiah shrugged. "If you say so, my dear."

"I do."

He stared down at the wharf in silence, then looked at her. "Your mother has never quite forgiven me for not loaning you the money you requested. She is right to be upset. I underestimated you. I apologize. I'll take care of them as you ask."

*   *   *

"Caroline! Oh, I mean Fancy, dearest. I'm so glad to see you." Blanche embraced her daughter with more enthusiasm than she had shown when Fancy arrived in Boston some nine months before. "You're so—so tan. Your skin looks . . . very beautiful."

"Thank you, Mother."

"And . . . welcome . . . to you . . . er . . ."

When Blanche cleared her throat for the second time, Holy Dulcibella took pity on her. "May I be shown to my room, maitresse?" she asked quietly. "I am very tired."

"Surely you can wait until we have had tea, Dulci?" Fancy protested. "I know you're just as tired as I am of shipboard fare."

"Oh, we can have Canham send a tray to her room," Blanche interceded. "That is"—she took a deep breath and smiled a little wanly—"unless you would prefer to remain here with the . . . family."

Josiah's mouth dropped open. "Mrs. Shepperton, I hardly think—"

"Holy Dulcibella accompanied my daughter on her journey, Mr. Shepperton. I'm sure Caroline thinks of her as part of her family."

"Thank you, Mrs. Shepperton," Holy Dulcibella replied smoothly, "but I am too old to go long without rest. If you will excuse me." She inclined her head graciously and walked out.

"Extraordinary," Josiah huffed to no one in particular.

The door had scarcely closed behind her when it burst open again and Alex came rushing in. "Mama!" He flung himself into her arms, staggering her sideways in his excitement. "Mama. You're home. I didn't think you were ever going to come back. I've missed you so much."

"Alex! You've grown so tall." Fancy could have

wept. During her absence her little boy had grown taller than she. His eyes were now an inch above her own. She shot Hunter a swift glance of amazement.

"I'm five feet four now." He looked accusingly at his parents. "You ran off without telling me or anyone, Mama, and Dad wouldn't take me with him because he said he'd be going into danger."

"We were in danger, Alex." His father came up to clap his son on the back and shake his hand. The boy returned the manly greeting, then put his arms around his father's waist and gave him a quick, embarrassed hug.

"I wish I'd been there."

"I thank God you weren't. I was captured and almost killed by the pirates. Your mother rescued me."

"Oh, my goodness." Blanche began to fan herself vigorously with the lace handkerchief she plucked from her sleeve. "Oh, how could you do this, Caroline, running off without telling us, taking Josiah's ship without permission, and getting yourself attacked by pirates?"

"I did what I had to do, Mother." Fancy looked at the three pairs of troubled eyes. "Josiah knows why I did it."

A slow flush rose in the Bostonian's cheeks. He dropped his eyes and turned away. "Yes. I could not believe . . . that is, I had not credited you or any woman with such strength and determination, my dear."

A small uncomfortable silence ensued, broken finally when Canham arrived with tea.

As he helped himself to two slices of jelly roll, Alex nudged Hunter. "Did Mama really save your life?"

"Yes, she did. And a braver woman never lived. You're very fortunate to have her for your mother, Alex. She has great courage and loyalty. I'm very

493

fortunate to have her for my wife." He lifted the delicate china cup in a salute to her.

After dinner that evening, Josiah led the way to his library. His face was grave as he assumed his most formal stance beside his desk.

Fancy and Hunter exchanged puzzled glances as they took the matching leather chairs in front of him. Blanche sat in a third chair, completing the circle. Rather than look at anyone in the room, she studied the lace edge of her handkerchief.

"Ordinarily, I would have discussed this matter with you alone, sir," Josiah began, frowning heavily at Hunter. "However, Mrs. Shepperton has . . . ahem . . . convinced me that I should include your wife and mine in this conversation." He looked at his wife with apparent disapproval.

Abandoning the handkerchief, she lifted her chin at a slightly defiant angle. "That is so, Mr. Shepperton," she said firmly.

He sighed. "Then not to prolong the unpleasantness, I will get to the point." He reached into his jacket to get a cigar, pulled it half out, realized ladies were present, and pushed it back into his pocket. He cleared his throat noisily. "Sir." The word was unnecessarily loud. "You may recall a young woman from South Carolina whom you had . . . found lodgings for here. That is, you had promised to . . . escort her to England to rejoin her husband."

Fancy stiffened and glanced at her mother. Blanche was sitting bolt upright and looking straight at her husband. Her mouth was tight; a light flush stained her cheeks.

Hunter cleared his throat. "You mean Jessica Rutledge. Yes, I left money to pay for lodgings here

494

in Boston."

"Exactly. The truth is—"

Hunter half rose. "If I didn't leave enough, I'll certainly make immediate reparations."

"No. No." Josiah held up his hand. He started to speak, hesitated, then fumbled for his cigar again.

"Oh, for heaven's sake, Mr. Shepperton," his wife burst out. "Smoke it. We are all adults here, and I'm sure that both my daughter and I will not be irreparably harmed."

He threw her a look mixed with reproach and gratitude, then drew the cigar from his pocket. The process of lighting it went on and on, while Hunter and Fancy waited helplessly. At last he puffed on it rapidly, drew the smoke into his lungs and exhaled it toward the ceiling.

It seemed to give him courage. "The truth is, Hunter, that Jessica Rutledge has already sailed for England. I myself put her on a Shepperton Lines vessel sailing directly for Portsmouth."

"Then I'll—"

Josiah raised his hand. "That is not the problem. The truth is that—that she—"

"For heaven's sake, Mr. Shepperton." Blanche rose abruptly. Color high in her cheeks, she clasped her hand firmly. "Mrs. Rutledge had a baby before she left. She claimed that it was yours."

Hunter fell back against the chair as if a great blow had struck him in the chest. Fancy stared open-mouthed at her mother and then at her stepfather. Blanche pressed the lace handkerchief to her lips, then crumpled it into a ball. Josiah regarded the ash at the end of his cigar.

At last Fancy spoke. "Where is the child now?"

"Upstairs." Blanche supplied the information with an air of defiance.

495

"Upstairs?" Hunter croaked.

"I did not think this a good idea at all," Josiah blurted out. "I told Mrs. Shepperton that the boy should be placed in a good home. Mrs. Rutledge did not want to take the child with her to England. She felt sure that she could be reconciled with her husband if she were to go to him . . . unencumbered. This is a most unfortunate business. Most unfortunate." His eyebrows drew together in an angry frown directed at Hunter.

"Jessica was pregnant," Hunter muttered.

"Sir . . ." Josiah began, his voice sounding shocked.

"We've all heard the word," Blanche cut him off. "She was pregnant, Hunter, but she did not know she was until after you had sailed. The poor woman came to me, and I could do nothing else in the name of Christian charity other than help her."

Beneath his dark tan, Hunter's face turned white. "Thank you," he murmured. He looked at Fancy with dead eyes.

She took a deep breath. A pulse throbbed in the side of her throat. "A boy, did you say?"

"A beautiful baby boy, with blond hair and the most unusual dark brown eyes. The very image of you, Hunter, despite his fairness," Blanche stammered slightly.

After another uncomfortable silence, Fancy rose deliberately. "Shall we go up and see him?"

The two men looked at her as if she had lost her mind. Then Blanche rose, too. "I think that would be a good idea, although he's probably asleep. He's a very good baby, the nurse says. Sleeps well, eats well, seldom cries."

Hunter rose and followed them out of the room. Josiah trailed behind him, his expression clearly conveying his misery and disapproval.

Suddenly, at the top of the stairs, Holy Dulcibella appeared. "I heard you coming." Her voice was deep and steady. Her eyes met Fancy's.

"Oh, see here . . ." Josiah protested from the bottom, but the other three paid him no heed.

Both Holy Dulcibella and Fancy stepped aside to let Blanche lead the way. Hunter trailed after them and Josiah brought up the rear. Quietly, Blanche tapped at the door at the end of the hall. A young woman in a black dress and white starched pinafore opened it. "Is he asleep?"

The nurse shook her head. "He's lying in his bed playing with that little silver rattle you gave him and cooing to himself."

Fancy looked beyond her at a white and blue draped bassinet. A soft tinkling sound came from it. Slowly, she walked across the room. The partially veiled light left the interior of the bassinet in shadow, but Fancy could see the little face. The baby's eyes were open; his fist clutched a small ivory ring with a little silver bell attached. He suddenly swung it back and forth with an uncertain wobbly motion. The little bell jingled.

Fancy put her hand in to nudge the other little fist that lay clenched on the coverlet. "Can you make it go?" she asked softly.

The baby looked up, his dark eyes searching, finding her, and focusing uncertainly. The little hand closed round her index finger. Suddenly, Fancy felt the tears start in her eyes. "Will you come to me?" she whispered.

The baby tugged at her finger.

"Will you?" she asked again. "Will you?"

Her hands slipped under the little body, one going under the head with its wispy silky hair, the other sliding under the tiny bottom. Gathering blanket and all, she lifted him out of the bassinet and held him out in front of her.

By the light, he might have been a blond edition of Alex. His features were so like his father's. He stared at her uncertainly. His father came up behind her. The movement caught the baby's attention, and his focus shifted.

The sight of his own son held so tenderly in the arms of the woman who was not his natural mother clamped a vise around Hunter's heart. He tried but failed to draw a breath. His own blood, his own flesh, his second son stared up into his wife's face and waved the tiny silver bell. Overcome with love and pain, Hunter clenched his fists.

Unaware of his torment, Fancy smiled at the baby, whose eyes shifted back to her. The silver bell tinkled in the chubby fist. "Oh, you are so clever," she crooned. "So clever."

As if he understood that she had paid him a compliment, he lifted the corners of his mouth in a tiny smile.

She smiled in answer. "Hunter . . ." She turned into his arms. "Hunter?"

Instinctively, she drew the baby to her shoulder. "Hunter?"

Only his eyes, demon-black pools of emotion, pierced her. The living proof of his adultery, his damnable sin, cuddled sweetly into the curve of his wife's neck. Finally, he managed to speak. "Can you ever forgive me?"

"I've forgiven you already."

"How? . . ."

The baby cooed again. She rubbed his back with a gentle circular motion. "We'll take him home with us."

Hunter could not believe his ears. "Angel," he choked. "You'd do that for my son?"

The baby cooed softly. Whether reflexively or not, his arms tightened around her neck.

"He'll be *our* son," she declared.

Hunter put his arms around them both. "Of course."

"I was hoping you would want to, Caroline Fancy," Blanche murmured somewhere behind them.

"Here. What's this?" Josiah asked.

"Praise God," Holy Dulcibella pronounced.

Josiah had reserved four of the most luxurious cabins on the *Cambridge* for their voyage home. After Hunter's assuming command of the brigantine *Cassandra*, Josiah had sent the merchantman *Carolina* on her way, but arrangements had been made for her to dock at Charleston on her return voyage. At that time, Hunter could make his decision as to whether he planned to resume command or to remain at England's Fancy as a planter.

Fancy stared around her in amazement at the half-dozen trunks someone had crammed into her cabin. She shook her head. Where had all this stuff come from? Puzzled, she mentally reviewed her belongings. Her clothing, much of it new, a gift from her mother. Clothing and personal items for the new baby Richard Quennell, named after her father and Hunter's father. Clothing for Holy Dulcibella, although her trunk should have been placed in her cabin. Clothing for Hunter, although his trunk should have been placed in his cabin. Clothing for Alex in his cabin. Two trunks of clothing and personal supplies for the people of England's Fancy, both of which should have been placed it the hold. What were these?

A quick knock sounded at the cabin door, but before she could answer, it swung open.

"Otis!"

"Shhh, Captain England. I'm not supposed to be down here."

"Otis Greene. You can come anywhere on any ship I'm on." She took his big rough hands in hers and drew him into the center of the cabin. "It's good to see you."

"Good to see you, too, Captain."

"We didn't have much chance to talk on the voyage home and I've hardly seen you over the last two and a half weeks. I'm so glad you're on this ship. We'll have—"

"I'm not sailing on the *Cambridge*."

"You're not?" Her disappointment was evident in her face and her voice.

"I'm to be first mate on a Shepperton Lines ship bound for the Orient by Cape Horn. She sails in a couple of weeks. I'm much obliged to you and Captain Gillard for making that up for me."

"Shepperton Lines doesn't know what a wonderful employee they're getting," she assured him. "They should be the ones to thank us."

He flashed his teeth in a half-cynical smile. "Sure thing . . . if you say so. But until they get around to it, I'm thanking you."

"You're entirely welcome."

They stared into each other's eyes for a moment, then Otis broke the contact. "Looks like you're travelin' with enough luggage," he remarked, looking around him with a smile of amusement.

"I can't understand it," she agreed. "I've never seen so many trunks. Somebody's made a mistake. I'm sure most of the belong in the hold."

"Nobody's made a mistake," he replied significantly. "I loaded all three of those trunks on here myself." He pointed to three huge brass-bound chests, each set down in a different part of the cabin, each looking quite different, as if they were in no way related.

"You! What are they?"

He stepped close to her. "Come here." He took her

500

by the arm and led her to the first. From the pocket of his seaman's canvas trousers, he pulled a set of keys. Selecting one, he unlocked the trunk and lifted the lid. While she gaped, he stooped and pawed aside unfamiliar clothing, a couple of blankets, and a heavy canvas.

At last he straightened and held out a long flat box that looked to have been cobbled together out of rough white oak.

"What is this?" she asked.

"Open it and see," he suggested, grinning hugely.

Wonderingly, she slid back the lid, then gasped. Her heart took a leap in her throat as she closed her eyes, then opened them again. The box was full of tarnished Spanish doubloons.

"Great Edward's treasure."

"Shhh," Otis warned. "There are two dozen boxes like this, packed eight in the bottom of each trunk."

"But how?" The tears had started in her eyes; now they poured down her cheeks. "How?"

The big man thrust the box into her hands and hurried to lock the cabin door. When he returned, she had sunk back on the lid of another trunk and cradled the box in her lap.

"The boys and I made the switch while you were unconscious. It was a trick of Great Edward's that my grandfather told me about many a time. Putman had heard the story, too. There were two ships, the *Argos* and the *Redoubt*."

Fancy shook her head. She could not remember ever having heard of them before.

"You passed out just after I said their names," he reminded her with a chuckle.

"Everyone thought the treasure was in the *Argos*. Great Edward had stored it there practically in plain sight. Sometimes he'd pick up a bag from the top of the

501

chest and open it and show everybody. But the treasure hoard on the *Argos* was just a thin layer; beneath the second layer of bags were rocks."

"And the real treasure was on the *Redoubt*."

"Right. My grandfather knew. He'd been the man that Great Edward trusted to help him pack the chests. My grandfather would have given his life for Edward England. He told me to do the same, if need be, for Great Edward's granddaughter."

"I would love to meet your grandfather."

"He's dead now, God rest his soul. He died last week." Otis swallowed hard. "I think he only wanted to wait until I got home so I could tell him about it. He listened and listened and laughed and laughed. Mother told me after he was gone that she thought he was over a hundred years old."

Fancy put the box aside and stood up. Her own face was wet with tears as she put her arms around the huge chest and pressed her face against his.

"Captain England!" he protested.

She tightened her grip, then gave a watery chuckle. "Surely this must be a first for Shepperton Lines. A captain hugging her first mate."

His great hands patted her shoulder awkwardly, and then she stepped back.

To cover his confusion, he scooped up the treasure box, slid the lid back in place, and reburied it in the depths of the trunk.

When he stood up again, she had regained her composure. "Did everybody get a share?"

"Aye, Captain. We all took shares, Beany most of all. We put it in the bank for him and are sendin' him to school. He wasn't real happy about it when we were first discussin' it, but he seems to be takin' to it now."

"That's good."

He wiped his hands on the sides of his trousers.

"Well, I'll be leavin' you now. You'll want to get settled before the ship sails."

"Yes."

He unlocked the door, but before he could open it, she put her hand on his. "Otis Greene, you will please come to England's Fancy in a couple of years, won't you? I'll want to take a ship to Madagascar and I'll need a first mate."

His face split in a smile. "With pleasure, Captain England."

And then he was gone.

Epilogue

The nightingale sang at midnight and warm summer rain spattered gently against the jalousies.

Fancy England writhed and moaned in ecstasy as Hunter lifted her hips to his mouth. "Not again," she begged. "No. I really can't. No."

He chuckled deep in his throat. "But you love it so. In a minute you'll be saying yes."

Pushing herself up on her elbows, she struggled halfheartedly to rise; but he chuckled and pushed her down, his big hand splaying out across her breast. "Hunter," she whispered desperately as he bent to his work again, "I can't."

"Shhh." He blew his breath into the silken tangle of red hair at the bottom of her belly.

She whimpered as his lips followed his breath, then cried out as she dug her heels into the bed on either side of his body and arched ecstatically. For the third time since he had carried her to the bed, heat built in her body. Every muscle sang and leaped and shuddered.

"Hunter!"

He lifted his head and grinned at her. "What?"

"Don't stop."

"Never, sweetheart."

With lips and tongue and teeth, he drove her to the edge of ecstasy. Just before he administered the *coup de grace,* he reared himself on his knees. She was incredibly beautiful, her body so slim and golden, her skin glowing with perspiration, her breasts hard, their nipples swollen and blushing rose.

Her eyes flew open, dazed, questioning. They stared at each other for the space of a breath. She lifted her hips, whether involuntarily or in invitation he could not tell, but he laughed.

"Tell me yes," he commanded.

She clutched her hard breasts and offered them to him with the thought of trapping him with his own desire. A minxlike smile lifted the corners of her mouth as she stubbornly shook her head.

"Then I'll leave you." He set his foot on the bed where his knee had been and started to rise.

"No. Please no."

"Then tell me."

"Yes." Her voice was the merest whisper of breath.

"Louder."

She clamped her lips together with another show of stubbornness, but he touched his index and third fingers to the nub of pleasure between her widely extended thighs. "Louder," he teased.

"Yes!"

He slipped his hands under her buttocks again, then bent to her. His mouth and tongue and teeth adored and assailed her.

Her climax was instantaneous and intense. She writhed and twisted against the silk as her body shivered and convulsed.

He waited until she was completely still, until she had managed to open her eyes, mere golden slits glinting in the soft lamplight. Then he kissed her deeply, putting his tongue into the very back of her throat and drawing it out slowly. When he felt her back arch upward, he thrust into her.

His hardness and heat sliding into the readied chamber aroused her again. She moaned in pleasure and pushed up weakly. Again his thrust, and again and again, while her own excitement built. Then, as suddenly, he stiffened, shuddered, and dropped his forehead to the pillow to gasp out his ecstasy and pleasure in her ear.

He dozed for a time, then awakened to nuzzle her breasts and run his fingers and tongue over her nipples.

"Hunter," she protested. "I really can't. Please. You'll kill me."

"What a lovely way to die," he chuckled. "But I doubt that you'll die, Angel. I've never known it to happen. And besides, angels are eternal creatures." His fingers slid down over the flat plane of her belly to the edge of her mound. Then his hand cupped her, his third finger winding itself in her tangled hair.

"Hunter," she pleaded.

"Just one more time, Fancy. Then you can sleep. I promise I'll let you sleep. I'll even cover you up."

"Hunter, for heaven's sake."

He rotated the tips of his two fingers. To Fancy, it seemed that she could feel every ridge and valley of his fingerprints. "I remember when you made love to me in Boston. You tied me to the bed. I've never forgotten that. You were raging. A devil, not an angel at all. I promised myself that I'd love you until you couldn't move." He changed from the tips of his fingers to his nails.

She cried out and arched desperately.

He sheathed his claws. "You told me you were a devil, and you swore I'd never leave you. And you were right. I can't leave you. No matter where I go or what I do, you're with me. I love you. And worse than that,

I'm obsessed by you." He stretched out beside her, never ceasing his touching, never increasing it one iota nor decreasing it.

She was gasping for breath. A hot blush suffused her breasts and throat.

"How red your nipples are," he whispered, touching her earlobe with his lips. "You must be very excited."

"Hunter," she pleaded. "I can't stand any more of this." Every muscle of her body was quivering uncontrollably. Her thighs lay shamelessly open, uncaring that he see how desirous she was of his touch. She was his creature to do with as he willed.

He smiled his dark, demonic smile. "Are you sure you can't stand any more? Are you quite, quite sure?"

She was silent, admitting by her silence that she did not want the torment to end.

He chuckled against her neck. "Oh, my sweet Fancy. How you do love it. How long have you lain here now, unable to move except as I guide you?"

She set her teeth. The torturous movements went on and on. Then something broke inside of her. The tight coiled spring unwound with a fierce burst of power. She screamed once, then began to sob wrenchingly as he continued his motion, until she slumped completely, all sound, all motion, all senses shocked by the power of her reaction. . . .

It had been as he had promised. Hunter gathered her into the huddle of his body to sleep the rest of the night.

She rose and wrapped her green silk robe around her. In the disordered bed, Hunter slept the sleep of the thoroughly exhausted, thoroughly satisfied male. Occasionally, his breathing would deepen until it was almost a snore. Then he would stir slightly and it would even out again. As she opened the door to the hall, she looked back at the sleeping man—the one and only true love of her life.

The summer had been as nearly perfect as she could ever remember. The quarters, the curing barns, the docks, the tool sheds, MacCullough's cabin, all had been rebuilt. The tobacco—a good crop—was even at that moment curing in the dry heat from trees felled by the great storm of the year before. Nothing bad ever happened but some good would come from it.

She opened the door to Alex's room. Her dark-haired son lay in almost the same position as his father. Deeply tanned from riding in the fields beside his parents, his face was a dark shadow on the white pillowcase. Even as she looked at him, he stirred restlessly, turning over and brushing the sheet aside. She did not waste her time in covering him up again. He was bursting with health and the night was warm. His thin nightshire was more than sufficient.

When she opened the door to Richard's room, he bobbed up immediately. "Mama."

His sweet birdlike voice gripped her heart. She closed the door silently behind her and came to the side of the crib.

"Mama." He held up his arms, a delighted smile on his face.

Richard was a night owl. More than half the time when she went in to check on him during the night, he was awake, playing with stuffed toys and blocks that she left in the crib for the purpose. Likewise, she kept a small lamp turned very low on a table near the door. Amazingly, he seldom cried in the night. She could almost believe he knew that his hours did not coincide with everyone else's and intended to be considerate.

"So you were playing and you are glad to see me come in and keep you company," she teased him, checking his diaper and finding it soaked as usual.

509

While she changed him and he played with his toes, she talked to him of inconsequential things.

Dry and smiling, he held up his arms to be walked. Obligingly, she picked him up and walked back and forth across the room with him for a couple of minutes, a little gesture that had turned into a ritual between them. When she returned him to his crib, his face screwed up, but she shook her head and put his favorite stuffed toy into his arms. He whimpered a bit but stuck his thumb in his mouth and turned his head away as she kissed him on the forehead.

"Good night, love," she whispered.

The house was dark and quiet, the moon covered by mountainous thunderheads that rolled away only briefly from time to time. She could smell the honeysuckle in the warm air as she mounted the steps of the folly and entered its latticed walls.

When she had returned home, nothing would deter her. The carpenters who had come to construct the new buildings were ordered to erect this replica of the little summer gazebos so popular in England. Hunter had protested mildly at the expense but had let her have her way. Now she sometimes sat inside it for hours. At any time of the day or night she could look out her bedroom window onto its shake-shingled roof.

Inside, she knelt, her hand touching the clean-swept floor. There, beneath the foundations of the lovely summer house, wrapped in oiled skins and locked in a brass-bound trunk, rested the white oak boxes containing Great Edward's treasure.

Like a touchstone, she brought herself back to it again and again. And felt secure in its nearness.

For perhaps a full minute, she stayed there, her hand touching the floor, then she rose and came back to the door of the folly. It pleased her to call it that, since she hoped by the name to further throw off suspicion.

All around her stretched the boundless acres of England's Fancy, the plantation that belonged to her forever, protected from Armageddon itself by the treasure of Edward England buried in its rich earth. The location was coded on parchment and slipped beneath the plate of the jewel case as the original location had been. Only she and Holy Dulcibella knew of its existence, and one day she would tell others. When the boys were old enough and wise enough, she would tell them.

She wrapped her arms around her well-loved body and shivered. Perhaps before then she would be able to bring herself to tell Hunter of its existence. Perhaps one day . . .